When the *Glitter* Fades

When the *Glitter* Fades

JACQX MELILLI

Escribano Publishing

First published in Australia by Escribano Publishing in 2024

This is a work of fiction, although loosely based on Alf Broadway's Pantomime Players touring circuit and certain events experienced by Shirley Broadway. Names and characters are fictional and bear no resemblance to any real life individuals, living or dead. Any resemblance is entirely coincidental. Businesses, places, events, and incidents are used in a fictitious manner.

The author and the publisher have made every effort to contact copyright holders for material used in this book. Any person or organisation that may have been overlooked should contact the publisher and they will be glad to rectify in future editions any errors or omission brought to their attention.

Cover design by Michael McDermaid and Jacqx Melilli
Back cover photographs courtesy of Shirley Barnett
Author photograph by Aida's Photography
Edited by Tricia Dearborn

ISBN 978-0-9756800-5-6 (paperback)
ISBN: 978-0-9756800-6-3 (eBook)

A catalogue record for this book is available from the National Library of Australia
https://catalogue.nla.gov.au

Contents

Preface

When the Glitter Fades is dedicated to Shirley Barnett (née Broadway), a seasoned show business veteran who kindly shared her life stories of growing up in a family of vaudeville performers. Shirley was born on 7 January 1931, in Melbourne, Victoria, during the Great Depression.

Shirley's life story became a research project for one of my Master of Arts degree units. Initially, I had planned on writing Shirley's biography, starting from her childhood until the late 1950s, when Australian television made its debut. Alf Spargo invited Shirley to audition at HSV-7 (Channel 7) where she worked as part of the variety act team and on the game show *Stop the Music*. She later worked on *The Late Show* with Bert Newton and then on *In Melbourne Tonight* at GTV-9 (Channel 9) with Graham Kennedy. One of Shirley's highlights was working on the *Flood Tide* episode of the *Whiplash* series starring American actor Peter Graves.

One of my aims when writing *When the Glitter Fades* was to preserve Australian entertainment history to the best of my ability. I started by recording Shirley's experiences. Whatever she couldn't recall in specific detail, I researched in the newspaper archives. I was able to piece together accurate information and dates recorded through advertisements Shirley's father, Alf Broadway, had placed to announce their shows.

After researching extensively, I found the Association for the Advancement of the Blind advertisements in the *Healesville and Yarra Glen Guardian* dating from 1921, mentioning Alf Broadway as 'a dexterous digger in juggling, racquet spinning, balancing and ball bouncing extraordinaire'. Since Shirley could not recall much about her parents' early start in show business, I was finding it difficult to come up with content that was going to be engaging, entertaining, and would preserve the art of Australian entertainment of that era. That's when a story began to formulate, of two men falling in love with the same woman, and I decided to create a fictional story, loosely based on Shirley and Alf Broadway's show business troupe using Alf's newspaper advertisements as a guide.

I made three trips to Melbourne to research at the State Library of Victoria and to visit some of the regional towns recorded in the diary of one of Alf's dancers. Shirley gave me a copy of the diary, which had meticulous notes and dates recorded of each regional town Alf's troupe performed in from 1933 to 1935. I visited the towns of the tour circuit that ended when Alf's touring truck crashed, although the true cause of the accident was not as described in *When the Glitter Fades*.

Some other true facts are that Shirley did start performing at age three and around a year later won the Shirley Temple Competition, where she was contracted for a time to perform at Hoyts Cinemas in Melbourne in replica Shirley Temple costumes to promote Shirley's latest films. The offer to renew the contract is fictional, as is the performance at Luna Park. Shirley did get polio and the outcome was as described in *When the Glitter Fades*.

The rest of the story is fiction, as are all the characters and their names. Unfortunately, Shirley passed away on 7 February 2021, so she was not able to read the story that unfolded. However, her daughter, Sue Broadway, founding member and Artistic Director of Circus Oz, gave it the thumbs up and assured me none of the characters resembled any of her family members.

As a tribute to Sue, who followed in her mother's and grandparents' showbiz footsteps, I included her teacup skit in *When the Glitter Fades*. Sue pointed out that the skit was not of the era, as she invented it in 1996 for her show. But, in 2016, after seeing Sue perform it in the variety show *The Classics* at Coffs Harbour Jetty Theatre—where sixteen years earlier, I met her mother, Shirley, I enjoyed it so much Sue agreed for me to include it in the story.

If you ask me why I chose to write about vaudeville performers, I'd say my fascination with show business started when I was young. My favourite thing to do was to watch entertainers like Bojangles (Bill Robinson) and Shirley Temple perform their impressive tap dancing routines. I was bedazzled by the illusion and glamour of show business created by entertainers with their big smiles, extravagant costumes, incredible energy, and captivating talent. Their apparent lavish, whimsical and eccentric lifestyles made you want to strive for fame, worldwide adoration, an abundance of money, and an immortal legacy of your existence.

But throughout my writing journey, the more I wrote and delved into research, the voices of my characters began to take over. They were screaming to tell their story—their truth that all that glitters is not gold, and when the glitter fades, they're left with the truth of who they really are behind the mask and elaborate costumes. Who would love them then?

1

A Criminal on the Run

Rural farm, Victoria, Australia, 1920

It was never Vinnie McIntyre's intention to commit a crime. On that brisk, starry night, he was lying in the stable to escape the cold. Listening to the rhythmic breathing of the horses, he snuggled against his favourite, Trixie, for warmth. As he was succumbing to the lull of sleep, the sound of someone entering the stable disturbed him.

Terrified his owner had found his hiding spot, he hid under the hay and peered towards the moonlight streaming through the open door. The scuffle of footsteps and the shadow of his owner moving in his direction made Vinnie's heart beat furiously. He ducked as a torch beam swiped at his head. His owner made his way to a corner of the stable that was stacked with crates. He pushed them aside until he located a particular one. Pulling wads of pound notes from his pocket, he shoved them into the crate, then rearranged the others to hide the one with the treasure.

Seconds later, the stable door closed, swallowing Vinnie in darkness. He quickly put on his boots and fumbled his way to the door, slowly opening it to let the moonlight in. He saw the faint shadow of his owner walking towards the shed Vinnie was meant to sleep in. Realising he had little time to spare before his owner found he wasn't there, he hurried to locate the crate and pried it open. Racing against time, he stuffed every wad into his pockets and undergarments.

'Thief!'

Vinnie's blood turned to ice as a torch illuminated his face. His owner's fist was raised, ready to strike him. Knowing he would be beaten more severely than usual, Vinnie panicked and picked up a hoe. In a swift motion, he struck his owner across the head, sending him crashing to the ground. Horrified at what he had done, Vinnie ran to the jalopy parked outside the stable and attempted to start it. The engine did nothing more than cough and splutter, making enough noise to stir the dead as it cut through the stillness of the night. He heard the farmhand's voice calling out from the darkness. Finally, the stubborn engine cranked to life.

In his panicked state, he crashed the jalopy into a fence post. The commotion, and the light of the moon, guided the agitated farmhand towards the jalopy. With adrenaline infused into every fibre of his body, Vinnie slammed the gearstick into reverse and backed away from the fence post. Just as the farmhand grabbed at the door, Vinnie jammed the gearstick into first gear and revved the engine to a screeching point as it bounced forward and out towards the mile-long driveway. The farmhand had managed to open the door and was being dragged along the dirt. Vinnie felt his heart would burst out of his chest, but out of crazed fear, he held the accelerator to the floor. Bouncing over potholes got the better of the farmhand, and he finally lost his grip and fell to the ground with a pained groan.

Vinnie tried to hold back his emotions as the enormity of what he had done sank in. There was no turning back. It was surprising the jalopy was going as fast as it was. Vinnie caught sight of wisps of smoke escaping from under the bonnet and noted the temperature gauge was reading hot. He had stopped praying sometime during his first year of enslavement when he realised no one was going to rescue him, but at that moment, he prayed the jalopy would make it to town. In his desperation, he found himself making deals with God. He thanked God for the moonlight, for without it his escape would not have been possible. His mind was racing as he tried to work out what he would do once he got to town at this late hour. At least this time he had money. The thought of being caught and imprisoned for his crimes weighed heavily on him as he contemplated how he would lie low in a small-town community where everybody knew each other's business. He kept repeating his deals to God, just in case He hadn't heard them.

Miraculously, the jalopy made it into town. *Thanks, God, Sir.* He headed for the train station. The arrival and departure board stated the next train was the following day at noon. Vinnie found a discreet location amongst the bushland to park the jalopy. The hissing of the punctured radiator was accompanied by the acrid smell of smoke and oil. He spent a wakeful night on high alert.

At sunrise, he abandoned the jalopy and walked into town. It didn't take him long to spot the farmhand on horseback—he had searched for Vinnie multiple times before when he had tried to escape. Panicked, Vinnie ran in search of a place to hide. His eye caught some men loading a truck with musical instruments. In a split second, when nobody was watching, Vinnie scrambled into the back of the truck. His heart was pounding as he searched for somewhere within the tightly packed area to hide. Moments later, voices approached the truck, prompting him to press himself as hard as he could into a small space, ignoring the pain of objects stabbing him in his attempt to conceal himself. He held his breath, hoping it would quiet the thunderous beating of his heart. The men packed more equipment into the truck, encasing him in complete darkness. His body jerked from the sudden fright of the truck door slamming shut. He felt a moment of relief, but it wasn't until he heard the rumble of the engine and the movement of the truck that he began to relax.

The realisation that he was finally free of the tortuous misery he had endured for the past eight years overwhelmed him, yet he refused to shed a tear. His thoughts drifted to seeing his mother again, but were dampened by the realisation that he was now a criminal on the run with only the clothes on his back and stolen money. He wondered if his mother was still living in London, or whether she had moved back to Scotland after what her stepfather had done to Vinnie. *I'll kill the bastard if I can just get back there,* thought Vinnie. But how would he return to England when he had nothing to prove his identity? As his body relaxed, his physical and mental exhaustion lulled him into a deep sleep.

The tension in his body returned when he awoke many hours later at the clanking of the truck door as it was swung open. Men began to unload the truck. As much as Vinnie tried to squeeze himself into invisibility, hoping he could run off when no one was looking, his effort failed and eventually, he was exposed.

'Mary, mother of Jesus! What the bloody hell are ya doing in here?' boomed one of the men, whose body blocked the sunlight.

Vinnie tried to make a run for it, but the giant hovering over him grabbed him by the scruff of his neck and, with an effortless swoop, flung him to the ground, pinning him down with the weight of his Swiss cheese boot held together with shredded rope.

'Who in hell are ya?'

'Vinnie McIntyre, sir,' he said, as his vision adjusted to the sudden jolt and brightness of day.

'What're ya doing in our truck?'

'I'm looking for work, sir. I'll do anything.'

'Work! We ain't looking for workers.'

'I'll work for food and lodging. I won't be no trouble. I'm a solid worker.'

'I said we ain't looking for workers, and the last thing we need is another mouth to feed. You got yourself a free ride, now get outta here.'

'Sir, at least let me repay you for my ride by helping unload the truck.'

The man looked Vinnie up and down. His body was as solid as a pit bull's with a jawline to match and a face etched with the markings of a young man forced into maturity before his time.

'Yeah, righto, but stop bloody calling me, sir.'

'Yes, sir, … um?'

'Reg. You sound like a bloody Pom.'

'I'm Scottish.'

'Same bloody thing.'

It took just over an hour for Reg and Vinnie to unload the truck and set up the equipment and props for the night's performance.

'We're done, kid. Now get outta here.'

'I ain't sure where to go. I dunno where I am.'

'Where's ya family? And don't lie to me.'

'I got took from my family and made to work on a farm. I ran away 'cause I was getting beat up.'

Reg eyeballed him, his forehead creasing into a mass of fleshy waves.

'Fibber!'

'I ain't fibbing, sir, I swear!'

'For the love of God, come on, then,' said Reg, as he walked off in search of his boss. 'Mack, this kid here needs some work.'

'Yeah, well, I need ticket sales or none of us'll have work,' replied Mack.

'I can go out right now and sell tickets for you,' said Vinnie.

'Who're you?'

'Vinnie McIntyre, sir. You won't have to pay me. I'll work for food and lodgings 'til I prove myself.'

'How old are you?'

'Sixteen, sir.'

'Ya look like a criminal on the run,' said Mack, eyeing the copper stubble of Vinnie's shaved head and his shabby clothes.

'He's got no family, Mack,' said Reg.

'Give me a chance. If I don't sell at least twenty tickets, I'll be on my way.'

'Make it thirty and ya got yourself a deal.' Mack handed Vinnie a stack of handbills.

'Go hand these out to the folk in town and tell 'em to bring the handbill to the ticket box so I know how many tickets ya sold.'

'"The Association for the Advancement of the Blind concert's variety acts",' read Vinnie. 'Are the performers blind?'

'Not all. We got a mix. Read the handbill and go sell some tickets.'

Vinnie lost no time in positioning himself in front of a small department store that seemed to be generating a reasonable amount of foot traffic. While he was conscious of his appearance, he was too scared to use the stolen money to buy new clothes in case it raised suspicions and confirmed his criminal status. He did his best to tidy himself by tucking his shirt into his pants and rolling up his sleeves to hide the missing buttons from the cuffs. He did up the top button of his shirt and loosened his braces so his pants would cover most of his muddy boots. The most valuable thing he possessed was his burning desire to get back to his mother. Puffing himself up with fake confidence, he began his mission to sell tickets in a desperate attempt to gain himself a new life. Recalling the spruikers he'd seen as a young boy in London, he mimicked them to the best of his knowledge.

'Hear ye, hear ye! Listen up, folks!' he called out. 'The best show on earth is here in town. Ya won't want to miss this. Come listen to blind musicians perform. Aye, folks, you heard me … *blind* performers with incredible talent, as well as a comedian, acrobats, an impersonator and singers! Only twopence a ticket for this extraordinary show, with money going towards helping the Association for the Advancement of the Blind.'

He sold forty-three tickets. Mack hired him, cementing Vinnie's freedom from a past he would prefer to forget. He repaid his gratitude by working hard to promote the Blind Association concerts. Never had he imagined he'd find work he enjoyed so much regardless of the long hours and hard labour involved in setting up and packing the trucks to move on to their next town, ready to do it all over again. He learned as many skills as he could through keen observation of each person's role and was soon a valued member of the troupe.

***

Over the next four years, Vinnie discovered that the tomfoolery of his youth had made him a natural comedian. Being part of the troupe gave him the opportunity to learn the art of performing comedy and the thrill of making cameo appearances until eventually he had even the toughest audience laughing as he recounted the shenanigans that had landed him in hot water once too often as a young boy. Not only had he proved his worth, but Mack noted he had a good mind for business and promoted Vinnie to managing the concerts after announcing he was leaving the Blind Association to start his own enterprise.

This opportunity was another major turning point in Vinnie's life. It would cost him more heartache than he'd ever imagined.

2

Escaping the Family Business

Yarra Glen, Victoria, 1924

'Hurry up, Artis. Pa said you're aiming for a belting.'

Artis frowned at his brother, who'd been loading the bread into the van, ready for delivery.

'I'll be glad for the day I'm outta here,' said Artis, swallowing the last mouthful of his bacon and egg roll as he finished tying his shoelaces.

'You've been saying that forever,' said Larry.

'Yeah, well, I'm sixteen now, and I'm done with getting belted.'

'You figured out where you're gonna go?'

'As far away from Yarra Glen as I can get.' Artis gave his brother a playful punch in the arm before heading to the bakery at the front of the house.

'Come on, Art! Stop dragging the chain!' Hank Newman let out an ear-piercing whistle.

'Coming, Pa!'

Artis grabbed a crate of freshly baked bread and pushed open the bakery door with his foot. The orange tinge of sunrise was beginning to break through the darkness. He made multiple trips back and forth before plonking the last crate into the back of his cart. The aroma of the freshly baked loaves wafted through the air. He swung his lanky body onto his bicycle and gave his father a wave as he forced the pedals into momentum. Within minutes, Artis's sandy hair, which he liked to slick back to make himself appear older, was ruffled into an unruly mess as the wind whipped it in every direction.

The family bakery business was doing well. Hank, always full of ideas, had built a cart that attached to the back of Artis's bicycle so he could make deliveries to the old folk who found it hard to get to the bakery. Hank would also deliver to other businesses and stores in town in his van. It was this kind of service that had made Hank's bakery prosperous.

Once Artis had finished his deliveries, he stopped to get a soft drink. The town clock struck nine, reminding him he'd be late for school again. To his advantage, he knew how to charm his teacher with a yarn about one of the old folk needing his help, hence causing the delay. Sitting on his cart, legs sprawled, he downed the drink, feeling the gas bubbles tickle his nostrils as they rose in his throat. Ensuring nobody was within earshot, he let out a drawn-out burp which would have normally resulted in a clip to the ear from his mother or an outright belting from his father.

The sound of a trumpet and saxophone followed by singing caught Artis's attention. He spotted musicians staring ahead while playing their instruments and a man singing a jazz number in front of the Grand Hotel. Beside them, another man was performing magic. Fascinated, Artis crossed the road to take a closer look. Once the musicians finished their number, the magician stood on a soapbox and rattled off a spiel about the upcoming matinee and evening show. Artis was intrigued. His eye caught the poster behind the men.

CONCERT BY THE BLIND

The Association for the Advancement of the Blind is pleased to present comedian Vinnie McIntyre and concert tenor, Aaron Porter, and Paul Lawry, in an act of paper manipulation and sketchy cartoons. Favourite, Fred Bunting, accompanies the quartet party. The purchase of tickets for this entertainment will go towards paying off the heavy debt of nearly £4000 for the new wing built at the Brighton Beach home.

The musicians struck up another number. Time stood still as Artis watched, mesmerised by the incredible talent of these entertainers. When they stood up to take a break, Artis noticed two of them reach for their walking stick.

'So they're really blind! said Artis.

'Course! This is just a teaser, son. Do yourself a favour and buy a ticket.'

Artis felt the weight of his morning's takings in his pocket and impulsively bought a ticket.

'Mind if I hang around and watch?'

'Only if you make yourself useful,' said the magician. He handed Artis some flyers. 'Here, go hand these out and see if you can sell us some tickets before the matinee starts.'

'Okey-doke,' said Artis, with the enthusiasm of a puppy. He bounded off down the road, waving the flyers as he called out to anyone who would listen how the greatest show on earth was in town and they would be crazy to miss it. The downside to living in a small town when you're doing something you shouldn't be is that everyone knows everyone, and each person questioned why Artis wasn't at school.

'I've got special permission to have the day off to sell tickets to support the Association for the Advancement of the Blind's important charity concert,' he lied, then felt totally ashamed of himself. He averted his eyes and tried to ignore the prickly sensation crawling under his skin.

'Oh, in that case, I'll buy six tickets for the family,' said the butcher with a smile.

Artis's zeal paid off. In a matter of hours, he'd sold thirty tickets for the matinee and evening show. This impressed Vinnie McIntyre, the Blind Association troupe's manager.

'Well done, laddie,' said Vinnie. 'You've earned yourself a front row seat.'

'Thank you, sir,' he said, fishing through his pocket for the crumpled ticket.

While Artis could barely contain his excitement, he was battling his conscience, which was blaring a warning of the aftermath of his blatant disobedience and lies. He was doing his utmost to shoo away the nagging voices of his parents and pastor yelling, *"Secular entertainment is of the devil!"* Without a doubt, his father would not spare the rod once some busybody blabbermouth in Yarra Glen's small community informed him of what he'd been up to instead of being at school. Considering the number of beatings he received, sometimes for the slightest transgressions, Artis thought this whopper sin was well worth the impending flogging. He resented the grip the church had on his father, that made him believe children had to have sin beaten out of them. Artis was desperate to escape the oppressive conformity of religion, which made no sense to him. If that was the doctrine of a loving God, he wanted no part of it.

People poured into the hall for the matinee performance and took their seats. Once the doors were closed, the audience quietened down. A rustle of excitement escaped when Vinnie McIntyre stepped out into the limelight dressed in knickerbockers, a Scottish plaid vest over a white shirt, and a matching plaid bowtie and socks. A cap, perfectly centred on his head, tamed his unruly mass of ginger ringlets. After positioning himself downstage centre, he introduced himself and gave a short spiel about the association's efforts to raise much-needed funds.

'Ladies and gentlemen, I'm sure you're gonna love the show, so if you feel moved to donate a little extra to help us pay off the new wing built at the Brighton Beach home, it would be much appreciated. And now, without further ado, I present the Association for the Advancement of the Blind concert!'

The next two hours were bliss for Artis. Between musical numbers, the concert was peppered with performances from a sketch artist, a magician, and a dexterous juggler. Vinnie's comedy routine was a corker.

'My sister spent two hours at the beauty shop,' he said. 'She looked fabulous after getting a mud pack on her face. But then the mud dried up and fell off her face!'

Throughout the show, an intense desire was brewing in Artis's mind. Once the show ended, he sprang into action to find Vinnie.

'Sir, that was the most fantastic show I've ever seen in my life! I'd like to join your troupe.'

'We ain't hiring,' replied Vinnie. While he may have had the audience in stitches with his comic routine, he was no pushover. Artis's charm, however, was a force to be reckoned with. His barrage of compliments had softened the Scott a 'wee' bit.

'I sell bread for a living, sir, so I figure I can sell your tickets like I did before.'

'Laddie, what's possessed you to want to join a troupe?'

'I just realised that I don't want to spend the rest of my life selling bread.'

'What's wrong with selling bread?'

'There's no dough in it, sir.' Artis surprised himself with his comic answer. It worked. Vinnie howled.

'How old are ya, laddie?'

'Sixteen, sir.'

'You've gotta be able to do more than sell tickets to earn your keep. What entertaining skills have you got?'

The question stumped Artis for a few seconds.

'Er, well, I got the gift of the gab, and I've got some juggling skills.' His face flushed red, and he began to fidget. Vinnie picked up on the lie. Artis's eagerness triggered a memory of how he'd begged for an opportunity to join the troupe four years ago, when he was a desperate sixteen-year-old running from enslavement and a crime he had never intended to commit. *Perhaps it's a sign*, he thought.

'What are you running from, laddie?'

'Religion.'

'Religion?'

'Yes, sir. I'm done getting the sin beaten outta me.'

'What crime have you committed to be getting the sin beaten outta you?'

'A bad report from my teacher, skipping school, fighting with my brother, sneaking outta Sunday School, swearing, using the Lord's name in vain. How long's a piece of string? I figure I'm going to hell, so I may as well go on my terms.'

'You shouldn't say things like that, laddie. You get just enough of a taste of heaven and hell here on earth to help you decide where you want to spend eternity.'

'Well, I may as well get a taste of heaven before I make up my mind.' Artis smiled.

'You better hope you don't die anytime soon, then.'

'So you're a believer?'

'More of a lost cause. Some sins can't be forgiven,' said Vinnie. He looked Artis up and down and scratched his head. 'Well, laddie, here's the deal. I can't pay you a wage. I'll be needing a forty per cent increase in sales to make it worth my while and to make sure we can cover the cost of another mouth to feed and accommodate. I can only give you a month to prove yourself, then you're on your own.' Vinnie expected his response to wipe the smile from Artis's face, but instead he jumped for joy.

'That's a deal, sir. Ya won't regret it!'

'You got one month and I'm not guaranteeing you nothin', considering you've got questionable entertaining skills.'

'I won't let you down, sir.' Artis beamed.

'Go sell some more tickets, then pack light and be back here for the evening show. We'll be packing up and moving on as soon as it's over.'

'Yes, sir!' Artis jumped on his bicycle and sped off with the nervous energy of a greyhound, pedalling with intensity, as if that would make the hours pass quicker. After selling more tickets for the evening show, he rode to the school and hid in the bushes, waiting for the bell to signal the end of the school day. While he was waiting, he found two palm-sized rocks and practised juggling, with limited success. The school bell rang and a few minutes later he saw his brother Larry approaching. He threw a stick in Larry's direction, hitting him on the shoulder.

'Where on God's earth have you been?' said Larry.

'A concert with blind musicians!'

Larry squinted in disbelief.

'You should have seen these guys, Laz,' Artis said. 'They're unbelievable.'

'Have you gone stark raving mad? I can't keep lying for you every time you miss school, Art!'

'Well, you won't have to anymore. I'm joining the troupe and leaving town tonight!'

Larry's mouth dropped open.

'Tonight?'

'I've been telling you for years, Laz. I finally got my chance.'

'You can't leave me, Art. What am I gonna do without you?' Tears welled in Larry's eyes.

'Don't go soft on me, Laz. I'll come get you in a couple of years, when you're old enough.'

'Pa's gonna kill you, Art. Don't go!'

'That's the whole problem, Laz. I'm done with beatings, church, and stinking religion. If Jesus already paid the price for our sins, then why the hell do I need to keep getting them beat outta me?'

'Cause you're not meant to keep sinning.'

'It's not like I'm a bad person, Laz. I ain't killed anyone or done anything really bad. Anyway, this is the most exciting thing that's ever happened to me. Look, I've been practising my juggling skills.'

But Artis's attempts to juggle the rocks were comical. He gave up and threw the rocks into the bush.

'I can't believe he's giving me a chance.' Artis got on his bicycle and motioned for Laz to get on. 'To think I'm gonna be on the road with a professional troupe!'

'Once they see your juggling skills, you won't be going nowhere.'

'Hop on and shut ya gob.' Artis manoeuvred his bicycle onto the path. 'You can't tell a soul, Laz.'

Larry positioned himself on the handlebars, and within seconds, Artis was pedalling like a lunatic, his legs burning with the exertion, as if speed would make time pass quicker. Despite Artis's disillusionment with religion, he had no doubt God existed and did not hesitate to pray, especially when he needed to get out of trouble. *Heavenly Father, I need you to help me get out of the house without my parents seeing me tonight. This is a once-in-a-lifetime opportunity and you'll be pleased to know I'll be helping raise money for a charity, so I'm doing a good thing. And can you make sure no busybody who saw me today reports me to Dad, so I don't get a belting and have my plans mucked up? Amen.*

When Artis and Larry got home, Artis noted that his father seemed none the wiser about his day's antics. It was business as usual. *Thanks, God!*

'Boys, get cracking. Pastor Paul's expecting the leftovers at the church before tea,' said Hank.

'Right on it, Pa.'

Artis and Larry loaded the cart with the bakery's leftover bread, which would be distributed to the needy in the community, and headed towards the church. When they returned home, Artis took three bread rolls he'd stuffed into his pockets and started juggling them.

'Watch this,' he said to Larry.

Larry laughed as Artis kept dropping the rolls.

'Boys, get inside for tea!' yelled Hank. 'Art, what the heck have you got in your pockets?'

'Uh … just some bread rolls, Pa. I accidentally dropped 'em, so I was gonna feed them to the chickens.'

'Are you outta your mind, boy, walking around with your pockets bulging like that?'

Larry tried his best not to laugh as they made their way inside. They got a whiff of Betty's dinner and, realising how famished they were, raced to wash their hands before sitting at the table.

'Did you make Shepherd's Pie, Ma?' said Larry.

'You'll eat what's put in front of you and be happy about it. Elbows off the table and bow your head for grace,' said Hank. 'Heavenly, Father. Thank you for everything you do and provide for us. We thank you for this food and the hands that prepared it, and we ask that you bless it to our bodies. Lord, help us to stay humble as we look to you for everything. And steer us towards your purpose for our lives. In Jesus's name …'

'Amen,' said the family in unison.

Artis squished his vegetables with his fork and blended them into his mashed potato and gravy to dilute their taste. He was leaving his corned beef until last so he could keep the flavoursome taste in his mouth for as long as possible. As he checked the clock on the wall, his mind wandered to the Blind Association concert that would start at half past seven. Larry gave him a look to signify that Artis was fidgeting. Not wanting to draw attention to himself, Artis settled himself down, despite his growing apprehension about how he was going to pull off his escape. His stomach knotted up when he noticed his parents looking at each other in a way that meant they were about to announce something major. Artis looked at Larry, who shrugged his shoulders.

'Artis, your mother and I've been talking and we've decided it's time you finish school and work full-time at the bakery, learning to make bread, so as you're ready to take over from me when the time comes.'

'Well, I was thinking about joining a blind musicians' troupe!' said Artis, his skin prickling in anticipation of the impending explosion. Larry's eyes almost popped out of their sockets.

'You what?' said his mother, pausing her fork, skewered with roast pumpkin, in mid-air.

Hank let out a chuckle that gathered momentum when he saw the look of complete horror on Betty's face.

'He's pulling your leg, love.' Hank snorted through his chuckle and continued to slice through his corned beef smothered in gravy. He layered the meat with mashed potatoes speckled with freshly chopped parsley and shovelled it into his mouth with gusto.

'I'm not pulling your leg, Pa. I don't want to be a baker,' said Artis, flinching from the kick Larry gave him under the table.

Betty, who had seconds ago relaxed, tightened up again as she sucked in her breath. Hank dropped his fork, the smile now wiped from his face.

'Have you lost your mind?'

'No, Pa.'

'You'd rather live the life of a rogue and vagabond, listening to the devil's music?' boomed Hank. 'I know you're coming to the age of manhood, but the last thing you want is a spirit of rebellion in you. Leaving a secure home to be with vagabond strangers is taking things too far. I forbid it.'

Betty's eyes filled with tears.

'Didn't you say we should go where the Lord guides us?' said Artis.

Hank pounced on Artis, grabbing him by the scruff of the neck and dragging him out of the room.

'The Lord does not guide us into the devil's playground!' He took the strap from the sideboard and laid it into Artis. Betty bowed her head and Larry blocked his ears with clenched fists, his chest heaving.

***

The thrashing propelled Artis to pack his few clothes and belongings into a canvas bag as soon as he was in his room. The swelling from his beating slowed his movements. He also took a small coin pouch containing his meagre savings and his leather-bound Bible, gifted to him when he was a child.

Larry gave his usual knock on the door after an episode before opening it. The sadness evident on his face increased when he saw

Artis's packed canvas bag.

'Please don't go, Art. Can't you just fight him back now you're older?'

'I can't fight my Pa, Laz. I love him and I know he loves me. He was crying when he was beating me, like it was hurting him more than me. I think about all the good things he does for us, like building us billy carts and fixing our bikes. I don't wanna leave mad at him. It's not a burden I wanna carry around with me.'

Larry and Artis got into bed and switched off the light. A sliver of light shone under the door, indicating that Hank and Betty had not yet retired.

'Why do you have to go?' said Larry.

'I just have to.'

'I wish you'd never gone to that concert.'

'It was meant to be, Laz.'

'So there's no use trying to talk you out of it, then?'

'Nah, mate. Not a bloody chance.'

'I wish I could go with you.'

'You're still an ankle-biter. Pa and Ma couldn't deal with losing both their sons in one go.' Artis felt the full force of Larry's pillow hit him across the face.

'I ain't no ankle-biter. I'll be fourteen in a couple of months. Take that back!'

'No chance, squirt.'

Within seconds, the boys were locked in a brotherly wrestle, Larry trying to prove he had equal strength.

'I'll let you win this time, Laz, 'cause I'm too sore.'

'Sissy.'

'Go to sleep now, Laz.'

'You're gonna be gone when I wake up, aren't you?'

'Yes, Laz.'

'Well, I'll be praying you change your mind, just so you know.'

It wasn't long before Artis heard Larry's breathing change to a sleeping rhythm in the bed beside him. The sliver of light was gone from under the door. Artis opened his bedroom window and jumped out, his canvas bag in hand. His heart was galloping before he'd even started running. He winced from the pain in his body, a reminder that he was making the right decision.

By the time he got into town, the show was ending. Waiting out of sight, he made sure to stay hidden until the audience had left the hall, to avoid being recognised. Then he sought out Vinnie, who seemed to forget who he was.

'Ah, you came back, then,' said Vinnie. Artis nodded. 'You sure you wanna do this? You'll be living by your wits and working harder than you ever thought.'

'I'm sure, sir.'

'There'll be no cosy bed and Mama's cooking.'

Artis swallowed hoping it would calm the fluttering sensation rising in him.

'Yes, sir.'

'Righto. You can start by helping load the truck,' said Vinnie.

So began Artis's journey of independence. He was no longer under his parents' protection. His survival would depend on what he'd learned in life so far and his sheer determination to succeed.

What have I done?

3

Belle of the Ball

Melbourne, Victoria, 1929

A month turned into five years. Artis worked hard to prove his worth. The work was arduous. It involved constantly setting up, packing up, selling tickets, negotiating venues, preparing meals, and arranging accommodation and transportation. In addition, Artis put in hours of practice to perfect a racquet spinning and ball balancing act with tutoring from members of the troupe. Learning magic tricks had also become an obsession. Vinnie gave him opportunities to perform whenever someone was feeling under the weather or injured. Once Artis got a taste for performing and hearing the audience's appreciation, he was hooked.

Vinnie, although a taskmaster, had taken a liking to Artis and over the five years had invested considerable time training him to be a competent manager. In October 1929, Prime Minister James Scullin declared America's stock market crash would cause a global depression, and sure enough, it didn't take long for the repercussions to rattle Australia. So it surprised Artis when Vinnie dropped his bombshell.

'Now that you're trained up, I've decided to start a vaudeville troupe and hand you the reins to keep managing here.'

'You're leaving the Blind Association?'

'Aye. Folks are lapping up the vaudeville shows. They love variety acts. Nothin' like dancers showing off some bust and legs to spice up the show.'

'Isn't this a risky time to start a business? Ticket sales have dropped since the stock market crash.'

'Business is always risky if you don't know what you're doing. I'm gonna put on a right spectacular show with costumes and sets that'll knock people's socks off. Dancers with sky-high legs, contortionists, acrobats, a strongman, magicians, jugglers, and singers that will take you to another planet. I'll make it the best show in Melbourne. No more touring one-nighters that suck the life outta ya.'

'How are you going to do that?'

'There's heaps of showbiz folks outta work willing to work for peanuts if they have to. I've got connections with theatre managers in Melbourne and enough savings put away now.'

'Well, thank you for handing over the reins here, but I'd be lying if I didn't wish I could join you!'

'Laddie, you've been like a brother, and I've trusted you more than anyone else. You can't leave the Association high and dry. They need the funds coming in. If you can train someone to take over from you and my business kicks off, I'll call on you to join me.'

'If anyone can make a business succeed even when things are iffy, it's you. I'll be looking to join you as soon as I can.'

Vinnie slapped him on the back. 'Go on then, get back to work. I know when I'm getting buttered up.'

Artis was pleased with the opportunity to manage the Blind Association. However, his envy of Vinnie's new venture gave him the burning desire to train up his replacement as soon as possible and hope Vinnie's business succeeded. Not only did vaudeville sound exciting, but he believed he had a better chance of meeting the girl of his dreams while running a vaudeville troupe.

Seven months later, Artis sent Vinnie a telegram informing him that he had trained a replacement and practically begging for the opportunity to join his troupe. Vinnie graciously offered Artis an opportunity to manage another troupe that would tour regionally, whilst Vinnie kept his troupe in Melbourne. Artis was required to travel to Melbourne to seek outstanding variety acts and hire dancers. Once Vinnie had approved the acts, Artis would organise a regional tour.

Whilst in Melbourne, he boarded at the home of a widow who kept an eagle eye on him, making it clear that there were to be no unaccompanied females on her property. During his talent search, he walked past a newsstand where his eye caught an advertisement in the *Guardian* announcing that the Glaciarium, an ice skating rink and one of Melbourne's hot spots for entertainment, fondly known as The Glassy, was holding its Annual Fancy Dress Ball. It was an extravagant event and some of the finest dancers in Melbourne were sure to have been commissioned for the Grand Parade.

The Fancy Dress Ball attracted close to 5000 people, who snaked along the almost one acre occupied by The Glassy, waiting to get through the doors. Artis was in awe when he finally entered and was guided to the second storey, above the ice skating rink. The orchestra was in full swing with a master pianist as the centrepiece on the grand piano. Artis revelled in the fine selection of beautiful women dressed in extraordinary, eye-catching costumes. At the climax of the Ball's Grand Parade, a group of dancers wooed the crowd with a spicy number. However, it was Belle Taylor who captivated every eye with her exotic dancing in a spectacular costume made of peacock feathers with a matching headpiece. At the climax of her dance, she pulled a string that released a tail of peacock feathers that spread out in a brilliant flash of rainbow magic. She continued to shimmy, ensuring the lights caught the full brilliance of her costume. The iridescent feathers trailed behind her as she masterfully danced and shimmied, stealing the limelight. Not only did she win the prize for best costume and most talented dancer, but she also won the complete attention of Artis Newman.

It was evident by the shape of her legs that she took mastering her craft seriously. Belle, with her stunning physique, oozed confidence when performing, but once the performance was over, she was unpretentious. Smitten, Artis made a beeline for her, almost knocking her over in his haste to reach her. When she turned to see who the stumbling fool was, his infatuation was reinforced once he saw her up close. Her eyes, shadowed by an umbrella of lashes, were pure gold with curious flecks of chocolate floating around the iris. She held so much power in her eyes. Lost for words, Artis stood gawking. Despite the goofy look on his face, he looked quite handsome in his top hat and tailcoat, a crisp white handkerchief immaculately folded in his breast pocket, and a spray of imitation white daisies pinned to his lapel.

'What's the matter? Has the cat got your tongue?'

'Uh, no, miss. No cat. Just me, Artis Newman.'

'Belle Taylor.'

'Belle Taylor,' repeated Artis, fidgeting with his tie.

An uncomfortable pause ensued before Belle's friend interrupted, tugging Belle's arm.

'Come on, Belle.'

Belle turned to leave when, in a quick-thinking attempt to impress her, Artis reached into his coat pocket and took out his magician's wand, motioning for her to take it. There was mischief in his blue eyes. Intrigued, she took hold of the wand, and as Artis pulled it away, a flower popped out from the end. She smiled. Before he could help himself, Artis pulled a ping-pong ball out from behind Belle's ear and wiggled it around his fingers, making it disappear and reappear. He pulled two more balls out from behind each of Belle's ears and juggled them with ease. When he had finished, he looked at Belle as if expecting a treat.

'Not bad.'

'Come on, Belle!' urged her friend.

In a quick motion, Belle twisted her body, sending a spray of peacock feathers from her tail into Artis's startled face. He watched her melt into the crowd, peacock feathers swaying to the rhythm of her hips. Fervently pursuing her, he hauled himself through the mass of bodies, trying not to lose sight of the bobbing peacock tail. Just when he was an arm's length from her, she disappeared behind a door. As he reached for the doorknob, a surly man grabbed hold of him. He was the size of a gorilla and almost as hairy.

'Where do ya think ya going?'

Artis's eyes focused on the 'Ladies' sign on the door. Embarrassed, he attempted to calm the beast by pointing his magician's wand at him. In a flash, the beast snatched his wand, broke it in half, and tossed it on the floor.

'That wand cost me ten shillings, I'll have you know!'

'Beat it!' growled the beast.

Artis dived into the crowd, ducked down low, and made a quick turn, crawling back to retrieve his broken wand as he grumbled to himself. The beast was standing with his hundred-pound arms folded across his bulging chest. Artis slid behind a tall potted plant. When the beast turned to harass a tipsy man, he jabbed one side of the beast's buttocks hard with the broken tip of his wand, then bolted in a crazed run, sending bodies splattering in all directions. The beast gave chase, facilitating Artis's plan to lure him away from the ladies' room door. Then he ducked and weaved his way back, hiding behind the potted plant where he kept a hawk-eye out for Belle's exit.

This unfamiliar sensation and the uncontrollable way his body was behaving over a woman he had just met was a little unnerving. *Have I lost my mind?* he wondered. After a few minutes, her reappearance caused his heart to leap, and he took pursuit once again. The possibility of public rejection and being made a fool of only dawned on him when she turned unexpectedly, causing him to bump into her.

'Are you following me?'

'Uh, no!' Mortified, he lost his composure. She wasn't buying it. 'Well … yes.' Beads of perspiration glistened on his forehead. He fidgeted with his tie again, this time causing the false shirt front that was tucked into his pants to release. It rolled up like a Venetian blind, striking him under the chin and jerking his head back.

Belle laughed at the shocked look on his face. 'Are you performing tonight?'

'Ah, no. This happens to be the only suit I own.'

'So you're a performer?'

'A magician and juggler, although I don't suppose I made much of an impression. You got me all worked up with that number you did with all those feathers flying everywhere. I came here looking for dancers, as a matter of fact. I manage a vaudeville troupe,' said Artis, trying to regain his confidence.

'I already work in a troupe. Tonight's a one-off. It's a good opportunity to be in the papers.'

'Well, I've no doubt you'll make the front page, having won a prize and all. How about coming to work for me?'

'I told you. I'm not available for dancing or romancing.'

'Are you betrothed? 'cause I don't see no ring on your finger.'

'That's none of your concern.'

'Well, I'm hoping there's still a chance for me.' Artis gave her his most winning smile.

'You're quite incorrigible, Mr Newman. I have to go. Reporters are waiting to take my picture.' She felt a flutter of excitement well inside her, and before she could help herself, she gave him a seductive smile.

'Incorrig …, what? Bit of a fancy word there, Miss Taylor.'

Belle's friends were calling out to her, trying to hurry her along. She turned to leave.

'Hang on a bit! You can't leave me high and dry! I need a dancer.'

She disappeared into a mass of fancy dress costumes. From that moment on, her image was imprinted in his mind; she was all he could think about. *I'm going to marry her, whatever it takes.*

4

Overseas Romance

Tasmanian tour, Australia, 1929

The day after the Fancy Dress Ball, Artis raced out to buy the newspaper. After a sleepless night of heavy praying, his heart leapt at the sight of Belle's beautiful smiling face under the title *Belle of the Ball*. The reporter had written a glowing review and revealed the crucial information Artis was looking for—Belle's association with May Downs School of Dancing. He wasted no time getting there.

The twanging of a piano accompanied by the tapping of steel-capped shoes permeated into the street, bringing the drab building to life. He peeked through the door's glass porthole, hoping to see Belle. Instead, he caught the eye of the middle-aged dance teacher.

Once the lesson had finished and the students dispersed, Artis introduced himself and gave his rehearsed spiel about needing some dancers for his start-up troupe. He requested Belle Taylor and another dancer who was available to tour. To his surprise, she read him like a book.

'What's your interest with Belle Taylor?'

'Ah, well. She's a fine dancer. I saw her performance at The Glassy and was very impressed.'

'There were several of our dancers at The Glassy. I don't recall you asking for them by name.'

'Ma'am, I'm a professional. I scout for talent, and Belle Taylor stood out above the rest. As you're no doubt aware, she won the award for best talent and costume. I'm looking for the best.'

'I can book you two dancers, but Belle still has three months remaining on her contract with Vinnie McIntyre's troupe.'

'Vinnie McIntyre?'

'Correct.'

'Blimey!'

'Is that a problem?'

'No, he's my boss.'

'Interesting. Maybe you both need to communicate better. He obviously hasn't told you he's asked about renewing her contract—for a year this time. A year is quite unusual during these uncertain times, so as I said, I can book you two other dancers.'

When he hesitated, she said, 'Mr Newman, I'm very busy. I doubt you could top that offer, considering Mr McIntyre is your boss. Please provide me with a contract, touring schedule, accommodation and travel arrangements and I'll provide you with two exceptionally talented dancers.'

'Contract?'

'Do you not read the newspapers? This Depression isn't going to disappear anytime soon. A contract guarantees security. If you're the businessman you say you are, a contract shouldn't be a problem. Or perhaps Mr McIntyre needs to be told about the limitations of your management capabilities.'

'No, ma'am. A contract's no problem.' Artis smiled through clenched teeth. He was still reeling at the news that Vinnie had contracted Belle.

'Good day, Mr Newman.'

Artis gave her a nod before placing his fedora on his head. He left the studio, deep in thought. How could he convince Vinnie to allow Belle to dance in his troupe without causing suspicion? If Vinnie found out how he felt about her, he would never agree to a working relationship between them. That was only permissible for married couples. So intense was Artis's infatuation with Belle that he would marry her in a heartbeat. Yet falling out of favour with Vinnie, who had quite the temper when crossed and could be unreasonably stubborn, was the last thing he wanted.

Mulling over how to work the situation to his advantage caused Artis some sleepless nights. The numerous excuses he'd thought up to drop in after Vinnie's show for the opportunity to see Belle again were abandoned. Vinnie was shrewd and would immediately notice his infatuation. Then, out of the blue, his prayers were answered when Vinnie was given a financially rewarding opportunity to tour

Tasmania, due to the favourable media coverage Belle gained at The Glassy's Fancy Dress Ball.

'I ain't setting foot on no ship. You'll have to go in my place,' said Vinnie to Artis. They agreed Vinnie would train Artis's new cast to take over the Melbourne circuit whilst Artis took Vinnie's troupe to Tasmania.

In the lead-up to preparing for the Tasmanian tour, it was a challenge for Artis to keep his elation under control, considering his infatuation was now seeping through every pore of his body. It wasn't until he was standing on the deck of the *Nairana* watching the shores of Melbourne fade into the horizon as they entered Bass Strait that he began to relax. In his enthusiasm, he manoeuvred himself so he was standing beside Belle, who was leaning on the deck railing.

'You look happy,' said Artis.

'Yes, I've never sailed on a ship before,' said Belle.

'We'll just pretend we're sailing off to perform in London, shall we?' said Artis, his joy evident. Her smile encouraged him. 'It's nice to know we have eighteen hours to get to know each other a little better,' coaxed Artis. The smile disappeared from Belle's face.

'Hold your horses, Mr Newman. Let's get one thing straight. This may be an overnight trip, but there'll be no hanky-panky on my part.'

The colour drained from Artis's face.

'I beg your forgiveness, Miss Taylor. It came out all wrong. I didn't mean to be disrespectful.'

Belle turned on her heel and left him standing there with his head bowed, angry and embarrassed over his idiotic choice of words. He cheered up at the thought that she was a girl with morals and strong-minded when she needed to be. It confirmed she was worth pursuing.

Not everyone in the troupe was as enthusiastic as Artis about spending eighteen hours sailing unpredictable waters, especially when the weather turned bad and a few of the troupe suffered seasickness and were confined to their small cabins. Belle steered away from Artis, although she observed how respectfully he interacted with the other women in the troupe when they met in the dining hall for dinner. Rose, one of the performers, was dominant in seeking his attention, as she had been with Vinnie. To Belle's surprise, Rose's flirtatiousness sparked jealousy in her. She was flattered when she noticed Artis trying to get her attention, smiling at her with apologetic eyes. After dinner, she relented and approached him when she found him alone on the deck, staring out at the ocean twinkling under the moon's rays.

'I'm sorry if I snapped at you earlier. My mother was very nervous about me touring. She drummed into me to be cautious of men's ill intentions.'

'I understand. I didn't mean to sound disrespectful. I get nervous around you and it's like my brain freezes up.'

'Why do you get nervous around me?'

'Well, you're the most beautiful woman I ever set eyes on.'

She smiled.

'Well, you probably hear that all the time,' he said, then wondered why she began fidgeting.

'There's something I need to tell you,' said Belle.

Artis began perspiring, despite the icy bite in the air, when he sensed the tension radiating in his direction.

'Belle, there you are,' interrupted Rose. 'Lizzy needs your help. It's urgent.' Belle hesitated a moment.

'Goodnight, then,' she said.

Artis's heart dropped as she left abruptly, and Rose made a beeline towards him.

'You want some company?' said Rose.

'Maybe I should go see what the urgent matter is,' said Artis.

'Oh, it's women's business. Nothing you need to concern yourself about.'

'Right. Then it's probably a good idea for you women to stick together. I'll see you in the morning.' Artis excused himself, leaving Rose looking deflated.

Once they disembarked in Tasmania, the flurry of activity and excitement swallowed up the rest of their day. The tour was to begin at the Academy Theatre in Launceston before moving down the coast and looping through to the Theatre Royal in Hobart, then back to Launceston.

Belle and Artis began an emotional dance that kept Artis on tenterhooks. As a novice to courting, he had not expected that love would be a battlefield of emotions. Whenever he thought things were going well between them, Belle would suddenly withdraw and cause him angst.

Word of mouth about the show was quick to get around once the reporters who had been given VIP seats published their reviews. Artis understood why Vinnie had been given such a golden opportunity to tour Tasmania. Belle was the troupe's major drawcard, and she didn't disappoint the Tasmanian audiences.

With only a week before the tour was to end, Artis felt confident enough to manoeuvre Belle into a backstage nook and reveal his true feelings. They faced each other timidly, sensing what was coming. Artis could no longer restrain himself and moved in to kiss her. In their nervous hesitation, their lips tingled as they brushed against each other ever so slightly, stimulating their senses. Satisfied their passion was mutual, the kiss intensified and lingered until it incited a fire within them that caught them by surprise. They attempted to pull away, but the force of their passion pulled them back together. Belle ran her fingers through his hair, arousing him further. Cautious not to ruin the moment by touching her in a way that might offend her, he put his hand on the arch of her back. His height allowed him to look down at her face. The sight of her surrender took his breath away. He brushed her cheek with his fingers and was about to kiss her again when a man's voice interrupted them.

'Artis!' They recognised Bert's voice—one of the performers who was a great help to Artis in keeping the tour running smoothly.

'I love you, Belle. I loved you the minute I saw you at The Glassy,' he whispered. Her heart leapt at his declaration.

'Artis!'

He gave Belle a quick peck on the lips as they left their hiding spot and feigned packing costumes into their travel crates.

With the weight of his feelings for Belle released, he felt like he was floating. *I think she loves me too.* He gave his leg a shake and hoped his baggy trousers did their job of concealing his moment of arousal. He picked up a prop and held it in front of him as he met with Bert.

'There you are! You keep disappearing on me. The theatre manager wants to see you,' said Bert.

'Yeah, righto,' beamed Artis.

The rest of the tour was pure exhilaration, fuelled by the potion of love. While Artis and Belle were infatuated, they tried to be discreet, but within seconds of meeting in their backstage nook, they would embrace, releasing their pent-up emotions.

'What are you doing, Belle? Vinnie's going to hit the roof when he finds out what you're doing,' Rose warned.

'You jealous, Rose, considering you can't get Vinnie's attention either?' Belle surprised herself with her curt reply and immediately regretted her words.

'You're a two-faced Jezebel,' sneered Rose. 'You better watch your back from now on.' Her threat cast a shadow over Belle, although she acted nonchalantly.

The unease building up inside Belle as the tour came to an end clashed with her newfound passion. Although nobody said anything, Artis sensed the troupe was gossiping, and there was an air of tension that he couldn't quite put his finger on. He was beyond smitten, and nothing else mattered except being around Belle. Little did he know Rose had sent Vinnie a telegram and a hell-fire storm was brewing.

On their return to Port Melbourne, a swirl of menacing slate clouds dominated the sky. The crisp, salty air left Artis and Belle's faces tingling as they stood on the deck of the *Nairana*. They sensed their own dark cloud forming at the prospect of being apart.

'I'm gonna ask Vinnie straight out to swap troupes,' said Artis.

Belle stiffened. 'I better go pack my port,' she said, her eyes lowered. Artis felt his stomach twist with a pang of anxiety. He tightened his coat belt and adjusted the collar snugly around his neck. The warmth had drained from his body as soon as Belle left. He dragged his weight behind Belle's invisible trail to seek warmth indoors.

Artis was confused at Belle's sudden aloofness when the *Nairana* docked at Melbourne's port. To his surprise, Vinnie was waiting for them at the dock. By the look on his face, it wasn't difficult to guess there was anger simmering beneath his tweed cap. Artis puffed himself up with bravado and walked boldly towards him, his hand extended and a wide smile plastered on his face. In a split second, Vinnie punched Artis in the jaw with such force that he fell to the ground.

'Stop!' screamed Belle as she ran from the boardwalk just as Vinnie picked Artis up by the scruff of his neck, flailing him about like a rag doll. Artis was trying to get his bearings when Vinnie struck him again. Blood splattered from Artis's nose.

'What the bloody hell's got into you?' said Artis.

'Into me? What the hell are you doing messing with my girl?'

'What do you mean, your girl?' Artis turned to Belle. Her face was pale.

'Vinnie ...'

'You didn't tell him?' Vinnie cut Belle off.

'Tell me what?' Artis looked from Vinnie to Belle. Acid filled his stomach as Vinnie's words registered.

He stared in disbelief at Belle. She burst into tears. Vinnie pushed Artis with such force he fell back down to the ground.

'I'm through with you, Newman. Don't show your face around me again, or I'll be tempted to rearrange it good and proper.'

He snatched Belle's port and led her to his car. Artis cradled his head as he tried to absorb the shock of what had just happened. Bert, who was still disembarking when he witnessed the assault, approached Artis and helped him up.

'Why the bloody hell didn't you tell me Vinnie and Belle are sweethearts? I thought we were mates. Why didn't she tell me?' He dusted off his pants.

'We are mates, but it's not like you came clean with me, sneaking around like you did. And don't tell me you wouldn't have denied it.'

'Yeah, righto. But it's 'cause I didn't want Vinnie to find out and stop me seeing her, the rules being what they are. I sure as hell didn't know he was sweet on her, though.'

'He's more than sweet on her. He's well and truly lovestruck, just like you, mate.'

'So, Belle's been playing me?'

'Belle's a hard one to read. She seems pretty focused on getting famous. But, to be honest, seeing that look in her eyes when she's with you made me think she's sweet on you.'

'You think so? Cause it sure didn't look like it when she up and left me just now.' Artis straightened his bloodied clothes, whining at having his suit ruined. Taking a handkerchief out of his pocket, he rolled up the ends and plugged up his nostrils to stop the bleeding while pinching the bridge of his nose. 'What a bloody fool I've been.'

'Mate, what do you expect her to do? Vinnie's her boss, and he kept harping on about how he's going to make her famous,' said Bert.

'Well, right bloody mess this has turned out to be. How the hell am I going to sort this out?'

'Mate, if you love each other, nothing should stop you from being together.'

'Yeah, well, I got a feeling I've awakened the beast in Vinnie. She may not love him, but by his reaction, it's clear his feelings are pretty damn strong for her. I may end up at the bottom of the river wearing concrete boots.'

'Ain't a good woman worth fighting for?'

'Bloody oath!' nodded Artis. 'She's even worth dying for.'

'Well, let's hope it won't come to that,' replied Bert.

5

Fame or Love?

The next few weeks were torture for Artis. He hadn't been able to communicate with Belle, and he was now unemployed. In his desperate mission to win Belle back, he decided to put together his own vaudeville troupe and make her an offer she couldn't refuse. The Depression had reduced the price of merchandise, making it affordable for Artis to purchase all the equipment he needed to get him started. He calculated it was going to take every last penny of his savings and a lot of wheeling and dealing. Anything to get Belle back.

A surprise visit from Bert perked up Artis's spirits.

'How's Belle?'

'Well, I'm not surprised that'd be the first thing you asked instead of "Good to see ya, Bert. How've ya been?"'

'Yeah, course, mate. How've you been?'

'Oh, shut up! As for Belle, she looks as miserable as you.'

'Can you ask her to meet me at The Glassy on Friday afternoon at half past five?'

'I'll do my best. She's keeping her head low, and Vinnie doesn't let her outta his sight, so don't hold your breath.'

Friday afternoon couldn't come quickly enough. Artis arrived at The Glassy fifteen minutes early, a bouquet in his hand. He paced the sidewalk, mentally rehearsing his speech. All the while, his eyes flitted about the bobbing heads of the crowd in search of Belle's soft golden curls. Those fifteen minutes were spent worrying about whether Belle felt too intimidated by Vinnie to come. Or worse, if she even cared for him and had maybe led him on to make a fool of him.

All his fears melted away when a break in the crowd revealed his beautiful Belle. As their eyes met, their faces were illuminated with matching smiles. A surge of energy shot through him, and he hastened towards her. Their steps quickened as they weaved through bodies and connected in a lingering embrace. Belle noticed the faint yellow remnants of bruising around his eyes and nose. She smoothed his skin with her fingers as if she had the power to make the bruising disappear. Sensing Artis's embarrassment, she hugged him.

'You look very handsome,' she said, running her hand down his jacket sleeve. Admiring the extra effort he had put into his grooming, she brushed her fingers across the red and white carnation on his lapel. A stray strand of his hair had draped over his forehead when he removed his fedora. She repositioned it, noting the distinct scent of the Brylcreem he'd used to style his hair.

'They're not as beautiful as you,' he said, 'but there you go.' Her eyes sparkled with appreciation as he held out the bouquet. 'Let's get out of the cold,' he said, leading her across the street to a restaurant.

The waiter took their coats and hats and led them to a private booth. As soon as the waiter had left, Artis said, 'Belle, I need to know if you love him.'

'I'm so sorry. I should have said something. He just came on so strong, promising to make me famous, then offering me a one-year contract. The next thing, he's at my house speaking with my mother, who's pressuring me to sign it, saying opportunities like this are hard to come by.'

'It's okay, love. You came. That's all that matters.'

'Oh, Artis. I'm so sorry.' Tears spilled from Belle's lashes. She searched her handbag for a handkerchief, dabbing at her tears before they ruined her make-up.

'Love, I can offer you better than a one-year contract. I'm starting my own troupe and I want you starring in it.'

'Artis, I can't join your troupe.' Fresh tears pooled around her lashes.

'What?' Artis looked at her in disbelief.

'Vinnie expected you might try to start your own troupe. He's furious with you. Said he took a chance on you when you were sixteen, trained you and trusted you, and this is how you repay him. He's vowed to destroy you and anyone in his troupe who even thinks about joining you.' Belle's tears were now flowing down her cheeks.

'It's true. I owe him a lot, but who would've guessed we'd both fall for you like a ton of bricks? I don't feel good about what's happened, Belle, but you can't live in fear, love. I promise to look after you.'

'My mother forbids me to leave Vinnie's troupe. Since my father died, we've been struggling to make ends meet. When Mother couldn't afford to keep paying for my dance classes, the opportunity to work for Vinnie was a godsend. He convinced my mother he was going to do everything in his power to make me famous. You know how pushy he can be. Next thing, I feel as though he had my entire life planned out as if I belonged to him.'

'Did he ask to marry you?' Belle bowed her head as fresh tears surfaced. Artis's heart sank. 'Did you accept?' She nodded weakly as her shoulders bobbed in rhythm to her weeping. 'Oh, Belle,' he whispered, his blood turning cold. They were silent as they battled with their thoughts.

'I don't know what to do,' said Belle, breaking the silence.

'How about I meet with your mother and tell her my proposal?'

'My mother's convinced Vinnie has the reputation to make me famous.'

'Strewth! It's come down to either fame or love, then, has it?' His words weighed on her heart. Her chin began to quiver and tears welled in her eyes. 'I love you, Belle, and I'll make you famous.'

'If it were my choice, I'd choose you, but my mother has her heart set on my success. I can't let her down, Artis. I made her a promise.'

'I don't understand. How can you marry a man you don't love just to please your mother?'

'It's for my sister as well.'

'You never mentioned you had a sister.'

'She died.'

'Strewth!'

'She was my parent's little star. We both started dancing from the time we could walk. I idolised her. I wanted to do everything she did. My mother would enter her in every talent competition, and she won most of them. Everyone adored her. Then she got the poliovirus and a few days later she died.'

'Strewth, Belle. How old were you?'

'Twelve. I remember feeling as if a light had gone out. It devastated my parents. Then, nine months later, my father died, and I was terrified my mother would too and I'd be alone.' As much as Belle tried to catch her tears with a handkerchief, some escaped, dotting her silk blouse with dark spots. Artis felt the dreaded lump in his throat, which was his warning that tears were surfacing. Hearing Belle's story made him love her all the more. He reached across the table and held her hands.

'Belle, I dunno what to say, love, except that I'll look after you from now on. You won't ever be alone while I got breath in my body.'

'After my sister died, I promised my mother I'd get famous and make her proud.'

'I'll make you famous, Belle, and I'll love you along the way. I've come alive these last few months. You've lit a fire in me and given me the drive I need to create the best show around.' His intensity excited her. 'Let's do this together, love.'

'What about Vinnie?' Artis took her handkerchief and dabbed her tears.

'Don't worry about him. I can handle him. Do you trust me to look after you, Belle?'

'Yes, I trust you.' She surrendered with a smile.

'Finally, a smile! I was beginning to wonder if I was hiring a sourpuss.' Artis lifted Belle's chin and gazed into her eyes. 'You're such a beauty.' Belle saw the love in his eyes and blushed. 'I got a surprise for you.' Belle's spirits lifted. 'We met across the road there at The Glassy, remember?' Belle nodded, a reminiscent smile softening her face. 'Well, I asked you to come here 'cause I wanted to celebrate our new beginning.'

'What made you so sure I was going to agree to work with you?'

'I made a deal with God.' Artis smiled and Belle raised an eyebrow. 'I'm also good at begging,' he said, laughing.

'Well, I wasn't expecting a long engagement this afternoon,' said Belle. 'I was planning on catching the tram at half past six.'

'I wasn't planning a long engagement either,' said Artis with a cheeky look on his face. 'You're here now, and like I told you, I'll look after you and accompany you home. What do you say?'

'I get the feeling you're not going to take no for an answer.'

'You're a fast learner. I might have to up your wages already.'

'Can I get that in writing?'

'Your mother's taught you well.' Artis chuckled. He paused a moment before saying, 'You might like to go powder your nose or whatever you ladies do to freshen up. You have a little smudge just here.' He pointed to his cheek.

'Oh dear, I'm sure my face is a mess.'

'It looks beautiful to me.' Artis helped Belle out of her chair, then indulged in watching the gentle swaying of her hips as she walked towards the powder room. Her heels emphasised her shapely legs, encased in seamed stockings.

When she returned, she noted an impish look on Artis's face. He stood and motioned for her to sit as he pulled out her chair. As soon as she sat down, she jumped back up when she felt a hard object on the seat. Her reaction almost knocked the table over, much to the amusement of onlookers. Artis laughed heartily at her startled face. Hands on hips, eyes narrowed, she was about to give him a piece of her mind when she saw that the object on her chair was a jeweller's box tied in a red and white ribbon. Her heart skipped a beat, and a surge of nervous energy made her shaky.

'Go on, open it!'

Belle fumbled with the ribbon as she tried to restrain her tears. Artis got down on one knee as she opened the box and gasped at the ring.

'Belle Taylor, will you marry me?'

'Oh, Artis!'

'Is that a yes?'

'Yes!' Fresh tears sprang to her eyes. Artis leapt into the air and clicked his heels together. Diners who were watching with interest clapped.

'So, Belle, since you mentioned you weren't expecting a long engagement, how soon can we tie the knot?' Belle laughed.

After dinner, Artis accompanied Belle home. There was an aura of peace and happiness between them. Belle's mother, Olivia, was listening to the wireless with knitting needles clacking at an impressive speed when they bounded into the lounge room.

'Mother, this is Artis. He was my manager during our trip to Tasmania.'

Surprised at the unexpected visit, Olivia put down her knitting and switched off the wireless. She noted the bouquet Belle was holding and the radiant expression on her face.

'Nice to meet you,' she said, with reservation. 'Excuse my appearance. I wasn't expecting company.'

'You look just fine, Mrs Taylor. I can see where Belle gets her looks.'

Olivia smiled. She raised her shapely medium frame from the chair. Filaments of silver shone through the gentle waves of hair framing her face. There was a hint of melancholy in her caramel eyes, which were encircled by the fine lines of time. Her once porcelain skin was marred with faint blotches of pigmentation.

'I'll make us some tea and put these flowers in a vase,' said Belle.

Olivia invited Artis to sit. Her stiffness and pursed lips clearly stated she was not comfortable with the unexpected visit. An awkward silence followed. After scanning the room to find something that might serve as an icebreaker, Artis's nerves got the better of him. His leg began to jiggle. He bit the top of his thumb. Olivia noted the droplets of perspiration collecting on his forehead.

'Mrs Taylor, I'll get straight to the point.'

'Please do.'

'Yes, ma'am.' Artis loosened his collar. 'The thing is, Belle and I are very much in love, and I want nothing more than to marry her. With your permission, of course.'

'Marry!'

'Please hear me out. I know you want the best for her, and so do I. I promise to do everything in my power to make her famous, like you want for her. I'm planning on putting on a spectacular show and making Belle the star she deserves to be.'

'Mr Newman, I applaud your enthusiasm, but Belle has commitments she needs to honour.'

Belle returned to the room with a tray of refreshments.

'Mother, I know we've sprung this on you, but Artis has proposed, and I've accepted. We're asking for your blessing.' Belle held out her hand to display her engagement ring.

'You've accepted! Considering Mr Newman is asking for my permission, I can't permit it. You're still under contract with Vinnie McIntyre, and you've also accepted *his* marriage proposal. He is very well known in the business and has already provided you with excellent opportunities to advance your career.'

Tears welled in Belle's eyes.

'I only agreed to marry him because you both put so much pressure on me. I don't love him, Mother. I feel anxious around him.'

'He adores you, Belle. He might come across as a little overbearing, but that's because he adores you and wants the best for you.'

'Artis feels the same, Mother.'

'Yes, I can see that, but we've already made a commitment to Vinnie. He's already established and well known, and he's promised to make you a Hollywood star!'

'If I had to choose fame or love, Mother, I choose love. I don't want to marry a man I don't love. I want to marry Artis. Please give me your blessing, because either way, I will marry him.' Her defiant tone shocked Olivia, who realised she had no control over the situation.

'God help you both when you break the news to Vinnie. This will not end well for either of you. Mark my words. You're making a big mistake!' she said as she stood. 'Please excuse me.'

Olivia left the room. Belle burst into tears.

6

Performing Around the Traps

The wedding plans began immediately. Artis went back to Yarra Glen to face his parents. Not long after he'd run away at the age of sixteen, he had got in touch with Larry, who told him his parents were devastated. They had been so regretful that their draconian discipline had pushed him to run away that they had been prompted to find a less legalistic church and re-evaluate their parenting. Their change of heart made life for Larry tolerable, even though he continued to miss his brother.

Artis was warmly welcomed by his parents and the community after his long absence. His visit was one of celebration, especially when he gave them the news of his plans to marry. Plans were made for them to meet Belle and Olivia and to collaborate on wedding arrangements.

Belle's friends arranged an embroidery afternoon tea where she was gifted with a beautiful hand-embroidered quilt, tablecloths, sheets, tea towels, and a special nightgown to add to her glory box. Artis's mother Betty, an excellent seamstress, offered to adjust Olivia's wedding dress, which she had preserved for the time of her daughter's wedding. Betty also offered to make the wedding party's attire and the costumes for the show, which she would replicate from photographs of English music hall performers.

Despite Vinnie's threats to ruin them and Olivia's efforts to talk Belle out of the hasty marriage, Belle was adamant and wanted to move forward with their plans as quickly as possible. Not wanting to be separated from her daughter, Olivia expressed an interest in joining the troupe as their pianist. Prior to getting married, Olivia had worked as a movie hall pianist. She got to choose, and play, a list of music from hundreds of scores that would suit the mood of the movie scene playing on the screen. Olivia had perfected the art form over the years, allowing her to transform a silent black-and-white movie into a profoundly emotional experience.

Their life became a flurry of activities, from wedding preparations to securing a touring schedule, production planning and hiring performers. With Belle's help, Artis scouted and auditioned performers, and made all the touring arrangements. Bert asked to join the troupe with his new bride, Jean. They were masterful tap dancers and trained singers. Bert was also a talented comedian and musician.

'Mate, I appreciate your loyalty. But as much as I want you in my troupe, I don't need to infuriate Vinnie even more.'

'And I want no part of his vendetta. I know whose side I wanna be on.'

'Ta, mate. You're true blue.'

With so many entertainers out of work, it wasn't difficult to put together a talented troupe of comedians, jugglers, dancers, singers, musicians, acrobats, and contortionists. When Artis called his first meeting to brief his troupe on the planned tour, he felt an overwhelming sense of responsibility for them. The thought of failing his troupe and not being able to support Belle, let alone make her famous as he had vowed, caused him angst. And yet it was the motivation he needed to make sure he succeeded.

'Welcome to Newman's Pantomime Players,' said Artis, addressing the gathered troupe. 'This is both exciting and nerve-wracking for me. We've decided to perform *Puss in Boots* as it's a popular pantomime in England right now, and we're confident Aussie audiences will also enjoy it. I'll be playing the miller's youngest son, who's very upset at only having inherited a cat instead of his father's mill. Belle will play Puss, the cunning cat who proves to be a valuable asset. Puss knows that by securing great wealth for her master, she will also live in the lap of luxury, so she sets out with a plan to convince the King that her master is a Marquis and the perfect match for the Princess.'

Artis pointed out Giuseppe, who stood out with his six foot four, nineteen stone frame, oozing with solid muscles. He had been performing as the strongman in various troupes, adopting the stage name Samson, to justify his long wavy hair. His act included his beloved white and caramel Jack Russell, Metza.

'Samson has been cast as the ogre who lives in a castle and scares the living daylights out of the townsfolk by turning himself into any creature he desires. He meets his fate when Puss eats him after tricking him into turning himself into a mouse. Bert will play our Dame.'

The other troupe members listened with interest. Gracie, sixteen, and Tommy, eighteen, were inseparable sweethearts. Tommy was a musician, and also trained in carpentry, a valuable skill for building makeshift sets. Gracie specialised in ballet, jazz and tap. Her petite frame and childlike voice also enabled her to play children's roles. Fredric was a fifth-generation circus performer who'd migrated from Germany years prior. Dedicated to his craft as an acrobatic clown, he had created acts that were guaranteed to make him money. Birdie, who claimed to be eighteen, was a dynamo contortionist and gymnast with the temper of a stray cat.

'Now I'm gonna be straight out honest with you. I'm not rolling in dough, so we're gonna have to pull together to construct sets, make our props, and work the lighting. For starters, we need to make portable props for the King's carriage and throne, and painted backdrops for the ogre's castle.'

There were some enthusiastic suggestions and by the end of the meeting, Artis felt confident that he had chosen an exceptionally talented team who were as invested as he was in making the show a success.

Having learnt the value of good publicity, Artis got in touch with the newspaper journalists he'd formed relationships with over the years. They were willing to support him in his new endeavour and a few free tickets scored him an editorial feature to promote the show.

***

Upon learning of Artis and Belle's impending marriage, Vinnie did everything he could to ruin their reputation. This barrage of attacks included planting hecklers in the audience and bribing journalists to post negative reviews, which impacted ticket sales. The troupe's morale was low, and Artis was losing money.

'I'm a few weeks away from bankruptcy,' confided Artis over a pint with Bert at the local pub. 'I won't have enough money to even get married!'

'Mate, this isn't going to go down well with anyone, especially Belle and her mother. They had a pretty sweet deal with Vinnie,' said Bert swallowing a mouthful of ale.

'I don't know what made me think I could pull this off.'

'You were thinking from below and not above,' said Bert tapping his head.

'No, I was thinking from the middle,' Artis said, tapping his chest. 'What am I gonna do, Bert? I'm about to lose everything!' Artis grabbed a handful of peanuts and crunched them nervously.

'Buggered if know. Looks like we're all facing Poverty Point.' Bert gulped the rest of his ale and let out a long burp.

7

Kindred Spirits

'I can't believe she's marrying that scoundrel!'

Vinnie's rage was uncontrollable. He paced the dressing room, smashing anything within reach. Rose had known he would not take the news well when she had asked to see him in private, but was taken aback by the intensity of his outburst. 'She's supposed to marry *me*!'

'Artis pursued Belle from the moment we were on the boat to Tasmania,' said Rose.

'What's it to you, anyway? You were always complaining about Belle, from the minute you both joined the troupe. "Why does Belle always get the lead role? Why does she get to choreograph the dances?"' he said, mimicking her voice. 'Whine, whine, whine, that's all you ever do. And don't think 'cause you do it behind my back it doesn't get back to me. You've always had it in for Belle. That's clear as day.'

'I'm on your side. That's why I sent you the telegram,' said Rose, her eyes as dark as the sadness reflected in them.

Vinnie had never paid Rose any attention while Belle was around, though it had puzzled him that someone of her status had come to him looking for work. She came packaged in tailored clothes, fancy shoes, and jewellery dripping from her chest and wrists. And although her looks were pleasing to the eye, aided by heavy make-up, and raven hair cut in a bob with bangs that framed her elongated face, there was a sense of deep bitterness about Rose that had been brewing a long time and seeped through her personality to mar her beauty somewhat.

'What's it to you?'

'I want to help you,' she said. 'It's so wrong what they've done to you.' Rose's voice oozed sympathy. 'Artis has started his own troupe. All you have to do is make sure he fails.'

'Let's get this straight, Missy. I make the decisions around here! Is that clear?'

'I was just trying to help.'

'No, you're meddling.'

Vinnie lit a cigarette, contemplating how he would ruin Artis. Olivia had made Belle's desire to be famous very clear. She certainly had the talent, and with his monopoly over the booking agents and theatre managers, he had the means. If he destroyed Artis's business, and offered Belle the starring role in a London theatre production or a role in a Hollywood film, he was sure he would win her back. *I need more than connections to pull that off. I need a stack of dough to buy my way in to that level,* he thought.

'Can I propose taking Belle's place as the lead? I can work extra hours to train a new dancer to replace my role.'

'Ah, so there is an agenda. Seems like you've got this all figured out. What's in it for you?'

'I get the chance to shine with a man I admire.' Rose smiled.

'You realise how hard you're gonna have to work to get to Belle's level?'

The remark stung, but she focused on the fact that she now had his attention and was hell-bent on keeping it.

'You won't be disappointed,' said Rose.

'I already am,' he said and left the room.

Rose looked in the mirror, challenging herself to keep her emotions in check, searching her eyes for hints of weakness. Without batting an eyelid, she picked up tweezers from the dressing table and gouged her upper thigh in a new spot, releasing the pressure-cooked emotions that were bubbling on the surface. When blood trickled through her skin, she calmly placed a handkerchief over the wound and pressed hard on it until the bleeding stopped.

With Belle out of the way, she was determined to win Vinnie over. Regardless of her efforts to get his attention, he was captivated by Belle. Now that she thought she had a chance, she indulged in fantasies of Vinnie as her saviour. *He can protect me and cherish me. And I won't break his heart like she did.* In her desperation, she ignored his flaws, believing she could heal his broken heart. To Rose, his crude demeanour was overshadowed by his endearing Australianised

Scottish accent, his rusty smile, and the hint of buried sadness she believed made them kindred spirits. She had even convinced herself he needed her as much as she needed him.

From then on, Vinnie relentlessly pushed Rose during rehearsals to prove herself worthy. She worked herself to the point of exhaustion to please him. When he contacted his connections to get Rose on the front page of the newspapers, she thought she'd finally made a breakthrough in winning him over. His intentions, however, had nothing to do with Rose, but were intended to make Belle regret choosing Artis over him. His infatuation with Belle grew the closer it got to her wedding date. In his desperation, Vinnie began stalking her in the hopes he could talk her out of making a big mistake.

8

Tying The Knot

Melbourne, Victoria, & Tasmania, 1930

Belle and Artis were married on Saturday, 22 February 1930, at the Wesley Church in Lonsdale Street. Belle looked breathtaking in her mother's white satin and lace wedding gown, with a flowing veil. A peacock feather was the centrepiece of her floral arrangement. Artis's navy blue tuxedo boasted a peacock's feather in his lapel buttonhole, as did the groomsmen, and the bridesmaids wore a peacock's feather in their perfectly coiffed hair.

As the ice skating season had not yet started, Artis was able to arrange to have their wedding reception at The Glassy and was granted permission for Olivia to play the grand piano. Bert and Jean entertained the wedding party with Artis and Belle's favourite songs and a dance routine that rivalled Fred Astaire and Ginger Rogers' talent. The evening exploded in merriment as the newly formed troupe gave brief performances in honour of the bride and groom.

As a special surprise, Artis arranged a honeymoon in Tasmania, where he had also booked the troupe to tour. It was the only way Artis could keep the troupe going, knowing that Vinnie would not bother them in Tasmania. Nobody but Bert knew that he was on the brink of bankruptcy. He had managed to break even on a few shows and used the money his parent's had given him as a wedding gift to keep up the pretence that all was well. Artis had arranged for the troupe to sail across to the tiny isle after they'd enjoyed a short honeymoon.

Once the tour was on the road, the Tasmanian audiences welcomed Belle back and loved *Puss in Boots*. They received positive reviews and ultimately played to full houses. The costumes Betty created were outstanding and given a special mention in reviews. The role of Puss was perfect for Belle. She relished the role, moving about the stage with the graceful air of entitlement characteristic of a cat. She stretched and arched, moving in forward rolls, backward arches and cartwheels, whilst purring seductively in a bid for attention. Her boots had been specially designed in felt to allow her to do her acrobatics without them being cumbersome. Although Belle had a quiet personality and was gently spoken, she came to life on stage. A bubble of energy would burst from her delicate frame, wowing the audience.

One of the most hilarious scenes was when Puss convinced her master to remove his clothes and bathe in the river. The conniving Puss knew that the King and his daughter would be passing through. When

Puss saw the King's carriage, she ran over to stop it and get the King's sympathy by telling him that her master had been robbed of his clothes. The audience howled when Artis made a song and dance at being caught out naked. His beige bodysuit had well-rounded buttocks, exaggerated muscles, and painted six-pack abdominals. Jean, who was playing the Princess, won the audience over with her song and dance routines. She offered Artis a fig leaf to cover himself with and tried her best not to laugh at his antics. Fredric played the King with an amusing affinity for juggling whenever he picked something up.

When Artis was not on stage, he doubled as stage manager, flitting about, making sure everything ran smoothly backstage. He should have been feeling on top of the world as he watched his beautiful wife come to life on stage, but a knot of anxiety marred his joy. In the back of his mind, he was aware that his ecstasy was another man's pain, and he wondered how high a price he would pay for that.

***

A few months into the tour, everyone noticed Belle wasn't her usual self. She'd lost her stamina and enthusiasm.

'What's the matter, love? You look like you're down in the dumps,' probed Artis, as they were getting ready for bed.

'I don't know. I'm so exhausted.' She broke down sobbing.

'Why didn't you say something, love?'

'I didn't want to worry you any more than you already are. I thought I was coming down with the flu, but it's not going away.'

'Love, you're more important to me than anything. I'll take you to a doctor first thing tomorrow.' They embraced, and she snuggled herself under the crook of his arm. As he stroked her hair, it wasn't long before Artis was overwhelmed with love for her. Cupping her chin in his hands, he lifted her face to his and kissed her passionately. She responded, eager to give herself to him, all worrying thoughts vanishing at that moment.

After examining Belle, the doctor invited Artis into the room.

'You have a serious condition, Mrs Newman.' Belle and Artis held their breath, their eyes pinned on the doctor. 'You'll need to make some significant changes to accommodate your condition, starting with immediate rest. Your life will never be the same.' The doctor paused. The anguished look on their faces made him smile. 'Becoming parents requires making some major changes, especially in your business.' Belle and Artis released their stale breath in a burst of excitement.

'Parents!'

They left the doctor's office in high spirits.

'Oh, Art. This isn't good timing, is it?' said Belle.

'Love, you've made me the happiest man in the world. Don't you worry about a thing. I'll sort it. It's best we get you back to Melbourne.'

***

After investing the last of his money to revive the tour in Tasmania away from Vinnie's attempts to discredit them, Artis was managing to take in a small profit. He used the money to book venues in Melbourne and hired an advance man to print and display posters around town to promote ticket sales. They returned to Melbourne in high spirits only to discover that Vinnie's troupe had taken over their venue bookings and would be performing *Puss in Boots* in their place. Unbelievably, Vinnie had deceived the advance man and theatre booking agents with a story about Artis's troupe being delayed in Tasmania, saying that Artis had asked him to take over his venue bookings and prebooked ticket sales. The booking agents, knowing Artis and Vinnie's work history, didn't question this arrangement and the contracts were signed over to Vinnie.

'Bloody hell! He's hell-bent on seeing us lined up with all the unemployed actors begging for work at Poverty Point while he goes around town big-noting himself.'

Belle, Jean and Bert watched Artis pace the room, slapping the newspaper across his hand and waving it around for emphasis.

'So, we book a lower-end venue. That's not so bad,' said Bert.

'Yes, it bloody well is. We've worked too bloody hard to let some bloody Scotsman knock us down.'

'What choice have we got?' said Bert.

'That's bloody right. We're outta bloody choices. Not only that, but we'll have to work twice as bloody hard to put together a new show at short notice and recoup our ticket sales. Bloody Scotsman!'

'Why don't we perform *Hoity Toity* and *Snap Shots?*' said Bert. 'Most of us have got those pantomimes pretty much rehearsed. I can play the Dame and have Jean as the Principal Boy. Your juggling act with the billiard cues is always a winner and the troupe have got their sketches, songs and ballet dances in the bag.'

'Don't leave me out. I can still sing,' said Belle.

'Only if you're up to it,' said Artis.

'I feel better now that I've been drinking those ginger, turmeric, lemon and honey concoctions my mother's been making for me.'

'Seeing we won't be on stage at the same time, I can always back you up if you take sick,' said Jean.

'Sounds like a good plan,' said Artis. 'I'll get to work on booking another venue lickety-split. It'll probably be right outta town, so the troupe will have to pull their weight to get the word out by handing out performance bills and putting up posters if we're going to make any sales.'

They managed to pull it off after securing a lower-end theatre in the outer suburbs that happened to be available within a few weeks. Everything was back on track, although ticket sales were low.

9

Seduction

Melbourne, Victoria, 1930

After the evening show, Rose lingered at the venue until she and Vinnie were the last ones left. Her flirtatious behaviour since Belle left the troupe had not gone unnoticed.

'You look tired. How about I cook you dinner at your place?' she said, eyeing Vinnie with a smile.

'As long as you keep quiet. My landlord doesn't allow female visitors.'

Rose felt a surge of excitement as she entered Vinnie's home. They took their coats and hats off and placed them on the coat rack near the door. Rose peeled off her gloves as she scanned the room, noting the simple furnishings. Apart from a painting over the fireplace, there were no photographs or memorabilia.

'Nice painting. Where is that?'

'Edinburgh, Scotland. I couldn't believe my luck when I found it. My ma had one just like it.'

'Tell me about your childhood.'

'Nothin' to tell.'

She picked up on his tone and moved toward his gramophone.

'This is a beauty,' she said, stroking the gramophone, then sifted through the pile of records. After selecting a Bessie Smith record, she poured Vinnie a drink and unpacked the groceries she'd bought to cook dinner. After feeding him and getting nothing more than small talk, even after she'd fuelled him with whisky, she changed the record on the gramophone and manoeuvred him towards what she guessed was the bedroom door. He resisted and sat on the sofa, his eyes half-closed.

'I heard Artis replaced Belle as the lead in *Puss in Boots*.'

'And why would he do that?' Vinnie's eyes snapped open.

'She's pregnant,' she said, masking her delight at the expectation that Belle's condition would extinguish his infatuation with her. The pain in his eyes stirred her jealousy. Thankful that the whisky had sedated him enough to avoid one of his rampages, Rose pinned him with her eyes before hiking up her skirt and straddling him.

'Why don't you marry *me*? I can give you a baby and make you happy.'

'For Pete's sake! Have you lost your marbles?' Holding his gaze, she pressed her body against him and ran her hands through his hair.

Vinnie responded to her touch, the scent of her hair, her warm breath whispering in his ear.

'Take me,' she cajoled, cradling his head with her hands, her fingers twined in his thick curls. The light from the lampstand highlighted his emerald eyes; his pupils dilated in response to her touch. She had succeeded in melting the anger from his body.

She unbuttoned her blouse and watched him ogle her bare chest. A wave of lust engulfed him as she took his hand and cupped it over her silken breast. She felt a surge of energy run through his body. Lifting his head towards her, she kissed him deeply and sensually until he was completely aroused. They undressed clumsily and slid to the floor. His mind revelled in the pleasure she gave him as he took her lustfully. Rose worked her body hard, feeling triumphant. He had never experienced such pleasure, and like an addict whose mind had been possessed, he asked her not to stop. When they were both spent, they lay sprawled on the thick rug. Vinnie reached for his half-filled glass of whisky and lit a cigarette.

'Blimey, how many men have you had to perform like that?' Rose took the cigarette from his lips and inhaled slowly and deeply as she locked eyes with him before blowing smoke into the air. 'You've got yourself some mighty skills.'

'Skills to survive.'

'That you will. You give a man that much pleasure and he'll be at your mercy.' He eyed her lustfully. 'I still got enough in me for another round,' he said, grinning selfishly.

'Take me to your bed.'

'No.' Vinnie withdrew, downing the last of his whisky and lighting another cigarette. Like a feline entrapping her prey, Rose wrapped her legs around him.

'You haven't answered my question. Marry me.'

'You're damaged goods, Rose. Do you propose to every man after seducing them?'

Rose took the blow and immediately discarded it.

'What options do you have? Belle's married with a baby on the way. You'll never get her back now,' she retaliated, pleased by the cloud that came over Vinnie's face. To appease him, she used the softness of her lips to caress the sadness from his face. The electrifying tingle he felt as she traced his lips with hers was all-consuming. 'We're all damaged goods, Vinnie. We can wear a mask and pretend we're fine, but deep down, we're all hiding something. Your anger isn't just over losing Belle. I'm guessing you've had something else taken from you. Am I right?'

'What are you? A bloody psychologist as well?'

'No, but I'm a great catch. My family's got a ton of money.'

Vinnie's interest was suddenly piqued.

'What do you mean by a ton of money?'

'My father owns businesses all over town.'

'So why'd you never mention this before?'

'You took no interest in me. It was always Belle who had your full attention.'

'Your family's got a ton of money and you're performing around the traps for a living?'

'It's my escape. Something my father can't control.'

Vinnie eyed her suspiciously.

'Your father will approve of you marrying a man in the arts, will he?'

'He's never approved of anyone. I'm twenty now. He can't keep me locked up forever.' She ran her nails up and down his back as she pressed herself against him. 'Besides, you can convince anybody, Vinnie. And I can give you all the pleasure you want. All you have to do is marry me,' she said coquettishly, continuing her erotic play. 'So, you gonna marry me, or what?'

Vinnie groaned as she massaged his groin.

'You can't just spring something like marriage on a man.' She worked him harder.

'Marry me, or this will be the last time my body touches yours. I won't be your lover.' She looked him straight in the eye and when he was at the point of climaxing, she lifted herself off him, leaving him groaning in frustration. She covered her breasts and buttoned her blouse then took her panties, slip and pantyhose from the floor and finished dressing.

'Who'd a thought you had it in you, Little Miss Rose? You're a shrewd one with a heck of a lot of sexual experience for a twenty-year-old.'

'Are you gonna marry me?'

'What sort of business is your family in?'

'Mostly restaurants.'

'Could work. Line up a meeting.'

'It's not a business deal, Vinnie. You wanna marry me, or not? I'm not asking again.' Vinnie liked her spunk, wondering why he hadn't noticed it before.

'Yeah, why the bloody hell not?'

It may not have been the romantic proposal Rose had hoped for, but she felt victorious, even if it didn't ease her insecurities. For the first time since her childhood, she felt elated at the thought of finally being rescued by her Prince Charming. The thought of announcing the news to her parents, however, filled her with apprehension.

'I'll arrange for you to meet my parents over dinner. Have you been to the Italian Society Restaurant on Bourke Street?'

'Nah, not quite the artists' hangout. Why do we have to go there?'

'It's where my parents always dine. They own it.'

'Your parents are Italian?' Rose nodded. Vinnie eyed her suspiciously. 'What kind of Italians?'

'The business kind,' said Rose, diverting her eyes.

'So you want me to ask your father for your hand in marriage in a public restaurant?'

'Yes.'

Before he could ask any more questions, she worked him over again. When he was finally asleep on the rug, she peered into his bedroom. Her heart sank at the sight of a photo of Belle in costume on his bedside table. Fury rose inside her. She went into the bathroom and washed herself, then called a taxi to take her home.

10

A Deal with the Devil

Rose arranged for Vinnie to meet her parents after their midweek rehearsals. She changed her clothes in the dressing room and helped Vinnie with his bow tie. They were almost at the restaurant entrance when Vinnie noticed Rose was fidgeting. She gripped his arm.

'What's with the nerves?'

'My parents have no idea what this dinner's about. I've never spoken about you,' she said, biting her lip.

'You can't be serious! Why the hell not?'

'My father's not a fan of touring troupes. He only approves of the high-class performers at the Tivoli.'

'You tell me this now!'

'I'm sorry.' Rose bit her lip. 'He forced me to work for him before I left and joined your troupe.'

'What the heck have you got me into?'

'Please, Vinnie, you can win anyone over.'

The desperation and fear in her eyes made him uneasy. Who were these people? He put his arm around her shoulder and was about to guide her through the restaurant door when she manoeuvred him down a side alley and rushed him through a door that took them down into a basement.

Inside, they were swallowed by dim lights and stale air that reeked of cigarettes and liquor. Music guided Vinnie's eyes to a scantily dressed singer seated on top of a grand piano. From the waist down, she was painted with a silk scarlet skirt, beaded in diamantes. A shapely leg was exposed through a split that ran up her thigh. A diamante necklace dripped over her bare chest, covering her ample breasts. Vinnie was mesmerised as she slithered atop the piano before sliding off as the music changed tempo. His jaw dropped as she removed the diamante necklace, revealing silver threaded tasselled pasties concealing her areolas. She expertly gyrated her hips and shook her shoulders, making her entire body quiver. Turning her back to the audience, she flexed her buttocks to make them dance. Her grand finale was whirling her breasts, sending her tassels and onlookers into a frenzy.

'You used to work here!' said Vinnie. Rose blushed and pulled him away before he could ask more questions. She spotted her parents in their usual corner and led Vinnie to their table. The moment they arrived, Carlo's eyes pierced Vinnie's with the venom of undeserved hatred.

'Vinnie, these are my parents, Sofia and Carlo De Luca.' Their faces were stony. 'This is my boss, Vinnie McIntyre.'

'Pleased to meet you.' Vinnie extended his hand to Carlo, who ignored the gesture.

'You Irish?' shot Carlo, as if it was an offence to be Irish.

'Scottish.'

'Same thing. Sit down before you cause a scene,' said Carlo, giving Rose an icy look.

'I make my living from causing scenes and I don't sit where I'm not welcome.' Vinnie's steely stare cut through Carlo's arrogance. A tense pause ensued as they stood their ground. Sofia and Rose were transfixed. Finally, Carlo broke into a booming laugh. Vinnie didn't reciprocate. His dislike for the man was cemented.

'I was checking you had-a some balls. Sit down.' Carlo waved his hand at some chairs. Vinnie noted Sofia's poker face matched her stiff posture. Her eyes were sapphires, the pupils rimmed in gold. She was elegantly gift-wrapped in designer clothes and matching accessories. Her face, a portrait of fine art, was exquisitely painted in colour-matched make-up, and her hair was coiffed to perfection in a spiral horn. With a cigarette daintily balanced between her red-stained lips, she indicated to a waiter for a light. He promptly obliged. She inhaled delicately, tilting her head to one side before exhaling silvery swirls of smoke through puckered lips. There was an elegance in the way she held her cigarette between her slender fingers, her elbow tucked in close to her body, her hand flipped back, palm up, displaying a slim, white porcelain wrist.

A wave of impatience came over Carlo.

'Let's cut the crap. What do you want?'

'Rose and I are getting hitched.' Vinnie reciprocated the bluntness. A cloud came over Carlo's face. Sofia gasped. Rose stiffened.

'You didn't say nothing about an engagement, Rosa. Where's your ring?' said Sofia.

'We only decided a few days ago,' said Rose.

'What's the rush? You pregnant, Rosa?'

'No, Mama.'

'It's difficult to plan around the shows, so we're making the wedding part of the show. There'll be a lot of media coverage. It'll make Rose a star,' said Vinnie.

'A star?' said Carlo. 'I can make Rose a star!'

'Like your piano singer?' said Vinnie. Carlo locked eyes with him, then pinned them on Rose.

'You're good at keeping secrets, Rosa,' said Carlo.

'Yes, I am. You taught me that,' said Rose.

Carlo flashed her a look that sliced through her confidence. She looked away, afraid to meet his glare. There was a long silence as Carlo sat fuming, nostrils flaring as he digested the news while Sofia sucked the life from her cigarette, trying to pin Rose with a stare. Vinnie watched the scene with interest as Rose reached for a breadstick and proceeded to break it into pieces, then pulverised the pieces between her thumb and forefinger in an attempt to stop her hands from shaking. The mood shifted when Carlo, still deep in thought, finally calmed down and moments later broke the silence.

'I tell you what, Vincent. You are a businessman, yes? You and me, we do business.'

Rose became very uncomfortable and attempted to make eye contact with Vinnie, but he was fixated on what Carlo had to say.

'What kind of business?'

'You make a dinner show here.'

'Here?' Vinnie looked around. 'How many does it seat?'

'Two hundred. It's-a good for special night shows,' winked Carlo. 'Upstairs, it's one thousand. You can make bigger shows at matinee.'

Vinnie whistled. 'How would this business proposal work?'

'You make a show. I take fifty per cent.'

'Fifty per cent!'

'You don't pay rent. I bring the customers. You will make a lot of money. More than you can dream about.'

'You want to run vaudeville shows in your venue?' Vinnie was showing some interest.

'Nah, vaudeville!' Carlo flicked his hand in the air. 'Burlesque!' Vinnie felt a wave of excitement. Rose looked stony-faced, her eyes shooting him warning signals to no avail.

'Burlesque. I like the idea. But how do you make a lot of dough in this Depression? Our ticket sales have taken a dive. We've had to come up with ideas to keep audiences interested, like having our wedding as part of the show,' said Vinnie.

Carlo broke into a hearty laugh that irritated Vinnie.

'You are amateur businessman. I show you how to make money.'

Carlo smirked as his tongue slithered between his lips. He clicked his fingers for the waiter, who was at Carlo's side within seconds. Carlo proceeded to order the finest champagne, wine, lobster, and most exquisite food Vinnie had ever seen or tasted. It wasn't long before the atmosphere changed; Carlo's charisma had put a spell on Vinnie. The food and wine kept coming, and Vinnie and Carlo were conversing like long-lost friends as they became more intoxicated. Rose and Sofia played their part, with stony faces. *These people are loaded. I'm about to marry into the elite,* thought Vinnie.

***

One dinner was all it took to lure Vinnie into a new world that would transform his life in ways he could never have imagined. Swaying and in an alcohol-induced good mood, he leaned heavily on an unimpressed Rose as they walked back to Vinnie's car. He twirled Rose around and attempted some dance steps with her before opening the car door and helping her in.

'Are you serious about going into business with Carlo?' said Rose as Vinnie pulled out from the kerb, driving unsteadily.

'Bloody oath! There's a Depression going on and the man's rolling in dough. Why didn't you tell me he had so many connections?'

'You saw the kind of entertainment he offers. Do you really want to be a part of that?'

'If it's gonna make me a pile of dough, hell, yeah.'

'There's a reason I stopped working for him, Vinnie. His special nighttime shows are not what you think.'

Vinnie's prolonged silence made Rose nervous. He pulled the car over and shut off the engine.

'Listen, you sprung this whole marriage thing on me and now you wanna call the shots, too?'

'I'm in love with you, Vinnie. I fell for you the minute I laid eyes on you.' In a moment of impulse, her fragile mind had laid her desperate heart on the sacrificial table, exposing her soul to the wilderness of love. She would have said the same to any man who she thought might rescue her from her deep-rooted pain. Her heart was immediately torn when she saw the blank expression on Vinnie's face before he vomited out lies.

'Well, er, I'm fond of you too and I'm gonna make you a star.'

'Who said I want to be a star?'

'Every girl wants to be a star.'

'Most girls just want to be loved.'

'Everyone loves you when you're a star.'

'They love the star image.'

'What's wrong with that?'

'It's superficial. It's worshipping something that's not real.'

'You'd rather be a nobody?'

'I'd rather be your wife.'

Vinnie snorted.

'How do you propose to make me a star?' said Rose, stifling her disappointment.

'For starters, by making our wedding part of the show. You're already in all the newspapers. What better way to make the public love us than to invite them to our wedding?'

'And when you start my father's shows, what will you have me do?

Slither topless across a piano?'

'Don't play games with me, Rose. Do you want to get married or not?' Vinnie's tone was like ice in Rose's veins.

'Not if you make me work in Carlo's shows.'

Vinnie's silence escalated Rose's anxiety. It seemed like an eternity before he replied.

'Alright, you'll continue to star in the matinee shows and we'll hire someone else for the burlesque shows.'

'There's one more thing. Before our public wedding, I'd like a proper marriage ceremony at Scots Church.'

'You're kidding, aren't you? You can't possibly expect to have a church wedding when you've laid with men. Why do you think I came up with the idea of having a theatre wedding?'

His words cut Rose so deeply that she resigned herself to believe she was trash, as she'd been told repeatedly. *I should think myself lucky he's agreed to marry me*, she thought. Her mother's words echoed in her head: *A woman has no option but to rely on a man.* She suppressed the anger rampant within her as her childhood vision of a prince who would rescue, love, and protect her vanished. Vinnie leaned over and groped her breast.

'How about a nightcap at my place?' She stared out of the windscreen, wanting nothing more than to punch him in the face.

'Sure.'

***

When they were done for the night, Vinnie drove Rose home.

'Wow! Impressive,' he whistled as he parked his car in the

driveway.

Rose noted a shift in Vinnie's demeanour now that there was immeasurable financial gain for him connected to their relationship. Her vulva and breasts ached after performing to Vinnie's satisfaction. His fondling was heavy-handed, leaving her feeling more bruised than caressed. She had repeated the words *I love him* in her head to get her through the act. This became her mantra to ease the oozing pain of knowing deep down that her words were empty.

Vinnie pulled her to him and kissed her on the mouth, his fresh stubble irritating her silken lips. There was a jovial air about him as he stepped out of the car and walked around to open the door for her. It gave her a flicker of hope that she might, in time, win his heart and experience true love if she continued to love him the way he wanted. He walked her to the front door and pecked her on the cheek, as if someone could be watching.

'I'll see you bright and early tomorrow,' he said, noting her hesitation to enter the house and the flicker of apprehension in her eyes.

11

The Letter

After closing the door, Rose leaned against it, listening to the sound of Vinnie's footsteps, and moments later the roar of his car as he drove away.

The house was quiet. She hated it when it was quiet. Rose's heart was pounding, her apprehension building as she climbed the stairs to her bedroom. She prayed Carlo would not be waiting for her, knowing he would unleash the anger he had restrained at the restaurant. Her heart sank the minute she opened her bedroom door. Carlo was sitting in the corner, his shirt unbuttoned, baring his rotund belly flecked with grey hairs that cascaded from his chest. The light from the bedside table lamp cast an eerie shadow across his face. How she detested that face. Despite trying to hold them back, she felt hot tears stinging the back of her eyes. The dreaded silent pause he always used on her to build her terror was only broken when he could see her body shaking.

'What the hell was that stunt you pulled tonight?' He glared at her.

'He wants to marry me,' she said, trying to contain her emotions.

'You trapped him.'

'No, you need to let me go!' Rose cried.

'Let you go? You tried to kill yourself! I gave you freedom for six months and you go to be with this clown!'

'I can't work for you anymore. I can't do it. I'm getting married now.'

'No!'

'You're not my father. You have to let me go if I get married!' sobbed Rose.

'You are a bastard child that I made my own. You owe me respect for that.'

'You raped me when I was a child!' In a rage, Carlo jumped up and slapped Rose hard across her face, sending her sprawling to the floor.

'You dare to say this!' He raged as she lay crying hysterically on the floor. He kicked her with force.

'I showed you how to give a man pleasure. This is a skill that will serve you. You can have anything you want when you know how to please a man. But you already know this. You trapped him, didn't you?' Rose's sobs further angered Carlo. 'Answer me!'

'No.'

'You will not marry him.'

'Yes, I will.' Rose braced herself.

Carlo pounced on her, ripping her blouse to expose her breasts. She struggled to stop him from turning her over, knowing what was coming. He bent her over, leaning his weight on her back, one hand clasping a handful of her hair, causing her to face the ceiling, her eyes wild with terror.

Knowing that her pleas for help were always ignored, she mustered every bit of strength she had to free herself as he pulled down her panties. In a swift movement, she was free and ran to her bedside drawer, ignoring the pain as a tuft of her hair was pulled from her scalp. She fumbled through the drawer and just as Carlo reached for her, his fist ready to pound, she pulled out a gun and aimed it at him. It had the desired effect of stopping him in his tracks.

'Stop!' said Rose, trying to control her shaking as she positioned her finger on the trigger. Carlo stared her down, hoping to intimidate her. 'Don't move or I swear I'll kill you. I've written a letter exposing your illegal businesses and everything you've done to me since I was a child. I've included the photographs you sell of me and the other girls, as humiliating as they are, so I'm sure to be believed.'

'You lost your mind. I look after you. I buy you everything you want.'

'No, you buy me things to shut me up. You destroyed my life!'

'You said you like it. You say you love me.'

'You make me say that. I hate you!' In her fury, she aimed the gun at his head. 'It would feel so good to kill you.'

'You're crazy, Rosa. You're taking too many drugs.'

'You made me this way. Leave me and Vinnie alone, or I'll expose you and ruin you. You'll rot in prison for what you've done!'

The shock rendered him immobile for a few moments.

'You're a whore, Rosa. You service cops. They're on our side. You know that, you stupid girl.'

'Well, lucky for me, I had an undercover cop who wasn't looking for tricks. He's looking to bring you down. Said he could protect me if I gave him the information he needed and because I hate you so much, I put it in a letter with his name on the envelope.'

'Where is this letter?'

'Why would I tell you? It's my insurance policy. You've taught me a lot more than you realise. If anything happens to me, the letter will be handed to the undercover cop.' Carlo weighed up her words, his eyes slits of fury.

In an instant, Carlo snatched the gun out of her hand and slugged her in the face, knocking her to the ground. He picked up the gun and held it against her temple as he pinned her body down with his knee.

'Give me the letter or that clown will have an accident. Capisce?'

'No, the letter will protect us both,' said Rose, blood flowing from her nose. She had urinated from the shock and was shaking uncontrollably as he pressed the gun hard against her temple.

She braced herself as he unleashed his fury on her, demanding that she tell him where she'd hidden the letter. No matter what he did to her, she refused to tell him. After he defiled her in the most despicable way, he left the room wheezing from the exertion.

In agony from Carlo's torture, it was some time before Rose could move from her foetal position without being overwhelmed by sharp pain throughout her body. She cleaned herself up from Carlo's filth and put on fresh clothes, reeling with the pain of these simple acts. With pained, slow steps, she edged her way towards the telephone downstairs, then dialled a number, letting it ring three times before hanging up. Tearfully enduring the pain of the exertion, she made her way outside to wait at the street corner. Mercifully, it did not take long for her grandfather to pick her up.

'Bastardo!' said her grandfather. 'I will kill him!'

'I'm okay, Nonno. You don't want to start another family war,' said Rose, allowing her grandfather to help her into the car.

'You not go back this time. I forbid it. Your Mama must come too.'

'You know she can't, Nonno. He would kill her.'

'Ah, I kill him first!' he said, his face darkened by his mood. 'You marry a good man, yes?'

'Yes, Vinnie is a good man, but Carlo offered him a business partnership to put on shows at the clubs.'

'This is not good. He must not do this thing.'

'I know, Nonno, but Carlo is too clever. He made Vinnie a deal too good to refuse and is doing the usual of buying him luxury items. Vinnie is sold and I don't know how to stop it.'

'Ah, this is not good,' he said, using the road as his personal racetrack, unaware of the pain the velocity was causing Rose as he turned corners. She gripped the door handle to steady herself.

Her grandparents had sheltered Rose many times whenever Carlo was on a rampage. It was her safe place to heal, where her Nonna would fuss over her and cook meals with fresh produce from Nonno's garden. It wouldn't be long before Sofia called her back, in anguish over some drama with Carlo. Nonna would try to convince her to stay. Rose's relationship with her mother was complicated—a co-dependent pendulum of love and hate. At least she knew she was safe at her grandparents' house. Carlo would not dare to go there or send any of his men.

It took a few days for Rose to recover from Carlo's beating. She told Vinnie she'd fallen down the stairs and needed some time to recuperate. When she went back to work, Rose applied her Max Factor stick foundation a little thicker than usual. She had become masterful at using the right shades of colour to camouflage any evidence of abuse on her face or body. Everyone was used to seeing her heavy-handed make-up and thought nothing of it. Although the cuts on her wrists, from the last attempt to end her life, had healed months prior to joining Vinnie's troupe, she covered the scars with foundation and bracelets. Alarming Vinnie about the true nature of Carlo was not in her best interests if she wanted to ensure the wedding went ahead.

Introducing Vinnie to Carlo had been a fatal mistake, although a necessary step if she was to marry Vinnie. She had never expected Carlo would propose a business deal. The very entrapment she so desperately wanted to escape had now ensnared her husband-to-be, ensuring she would never escape the clutches of Carlo and his mob.

'Vinnie, I'm begging you to reconsider going into business with my father.'

'Why would I? There's a Depression going on and the man's raking in money. In fact, Carlo just told me if things work out in the next month, he'll up my share to sixty per cent. This is my chance to pay back that dog Artis for messing with me. I'll ruin him while he watches me living in the lap of luxury.'

'Once you work for my father, there's no turning back.'

'For Pete's sake! Do I have to keep reminding you, you're the one that hauled me into this? For better or worse—ain't that the marriage vows?'

Rose remained silent, deciding to keep her secrets buried a little longer. Her letter was the only way out, but Carlo was playing his cards right. The possibility that things could go horribly wrong was becoming a real concern.

12

Avoiding Poverty Point

Melbourne, Victoria, 1931

Belle gave birth to their daughter, Shelley, in the dry, sweltering January heat. The newspapers' doom and gloom stories about the Great Depression did not dampen Artis and Belle's happiness over their firstborn. While competing with Vinnie meant they were barely breaking even, Artis was at least making a name for himself.

The delight Artis expressed towards his darling daughter was heartwarming, though watching him dance around the room while holding Shelley caused Belle some concern.

'What on earth are you doing? She's going to throw up her milk!' said Belle.

'I'm teaching her to dance. She'll be performing in no time.' The motion caused Shelley to projectile vomit. Then she proceeded to scream the house down. With flecks of sour milk stuck to his hair and running down his face, Artis panicked and immediately handed her over to Belle.

'Well, what did you expect? It made me dizzy just watching you,' laughed Belle.

Belle's protective maternal instincts made her hesitant to leave her precious baby in the care of a clueless husband. What she didn't expect was the shock she was about to receive on a balmy February night when Shelley was just six weeks old. The troupe was performing at the Apollo and Artis insisted Belle come to see the show with Shelley. The stuffy air of the theatre, mingled with perspiration, greasepaint and decades of dust, made it particularly stifling, especially backstage in the wings, where Belle sat holding Shelley.

Jean had taken over Belle's role until she was ready to return to the stage. She approached Belle in a flurry.

'Ooooh, let me have a cuddle.'

'Aren't you about to go on?'

Before she finished her sentence, Jean had whisked Shelley to centre stage, where Artis, Bert and Fredric were sitting at a table with a deck of cards fanned out in front of them. Jean breezed in, looking very elegant in a cream mid-calf rayon dress, thick beige nylon stockings, and black side-buckled court shoes. Rich, soft caramel curls poked out from under her hat.

'Look, fellas. Isn't she just divine?' She held Shelley out for the men to see. They craned their necks and nodded in unison. Jean then showed the audience, who let out 'aws' and 'ahs' while Belle watched in shock from the wings.

'She's sweet as punch,' said Artis.

'Now, dear, I have to run a few errands. As this is the first time I'm leaving her in your care, you need to promise me she'll not leave your sight.'

'Course, love, but what am I supposed to do with her?'

'If she wakes, you'll need to comfort her until I get back.'

'Fine, dear. Can you put her in the basket?'

'It's not a basket, it's a bassinet.'

Jean wiggled over to the bassinet and bent over to place Shelley inside. The men gawked at her derriere and shapely calves, unaware that they were all leaning almost horizontally from their chairs. Jean placed Shelley in the bassinet, turned on her heel, and, with an elegant flourish, exited the stage. The men followed her movements, straightening themselves up from their horizontal position until they were sitting bolt upright, their heads turning in unison as they watched her exit.

'Cheerio!' said Jean.

Artis noticed Fredric and Bert's lustful gazes and slammed his fist on the table.

'Oi! That's my lady you're looking at. Get a grip!'

The men snapped out of it and continued their card game. Within seconds, Shelley started to cry. The men continued playing, oblivious to her cries. The wailing became louder.

'For crying out loud, I can't think with all this racket!' said Fredric.

Artis set down his cards and stood up.

'What am I supposed to do with her?'

'Stick a dummy in her mouth,' said Bert.

Artis moved over to the bassinet and peered inside. He reached into the bassinet and pulled out a dummy. It was the size of a small football.

'How am I gonna fit this in that wee mouth?'

Shelley's screams reached an ear-piercing level. Artis dived the dummy into her mouth. Within seconds, the dummy was projected through the air and landed on the floor. Fredric and Bert looked astonished. They covered their ears as Shelley's screams continued to escalate. Artis picked up the dummy, blew off the dirt, spat on it, and wiped it on his trouser leg before attempting to stick it back into her mouth. Again, the dummy was projected into the air. They covered their ears as Shelley continued to scream.

In frustration, Artis picked her up and jiggled her in his cradled arms, but she continued to scream. In desperation, Bert and Fredric plugged their fingers into their ears. Unable to stand the shrieks any longer, Artis passed Shelley to Bert and stuck his fingers in his ears. The men took turns cradling her. They paced the room, trying to pacify her. When jiggling did nothing to console her, Fredric tossed her across the room towards Bert.

'Catch!'

The audience and Belle gasped as she watched from the wings, wondering whether to intervene. Bert skilfully caught Shelley and passed her from one man to another, like a football. The only time Shelley was quiet was when she was flying through the air. They continued to hurl her across the stage, letting out a triumphant yell each time she was caught. They called out their passes as if they were playing football. Once they stopped, Shelley screamed again. Artis put her back in the bassinet and slumped into a chair.

'What now?'

'How long do these things take to grow?' said Fredric.

'Maybe if we put her in the oven, she'll come out grown!' said Bert.

'Don't be ridiculous! She's not a loaf of bread!' boomed Artis.

'Trust me, I've seen it work,' said Bert.

'Let's try it. I won't be able to stand all this crying much longer!' said Fredric.

'What if she comes out toasted? My wife'll kill me!'

'If you don't do something to shut her up, I'll kill you myself!' said Fredric.

'Why, I oughta punch you in the nose!' said Artis.

Shelley continued screaming, and in desperation, Artis took her back out of the bassinet, put her in the oven, and closed the door. Bert set the timer on an alarm clock, and they went back to playing cards. Artis looked nervous as he listened to the muffled sounds of the crying baby diminishing. The alarm went off with a loud ring. Artis jumped up and ran to open the oven door. He let out a mighty shout as an enormous baby crawled out, sucking on an oversized dummy, wearing a bonnet, miniature dress, and nappy.

A roar of laughter filled the room, followed by thunderous applause. Belle, whose suspicions were confirmed, smiled at the gag. Artis, a master of improvisation, was always thinking of novel ways to shock the audience. He had placed a prop doll inside the bassinet to be used as the football-throwing doll. Backstage, Gracie, dressed as the grown baby, was emulating the baby's cries. One of the backstage crew had retrieved Shelley from the bassinet, which was rigged with a secret opening at the side. Gracie threw the oversized dummy out during the gag and then crawled into the backless oven.

Relieved to have Shelley back in her arms, Belle wondered what was to become of her daughter, who had just made her first stage appearance at the tender age of six weeks. She seemed quite unperturbed by the roar of the audience, the stuffy air of a well-worn theatre, the bright lights, music and rapid backstage hustle.

Gag aside, for the past few weeks Belle had sensed something was amiss with Artis and no amount of probing would get him to open up. As much as she tried to focus her attention back on the performance, she could see Artis was particularly unsettled and fidgety.

Back on stage, Artis, Bert, and Fred gathered around Gracie, who was sucking the oversized dummy with gusto.

'Honey, I'm home!' Jean re-entered the stage, her presence freshening the stale air like a cool ocean breeze. 'How's my darling Shelley?'

The men formed a circle to hide the oversized baby. Jean walked over to the bassinet and peered in.

'Where is she?'

The men scratched their heads and shrugged their shoulders in unison. Jean moved in closer. They crab-walked in unison to hide Gracie. Jean moved to the other side of them to get a look at what they were hiding, but they followed her steps in a crab walk. Their pace quickened as Jean tried to outsmart them, stretching out her neck to see what they were hiding. Gracie let out a loud cry. The men froze. In a mighty heave, Jean pushed them aside and screamed at the sight of Gracie. She fainted in grand style.

The wave of laughter and applause from the audience was intoxicating. It lifted the cast and crew's morale and validated all their hard work. As the curtain closed, the performers scurried about backstage, as quiet as mice. Birdie, the contortionist, was on stage within seconds of the curtain closing as the front-cloth performer. The audience watched with amazement as she twisted her body into pretzel shapes with ease. After bending backwards and forwards with her head peeking through the opposite side of herself, she lay face down on the ground arching herself into a circle with her feet touching her head and then shot forward into a C shape. She then did a handstand and folded her back in half whilst balancing on one hand. The crowd stared in wonder, mesmerised by the rubber girl in her vibrant leotard and slippers.

In the meantime, behind the front curtain, the scene was being set for the Big Scena.

'Honey, can you pin me? My zipper broke.' Jean rushed over to Belle and handed her a safety pin. 'What's up with Artis?'

'What do you mean?' said Belle.

'He's wound up tighter than a two-dollar watch.'

'You noticed too. I wish I knew. He thinks by telling me to leave the worrying to him it stops me worrying.'

'Men have no logic,' said Jean.

Belle handed Shelley to Jean and pinned her bronze strapless taffeta dress to secure the zipper. It was an elegant garment that trailed behind her like flowing water. The bodice and hem had black satin ribbon woven through them, which made it even more striking. As much as Belle loved being a mother, she missed performing and was looking forward to returning to the stage.

Jean winked at Belle as she positioned herself at the left wing and waited for her cue. Birdie finished her contortionist act by passing her body through a metal hoop whilst balancing a glass of water on her forehead. The audience's tension subsided once Birdie took the glass off her forehead and drank the water. She left the stage to the sound of applause. The curtain reopened to reveal a different backdrop and set for Jean's act.

The orchestra sprang to life as Jean floated on stage singing 'Give My Regards to Broadway', with her dancers in tow. She masterfully seduced the audience into singing the chorus with her. A larrikin in the audience let out a wolf whistle that prompted a slap from the woman sitting next to him. Artis knew the value of spectacular costumes, especially when they were designed to accentuate certain parts of the female body. Apart from talent, a pair of well-toned legs and ample cleavage was a performer's best asset.

With each act, the audience's mood changed. Artis watched from the wings, unseen by the audience. He evaluated the audience's appreciation of each act and ascertained what needed changing or improving, or what needed to be scrapped. Bert and Artis were next in line to perform. Bert was dressed in baggy pants and a checked shirt, with a long, thick red tie around his neck and his red clown's nose resting on his forehead, ready to be put in place before he got on stage. His heavy make-up highlighted his comical face. They nodded to each other in a silent greeting.

Jean's voice rose to a climax, holding the audience captivated. The orchestra faded out as the applause rose. Jean and the dancers exited the stage as the curtain closed. When the applause died down, Bert adjusted his clown nose and entered the stage in a series of somersaults. He took several balls out of his pockets and juggled them. Artis, who was playing the straight man, walked onto the stage and began announcing the next act when he noticed Bert.

Artis: Oh, so there you are!

Bert: Where?

Artis: There! (pointing to Bert)

Bert: Oh, so I am. I wondered where I'd got to.

Artis: I've been looking all over for you.

Bert: Well, I was there.

Artis: Where?

Bert: Where you never looked. As a matter of fact, I've been for a walk to let the summer breeze blow on my face.

Artis: Well, here's another kind of blow on your face.

Artis slapped him across the face, sending him hurtling sidewards into a cartwheel. The audience roared with laughter.

Artis: And what a face! Do you know what I'd do if I had a face like yours?

Bert: (rubbing his cheek) No, what would you do if you had a face like mine?

Artis: I'd put it up against a wall and throw a brick at it.

Bert: Oh, would you now! Well, do you know what I'd do if I had a face like yourrrrs?

Artis: No, what would you do if you had a face like mine?

Bert: I'd put it up against a brick and throw a wall at it. And not only that, I'd fry it.

Artis: Indeed!

Bert: No, in dripping!

Laughter erupted from the audience as the men chased one another around the stage. Bert was jumping and back-flipping, trying to avoid Artis's clutches. Artis stopped suddenly and held out his hand, palm facing forward. Bert ran into his hand and did a backflip before falling onto the floor. He quickly stood up and straightened his jacket.

Artis: You know, I read in the paper that they're gonna have women on the juries.

Bert: You can't have women on a jury.

Artis: Why not?

Bert: Just imagine three men and three women locked up together all night. Then they come out the next morning and say, "Not guilty!"

The gag was well received, with hearty laughs and applause. Artis and Bert made a wonderful team. Their timing was perfect, and they knew how to use their facial expressions and bodies to enhance their performance.

Artis: Now, on a more serious note, I've had a request from a member of the audience to recite the poem called 'The Boy Stood on the Burning Deck'.

Bert: Ah, yes. A very tragic piece, that is. You go right ahead. I'll just stand over here out of the way.

Artis: Thank you.

With a serious face, Artis starts reciting the poem.

The boy stood on the burning deck
Whence all but he had fled
The flame that lit the battle's wreck
Shone round him o'er the dead.

Bert let out a scream that jolted Artis.

Bert: Oh, it's alright. I thought my tongue was hanging out!

Bert pulled at his red tie and then plastered it down onto his shirt. The audience laughed.

Artis: Please, you're ruining the mood!

Bert: Terribly sorry. Please do go on.

Artis: Thank you.

Turning back to face the audience, Artis opened his mouth to continue when Bert interrupted him again to recite his variation of the poem.

The boy stood on the burning deck
Playing a game of cricket,
The ball flew down his trouser leg
And hit his middle wicket.

The audience howled. Artis pushed Bert to one side.

Artis: Right, you need to stand there and not say a word, or, so help me God, I'm going to punch you right in the nose!

Bert covered his nose in fright and by the time Artis walked back to centre stage, he had begun picking his nose, using exaggerated digging motions and comical facial gestures, indicating he was on to something big. Meanwhile, Artis positioned himself centre stage and was smoothing out his suit and patting down his hair, ready to continue his recitation. By this time Bert had rolled his findings between his thumb and index finger and with a mighty flick aimed his booger ball at Artis. He made a whistling sound and rolled his head, following the direction of the booger as it landed smack on Artis's face. With an exaggerated gesture, Artis reacted as if the booger had almost bowled him over. He clasped his hand to his face.

Artis: Why, you rotten scoundrel!

Artis got a handkerchief out of his pocket and tried to wipe his cheek, but the hanky got stuck to his cheek. The audience was laughing hysterically as Artis chased Bert around the stage with the hanky on his cheek. He took a swipe at Bert, who did a backflip. Artis continued to swipe at him as Bert backflipped off the stage into the wings.

The curtain closed. The audience continued to clap and laugh uproariously. Belle caught Artis's worried look as he peered through the curtain to see the audience.

'Artis, tell me what's going on.'

'Not now, love. You'll know soon enough.'

When the show ended, everyone busied themselves with removing their costumes and make-up and packing all the props, equipment, and backdrops. Belle looked everywhere for Artis and found him at the back entrance door. He was speaking with a man she didn't recognise. The man was shrugging his shoulders and shaking his head. Artis threw his hands up and walked away. His mood was heavy as he walked backstage.

The troupe waited for Artis's usual debriefing once everything was packed, and everyone was ready to leave the theatre. The atmosphere was electric with the buzz of well-received performances. Performers, musicians, and crew were all energised and chatting about highlights and moments that hadn't gone according to plan. The mood shifted when Artis entered with a dark cloud over his head. He looked queasy. Instead, the dreaded words ejected themselves from his mouth.

'Our shows have been cancelled,' he said, pained at the devastated expressions the news caused.

'Is this Vinnie's doing again?' said Fredric.

'No, this time we can blame the economy.'

Artis lowered his eyes when he saw the fear on the faces of his troupe. The severity of the Depression was becoming a harsh reality. They had dodged it for a while, but finally, the dark cloud rained down on them. Artis couldn't bear to look at them, knowing he'd given them hope they would make it through. What hurt him most were the promises he'd made to look after Belle and make her famous. The weight and embarrassment of failure pressed down on him. Everyone's worst fear during the Depression was to be out of work.

'Is there anything we can do?' said Bert.

'I just spoke with the theatre owner. The bloody bank's forcing him to close his theatre 'cause he's six months behind on his mortgage payments, plus he has a massive tax bill to pay. He's doing what every other theatre owner is doing these days—switching to showing talking pictures. Talkies are easy money, and they can have as many showings a day as they can fit in. Apparently, it's all the rage and what city folk want.'

Even the majestic Tivoli Theatre was barely surviving, and the King's Theatre had suffered a backstage fire. The deathly silence of the troupe was excruciating for Artis.

'What about the Melba or Garrick Theatre, the Trocadero, the Windmill? Or even the town halls?' suggested Jean.

'I've tried them all. We're not exactly on the elite performers' list. I got nothin' to offer you. I hoped I could talk the owner into letting us finish the tour, but he stood firm, so now I'm gonna have to refund the pre-sold tickets. A bloody mess is what it is.'

'You can thank our government for the high tax on live shows,' said Bert.

'What chance have we got against the talkies? Everyone's curious to see them,' said Fredric.

'They're cheaper than putting on a production with costumes and sets and wages for performers and crew. It means we have to charge higher admission prices,' said Artis.

'I still can't believe they've turned the Theatre Royal into Manton's Drapery Store!' said Jean.

'Even worse, I read in the paper that they turned the Palace Theatre in Sydney into a miniature golf course!' said Bert.

'It's a crying shame,' replied Artis.

The troupe started loading Artis's truck at the theatre's loading dock with all their costumes and props. Artis looked at the empty theatre, depleted of all the vibrant energy that had made it come to life less than an hour before. The stage was bare except for the beautiful velvet red curtains. When they finished loading the truck, they switched off all the lights. It was all over. Just like that.

13

A Public Wedding

Melbourne, Victoria, 1930

The next few weeks were a whirlwind of wedding arrangements for Vinnie and Rose. Vinnie contacted every reporter in town to create a buzz. He was offering wedding show memorabilia with every ticket sold and suggesting people wear their wedding day best for their chance to be caught on camera by the reporter commissioned to take photographs. The enticement included the possibility of being caught in a shot that ended up as front-page news—something everybody would love to have in their scrapbooks.

Rose got caught up in the excitement of being hounded by the press for photographs whilst she shopped for a wedding dress. The public's admiration gave Rose a sense of euphoria she'd never experienced before.

The wedding day performance had the theatre packed to maximum capacity. Once the band struck up their tune, and the curtains were peeled open, the restlessness of the audience subsided. A freestanding coat rack on which hung a trench coat and fedora was spotlit on centre stage. The spotlight darted around the stage and then returned to the coat rack just as the trench coat came to life, sprouting arms and legs and a head that popped into the fedora. Vinnie shook himself loose from the coat rack and paraded downstage with a radiant smile. He took off the trench coat and fedora and placed them back on the coat rack. Offstage, he kept his hair slicked back with lashings of Brylcreem, but the onstage persona he'd created capitalised on his trademark ginger ringlets. His purple suit with orange and purple polka dot bow tie completed his comical look. Onstage, he accentuated his Scottish accent and liked to tell Scottish jokes.

'Ye know, I wanted to be a copper before I became an entertainer. I applied to join the Victorian police force and managed to get an interview. One of the questions the inspector asked me was, "How would I disperse a large, unruly crowd?" Well, I answered, I'm not too sure how ye do it here, but in Scotland, we just pass the hat around for donations, and they soon begin to shuffle off.' The audience clapped.

'A couple of weeks ago, I caught up with my mother. When I asked her where my father was, she said he'd started a new job where he had hundreds of people under him. 'That's very good news,' I said. 'How did he manage to get a job like that?' 'It was easy,' said my mother. 'They needed someone to mow the lawns at the local cemetery, and nobody else wanted to do it.'

Peals of laughter rose from the audience.

'Now, who here likes a bacon and egg breakfast?' A show of hands went up. 'Well, think about this next time you're hoeing into your breakfast. A chicken and a pig were passing a church. They stopped to read a large sign that announced a bacon and egg breakfast, with the proceeds going to the missions. "A fine idea," commented the hen. "I think I'll attend."

'"That's an easy decision for you," the pig replied. "You only have to give an offering. I have to make a sacrifice."'

The gag was followed by applause and laughter.

'Now, ladies and gentlemen, I have a special announcement.' He paused for the drum roll. 'First, let's welcome the beautiful Rose De Luca to the stage. Please give her a round of applause.' The audience obliged as she entered the stage wearing a pale blue chiffon frock speckled with diamantes. Another drum roll resounded as she stood alongside Vinnie, and he lowered himself to one knee. That was the cue for the flashlight bulbs to start popping from the reporters Vinnie had invited for publicity. Rose acted surprised and teary as she watched Vinnie get a ring box from his jacket pocket.

'Rose, will you marry me in about 20 minutes? And I won't take no for an answer 'cause I ain't refunding no tickets.'

The audience howled.

'I will, but I'm going to need at least an hour to get ready!' she said.

'I'll give you a half hour.'

'How about three-quarters of an hour?'

'Thirty-seven minutes is my last and final offer! I've got a show to run!'

'I'll take it, but don't blame me if I don't look my best.'

'This is all you need to look your best.' Vinnie put the glistening diamond ring on her finger and the crowd went wild.

'Now all I have to do is ask your father's permission. Where do I get a hold of him?'

'I don't know. He's awfully ticklish.'

The audience loved it. Rose took her place centre stage and performed *I Wanna Be Loved By You*. Dancers joined her in chiffon frocks. Once she'd finished to explosive applause, she exited the stage for her wedding costume change.

Vinnie announced the next act and prepared himself for the grand finale wedding scene.

The announcement of the wedding scene elicited thunderous applause and foot stomping. The curtains were drawn back, unveiling the inside of a church. A barrage of flashbulb explosions photographed Vinnie, who stood downstage right. Rose walked down the aisle from upstage left as the band played and dancers performed. Once Vinnie and Rose completed their vows, the audience responded with howls, claps, and whistles. They closed the ceremony by walking downstage, holding hands, before taking a bow and exiting the stage.

The wedding was a huge financial success, and the media coverage cemented their top-billing status in Melbourne's entertainment circuit.

***

As a wedding gift, Carlo bought Vinnie a brand-new Plymouth and provided them with a stylish house not far from Carlo and Sofia's house. Vinnie could not understand Rose's protests and why she would want to live on the other side of town in Vinnie's cramped, rented apartment. He had never lived in luxury, and he'd never met anyone as generous as Carlo.

'These are not gifts, Vinnie. They come with a price,' said Rose.

'You're a killjoy, Rose. Can't you just be happy for me?'

Vinnie began running clean dinner shows and burlesque late-night shows for Carlo's special members in his multiple restaurant venues.

'Marcello will take you to the bank to open a bank account for the business,' said Carlo.

'Why do I need a separate bank account?' said Vinnie.

'You gonna make a lot of money. We set up a company with you as director and Marcello will look after the books. It's too much headache for you.'

'I've run a business before. I know what I'm doing.'

'You make chicken feed. Marcello is accountant. He will help you not pay taxes.'

The flow of money coming through the late-night shows took Vinnie by surprise. He chose not to ask questions, considering everything he touched was turning to gold. Vinnie nudged away the niggle in his conscience as he submitted control of the finances to Marcello and focused on making a ton of money. He visualised returning to England as a rich man to visit his mother and make her proud. And make Belle regret choosing Artis over him.

***

'Your father's a force to be reckoned with,' said Vinnie.

'Most people are afraid of him. I'm surprised you're not.'

'I've never met a businessman like him. He wants me to hire international stars for the dinner show so we can charge premium prices.'

'He wants to compete with the Tivoli,' said Rose.

'He's looking at some Hollywood film deals as well. That man's got connections everywhere.'

'There'll be a high price to pay. I won't sell my soul for one of his Hollywood deals.'

'Hollywood isn't burlesque.'

'What they'll make me do to get the part is worse than burlesque. I won't do it.'

'You'd give up a chance for international stardom?'

'It's not the kind of deal you think it is.'

'Well, as your husband, I'm telling you to do it. I'm sick of you fighting me every step of the way. I'm trying to run a business, for God's sake.'

'There's no God in this business.' Rose left the room, slamming the door behind her.

But she basked in the special attention Vinnie paid her in public, holding her hand and kissing her whenever there was a photographer in sight. He insisted she keep on top of the latest fashion and hairstyles and always look her very best when in public and invested in promotional photographs that featured her in provocative gowns. These were strategically placed wherever Artis's troupe was playing, and Artis's promotional posters were removed.

Rose's popularity in the matinee performances continued to grow. All the attention she was getting from Vinnie made her believe he was falling in love with her. The satisfaction of knowing he was her husband, not Belle's, made her happy, and the fame that he'd meant for Belle was hers to relish.

***

It didn't take Rose long to get pregnant thanks to Vinnie's naivety about contraceptives. The memories of Carlo's questionable contraceptive methods and forced abortions were fresh in her mind. If his multiple punches to her abdomen didn't work, she was butchered by a questionable doctor whose barbaric method caused her to have recurring nightmares after she witnessed him pulling pieces of flesh from inside her. These experiences heightened her protective instincts to keep her baby safe.

As if cursed by Carlo, Rose's pregnancy caused her misery. Her damaged body struggled with hormonal upheaval, causing her to be violently ill and exhausted for most of the day. The doctor ordered complete bed rest to avoid a miscarriage.

Frank was born six weeks premature after an arduous and risky labour. Regardless of the ordeal, Rose's world changed that day when she experienced her first sense of pure love as she held her tiny creation. The change in Vinnie was also noticeable. His chiselled face softened at the sight of his son.

In show business, married women were not bound by the conventional expectation to quit work and focus solely on their role as a mother and homemaker. Although Vinnie seemed pleased about the baby, he wanted Rose to continue working as Belle had after the birth of her child.

'Well, you don't want Belle to outshine you, do you? Ye need to get back in the game,' he said, showing Rose newspaper clippings of Belle he'd been collecting.

'She hasn't made the front page like I have.'

'That's because she married an idiot,' said Vinnie. 'She's wasting her talent with him.'

His comments refuelled Rose's resentment towards her. Marriage and fatherhood hadn't changed Vinnie's obsession with Belle. Rose realised everything he was doing was to impress Belle. She knew then that she had to keep a closer eye on him.

'I know someone you could hire to spy on Artis. He can find out their touring plans and what they're rehearsing, so you can intervene and put them out of business,' said Rose.

'Who?'

'Stan.'

'And why would he do that?'

'He's desperate for money. Got himself into a pile of debt he couldn't pay back when he lost his job and he had to farm his family out to relatives after getting evicted. All he's got left is his motorcycle, which means he can get around cheaply and fast.'

'Where do you find these people?'

'Carlo.'

'Why do you call your father by his name?'

'He's not my real father.'

'That explains a lot.'

'Explains what?'

'You look like you're scared to death of him. I'd go so far as to say you hated him.'

'Maybe I do.'

Not wanting to disclose anything further about Carlo's abuse, Rose distracted Vinnie by putting one hand down his pants while the other cupped the back of his head, drawing his mouth to her lips. As much as Vinnie's heart longed for Belle, he was helpless to the allure of Rose's sexual prowess. Their lovemaking was lustful and impulsive. There was an animalistic wild abandon to their act, which would take place in any hidden corner wherever and whenever they succumbed to the urge. Rose used the power of seduction she had mastered to work in her favour. It was her most powerful drawcard to keep her husband satisfied. Her next step was to convince him to hire Stan so she could also use him to spy on Vinnie and Belle, and ultimately get Artis and Belle out of their lives.

14

Hitting the Road

Artis sat on the edge of his bed, looking through the bars of his daughter's crib. The weight of his responsibilities tormented him, making it difficult to sleep. His mind was racing as he sought a solution to his predicament. Closing his eyes, he listened to Belle and Shelley's gentle breathing. It helped him relax. The two most precious people in his life, lying in peaceful slumber, were relying on him to make things right. He had never imagined the depth of his love could cause him both ecstasy and pain. Exhausted with carrying the burden alone, he recalled his parent's beliefs about the power of prayer and fell to his knees. *God, I know I've turned my back on you, but if you're listening, I need you to tell me what to do. I got so many people relying on me.*

Nothing happened. Unlike the Bible stories he'd read, there was no booming voice instructing him. While his mother had encouraged him to always keep praying, she also reminded him that God wasn't a genie in a bottle, granting every wish. His heart must be pure, his motivation unselfish, and his belief unwavering. *I'll do my best, God, from now on. Just help me, please, to look after my family and troupe.*

The heaviness of sleep pulled his eyes closed. He curled himself around Belle, allowing the warmth of her body to relax his muscles. A sense of peace came over him, and he fell into a deep sleep. When the morning light woke him, it came with a plan. Artis brushed the hair from Belle's face, causing her to stir.

'Love, I've thought of a solution.' He watched Belle's eyes flickering behind her lids before she opened them in a sleepy squint.

'What? What time is it?' She peered through the bars of Shelley's crib to see her still sound asleep.

'I'm not sure, but I've figured out our touring plan.' Even when she wasn't made up, Belle's beauty took his breath away. He relished the sight of her tousled hair cascading across the pillow, her eyes sleepy and pale rose lips slightly parted. When she rolled over to face him, her nightgown tangled itself around her body and parted across her chest, revealing her milky skin and the curve of her breast. The sight stirred Artis.

'Well, seeing as Shelley's still asleep, how about a bit of hanky-panky before I tell you my plan?' He gave her a hopeful smile. She playfully rolled on top of him, her hair cascading around their faces as she kissed him passionately.

The Depression forecast an unforgiving economy with an

undetermined end date. For many, it was a soul-destroying time. Those who were unfortunate enough to have lost their job had to find any means to make money or face losing their home and possibly their family. Some had begun to grow their own vegetables, keep chickens, hunt for rabbits and fish to provide for their families. Entertainment was the balm that eased the pain of the situation and allowed people to forget about their troubles for a couple of hours during a show.

A week later, Artis met with the remaining sixteen members of his troupe, their faces pinched with anticipation.

'As you all know, we've run out of options for performing in Melbourne, and Vinnie has poached some of our performers. He's now managing several shows which are dominating the Melbourne circuit, and he's secured a higher-class clientele by offering a dinner and show package, with international stars, through multiple restaurants and clubs.'

'The dirty rotten scoundrel,' said Fredric. The troupe mumbled their agreement.

'After working so hard to bring our show to such a professional standard, the last thing I want is to face public humiliation. So I'm gonna put an ad in the paper announcing that due to public demand, our show will be touring regional Victoria.'

'I don't think making a public announcement is a good idea. Ain't it better if Vinnie doesn't know what we're up to?' said Bert.

'It's the professional thing to do, mate. It shows we value our audience, and we don't want to burn our bridges for when we're able to return.'

Artis drew their attention to a map that he had pinned to the wall. 'I've mapped out a touring circuit that will cover approximately 3000 miles. I know it looks like a lot of ground to cover, but I've done this circuit before, when I worked with the Blind Association. We'll start in Kilmore, then head north to Echuca, cross the border into New South Wales as far as Moulamein before heading back down through Deniliquin, and back into Victoria via Cobram. Then we'll continue to the north-east region, through Beechworth, Bright, Wangaratta, Myrtleford, and back into New South Wales to Wagga Wagga. Then we head back to Victoria through Wodonga before finishing in Longwood. Over those three months we'll perform in 75 towns. Now, I know that's a hard slog, but keeping the show moving is the only way to make money. Folks won't want to miss the show, so they'll make the effort to come. We'll rest on Sundays and keep moving the rest of the time. After each tour, we'll return to Melbourne for a short break before heading out on a new circuit.'

Artis scanned his troupe's faces. He saw mixed emotions. Some expressed enthusiasm at the prospect of touring, and others were not keen on leaving their families for such an extended period.

'How're we gonna sell tickets, and where are we gonna stay?' asked Tommy.

'I'm hiring an advance man. His name's Jonesy. I worked with him years ago with the Blind Association. We'll tour the same circuit 'cause he knows all the theatre managers, newspaper reporters, mayors, and tourist parks we can camp at. He'll arrange our venues and accommodation, which will be mostly in the trucks or tents. He'll travel ahead to make sure the show's promoted and have the playbills printed and posted up to get the buzz going around town.'

'What's the guarantee we can sell tickets? The economy's gone to hell,' said Fredric.

'There's no guarantee of anything, mate, not even your wages. If worse comes to worst, you'll have a roof over your head and a feed.'

'How do I support my family? They need money for rent and food.'

'I understand this ain't gonna work out for some of you. I'll do my bloody best to pay you, but I don't know what's ahead—except financial ruin if we don't give it a go. There's no way around it. You're gonna be away from family for roughly three months at a time, so if you can't commit, then you need to let me know now.' He scanned the solemn faces.

'How do we keep our costumes clean?' said Jean.

'I'll ask Jonesy to pre-book laundering services. Some things you'll have to handwash.'

'How you gonna feed us all?' said Tommy

'Olivia has agreed to tour with us as our pianist and cook. She's offered to preserve a supply of eggs in waterglass and make preserves, jams and sauces that should last us through the tour. We'll get flour for damper, and I can barter for meat, milk, eggs, vegetables, and butter from farmers in exchange for show tickets.'

'I got nowhere else to go, so I'm in,' said Tommy.

'Good to hear, Tommy. It's up to us to keep this show going. Regional folks appreciate a show. It's an escape from what's happening in their lives. And we can take the show to them. It's the best I can offer you, so I need to know who's in.'

The thought of lining up at Poverty Point meant most agreed to Artis's plan.

'I've invested the last of my money to buy a truck and a marquee for when there's not a big enough hall to perform in. My brother Larry here is joining us. He's also got a truck, mechanical skills and a knack for building things. We're having both trucks modified so we can load our equipment, costumes and props when travelling and once we unload, they'll double up as sleeping quarters. If you want private sleeping quarters, you'll have to bring your own tents, which I highly recommend.'

'I started juggling bread rolls after you left all those years ago. I'm real good now. Maybe you'll give me a spot in the show,' said Larry.

Artis raised an eyebrow. 'We'll see.'

'I will bring a tent and Metza,' said Samson.

'I'm glad to hear it.'

'My cousin and his family got evicted after he lost his job and couldn't pay the rent,' said Bert. 'Their kids had to live with relatives while he went on the wallaby looking for work. This country's a bloody mess, so all I can say is I'm grateful for this plan of yours, mate. You can count me and Jean in. At least we'll be together.' Jean agreed, then asked, 'So, what's the show we're putting on?'

'*The House That Jack Built*. It's currently England's most popular pantomime,' said Artis, trying to lighten the mood. 'It's two acts and twenty scenes of non-stop energy. A sure winner.'

As the meeting came to a close, and he knew who could commit to touring, he gave them a start date for rehearsals and the tour.

The following day, Artis and Belle scouted Melbourne's community singing sessions for talent that would bring the house down, to replace those who had chosen to leave. Artis purchased a songbook for sixpence and led Belle to a seat near the back of the hall so he could check whether a singer's voice had the power to reach the back seats. An outstanding performer had to not only sing well, but to ooze personality and presence and, most importantly, connect with the audience.

'Let's begin, shall we? I've picked some bonza songs for you!' said the compere, waving his pointer in preparation for guiding the singers by tapping the words projected on a screen. Although everyone would sing their hearts out, the loudest singer was always someone who knew all the words. Belle watched the bobbing heads, adorned with an assortment of hats. Regardless of the poverty some people were enduring, wearing a hat and gloves seemed to preserve a person's dignity. It amused Belle how many women would knit while singing.

A man who appeared to be in his early twenties caught Artis's eye with his bright orange suit and purple bow tie. He sang with such gusto, using passionate hand movements and facial expressions, that it was impossible not to be mesmerised. The most endearing thing about him was that he was completely tone deaf and sounded like a dying animal. The audience watched in disbelief mingled with amusement and pity.

'He's brilliant,' said Artis. Belle raised an eyebrow, but before she got an explanation, Artis was making a beeline towards the orange glow. Belle followed him, perplexed.

Artis offered the man a handshake. When the man reached out to shake his hand, Artis pulled his away. The man looked shocked until Artis broke into a broad smile, then he reciprocated with a goofy smile and a nervous shuffling of his feet. He held his hand back out to Artis, who reached to shake it. The man pulled his hand away and broke into a guffaw that jerked heads in his direction. Belle and Artis burst out laughing at the ridiculous look on his face.

'What's your name, matey?' asked Artis.

'Charley.'

'Gidday, Charley. I'm Artis Newman and this is my wife, Belle. We came here looking for talent.' Charley's eyes widened in anticipation. 'Charley, mate, you can't sing for peanuts.' Charley's face drooped. 'But you're one hell of a funny guy. Have you ever thought about doing a comedy act?' Charley shook his head. 'I'd like you to join my troupe. You gave me a great idea for an act. You wanna talk about it over a beer?' Charley nodded, still dumbfounded. Belle knew Artis already had him in the bag.

Artis and Belle also approached five of the most outstanding singers, who could also move their bodies to a beat, with a request for an audition the following day. The audition was to include a simple dance routine choreographed by Belle and a one-page script to test their acting abilities.

After a full week of scouting and auditions, Artis had narrowed it down to the best two singers. One had a sweet voice, and the other belted out songs like she was going to devour the audience. It was the exact balance Artis knew the show needed to keep the audience entertained. He used his most impressive powers of persuasion to dazzle his preferred two performers and convince them to tour with them.

***

Preparing for regional touring required many adjustments to compensate for not performing in a theatre. The singers relied on acoustics to optimise their voices, and the dancers were particularly concerned about floor surfaces. Larry proved himself to be an invaluable asset. He was incredibly innovative and satisfied the tap dancers' requirements by making portable tap mats eight feet by four feet in dimension out of one-and-a-half-inch thick wooden slats. The sides were planed and bevelled and each slat was held flat and firmly together by furniture strapping that was nailed underneath the slats, with all the nails countersunk. After sanding and lacquering each mat, he managed to impress even the most sceptical dancer once they tested a mat out. His invention created a resonant sound and, best of all, the mats could be rolled up like a piece of lino.

Each performer was expected to have their own costumes, shoes, props, and make-up. Tins of gold and silver paint kept shoes looking shiny and new. They also came in handy for freshening up props. A variety of taps for the tap dancer's shoes were kept on hand. The acrobats had their own resin boxes. Every act was particular about their props and did not want anyone except themselves handling them. Without their props, they had no act. Props ranged from ventriloquist dummies, juggling balls, clubs, rackets, hoops, pistols and blanks, dance mats and acrobatic equipment. All props had to be carefully packed to avoid damage.

Realistic scenes such as gardens, street settings, storefronts and interior settings were painted on canvas drop curtains by some of the more artistic performers. The stage cloths were secured to wooden battens with ropes and pulleys to raise and lower them. Wooden battens were glued to the bottom of the cloths to help them hang straight. A strip of black material was attached at the bottom of the drop to block out light that might peek through.

It took a lot of detailed planning to transport everything required to stage a show. The most cumbersome necessity was a piano that had to be carefully loaded and fine-tuned before each performance. A set of drums was also necessary for the dramatic drum rolls.

Preparation for the tour was arduous. The new troupe consisted of twenty-five cast members. Rehearsals were gruelling as the tour date was fast approaching and the new performers needed to train to the high calibre Artis expected. Belle was cast as Jack, the principal boy role. Jonesy, their advance man, had contacted the regional newspapers in each town and placed an advertisement announcing their show. A couple of weeks before the tour started, Jonesy would travel ahead to make sure everything ran smoothly. He suggested running a painting competition for the children and awarding the three best paintings with a fountain pen presented to the winners at the end of the performance. It was a clever publicity idea and certainly helped fill up the matinee performances, which were timed to start after the school day finished. Jonesy had a lot of connections with regional reporters and was able to get them some pre-show publicity write-ups in exchange for free tickets. He approached all the VIPs in town, offering them the best seats in the house. 'We have the best talent in Melbourne touring with us and international artists from Germany and Italy,' he'd say. 'There'll be only two performances before they move on to the next town, so folks won't want to miss this spectacular show. Do the town a favour and spread the word.'

He was a master at stirring up excitement and had the reporters clacking away at their typewriters as he gave them details of what to expect from the show. '*The House That Jack Built* has already enjoyed a record season at the Theatre Royal in Hobart and the Academy Theatre in Launceston. It's been quite an achievement to keep this touring company successfully on the road during this Depression. This town is in for a real treat!' Jonesy would peer over the reporter's shoulder to check the wording. 'Oh, and make sure you highlight Samson, the strongman. He can pull a truck along the road with a rope between his teeth.'

There were only a few days left before touring began. Artis and Belle had sold most of their furniture and belongings and stored the rest at Olivia's house, where boarders would live until they returned. Belle was reluctant to be touring with a baby. Artis made it sound exciting, but as a new mother, she wanted stability and routine. However, with few choices open to them, touring was their sole means of making a living for the time being. As she swept her eyes over her empty house, her stomach knotted with apprehension.

Artis had left Belle to finish up the last of the packing at home while

Olivia minded Shelley. A knock on the back door resonated through the empty house. Belle opened the door.

'What are you doing here?'

'I've come to talk you out of making another big mistake. Why would anyone in their right mind want to tour in a truck like rogues and vagabonds?' Vinnie pushed through the door and locked it.

'It's because of you. You're taking things too far.'

'What do I need to do for you to leave him? I can make you famous. I did it for Rose, and I can do it for you.'

'We're both married now. This has to stop.'

'I love you, Belle. You know that. I'm rolling in dough now. I can give you anything you want.' He moved towards her, his face so close she caught the scent of his aftershave. 'Give me a chance, Belle. Artis can't do nothin' for you. Look at the life you're living. Is this what you want?'

'No, it's not what I want. You've made things very hard for us.'

'I'll make it right, Belle. Just give me the word and I'll sort everything out.'

He put his arms around her and kissed her, neither of them noticing the man peering through the curtainless window.

15

Rogues and Vagabonds

Touring regional Victoria, 1931

Artis stood beaming at the freshly painted lettering that read *ARTIS NEWMAN'S PANTOMIME PLAYERS* on both sides of the Dodge Brothers touring trucks. The trucks had been fitted out with panels that folded down as bunks and doubled up as seats. Jonesy had arranged for some publicity shots. It wasn't long before the sound of tyres crunching gravel caught their attention as a car pulled up. A reporter strode towards them with a Nagel Fornidar 30 camera in his hand.

'I'm under the pump, folks. I've got five minutes.' He barked instructions to get the troupe positioned in front of the touring trucks as quickly as possible. Within five minutes, the reporter had taken the photographs he needed.

'Tell Jonesy they'll be ready for him to collect next week,' said the reporter as he got back in his car before speeding off, leaving a puff of dust on the horizon.

'Well, then, I suppose it's time to hit the road,' said Artis.

Only Bert and Samson had cars reliable enough to join the entourage. Samson's attempts at enticing the young dancers to ride in his car were politely declined. Despite his ruggedly handsome appearance, he was unaware of his body odour and salami breath, which was tolerable in an open space, but not in the confines of his car. Even the adorable Metza wasn't enough to attract female company. Instead, he loaded up his car with testosterone-fuelled males where body odours could intensify without offending anyone.

Larry couldn't contain his excitement as he got into his truck with some of the troupe. In Artis's truck, Belle sat in the front seat next to Artis, with baby Shelley nestled in her arms. She was quiet and withdrawn, and no amount of probing would prompt her to reveal what was bothering her, so Artis put it down to her hesitation to tour.

'Come on, love. Give me a smile,' he coaxed. She continued to stare out of the windscreen, oblivious to his words. 'I'll look after you,' he said as he stroked her cheek. She glanced in his direction. The corners of her mouth lifted slightly to let him know she'd be alright. He smiled and broke into song. Within seconds, Artis had his heavy-laden truck's engine percolating. He jammed the gearstick into first gear and released the handbrake. The engine strained from the weight of the truck before gaining momentum and bouncing into a comfortable roll. Checking the rear-view mirror, Artis noticed the bobbing heads of the passengers in the back of the truck, who were singing along with him.

The side mirrors revealed that Larry, Bert, and Samson were trailing behind him. What he failed to notice was a motorcyclist pulling out to join the entourage.

They headed for Kilmore, 46 miles north of Melbourne. Once they reached the outskirts of Melbourne, the road became rougher, causing them to bounce around in their seats. This resulted in a few complaints of motion sickness, and the reality of touring sank in. Artis noticed a bundle of inhospitable clouds building up on the horizon. The worst-case scenario was setting up the marquee and campsite in a storm. He glanced over at Belle, who was nursing Shelley. His heart swelled with love at the sight of them.

Splashes of rain dotted the windscreen as they approached Kilmore. It was inevitable they were destined to be greeted with torrential rain.

'What a bloody damned way to start a tour,' said Artis, as the rain fell in a crescendo. Unable to see through the fogged windscreen, they had no choice but to pull over and sit in the trucks to wait for a break in the downpour. The hammering rain against the metal roof woke Shelley, who began to cry, adding to their stress. There were whines about toilet emergencies. It wasn't long before morale was dashed. Each minute they waited for the rain to ease cut into their setting-up time and their chance to unwind before the show. The minutes dragged. Shelley needed her nappy changed and was wailing. By the time the rain calmed down enough for them to proceed, their nerves were shattered, and moods were dark. It was nearing lunchtime. Everyone was tired and hungry. Setting up for the matinee show was going to be a slog. Belle looked as if she was holding back tears.

'I'll ask about accommodation,' said Artis.

'Thank you.'

Artis had budgeted for such situations when Belle expressed her concerns about travelling with a baby. They made their way to a local hotel where Artis made a deal with the owner that included tickets to the show. The rest of the troupe would have to make do with sleeping in the trucks, under the marquee, or in their tents. Setting up the marquee became a slippery, muddy mess that had the men cursing under the strain. Unloading the musical instruments, lights and props had to be done as quickly as possible and precious time was wasted wiping everything dry. They then set up the makeshift stage with backdrops, lighting and sound while the women attended to preening their costumes and headpieces and repairing any tears or loose buttons.

Stan had parked his 247cc Waratah motorcycle down a side street, out of sight from the venue. He took off his helmet and goggles after positioning himself under an awning opposite the venue. He rolled a cigarette as he watched the troupe unload the trucks. His soaked jacket and pants clung to his skin. He was contemplating the best plan of attack when his eye caught a beautiful woman dressed the way he liked them. Flicking the butt of his cigarette into a puddle, he made his move to find a bed for the night.

It didn't take long for word to get around that the troupe had arrived once they set up the marquee. Artis checked in at the box office.

'Gidday, Artis! Good to see ya, mate. Been a while,' said Bill. They shook hands.

'Yeah, mate. Too long, hey? About time we dazzled you with some mighty fine entertainment.'

'Yeah, mate. The kids have been talking about it all week.'

'Good to hear. You mind switching off the bloody rain?' said Artis.

'I'll have a word with the man upstairs, hey?'

'Bloody oath!'

'So what's this I hear about you getting hitched to Vinnie's girl?'

'Strewth, Bill!'

'Listen, mate. I know you ain't been around these parts for a while, but as a mate I gotta tell you that Vinnie went to the trouble of phoning me the other week. He's been painting you black. Said you stole his woman. Rants about how he gave you a chance to start out in the business and this is how you pay him back.'

'For the love of God!' Artis exclaimed. 'I never knew he was sweet on her. And if you ask Belle, she sure as hell wasn't sweet on him!'

'Mate, calm down. Don't get your knickers in a knot. I'm just telling you what rumours are going around.'

'Yeah, yeah, I know. Every bloody where I go, I get the same bloody story. The man's out to ruin me. Doesn't bloody matter where I go, he's poisoned the whole bloody state of Victoria against me. The only place I don't get an earful is in Tassie.'

'Yeah, righto. Tone down the language, mate. This storm'll blow over and things'll be right as rain again.'

'Sorry, Bill. It just gets me wound up every time I hear it. That's not the kind of man I am. I wouldn't do something like that intentionally.'

'Good to know, mate. We won't have to worry about locking up our wives then, hey?' Bill slapped him on the back and laughed.

'Ya rogue!' laughed Artis. 'So what did Vinnie ring you for? Just to tell you that?'

'He was trying to discourage me from selling your tickets. Said your show was second-rate.'

'Scoundrel! By the looks of the pre-sales, you must have believed him.'

'You can't blame me, can you?'

'I suppose,' said Artis. 'I better make a move. Setting up in the rain is never a great start to a show. Takes us nearly twice as long. You gonna write up a review for us in the local rag?'

'Yeah, mate. Ya better impress me!'

'Guaranteed, mate. The evening show might be more to your liking if you're not a fan of *The House That Jack Built*.'

'The mother-in-law's taking the kids to the matinee, and Lizzy and me will come tonight. Now that you've set the record straight about Vinnie, I'll spread the word. I know a few people were holding back. Might be able to get you a sell-out show.'

'Thanks, mate. You're a bloody legend.'

'Language, mate … geez!'

Pre-ticket sales only filled half of the marquee, but by opening time, the rain had ceased, and the marquee was almost full. Artis was sure Bill had something to do with that and made a mental note to thank him before they left town. Backstage was a flurry of activity as the performers and crew prepared for the curtain call. Tommy, who was doubling as the call boy, called the time. The acrobats opened the show as the sight act. Olivia was at the piano alongside the drummer and violinist, ready to strike the first key on cue before Artis strode out to announce the show. Precisely on cue, the spotlight traced his steps to downstage centre, casting a heavenly glow around him.

'Welcome, ladies, gentlemen, and children. It's such a pleasure to be visiting your beautiful town again. Some of you may recall my previous visits with the Blind Association. As you can see, I've formed my own company of performers, specialising in pantomime and variety acts. Today, we're pleased to be presenting to you, by popular demand, the pantomime *The House That Jack Built*. I'm sure you'll be delighted and will show your appreciation with hearty applause and spread the word about our eight o'clock evening show. We've made our tickets very affordable, with prices ranging from 1 to 3 shillings, plus tax. Families will appreciate our special matinee prices. We'll also be announcing the winner of our painting competition. We've received some impressive paintings of *The House That Jack Built* and I'm looking forward to presenting the lucky winners with their prize at the end of the show. And now, without further ado, please enjoy the show, *The House That Jack Built*!' He boomed these last words for dramatic emphasis.

Music burst through the air as bodies in the audience shuffled in anticipation and children's necks craned. The atmosphere changed the moment the performers appeared on stage and connected with the audience. Artis knew the sign of an extraordinary show was when the audience became transfixed. Their worries melted away and their bodies relaxed as they relinquished their minds to the glamour of entertainment. From behind the curtains, Artis always kept his eye on the audience so that if there was any change in mood, he could rectify it by switching around the acts. This was something he had become quite skilful at over the years, thanks to Vinnie's training.

The show ran smoothly with only minor hiccups, such as a missing prop or forgotten lines, that were masterfully covered up. Hearty laughter and applause echoed outside the marquee, enticing townsfolk to purchase tickets for the evening performance. The buzz in town was infectious, ensuring the evening performance had the marquee swollen with bodies. The grand finale included Samson highlighting his feats of strength by lifting the platform that held Olivia on her piano, with the musicians, onto his back. He rotated the platform in a complete circle to the admiration of the audience, who were holding their collective breath, anticipating something going horribly wrong. Samson acted the part by using facial expressions that hinted at the possibility of disaster. The musicians performed a number designed to increase the tension. On cue, Metza ran on stage and sat up on her hind legs with her front paws outstretched. Then she jumped in circles and barked as if she was begging Samson to put the platform down. Once Samson placed the platform back on the stumps, it broke the tension, and the audience applauded in appreciation. As Samson took his bow, Metza jumped on his back and, after positioning herself on his shoulders, licked his face, much to the delight of the audience. They exited stage right just as the closing contortionist act entered from stage left, allowing for a smooth transition as the applause simmered down. When the last act took their bow, Artis strode downstage centre to close the show.

'Ladies, gentlemen and littlies. Did you enjoy the show?' There was a loud, positive response. 'Thank you very much! We were certainly delighted to have the opportunity to entertain you. You certainly made a fuss over Samson's feats of strength.' The audience clapped their agreement and there were a few shout outs of appreciation. 'Well, I have some very exciting news.' A drum roll followed the statement. 'After pleading with Samson, I've convinced him to perform one of his most dangerous stunts, as a special treat for you.' Artis paused for emphasis and to allow for another drum roll. 'Ladies, gentlemen and littlies, Samson has agreed to pull one of our touring trucks through the main street of town with his teeth!'

Kerboom! The drums were struck with force. The audience applauded and howled.

'Now, before we see this amazing feat, I'd like to announce the winner of our painting competition and present them with their prize. The Kilmore Free Press has kindly taken charge of displaying all our entries over the past week. They are all marvellous paintings, and it was very difficult to choose the winners. Please give a round of applause to the beautiful Belle as she presents three lucky winners with their prize.'

It was a brilliant way to end the show, along with having the cast mingle with the audience at the end of the matinee. This worked wonders in getting people to spread the word about the evening show.

'I envy you so much,' said a woman who approached Belle after the show. 'Your life must be magical, getting dressed up in beautiful costumes and travelling all over the country.'

'Thank you. Yes, it's quite special,' said Belle, not wanting to destroy the illusion by stating the difficulties. People either looked down on them as rogues and vagabonds or envied them as theatre stars living glamorous lives.

'I got nothin' to look forward to,' the woman said. 'My husband's at the pub most of the time and all I do is cook, wash, tend the garden and look after the kids. It's a treat when a show comes to town. And having a painting competition for the littlies gets them excited. And giving sweets to all the littlies so they don't feel like they're missing out if they don't win a prize is really good of you.'

'Thank you,' said Belle. 'We certainly enjoy seeing the children's artwork.'

Some townsfolk bartered scones, biscuits or vegetables they had grown for tickets. It was worth a few hours of merriment that lifted their spirits and kept them going, believing their dark days would pass. Men with large families would trade a chicken or a couple of rabbits so the whole family could watch the show.

The buzz created by the announcement that Samson would be pulling a truck with his teeth was a genius publicity stunt that would guarantee them filled seats to the evening performance and pre-sales to future shows once Jonesy got hold of the publicity photos and newspaper reviews. The time it took Samson and the crew to set up the stunt gave the local newspaper reporter a chance to cover this most unusual event. Word spread quickly, and the street was lined with townsfolk. Some peered out from first-storey windows, stood on car roofs, or climbed lamp posts or trees to get a view. Samson chose his shoes according to the condition of the road surface. The rope and mouthpiece he used were designed to withstand the weight he would be pulling.

The townsfolk watched as he rigged up the rope to the touring truck and attached the mouthpiece to the end of the rope. He inserted the mouthpiece into his mouth and positioned himself to pull the truck. There was deathly silence except for the clicking of the reporter's camera. Once his body was in position, Samson began pulling at the rope as the townsfolk watched in awe. They cheered him on as his muscles bulged and twitched with the exertion. Eventually, the wheels of the truck budged, and the townsfolk burst into an uproar as the truck followed Samson along the main street of town.

Stan heard the commotion from outside his motel window. He threw the sheet to one side of the bed, exposing the naked body of a buxom brunette who was lying on her back smoking a cigarette. After watching from the window, Stan took the brunette by the hand and dragged her out of bed.

'Get dressed. I want you to do a number on the strongman. Make sure he misses the evening show and find out what town the troupe's playing next.' He slapped her on the buttocks and shoved her in the direction of the bathroom.

'Give me my money first.'

'You'll get it when you finish the job.'

She eyed him with contempt.

'Give me my money or I'll call me boss.'

Stan swung around to look at her, a flash of anger in his eyes. She set her jaw.

'It's like that, is it?'

'Yeah, it's like that,' she said, hoping he wouldn't notice her body shaking. He stared her down before walking over to his bag and pulling out a note. Walking back, he raised the note to her face.

'Like I said, sweet pea, you'll get the rest when you finish the job.'

She snatched the note and quickly got dressed. Without looking at him, she left, slamming the door behind her.

After Samson's publicity stunt, the evening show sold out. The acrobats were first up to kickstart the show with backflips, cartwheels and impressive feats of balance. By the time the acrobats were halfway through their act, the last of the stragglers were seated. Bert then signalled for Charley to take his place for their entrance.

That was the trigger for Charley's panic attack. He had assisted the backstage crew during the matinee, and now it was his moment to shine in his debut performance. When he got a glimpse of the audience from the wings, it gave him a jolt and frazzled his nerves. He began to hyperventilate. In his orange suit with a purple bow tie and a matching purple and orange bowler hat the girls had made him, he looked quite comical in his panicked state. As he began jittering, Bert came to his aid and remedied the situation by giving him a swift slap across the face. It had the desired effect. Charley stopped hyperventilating.

'I can't do this!' he squeaked, wide-eyed.

'Yes, you can. We've rehearsed this for weeks,' whispered Bert.

'I can't!'

'Yes, you can. Just pretend you're singing in the Community Singing.'

'But I'm not!'

'Get a grip, mate.' Bert shook him by the shoulders, causing his bowler hat to drop to the floor. Bert popped it back on his head. 'Listen to the crowd. Their claps will guide you. You'll get to know the different sounds and you can pick up your game if you think you're losing them. Now get out there.' Bert gave Charley a mighty push just as the sight act finished. He followed behind him, continuing to shove him forward, improvising to help cover Charley's nerves.

Then something baffling happened to Charley, when he found himself centre stage, that only performers understand but can't quite explain. A galvanic current ran through him the moment he faced the audience. It was like a wave of energy connecting him to the audience as he realised that what they saw was a funny-looking man in an orange suit with a purple bow tie, matching bowler hat, and make-up that made him appear ludicrous. Within seconds, he was making them laugh as he attempted to sing with zest. Bert's guidance gave him the confidence to make it appear like he'd been performing for years. In a heartbeat, Charley was hooked. When his ears were assaulted with roaring laughter, it cemented his addiction to performance.

Once they exited, a new backdrop was released within seconds, and Birdie began her contortionist act. Holding a metal hoop and a glass of water, she curtsied before tilting her head back and placing the glass of water on her forehead. She proceeded to pass her body through the hoop whilst balancing the glass of water. Once through the hoop, she took the glass and drank the water before curtsying again to the audience's applause. Birdie then juggled hats and tin cups, popping the hats on and off, creating an elaborate pattern of hats and tin cups dancing through the air. Next, she spun plates on a long stick, creating tension as she added more and more plates, spinning them faster and faster. When they slowed to a wobble, someone in the audience called out a warning. Birdie gave them a smile and sped them up again. For her grand finale, she sat in front of a table set up with a milk jug, sugar bowl, teapot, cup, saucer, and spoon. She balanced a teacup on her head and poured milk from the jug into it, then reached for a lump of sugar. With comical facial expressions, she threw it up in the air, landing it in the teacup. The audience applauded. Reaching for the teapot, she picked it up. The audience held their breath at the sight of steam coming from the spout. With a worried expression and a shaky hand, she lifted the teapot to her head and teased the audience as she tried to find the right spot to pour the tea into the cup. After pouring it without spilling a drop, there was more applause from the audience. She took the spoon from the table and masterfully flicked it into the air, landing it inside the teacup. Waiting for the applause to subside, she stirred the spoon around the teacup, then took the cup and saucer off her head, and sipped the tea with a satisfied smile. A roar of applause accompanied her off the stage.

Belle was waiting in the wings for the grand finale, accompanied by four dancers. She looked exquisite in a red satin dress with black satin trimming that accentuated her figure. Belle had the ability to transfix an audience from the moment she stepped on stage. She radiated an electrifying energy that raised goosebumps. Her exceptional performance paid off. The high spirits of the audience were infectious. When Belle's voice reached its final climax, the audience was captivated in a heightened state of ecstasy until the music faded, bringing them back down to earth. They rose from their seats and gave her a standing ovation. Belle and the dancers exited the stage as the curtain closed. The waves of appreciation received from an audience who envied her gift gave her an extreme adrenalin rush. These accolades made touring difficulties bearable, and all negative thoughts evaporated.

'Encore! Encore!' shouted the audience. Those words were music to a performer's ears. She was more than happy to oblige, giving the audience a few more moments of pleasure to carry them through the next few days of personal burdens.

Samson was meant to close the show by lifting the musician's platform, but he was nowhere to be seen.

Halfway through the show, Stan had been lurking around the outside of the marquee. He eyed the troupe's trucks and cars, which were parked around the back of the marquee. Scanning the area to make sure there was nobody in sight, he edged his way towards the trucks, his dark clothes helping him blend into the night. The moonlight caught the silver blade of a large hunting knife as he slid it out of the leather pouch attached to his belt. Holding it close to his thigh, he peered inside each of the truck windows, straining his ears for the slightest sound. When he came to Artis's truck, he opened the door and quietly stepped inside. After searching through the truck, he came across Shelley, sleeping in a makeshift bassinet. The moonlight that penetrated through a window allowed him to see the blonde curls around her delicate face. He watched her sleeping until the sharp reality of what he was there to do dawned on him.

The sound of footsteps hurrying towards the truck jolted him. He buried himself in the darkness, hiding under a blanket, his head positioned to see the intruder, ready to pounce in his defence. Gracie, one of the young dancers, opened the truck door. She tiptoed over to Shelley and cocooned her in her blanket to keep her warm. Stan watched her intently as she rummaged around in the truck. Her hand brushed past Stan's leg, dangerously close to his knife, as she bent to pick up a bag close to his feet. Relying on the sliver of moonlight streaming through the truck window, she fished around in the bag until she found a lollipop. Unwrapping it, she popped it into her mouth and sucked on it as she watched over Shelley. The sound aroused Stan. Her silhouette outlined the small curve of her breasts. He felt his heart quicken.

A wave of laughter and applause exuded from the marquee as the show came to an end without Samson's finale. The audience's energy as they meandered out of the marquee disturbed the stillness of the night. The troupe began packing up their props and costumes and dismantling the lighting and sound equipment in the marquee when they heard Larry's shout from outside. Their high spirits were soon extinguished as the realisation of what Stan had done confronted them.

'Mary, mother of God!' The troupe rushed to where Larry was standing, holding his head in disbelief. 'Who in hell would do such a thing?'

16

Sinister Intentions

'What in hell's happened now?' said Artis as he made his way towards where some of the troupe were standing, searching their horrified faces for answers.

Larry shone a light on their vehicles. Every tyre was slashed.

'Bloody hell!' Artis threw down a stack of flyers he was carrying. Fredric approached the troupe and let out a barrage of swear words in German.

'They weren't slashed when I came to check on Shelley,' said Gracie.

'And you didn't see anyone hanging around?'

'No.'

'We're bloody cursed!' said Artis.

Samson walked over to where they were standing.

'And where the bloody hell have you been? You've never missed a show!' said Artis.

'Scusa, sorry. I fell asleep,' he said. His dishevelled state made his story believable, although questionable.

'Don't let it happen again. Fredric had to cover for you. It's just as well the audience didn't protest.'

Artis notified the police, who wrote a report and passed the details on to the media, with a request for any witnesses to come forward. Replacing the tyres turned out to be a bigger headache than first anticipated.

'Radio Motors on Sydney Street is your best bet. They've got the largest stock of tyres in Kilmore,' suggested the police officer. Unfortunately, they didn't have the correct tyres in stock for Samson's car, so their only option was to order from the stockist in Melbourne and wait the few days it took to deliver them. The cost to replace the tyres not only robbed them of their day's earnings but caused them to have to cancel their performances in Echuca, Moulamein and Deniliquin, their next scheduled towns. They made the most of their stay by putting on more performances while they waited for the tyres to arrive. The excellent publicity and reviews they received, especially after Samson's amazing truck-pulling feat, ensured they made good sales over the next few days. While Samson ensured he was never late for a show again, he continued to be enticed into the bed of the buxom brunette after the evening shows were over. He made sure Artis, along with everyone else, was none the wiser.

Their delay also disrupted Stan's plans to continue to sabotage the tour. After the brunette gave Stan the information he needed, he had headed off to Echuca early that morning, expecting the troupe to cancel the matinee but still make the evening performance. When they didn't show up, he lost the thread of the tour. He had no option but to return to Melbourne. Vinnie was pleased to hear that the disruptions were eating into Artis's profits and believed it was a matter of time before he would be forced to close the business. All he had to do was line up an irresistible offer for Belle to work for him.

***

The women had become quite masterful in creating a homely environment, no matter where they were. Unsightly crates were turned into alfresco dining tables by decorating them with makeshift tablecloths using old newspapers and candles. The men preferred to sit by the campfire on logs, balancing their plate on their lap. Metza was always close by, sniffing for morsels that may have dropped on the ground, never quite satisfied with her portion of food, which she always wolfed down, making little use of her teeth. Artis found a second-hand Coolgardie safe, which was a godsend in helping to keep their perishables cool and away from the wildlife and Metza's rumbling tummy. They placed containers filled with water under each leg to keep the ants away.

After dinner and the washing up was done, the women joined the men around the campfire. It was important to Artis that everyone got along and had time to relax. When tempers flared from time to time, the ritual of sitting in front of the campfire sharing a meal, a cuppa, and a song worked well in keeping temperaments composed.

Watching flames licking the logs had a calming effect. The flames stretched themselves as far as possible, searching to bite at anything within their perimeter. They snapped at the cold air, creating swirls of heat that were welcomed by the troupe sitting with faces flushed from the flames, whilst their backs endured the chilly night air. It did not take long for the logs to be devoured, leaving behind glowing orange coals waiting to ignite a fresh supply of logs.

'Who wants a cuppa?' said Larry.

All hands went up.

'I'd rather some bootleg,' said Fredric, holding up a bottle.

'Aye!' came the replies. Larry filled the billy can with water.

'Tea first,' said Larry as he counted out the number of tea scoops required and added an extra 'one for the pot' as his nanna had taught him to do for the perfect cup of tea. He balanced the billy can on some newly sacrificed logs and went to fetch the tin mugs, sugar, milk, and some Anzac biscuits that had been a barter exchange for show tickets. By the time they had their cuppa and bootleg, the fire had died down again, leaving logs with charred exteriors flecked with grey, and looking like the leathery skin of a crocodile. It was time for bed.

***

A few days later, the tyres arrived, and they headed to Cobram after Artis sent Jonesy a telegram telling him to inform the media that Samson was going to perform his truck-pulling stunt at eleven o'clock the next morning. It was sure to help make up for their loss of earnings by getting them maximum numbers for the matinee and evening show.

Jonesy and the townsfolk didn't disappoint. As predicted, Samson was a colossal hit, and both shows were packed to standing room only. The rest of the tour ran smoothly, the troupe unaware that it was because of Stan's absence. It helped morale to receive glowing reviews from the local newspapers:

For real good sparkling entertainment, the performance of The House That Jack Built would be hard to beat. Well known entrepreneur, Artis Newman, presented the ever-popular pantomime after many successful seasons in Melbourne, Hobart, and Launceston. His cast of 25 will keep you entertained from start to finish. Comedian, Bert McCarthy, was cast in the role of Dame Barleycorn who with her weak-kneed husband, kept the audience in good humour all evening, especially in the second half, when they had suddenly been transformed from poverty-stricken conditions to affluence. She was the woman who refused to go to hell with the demon because she had left her umbrella and her macintosh behind and she could not go there without them. Her song numbers included 'Where's The Face You Had on Monday, Mrs. Grundy', and 'Have a Little Drink with Martha'.

Baron Barleycorn, played by Artis Newman, was very much under his wife's thumb, and always worse off in his arguments with her. He shone especially in the scene in which the demon haunted their home, and he had to tell the story of the miser whose throat was cut from ear to there. His solo was Skipper Sardines, and he also appeared in a duet with his wife, singing 'Why?' Supporting him was Fredric Reif as Demon Despair. He had an effective baritone voice. His solo was 'The Demon of the Deep' and he also had a duet, 'Love and Hate', with the fairy. Coco Williams played the Principal Girl, Jill. Her voice was well heard in 'Here Comes the Sun', 'Sunny Side of the Street', and 'Be Careful with Those Eyes.' Jean Mayfield made a dashing Principal Boy, Jack. She has played the role on many occasions and is favourably known to radio fans for her many delightful renditions of songs and monologues over the air from 3LO, Melbourne. Her solos included 'You're Simply Delish', 'Old-Fashioned Girl' and 'Confession.' There was also a much-appreciated duet between Jack and Jill, 'If I Had a Girl Like You.' Miss Gracie Wells, who has a fine mezzo-soprano voice, played the delightful Fairy Prosperita, contributing some of the most attractive vocal work of the evening with her rendition of 'Here's to Love' being especially delightful.'

Ernie Smythe was the stony-hearted landlord, ready to play a trick to get Dame Barleycorn to accept service of a summons for rent, but not quite so ready for the trick she played on him in returning it. She gave considerable pleasure by singing 'Mother of Mine.' Tommy Williams played Sammy, the farmer's son. Myrtle the Cow with the crumpled horn was a two-man effort by Larry Newman and Charley Connors. She was aptly described as 'a cow of a cow' and provided more mirth for the audience, particularly when she gave a dance exhibition of the 'Charleston' after viciously kicking at Dame for sending the bucket flying. Perhaps the most amusing feature of the pantomime was the acting of 'Denis, the Pig'. He was brought onto the stage to receive a bath and resented the treatment with loud squeals, much to the delight of the juveniles. A bottle of milk, however, had a quietening effect and after being dressed in baby's clothes, the animal ran off the stage.

In addition, there are some very fine solo dancers, amazing and wonderful acrobats, and a host of pantomime specialities, including Artis and Larry, the Continental Jugglers, who performed in the second act. It's not everyone who can walk on a sphere and keep six tennis racquets moving at the same time, nor is it every couple who can fight and still keep three Indian clubs moving.

In addition to numerous dances by the Sunshine Girls (Belle Taylor, Jean Mayfield, Gracie Wells and Coco Williams), there was a clever acrobatic specialty and toe-dance by Miss Coco Williams. The production is on a lavish scale, with over 100 costumes, and there is not one dull moment during the two acts and the 20 scenes.

Popular prices will prevail, viz.. 2/-, 3/-. and 4/ reserved, plus tax, with children at half rates. There will be a special matinee performance of the pantomime on Thursday afternoon after school when the performance will be exactly as at night and children will be admitted for 1/1 and adults 2/2. Free sweets will be given to every child attending the matinee. Box plans are now available where seats may be booked without extra charge.

***

Belle's aloofness since they first started the tour did not go unnoticed. Not one to complain, she kept what was bothering her to herself and did her best to keep focused on completing the tour, as difficult as it was for her. Between looking after Shelley and performing, she was struggling with extreme fatigue, and the travelling was causing her to experience severe nausea. She managed to hold herself together until the last two weeks of the tour, when she collapsed backstage. As professional as Artis was, he abandoned his post, signalling for Larry to take over as he rushed to Belle's side.

'Are you alright, love? You look pale.'

'I'm fine.'

'Belle, you need to tell me what's wrong. You've not been yourself this whole tour.'

She burst into tears.

'I'm pregnant.'

17

Predator

Melbourne, Victoria, 1932

The news of Belle's pregnancy was a pleasant surprise for Artis, so her lack of enthusiasm and secrecy puzzled him.

'Why didn't you tell me sooner, love?'

'I was going to tell you when the tour was over.'

'I wish you'd just told me straight up. I knew something wasn't right from the get-go.'

'I'll be alright. You worry too much.'

'You could've lost the baby, Belle. I'm surprised you'd take such a risk.'

'Stop fussing.'

'It's my job to look after you, love,' he said, holding her hand. 'I had a talk with Olivia about you and Shelley staying with her in Melbourne 'til the baby comes.'

Belle agreed. The last three months had been a hard slog, and Artis could see Belle had been struggling, despite her efforts to conceal it. She seemed particularly emotional during this pregnancy, compared to Shelley's.

***

When the tour ended, the troupe headed back to Melbourne for a short break before starting their second tour in a new region. Artis met with Jonesy to discuss how they could maximise sales. Finances were tight, and he now had the added expense of replacing Belle and Olivia and sending money home to support them. Olivia kept one room for boarders and planned to teach piano from home to support herself, and Belle said she would teach singing to lighten the burden. They parted with heavy hearts. Belle lay on her bed, holding her belly. She cried until she felt as if her insides were being ripped to pieces. *God, help me! I don't know how I'm going to get through this.*

***

When Stan reported that Belle and Olivia had stayed behind, Vinnie and Rose gave Stan separate instructions to stay in Melbourne and report Belle's movements. Stan was in the difficult position of having to secretly give separate reports, knowing it meant betraying Vinnie if he was seen with Belle.

***

Belle left Shelley with Olivia and caught the bus into town for her medical appointment. After Stan's tip-off, Vinnie drove to the address

Stan had given him and sat out of sight in the doctor's waiting room, his fedora tilted to hide his face while he read the newspaper. When Belle left the doctor's room, he followed her to the elevator. Seconds later, it jolted to a stop, and he swiftly followed her in. Keeping his back to Belle, he slid the metal gating closed, then pressed the ground floor button. Seconds after the elevator began descending, he slammed the stop button, jamming the elevator between floors. She looked at him in total disbelief when he turned to face her.

'I thought I'd surprise you,' he smiled.

'Have you lost your mind, following me here?' Her coat parted as she stepped away from him, revealing her swollen belly. Vinnie gasped. As she reached for the button to restart the elevator, Vinnie made a move to kiss her. In a rage, she slapped his face and hissed at him.

'Don't touch me! Haven't you done enough damage? Do you want to publicly shame me as well by having us in the newspaper headlines!' She pushed him aside and slammed the elevator button, jerking it back into motion.

'We can make this work, Belle. Don't be afraid.' The elevator came to a stop. Vinnie stood in front of the gate. 'We can go to London. I've got connections there now with the major theatre production companies. I promise I'll look after you and the babies. I'll make your dreams come true.'

'Leave me alone!'

Belle pushed him aside and slid the metal gate open with a force sourced from nervous energy. Without looking back, she rushed out into the street.

'You belong with me, Belle!' yelled Vinnie.

Making her way to the bus stop, she saw a poster of Rose in a provocative gown promoting Vinnie's show. It made her blood boil. His media connections got him regular features in the newspapers. She passed a newsstand where a photograph of Rose and Vinnie holding their son had made the front-page news. Her rage increased as she hastened to the bus stop.

The minute Belle walked into the house, Olivia felt the atmosphere change.

'What happened?'

'Vinnie was waiting for me after my doctor's appointment.'

'What's so bad about that?'

'I don't want to be seen with him in public. We're both married. It'll cause a scandal.'

'He's still in love with you, even though you hurt him terribly.'

'That's not helpful, Mother.'

'Maybe you could appease him by agreeing to work with him after the baby's born. He can make you famous.'

'You can't be serious!'

'Look how you've ended up with Artis. Touring like gypsies, barely making ends meet.'

'Are you suggesting I leave my husband?'

'No, it can be a business arrangement. Artis can continue to tour, and I'll look after the children while you work with Vinnie.'

'I can't believe you'd suggest such a thing.' Belle walked into the bathroom and slammed the door. She prepared a bath, hoping it would calm her nerves. Grateful for the noise of the running water, she let her tears flow as she rubbed her swollen belly.

Once night had fallen, Vinnie drove to Olivia's house. Checking to make sure no one was watching, he opened the gate and peeped into each window until he saw Belle, through a sheer curtain, playing with Shelley on the bed. The outline of Belle's swollen breasts and belly underneath her nightgown aroused him. Mesmerised, he watched her with Shelley, listening to their laughs and fantasising about walking into the room and laying with her as her husband. When Belle turned out the light, Vinnie felt the emptiness of his soul. Surrounded by darkness, he returned to his car.

When Vinnie's car pulled into the driveway, Rose was seated in an armchair, with a book in hand, waiting for him.

'I was getting worried about you,' she said, loud enough to startle him.

'Why? I told you I was in a meeting?'

'With Rick?'

'Aye. What's with the questions?'

'Rick called in here, looking for you.'

'Well, our paths must've crossed. When I couldn't find him, I decided to go to the pub for a pint.'

'By yourself?'

'Aye, by myself. You got a problem with that?' said Vinnie, ignoring the hurt in her eyes as he headed up the stairs to the bedroom. Stan had reported Vinnie and Belle's meeting, and that she was pregnant. Rose calculated that Belle's pregnancy coincided with the photographs Stan had taken of Vinnie at Belle's house before she left for their tour months earlier. The fury she felt at this betrayal begged revenge. Publicly exposing them would cause a scandal that would ruin them all, and confronting Vinnie would alienate him further from her. She had to find a way to get Belle out of the picture. *At least he's still coming home to our bed. He's my husband and I know how to please him.* She peeled off her clothes as she headed towards the bedroom.

***

Artis returned home a few weeks before the baby's arrival. Shelley slept in a cot in Artis and Belle's room. Belle set up a makeshift bed for the baby, using a drawer from the chest in their room. The baby arrived five days early.

'Ah, he's just magnificent, Belle. What a beauty!'

The tiny 'dolly' intrigued Shelley and caused her to squeal with delight whenever he moved. Artis was in awe at having created such a beautiful family with the woman he cherished.

'I'm the luckiest man in the world!'

'Can we call him Joseph?'

'Yeah, sure, love. Joe for short, hey?' Belle's smile enticed Artis to kiss her. She let it linger to signal her desire for him to take her.

***

Not long after Artis returned, Vinnie drove to the house. He fumed at the sight of Artis's truck parked there and immediately went to peer through the bedroom window. The sight of Artis lying on the bed with

Shelley straddled across his stomach and Belle by his side made him bristle with jealousy. Vinnie fixed his attention on Belle, stretching his neck to catch a glimpse of her breast as she fed Joe. Artis interrupted Vinnie's moment of hypnosis when he put Shelley in her cot and Belle placed Joe in an open chest drawer she had padded with a blanket. Jealous rage pumped through him as Artis and Belle kissed passionately before turning off the bedside lamp, enveloping them in darkness. Vinnie strained to hear them, his imagination driving him to distraction until he could stand it no longer and left in the foulest of moods.

***

Vinnie sat on the floor beside his son's cot, listening to his rhythmic breathing as he slept. Frank was almost a year old. He closed his eyes and conjured up the fading image of his mother, laughing as she sat embracing him and his sister at his grandmother's house in London. Her joyous laugh could lift the spirits of even the most morose person. The recollections always ended with the image of his distraught mother wailing as she watched her son disappear into the distance. It still caused him intense pain and his hatred towards his step-grandfather would resurface.

His thoughts migrated to Belle, and how he could win her over while Artis was touring. As much as it tormented him to watch her through her bedroom window every chance he could, his obsession made it impossible to stop stalking her. The fantasies he created of them being together made him feel alive and hopeful. He held the image of Belle in his mind whenever he was intimate with Rose and when her name escaped his lips during lovemaking it incited Rose's hatred for her. Stan had reported to Rose that Vinnie's car had been parked a block from Belle's house most nights between shows. Confronting Vinnie would risk him leaving her. She had to find a way of getting rid of Belle without arousing Vinnie's suspicions.

18

A Golden Opportunity

When Artis returned from his latest tour, he was brimming over with excitement.

'Put on your best dress, love. I'm taking you out to dinner!'

'What are we celebrating?' Belle's eyes lit up.

'You'll know soon enough,' said Artis. Olivia agreed to mind the children. She refrained from asking what the excitement was about, guessing it must be major for Artis to spend precious dollars on dining out.

Belle had regained her slim figure and was wearing her favourite cream dress, with lace trim. The fabric was cut to accentuate her waist, and the calf-length folding panels flowed like ripples of water as she walked. Artis looked dapper in his double-breasted pin-striped suit, a white shirt with pale grey stripes and a black bow tie, his hair slicked back with Brylcreem.

As they drove to the restaurant, Artis tried to distract Belle by asking questions about the children. Even when they were seated at the restaurant, he continued to tease her.

'So, tell me already! I'm dying to know,' said Belle.

'Hold your horses. We haven't even ordered yet!' laughed Artis.

'How can you be so mean to keep making me wait? Tell me this minute!'

'A kiss would make me tell you right now,' coaxed Artis.

'Artis Newman, I'm not kissing you in public. Now stop teasing and tell me.' Artis let out a chuckle and reached out for Belle's hands. He was about to speak when the waiter interrupted them by placing warm bread rolls with a small dish of butter on the table. He handed them menus and advised them of the chef's specials before retreating.

'Quick, tell me already!'

'Belle, you'd never believe my luck. I ran into John Molloy at the Camperdown Mechanics Institute. He happened to be in Camperdown for business and came to see the show when he noticed we were playing. After the show, he sought me out to congratulate me and tell me how impressed he was.' He paused for emphasis.

'Well, go on!'

'Maybe we should order. The waiter's giving me the eye.'

'Artis! Give me the news already!'

'Did I tell you how beautiful you look tonight?'

'Yes, five times.'

'You light up the room, Belle Newman. You're the most beautiful woman I've ever set eyes on. I can't stand being apart from you and the beautiful children you've given me. I'm truly the luckiest man in the world. I'll do whatever I can to make you happy.'

The waiter returned, and they placed their order.

'You can start by telling me the news!'

'John Molloy proposed we put on the *Little Red Riding Hood* pantomime at the Playhouse in Melbourne. His mate Jim Stapleton's the new manager there.'

'Oh, Artis, that's wonderful news! Can we afford to put on such an extravagant show?'

'Let me worry about that. This is our chance to hit the big time.'

'I'm so excited! Did he say when?'

'He reckons he can book us into the Playhouse in six months, once the current show's finished.'

'Six months is such a long way away,' said Belle.

'I know, but without John's connections, it would've taken us a lot longer to get a venue in Melbourne. At least it'll give me time to wrap up this next tour and get the finances we need for *Little Red Riding Hood*. We're gonna have to get new costumes, props and backdrops made up, and we need time to rehearse.'

'I can get a start on that.'

'That's my girl. John specifically asked for you to be Little Red Riding Hood, if you're up to it.'

'Of course I am!'

Artis revelled in her excitement.

'Love, this is the chance for you to be the star you were born to be.

John produces tours that have sold out in London! If the show's a hit, there's a good chance we'll be touring in London!'

'Mother will be beside herself when I tell her.'

'How do you feel about going to stay with my parents while I'm on tour? I haven't asked them yet, but I want to ask Ma if she'd make the costumes for the show, with your help.'

'That's a good idea. You know Mother is going to insist on being the pianist, especially when she finds out we'll be playing at the Playhouse.'

'Of course, love. So, you're happy?'

'Very. We're finally getting our big break.'

'I know it's been a hard slog, Belle. There were a few times I thought you were going to call it quits after Shelley was born and we had to go on the road, and then before Joe was born, but you never complained, even when I wasn't around much.'

'It was hard, Artis.'

'I know it wasn't what you'd expected when you agreed to marry me. But I'm going to make it up to you.' He held her hand and looked into her eyes. The waiter returned with their order.

'Did anything funny happen on the tour?'

'There's always something funny happening.' He thought for a moment and then laughed. 'You know how Gertie Crockett replaced your mother on the tour, and how she's so religious and it's hard for her to crack a smile?'

A nod accompanied Belle's laugh.

'And you know how Jonesy always goes around town before the

show to see if any of the shops are throwing stuff out that we can use for the acts?'

Belle nodded, leaning forward in anticipation.

'Well, the bakery was gonna thrown out some flour that had weevils in it, so Jonesy brings it so we can do the Widow Twankey's Kitchen skit. Luckily, we planned to do it at the end of the show cause one of the crew left the sack of flour downstage left, right under the pit where Gertie's playing the piano. So, she's sitting playing like she's got a rod up her back, and she's got her hair in that tight bun. You know what I mean, not a hair outta place, looking so prim and proper with her doily collar and all. Well, anyway, one of the acrobats knocks the flour sack over and the flour projectiles all over Gertie.'

Artis's hysterical laugh infected Belle, and her shoulders shook with hilarity.

'Oh, Belle, you should have seen her. She's sitting there, rod-straight, and doesn't miss a beat. She just keeps on playing, completely covered in flour, like she's hoping nobody noticed. Even her eyelashes are white. She's sitting there looking like a snow cone when all of a sudden she can't help herself and she sneezes and flour just blows everywhere in a puff of white cloud. Nobody's watching the stage anymore. The audience is killing themselves laughing at Gertie, who, like the pro she is, keeps playing, glaring at me to do something.'

Belle teared up from laughing so hard.

'Well, didn't I get a mouthful about the damage to her keyboard and how many hours it was gonna take her to get all that flour cleaned out. Fair dinkum, you've no idea how hard it was for me to keep a straight face while she was piling her wrath on me.' Artis laughed.

The other diners frowned upon their boisterousness, but their mood was unshakable. They left the restaurant a couple of hours later in high spirits, not noticing Stan following them out.

19

A House of Cards

The next few weeks were a flurry of activities. Artis met with John to sign the contract. Everyone in the troupe was ecstatic about the opportunity to perform at the Playhouse. Once briefed on their new roles, they took a well-earned rest. Belle was so eager she made a start on arrangements. Olivia was consulted about the musical numbers and choreography. Betty agreed to make the new costumes for the show. She had an amazing ability to create masterpieces on a shoestring budget and suggested Belle scout the thrift shops for fabrics, buttons, sashes, feathers and hats they could recycle for the costumes. When the time came for the troupe to start their final regional tour, Belle and Artis's farewell was less melancholy.

As the days warmed up, Belle took Shelley and baby Joe to the local park every afternoon. Their visits were always at the mercy of the moody Victorian weather, which was as predictable as the ocean currents. On sunny days, the park was well dotted with mothers and their children. Shrill laughter and the occasional screams or wails as a child fell or was pushed by a rumbustious bully assaulted Belle's ears. To her horror, the park had become home to families who were suffering hardship from the severe economic depression. Their only resort was to pitch a tent in the park and hope for better days.

A group of boys were tormenting the homeless children with a despicable chant sung to those who were on government sustenance payments.

You're on the Susso now
You can't afford a cow
You can't pay the rent
You live in a tent
You're on the Susso now.

A fight was about to break out. Enraged by their cruelty, Belle intercepted them, her arms flailing as she shooed them away.

'Stop it this minute!' She gave the boys their marching orders.

A group of mothers gathered around her in support, and the boys left the park. The mothers then foraged through their handbags for snacks they had brought for their children. They gave them to the homeless children, whose faces were etched with shame as they took the offering.

'Do you have food?' said Belle.

'Ma's gone looking for some,' said one of the children.

'Are you here alone?' The children nodded. 'Where's your father?' asked Belle.

'Looking for work.'

Belle was heartbroken.

'I'll bring you some food tomorrow,' said Belle.

'Me too,' chimed a mother.

'We can take turns,' said another mother.

'We'll keep an eye on you as well,' said another.

The children ran off to play while the women discussed options to help these unfortunate families. Belle, with Joe on her lap, was engrossed in the conversation and failed to notice a man positioned behind a tree watching Shelley playing in the park. His fedora was tilted to overshadow his face.

'Shelley, come look!' he said, pulling out a colourful puppet. Shelley's eyes lit up, and she ran to take a closer look. The man swiftly lured Shelley away from the park into a thicket of bushes.

When Belle looked up to check on Shelley, she was gone. Panic gripped her as she called out her name. She handed Joe to one of the mothers and frantically searched the park. From the corner of her eye, she saw Shelley and the man in the distance and ran towards them. The man was entertaining Shelley with the puppet, uttering silly commentary. Belle snatched Shelley's hand.

'What do you think you're doing?' she yelled, trying to catch her breath. She swayed at the shock of seeing Vinnie.

'We were just getting to know each other,' said Vinnie.

'How dare you! Have you lost your mind?' she screamed.

'Calm down! I need to talk to you and this is the only way I could think to get your attention.'

'I told you to stay away from me!'

'You've been avoiding me, Belle, and I have a proposition for you. I'm producing a new show in London, and I want you as the lead. I'm lining up Hollywood agents for the premiere to give you a chance to get a film deal. It'll make you an international star, Belle! But I need an answer today.'

Belle looked at him dumbfounded. In a split second, Vinnie kissed her on the mouth, locking her into a tight embrace. Shelley watched, confused.

'Mama?' Belle broke away by pinching Vinnie on the arm as hard as she could.

'Don't you ever do that again!'

'Stop procrastinating, Belle. You need to make up your mind. I've lined this opportunity up for you. Don't make me look like a fool.'

'I'm not leaving him,' she hissed.

Vinnie signalled for Stan to come out of the bushes, camera in hand. Belle froze.

'Why won't you give me a chance, Belle? I can give you everything you dreamed about and take care of you and the children better than he can.' Belle tried to contain her fury as she saw the confusion on Shelley's face. She took her by the hand and turned to walk away.

'I'll have to show him the pictures.'

'If you do, I promise you'll regret it and you'll never see me again.'

Belle quickened her step, pulling Shelley along beside her until she tripped and grazed her knee. She howled in protest, resisting Belle's grip on her hand. Belle was so rattled, she yanked her up, swung her on her hip and continued to run, her heart beating so hard with the exertion that she felt she would pass out.

'Belle, what happened?' said the mother holding Joe. 'Who was that man?'

'I'm sorry, I have to go,' she said as she took Joe and quickly put him in the pram. She hurried home, looking around to make sure Vinnie was nowhere in sight.

Shelley was whimpering, her cheeks wet with tears, her knee trickling blood. When she got home, Belle was relieved to see Olivia knitting by the fireplace.

'Mother, can you please look after the children? Shelley fell and scraped her knee.'

'What happened?' Olivia noticed Belle was fighting back tears.

'I need a moment alone.'

Belle went to her room, collapsed on the bed, and let the tears flow. Her rage was aimed at a pillow that she pounded repeatedly, her body twisting with the force of her blows. She bit into the pillow to muffle the sound of her sobs. Her nervous exhaustion took her into slumber.

Hours later, she awoke feeling as if sleep had poisoned her. Thirst prompted her to get up. She ran her fingers through her knotted hair and smoothed out her crumpled skirt before opening the door. A sliver of light coming from Olivia's bedroom door caught her attention. She pushed it ajar and poked her head through. The children were sleeping on the bed as Olivia sat reading under a lamp. She looked up and gave Belle a faint smile.

'I'm going to get a drink of water,' said Belle. Olivia followed her to the kitchen. The noise from the rattling pipes broke the silence. Belle turned the tap off and drank deeply before refilling her glass.

'Shelley said a man kissed you.' Belle froze, annoyed that Olivia had wasted no time in prying information from Shelley. The last thing she needed was her mother's involvement to complicate things.

'It was Vinnie. He lured Shelley away at the park, then kissed me in front of her while someone hiding in the bushes took photographs.'

'Why would he do that?'

'He's trying to blackmail me to play the lead in his show.'

'Well, he shouldn't have kissed you, but that's wonderful.'

'Did you not hear what I said? He didn't just kiss me, he took photographs.'

'That a worry. But why wouldn't you want to play a lead in his show? I read in the newspaper that his wife's pregnant, so it makes sense he would want you in his show. This is a huge opportunity.'

'Artis has already lined up a huge opportunity, Mother!'

'Yes, but Vinnie has Hollywood connections. His wife has already played a part in a Hollywood film.'

'In a questionable role. Certainly not the kind of role I'd want.'

'It's Hollywood, Belle. You have to do whatever it takes until you get famous. Then you can pick and choose.'

'I can't believe you're saying this. I have a husband and children.'

'I told you to hold off from having children. If you'd only listened to me, you'd be famous by now.'

'I don't know what I want anymore.'

'Of course you do. Who wouldn't want to be immortalised at the peak of their youth and beauty? Hollywood stars are worshipped, like gods.'

'Mother, stop. Don't you like Artis?'

'Everybody likes Artis. But he doesn't have the right connections like Vinnie does. You made a mistake marrying him. You should have listened to me. Everything was lined up ready to go, and you turned everything on its head by getting involved with Artis. But don't let that stop you from taking up Vinnie's opportunity. Look at it as a business deal. Besides, Artis will benefit from your fame. It'll give him a foot in the door to Hollywood.'

'You're talking about Hollywood as if it's a done deal.'

'Vinnie's made his wife famous, and he can do it for you. Besides, if you don't comply, he'll use the photographs against you, which will ruin your marriage and your chances of fame. And now that Shelley knows, you have a house of cards that's ready to come down at any moment.'

'This is such a mess.'

'How many times do I have to remind you we live in a man's world? Just play the game, Belle. Use men, like they use us. Take up his offer.'

'I need time to think. Artis works so hard to make me happy and now we've finally got our big break with *Little Red Riding Hood*. Promise me you won't say anything to Artis about all this.'

'Fine, but it's a ticking time bomb trying to keep a child quiet.'

20

Little Red Riding Hood

Melbourne, Victoria

'I'm going to do everything in my power to put on the best show in town!,' announced Belle.

'Why would you be so foolish as to pass up Vinnie's offer?' said Olivia.

'Please stay out of it, Mother, and just trust me to make my own decisions.'

Olivia's disappointment was reflected in her eyes, but Belle's steely determination was clear. Belle set to work, making plans for the show. She challenged herself with complex dance routines that were much more physically demanding than those she'd done in the past, spending hours rehearsing every day. She was an exceptional tap dancer with a natural rhythm that was pure joy to watch.

'I want to dance!' said Shelley, attempting to copy her mother. Belle choreographed a few simple steps that were manageable for a two-year-old. To her amazement, Shelley picked most of them up first go, igniting her love of dancing.

Belle scanned the newspapers to size up their competition. To her chagrin, Vinnie's shows were receiving top billing. She went to the expense of attending current shows to get ideas, to ensure their production would be a standout amongst their competitors. A quick-change act particularly impressed her. She believed it would work well in the *Little Red Riding Hood* scene where the wolf changes into grandma. The duo master illusionist confounded Belle with the swift dance-like movements that peeled away one costume after the other in what seemed like magic. The costume change happened in a blink of an eye right in front of the audience, or the performer crossed behind a screen, or through a door, and emerged an instant later clad in a new costume. Mesmerised, she took mental notes about the performer's techniques. It appeared that the transformations were done through a series of turns during which the performer's costume unwound from one into another. It would require many rehearsals to master the quick-change technique.

Belle went so far as to attend Vinnie's matinee production to see what they were competing against. She disguised herself in a grey wig, no make-up, and clothes she borrowed from Olivia. The matinee featured an international performer and top professional local talent, with no expense spared on costumes and set design. Even the ushers wore gold-braided uniforms. The show was impressive and ended with a spectacular grand finale that she thought would work perfectly for their show.

*** *

Hank and Betty left Yarra Glen at the crack of dawn for the thirty-one-mile trip to Melbourne. Hank had some business to attend to whilst he was in 'the big smoke', as he called Melbourne, so Belle had arranged to meet Betty at the front of the Coles entrance on Bourke Street. Hank dropped Betty off, and after confirming a time when he would return to pick them up, continued down the busy street. The women complimented each other on their outfits and hats before proceeding through the bustle of lively shoppers.

'Oh my, this is so elaborate! There must be thousands of items on sale. You'd never guess we were in a Depression here,' said Betty.

'People with jobs are taking advantage of the discounts. And because they're buying more, it helps businesses stay afloat. Just wait 'til you see the size of the cafeteria. It takes up an entire floor and boasts a thousand seats,' said Belle.

Betty's delight made Belle smile as they entered it.

'Oh my! Just look at those beautiful tiles. Oh, and the ceiling! It's a work of art!' said Betty, raising her voice over the effervescent chatter of customers and the clinking of dishes.

They found a quiet spot at the far end of the cafeteria where the mingled smells of the cafeteria food were less prevalent. They purchased tea, raspberry jam tarts and scones to share. After peeling off her gloves, Belle bit into a dainty tart. The shortbread crust melted into a buttery paste in her mouth, mixing itself with the raspberry glaze that was bursting with sweetness.

'These are Artis's favourites,' said Belle.

'Mmm, they are delicious!' said Betty. 'Now, let me see the cast's measurements so I can calculate how much fabric we'll need.' Belle took out her notebook with the measurements and some of her sketches and photographs of costumes worn by Hollywood stars.

'I love this costume Ginger Rogers is wearing. For Red Riding Hood's first scene, I want to create a red sprigged frock of muslin with red piping and a bow, a white pleated muslin apron tied with a big bow, and a scarlet cape and hood,' said Belle. 'Little Red's mother is very glamourous. I've designed this silver-frosted lame frock with a fitted bodice of ivory satin surmounting a long fully flared skirt. I want the entire frock to be ornamented with opalescent coin sequins like the Ginger Rogers costume.' Belle showed Betty the design sketches.

'It sounds very high class,' said Betty.

'Yes, I've talked to Artis about putting a spin on the storyline so that it's extra spectacular. The story goes that Red Riding Hood is about to inherit millions from her sick grandmother, and the wolf is using Red Riding Hood to intervene and get her grandmother to sign her millions over to him. It also makes it more entertaining for the adults who are bringing their children.'

Belle showed Betty a photo of Clark Gable.

'This is how I want the wolf to look. Suave and debonair, like Clark. His tunic suit will be burnt orange silk, ornamented with wide straps of copper tissue and a belt, pochette, a cap of copper and silver-frosted lame, and a bright orange bow tie. A hood with ears will be attached to the suit collar, but his ears will be hidden under his cap, until he's exposed by the woodchopper. Now, the woodchopper is very handsome, and when he sees Little Red, it's love at first sight for both of them. He's going to be wearing a suit with a basque of pleated white satin to match his fitted coat and black vest when he rescues Little Red. Then there's a courting scene where he'll be changing into a coat of silver cloth with gauntlet cuffs bound with plain silver braid. In that scene, I want Little Red in a Dolly Varden frock with a pink taffeta skirt and pale pink hemline. Her panniers and bodice will be lavender silk printed with a pink and deeper mauve bell design. I want to doll grandma up for that scene in a long frock of pink floral silk with narrow flounces on her hips of plain silk to match the edging on her cape berthe. Little Red's mother is going to join them in that scene wearing an ivory georgette frock embroidered with crystal beads and diamantes.'

'Sounds spectacular. You've definitely put a lot of thought into every detail,' said Betty.

'I'm glad you like it. This is such an important opportunity for us. We have to make sure this is the best show in town. It could launch us into bigger things. John Molloy is a producer who's had sell-out shows in London, and Jim Stapleton, who manages the Playhouse, has connections with Hollywood agents. They're always scouting for new talent, so he always invites them to his shows.'

'Is it your dream to be famous?'

'Of course! Isn't that every performer's dream?'

'What happiness do you think fame will bring you?'

The question stunned Belle.

'Admirers all over the world, money to buy whatever I want, a glamorous life travelling to exotic places and staying in luxury hotels.'

'Performers are only as glamorous as their publicity photographs. Surely you're familiar with fans who admire you but don't really know you. It's an illusion you create on stage, isn't it?'

'I suppose, but why not aim high and get rich and famous? Then we could have everything we wanted and be immortalised and remembered forever.'

'Isn't it only a very small percentage of performers who reach that status? And it always seems to come at a price.'

'Do you disapprove?'

'I'm sorry, I didn't mean to upset you. I've learnt the hard way that all that glitters is not gold. It seems to me that film stars are beautiful illusions people worship as if they were immortal gods.'

'Yet film stars bring people so much joy and help them forget their troubles. Besides, it's what I love to do.'

'Yes, I can see that. You're very talented and it's good to pursue your dreams if that's what makes you happy.'

'It makes Artis happy too.'

'You and the children make Artis happy. You're all that matters to him. Unfortunately, he seems to have abandoned his faith along the way.'

'Pardon me for saying so, but it seemed to have been forced on him. He said he'd get beatings for the slightest things he did wrong and that's why he left home as soon as he was old enough.'

'Yes, you're right. We made mistakes with raising our boys, and we were devastated when Artis left. Even more so when Larry told us that was the reason he left. Larry was furious with us and threatened to leave as well. That's when we realised how wrong we'd been to follow such strict teaching from the church. We believed we were doing it to prevent the boys from going down the wrong path in life. We'd misinterpreted the Bible verse in the Old Testament that says, *"He who spares his rod hates his son, but he who loves him disciplines him promptly."* That's what the elders of the church taught us. We repented and asked Artis and Larry to forgive us. Thankfully, they have. But, unfortunately, our discipline had a detrimental effect on their faith—the reverse of what we were trying to instil.'

'At least you made amends.'

'Does he ever express his faith to you and the children?'

'He keeps a Bible by the bed, even when we're touring, but that's about all, really.'

'That's good to know. We all have our journey to pursue in life. Forcing faith onto anyone is wrong, no matter how good our intentions are. God wants people to seek Him with a willing heart. He doesn't demand that you love Him.'

'I know how that feels.'

'Do you feel we've forced God on you?'

'No, I was referring to something else. Never mind.'

'Well, as it's turned out, Artis found you and that's a wonderful thing.'

'Thank you. But now we have an enemy who wants to destroy us.'

'Never fear your enemies. Fear takes away your ability to protect yourself.'

'So what should we do?'

'Forgiveness has more power than revenge. Hurt people hurt others. And hurting others in retaliation is a trap. It never ends well for anyone.'

Belle changed the subject and discussed the quick-change costumes with Betty.

'I'm not confident in designing such complex costumes,' said Betty.

'Yes, they are complex, with many layers. While we're in town, I'll look into having them made to order. We'll be able to continue to use them for many acts and recoup our initial investment.'

They were completely oblivious to Stan, who was seated at the table next to theirs, listening to every word.

When they had finished their morning tea, they visited each fabric shop on Belle's list, completing their purchases just in time for Hank to pick them up. They drove to Olivia's house for lunch. Hank had brought some loaves from his bakery, freshly baked before they left that morning. Olivia prepared a delicious lunch of corned beef sandwiches with cheese and pickles, slathered in English mustard. Hank bit into the spongy bread, causing the filling to ooze from the edges of the crackly crust.

'Ripper sambos, Olivia,' he said, as he gulped his second cup of sugary tea.

'It's the bread that makes them so delicious,' she said, smiling.

When they noticed the mood of the sky had changed, they made haste to return to Yarra Glen before night fell. They loaded the car as quickly as possible before the impending downpour unleashed its load. Belle sat in the back seat with Shelley tucked under her arm and Joe snuggled on her lap, almost invisible under the array of fabric, hats, and props that could not fit in the boot amongst their luggage. The return trip took longer than expected as the rain finally came down with force, making it difficult to see through the windscreen. Hank slowed to a snail's pace and was forced to stop and wait for the rain to die down after the car swerved dangerously as it sliced through torrents of water rushing across the road. Thankfully, the children fell asleep to the drumming of the rain on the roof as nightfall enveloped the car.

***

Later that day, Stan reported back to Vinnie.

'She met some middle-aged woman at the Coles cafeteria. I heard them planning to perform *Little Red Riding Hood* at the Playhouse. They spent the morning tram hopping and buying a heck of a lot of fabric.'

'Where is she now?'

'I dunno. I started following them, but once it started pelting down rain, my motorcycle kept sliding all over the road and I lost them.'

After hearing Stan's report, Vinnie headed down to the Playhouse to meet with the booking manager.

'G'day. My name's Vinnie McIntyre. You're no doubt familiar with my shows?' said Vinnie, extending his hand to solicit a handshake.

'Jim Stapleton.' They shook hands. Vinnie noted the cool response. 'What can I do for you?'

'I've come with a proposal that will throw the Playhouse Theatre into the limelight and, at the same time, stop you from making a very big mistake.'

'A mistake?'

'Aye, I heard you've booked Artis Newman's production of *Little Red Riding Hood* to start in a few months.'

'What's it to you?'

'I know Artis very well and I believe they're not prepared to produce a show.'

'What do you mean, they're not prepared?'

'I've heard from a very reliable source that Artis is struggling financially and hasn't had time to prepare for the show. His wife's recently had a baby and isn't up to performing, and I believe he'll be losing a few of his star performers once he's finished touring. I'll be honest with you, I think you're taking a big risk.'

'What are you proposing?'

'I can guarantee you a top-notch production of *Little Red Riding Hood* with sold-out dates and standing room only. You'll make a lot of money from my production.'

'It that right?'

'Too right.'

'Artis called me a few days ago. He never mentioned he wasn't ready for the show. On the contrary …'

'With all due respect, Mr Stapleton, I've been in the business a very long time and believe me, I wouldn't have gone out of my way to come here if I didn't feel a duty to warn you of the mistake you're about to make. There's a reason Artis has had to resort to regional touring.'

'I may be new to managing this theatre, Mr McIntyre, but I've also been in business a long time. Just how far would you go to cut a deal to take over Artis Newman's contract?'

Vinnie grinned and proceeded to make Jim an exceedingly generous offer.

***

Once Stan processed the photographs he had taken of Vinnie and Belle in the park, he gave copies to Rose. Even though she hid her fury as she flicked through them, Stan sensed her emotions through her steely composure. He felt little compassion for her and resented taking orders from a woman. Especially Rose, considering Carlo was the reason for his predicament. He had loaned Stan money after he lost his job and couldn't pay the rent, and when he wasn't able to find work to pay Carlo back, his thugs had paid him a visit, wielding a sledgehammer. He was given the option of working for Carlo to pay off his debt or have both knees smashed. Stan was made fully aware that once he entered Carlo's circle, and had seen the dealings of Melbourne's underbelly, he was a marked man for the rest of his life.

After having to follow Artis's troupe through the countryside, he had lost touch with his wife and daughter and begun medicating himself with the bottle. Reporting secretly to Vinnie and Rose separately was also taking its toll. By giving them the photographs,

Stan had placed a weapon in both their hands. *I'll give them a taste of their own medicine,* he thought. *Let's see how they like having their lives destroyed.*

***

Belle and Betty got busy making costumes. They littered the house with butcher's paper as Betty created patterns and Belle cut up the fabric ready for sewing. Betty then sewed the costumes together and Belle fastened the buttons, bows, ribbons and other decorative features to the fabric. The results were outstanding costumes that were sure to dazzle audiences under the magic of brilliant lighting.

Once they finished making the costumes, Hank drove Belle and the children back to Melbourne, his car brimming with costumes, hats, and props. On their way through the city, they picked up the pre-ordered quick-change costumes, which were exquisitely crafted. Olivia welcomed them home with her speciality jam and cream pumpkin scones and a hot pot of tea. Belle had been rehearsing the musical numbers for the show and gave them a demonstration before Hank made his way back to Yarra Glen. Shelley had also learned some steps and was keen to perform with her mother.

'It looks like your mother has done a fine job teaching you to dance,' said Olivia.

'I can do rolls, too,' said Shelley, attempting a forward roll.

'Artis suggested I enrol her at the Melrose Violetta Dancing School. They also teach acrobatics and tumbling.'

'Watch, Mama and Nanma!' Shelley called out. Belle and Olivia laughed at her wonky side rolls.

'It'll help her with her balance and coordination. It looks like she'll be a right little star,' said Olivia.

'I'm going to enrol her at the Bourke Street studio in the city. Agnes Greenwood teaches there. She has an excellent reputation,' said Belle.

When the troupe returned from touring, everyone was in high spirits about being back in Melbourne for the next production. Intense rehearsals would begin within days. Belle handed Artis the telegram sent by Jim Stapleton, requesting him to call as soon as he returned from touring.

'Do you think there might be a problem?' said Belle.

'I bloody well hope not.' He hurried out the door, telegram in hand, to the phone box down the street. He cocooned himself inside, lifted the receiver, put his coins through the slot, and asked the switchboard operator to connect the call as he read Jim's phone number out to her, then waited for her to make the connection.

'Good afternoon, Mr Stapleton. This is Artis Newman.'

'Artis, how are preparations for *Little Red Riding Hood* going?'

'Everything's on track. Is there a problem?'

'I had a visit from Vinnie McIntyre a while ago. He seemed concerned that you were having financial problems and wouldn't be able to get the production organised on time for the opening. Said your wife just had a baby and wasn't up for the lead.'

'Mr Stapleton, I can assure you that the production will be one of the best in town. I don't wish to speak ill of Mr McIntyre, but the reason we had to go out on the road was because he was sabotaging all our booking opportunities. I'd hoped he'd got past that, so it's disappointing to hear that he's back to his old tricks.' Jim could hear the exasperation in Artis's voice.

'I'm not interested in the beef between the two of you. My job is to manage the theatre and make sure I have the best shows running, to ensure profitability. Can you assure me I'm not making a mistake?'

'Mr Stapleton, I can come by your office tomorrow and show you the newspaper clippings I've been collecting of rave reviews our show's received whilst we've been touring.'

'That won't be necessary. I've heard glowing reviews from trusted sources. The main reason I booked you is because your wife is playing the lead, and you have Samson playing the woodchopper—two unique talents I keep hearing about. Is your wife up for the challenge so soon after having a child?'

'Absolutely, Mr Stapleton. I've never seen her so excited about performing in a show. She's already put so much work into it. She designed and had the most glamorous costumes made, and she's put together some fine choreography. I guarantee you'll be very pleased.'

'I'm glad to hear it.'

'So may I ask what's Vinnie's position in this?'

'I've never seen the blood drain from a man's face as quickly as when I told him that your show's drawcard was your wife, and I wouldn't be making any deals that didn't involve her. It's what the public's been wanting after her absence,' he said. Artis felt an immense sense of relief knowing that Vinnie had lost out this time and that the show would go on as scheduled.

'I don't know what the hell's gone down between the two of you, but it's clear you need to watch your back with an enemy like McIntyre. That's another reason I didn't want to do business with the man. I simply don't trust him.' The switchboard operator interrupted their conversation to ask whether they would like to extend their call for a further three minutes.

'No need,' said Jim. 'Mr Newman, call into my office with your show program and publicity photos as soon as you can. I recommend you book Universal Studios to take your photos. They do a good job and will give you a discount if you mention me. They're in the Nicholas Building in Swanston Street, fifth floor.'

The line dropped out before Artis could thank him. Their booking at the Playhouse might be secure, but he had every intention of keeping his radar tuned to Vinnie, who would no doubt have plans to sabotage their production. He returned home in a jovial mood to find Belle awaiting the outcome of his conversation with Jim.

'*Little Red Riding Hood* is going to be a massive hit, I just know it!' she said with passion.

***

Jim Stapleton did an excellent job of promoting *Little Red Riding Hood*, with pre-sales exceeding their expectations. Artis had booked Universal Studios in Swanston Street to take their publicity photos and spent over a thousand pounds on wardrobe and scenery to ensure he honoured his word to Jim: that it would bring him the success he was counting on. Once the show's run began, he waited with bated breath for the first review to be published. The *Melbourne Advocate*'s read:

LITTLE RED RIDING HOOD
DELIGHTFUL PANTOMIME
AT THE PLAYHOUSE

Artis Newman's Pantomime Players' opening night of Little Red Riding Hood at the Playhouse on Saturday delighted the patrons by the standard of the production. The program was one continuous round of sparkling and clean humour, brilliant dancing, wonderfully dexterous juggling and some nice singing—just the kind of show in which a whole family can find enjoyable entertainment. A standout performance was given by Belle Taylor, as Little Red Riding Hood, who was warmly welcomed back after a break from the stage. She sang and danced superbly and was well supported by a cast of merry comedians. Jean Mayfield made an amusing grandma, and her make-up was excellent. There were many fine ensembles and dances throughout the show; the dainty and graceful butterfly ballet and the hunting scene being particularly fine. Everyone danced as if it were the one thing in life worth doing. The acrobatic displays of two of the ballet dancers, Birdie Davis and Coco Williams, were possibly the best that has been seen here for a number of years, while the 'Whirlwind Roman Offs' on skates were particularly clever and graceful in their movements. The costumes were exquisite and worth special mention. Samson, the Strong Man, played the part of the woodchopper to perfection, and Fredric Reif made a very convincing wolf who confounded the audience with his quick-change routine that had the audience in stitches. There is no doubt that Artis Newman's Little Red Riding Hood is one of the finest pantomimes seen for some time. Ballets and ensembles are by May Downs dancers and brilliantly choreographed by Belle Taylor.

Little Red Riding Hood gained momentum and continued to receive rave reviews. On the other side of town, Vinnie's matinee ticket sales declined. It wasn't long before he received a phone call from Carlo.

'I don't like losing money. Do something about it.' Vinnie heard the click of the phone before he could reply.

Damned son of a bitch. I should never have got involved with him, thought Vinnie.

21

A Deal to Kill

Melbourne, Victoria, 1932

Vinnie arranged to meet Stan at a rundown pub outside of town. Vinnie broke through the stale, humid air, polluted with thick smoke and the rancid smell of spilled beer. It took him a while to spot Stan amongst the crowd of staggering, rowdy bodies, diluting their worries with booze. By the smell of Stan's breath, Vinnie could tell he'd had his fair share.

'G'day, boss,' slurred Stan, his hand outstretched. Vinnie ignored the gesture, noting Stan's bloodshot eyes. He didn't ask about Stan's worries. It was better that he knew nothing about him.

'I told you not to call me boss,' said Vinnie. 'What are you drinking?'

'A dead soldier,' he said, turning his glass upside down. 'But some liquid gold will go down nice.' Vinnie looked in disdain at the pathetic figure hunched over the bar. He motioned for the bartender.

'Two beers and a bag of crisps.' Vinnie dug into his pocket and placed some coins on the counter. The bartender exchanged the coins for the beer and a pack of Smith's crisps.

'I want you to set up a show to play around the traps. I'll set up the venue and the program. All you have to do is hire a couple of face stretchers and wannabe actors scrounging for a bob. That shouldn't be hard to do down at Poverty Point.' Vinnie opened the packet of crisps, took the salt sachet, twisted it opened and sprinkled the salt over the crisps. He took a swig of beer, then shoved a handful of crisps into his mouth. The crackling crunch made Stan hunger for a bite. He eyed the packet, hoping Vinnie would offer him some. When he didn't, he took a long gulp of beer.

'I don't know nothin' about putting on a show or hiring talent,' said Stan.

'You're not listening, mate. I said I'd take care of it, and I'm not looking for talent. The worse they perform, the better.' He handed Stan a stack of handbills and posters.

'Newman Entertainers,' read Stan.

'I suggest you get to work. I got no time to lose. The show needs to start next week. I want these posted anywhere that'll take a nail. Come find me when you've got it sorted. And sober up, mate. I catch you pissed on the job and you'll be getting your marching orders. Is that clear?'

He placed Stan's usual expenses on the counter and left. Stan reached over for Vinnie's remaining beer and crisps. As he was sliding Vinnie's wad of notes into the inside of his jacket pocket, he pulled out a well-worn photograph. The edges were dog-eared. He stared at the smiling faces of his wife, Betsy, and three-year-old daughter, Lulu. A wave of emotion came over him as he recalled how Lulu's smile would melt his heart. She would hold his face with both her tiny hands and move her face close to his, asking for butterfly kisses. The sound of her voice and laughter echoed in his ears, and he wondered if she still remembered him. When he had left Betsy and Lulu at her parent's house, he had never expected them to be gone six months later, when he returned. The strangers living in the house had no idea where they were. He wept for a few minutes, weakened by the effects of the booze. He caressed the photograph with his thumb and kissed it before putting it back in his pocket. At least he was working now. Maybe he could win his wife back, he thought, if he could only stop drinking. After downing the rest of his beer, he released a liquid belch that he re-swallowed. He wiped his mouth with his sleeve and picked up the posters.

'Do us a favour, mate, and put this up on your board. Best show in town!' Stan handed the poster to the bartender and walked a wobbly line onto the street.

***

Much to Vinnie's delight, *Newman Entertainers* caused more havoc than he'd expected. Vinnie had advertised a very similar program to Artis's current one, causing confusion between the separate troupes. By the time the audience realised that Newman

Entertainers was not related to Artis Newman, it was too late. They had purchased their tickets and witnessed one of the worst shows imaginable. At a time when money was not to be wasted, it made for a furious crowd. Artis received complaints from so many people that he was forced to take out a newspaper advertisement explaining the situation.

A DISCLAIMER!

Mr. Artis Newman, who is presenting Little Red Riding Hood at The Playhouse, is the original Artis Newman, formerly with the Royal Blind Society, and begs to notify all interested that he has no connections whatsoever with a combination touring under the name of 'Newman Entertainers.'

***

Around the same time, Belle received a telegram from Rose.

Need to talk. Meet at Fitzroy Park Gardener's cottage. Monday, 4 pm.

Rose's request made her uneasy. They had not spoken since Belle left Vinnie's troupe. She wondered if Rose had seen the photograph and was out for blood.

Nobody else was in sight when Belle arrived at Fitzroy Park, so it was easy to spot Rose sitting on a park bench. Rose stood as Belle approached. Belle caught a whiff of port on her breath and noted she was unsteady on her feet.

'Well, if it isn't the prissy Belle Newman!' she said, a little too loud. Belle's instinct was to head back home, but in a flash, Rose had knocked her hat off and grasped a handful of Belle's hair, pulling down so hard it caused Belle to bend and smash her knees on the stony path.

'You low-life hussy, why are you messing with my husband?'

'He came to me. I—' Belle's words triggered Rose's full fury, and she weathered blow after blow across her head and body.

'You're not the ant's pants now, are you?' She kicked Belle, who was cowering on the ground. 'Stay away from my husband or next time I'll kill you!'

Belle sat on the ground gasping, her hair in disarray. Rose retreated, her body shaking with adrenalin as she disentangled clumps of Belle's hair from around her fingers and zigzagged along the pathway.

The shock of the beating rendered Belle immobile for a few minutes as she tried to stop herself from shaking. The tightness of her corset inhibited her efforts to breathe as she gasped for air. She stood and collected herself, looking around to see if anybody had witnessed the humiliating attack. As she attempted to tidy her hair, she noticed that the pins holding it in place had pierced her scalp on one side. It was painful to touch. Her head was throbbing. Moving towards the park bench, she sat down and noted the holes in her stockings. Both her knees were bleeding, her skin glued to her stockings. Checking to ensure no one was watching, she unclasped her stockings from their suspenders and peeled them off. Taking an embroidered handkerchief from her handbag, she dabbed her bloodied knees. Suddenly, a flood of tears burst forth releasing the pent-up tension in her body as she began to sob—the forceful energy emanating from deep within her soul. *I can't do this anymore.* Once the sobbing subsided, she headed back home, hoping Artis was still at the theatre attending to business.

Just as they were on the cusp of reaching the zenith of their careers as elite entertainers, it all came crashing down.

Carlo sent some of his men to pay Jim Stapleton a visit. They roughed him up just enough to convince him not to renew Artis's contract and warned him to keep his mouth shut about their visit if he wanted to keep his kneecaps intact.

'I don't understand. *Little Red Riding Hood* has performed a record season of sixty-four performances. It's been a tremendous success!' said Artis, devastated at the news and the thought of having to take the troupe back on the road again.

'You have some powerful enemies, Mr Newman. Had I known that earlier, I would not have signed you on. Your business here is finished,' said Jim. And that was the end of their dream of bigger and better opportunities.

***

The day following her altercation with Belle, Rose summoned Stan.

'You need to get rid of her.'

'What do you mean?'

'I mean, enough pussyfooting around with these pathetic disruptions to their tours. I'll pay you five hundred pounds to make her disappear.' Stan looked at her stony face, realising she was serious.

'I'm not a killer!'

'There's a first time for everything. Start by killing an animal.'

He turned away in disgust, declaring again, 'I'm not a killer.'

'If you ever want to see your wife and daughter again, you'll do what I ask.'

Stan froze and turned to face her.

'You know where they are?'

'You should know by now that the De Lucas can find anybody.'

'I won't be no good to them if I'm in the slammer.'

'Make sure you don't get caught, or you won't have the luxury of prison.'

'Is that a threat?'

'Yes.' Her ruthlessness made him uneasy. 'Relax. You should know by now we have lawyers to keep you out of prison. So, do we have a deal?'

Stan bowed his head as he mulled it over. He sensed Rose was getting impatient. The thought of seeing his wife and daughter again filled him with joy.

'I wanna see them first.'

Having anticipated his request, she produced a piece of paper with an address written on it.

'Do we have a deal?' she said before handing him the paper.

'I'll let you know after I've seen my family.'

'You know what'll happen to you if you go back on a deal with a De Luca. We can make your family disappear.'

He snatched the paper from her hand and left.

Rose's dirty deed weighed heavily on his conscience. His predominant thoughts were to find a way to disentangle himself from the De Lucas and make things right with his wife and daughter. The situation seemed hopeless. Without a job, he would be right back where he started, except he'd be a marked man on the run, putting in danger not only himself but his family as well.

The first thing Stan did after meeting with Rose was visit the barber for a haircut and shave. Back in his modest dwelling, he put on his best shirt, suit and tie and polished his shoes with a handkerchief and some spit. He found an old envelope and sealed a one pound note inside it. His eye caught the bottle of whisky on his bedside table. The demons in his mind lured him to take a swig to settle his nerves. But after picking up the bottle, his daughter's face came into his mind. He put the bottle down and left the room. His motorcycle was parked in front of the corner store, prompting him to purchase flowers and lollies.

The dappled sky dampened his mood as he rode the forty-five minutes to his wife's abode. His heart sank at the bleakness of the run-down homes surrounded by squalor. There was a strong odour of waste and there were makeshift tents in the yards. Children were playing outside in bare feet and soiled clothes. Silencing his Waratah, he unzipped his jacket, took the squashed flowers and lolly bag, and scanned the neighbourhood, searching for Lulu. A group of boys were playing marbles; some used the marbles as weapons they projected from slingshots. They immediately stopped their gang war when Stan barked at them. Girls were playing hopscotch, unaware of the wayward boys gawking as they caught a glimpse of a girl's underwear as she bent to pick up her rock or refresh the hopscotch markings with chalk. A few of the younger children were hooked on the hips of preteen girls. His heart leapt when he heard a child call out Lulu's name. He watched intently as a little girl ran over and sat down beside Lulu, who was making mud pies. Her grubby state overwhelmed Stan. Lulu was intent at her work, her long chestnut curls covering her face.

'Lulu!' His heart sank as she looked at him, her face void of recognition. He walked towards her and knelt. 'Do you remember me?' She shook her head. 'Where's your ma?'

'Working.'

'Do you know when she'll be home?' Lulu shrugged. 'I have something for you.' Stan gave her the lolly bag. The smile he remembered tore at his heart. 'And these are for your mum.' He handed the flowers to Lulu and tucked the envelope with the pound note in it between the stems. 'Can I come inside and wait for her?'

'I have to ask Pa,' she said.

'Who's Pa?'

'He lives with us.'

Stan's heart froze.

'Where is he?'

'Inside. You can come in.'

'No, I have to go. Tell your mum Stan called by to see her, and make sure only your mum gets the envelope. You understand?' Lulu nodded. Stan wanted to hold her. She was so beautiful. The emotions he had been drowning with liquor for years began to surface. He mounted his motorcycle with vigour, pushing the limits of the machine as he headed straight for Rose's house.

***

'I want two thousand pounds or there's no deal.'

Rose drew deeply on her cigarette and aimed the stream of smoke into Stan's face. The smell of tobacco mingled with bourbon and a heavy dose of perfume wafted around her.

'My family's living in squalor. I wanna make sure they're looked after.'

'Cigarette?' Rose stretched out a silver case packed with cigarettes in a neat row. Stan took one and lit it, his hands unsteady. 'That's a lot of dough.'

'Then there's no deal.' Rose tapped the ash from her cigarette against the side of the ashtray before extinguishing it. She looked up at Stan with lifeless eyes.

'I'll pay you one thousand pounds for Belle and Artis.'

The knot in Stan's stomach tightened.

'Are you outta your mind? These people have families.'

'Vinnie's going to ask you to get rid of Artis. He's not in a position to pay you what you're asking. Get rid of them both and you have a deal.'

Stan paced the room, sucking his cigarette to cinders.

'I'll take one thousand and all debts cleared with your old man, and I walk away a free man.'

'Done,' she lied, her jaw set, masking the icy spirit that dwelt within her. She threw him a jar of pills. 'Take a handful of those. It'll make your mission a breeze. And remember: there'll be a high price to pay if you fail.'

A feeling of doom entered Stan as it dawned on him that he had just sealed Artis and Belle's fates, and possibly his own.

214

22

Back on the Road

Hitting the road again at least guaranteed Artis a loyal following of townsfolk who had looked forward to the troupe's return. They knew they were in for a successful show and a welcome distraction from the hard slog of daily living in a rural community. Shelley, now three years old, pestered them for a part in the show. Belle and Artis agreed she was ready. She excelled in her acrobatic and tumbling classes and could pick up dance moves rapidly and memorise the words to songs with ease. Throughout the day, she tapped, sang, cartwheeled, and rolled as if it were the normal way to function. Artis had billed her in the newspaper advertisements as *Baby Shelley*, capitalising on the fact that audiences loved seeing young children perform.

The tour would begin in Meredith, a small town sixty-eight miles from Melbourne. It was late November and the weather was warming up, though there was a nip in the air that held some bite until the sun had time to throw a blanket of warmth onto the landscape.

The most unpleasant part of touring for the women was having to stop for a toilet break when there were no public amenities. They refused to bush squat anywhere near the trucks, so they had to find a spot far enough away in the bushland to be well out of sight. Occasionally, one would come screaming through the bushes, having come face to face with a kangaroo or a snake, or, heaven forbid, having run into a spider's web. The troupe would have a good laugh seeing the damsel in distress hopping about with arms flailing, their high-pitched screams echoing through the vast bushland.

It was always a relief to reach their destination without any mishaps such as blown tyres or getting bogged or lost. The worst mishaps were mechanical issues requiring costly repairs. The troupe had gained enough touring experience to have spare parts and some basic mechanical knowledge. When Samson's radiator sprang a leak, he poured a generous amount of finely ground pepper into it. The simple trick kept his motor humming for many more miles.

When they reached the town of Meredith, their entourage of vehicles created a dusty storm of orange dirt as they wheeled through Staughton Street. Curious heads turned as Larry announced their arrival on the loudspeaker. Faces lit up when they read the signage on the trucks, prompting a loud welcome. Excited children chased the trucks down the main road, squealing with delight as the troupe waved through the open car windows. Boys in billy carts attempted to race them down the street, the faces of the boys pushing them along flushed with the exertion.

'Today, I'm going on stage!' said Shelley, squirming on Belle's lap.

'Be still. You're hurting my legs. I can't dance with sore legs.'

'I can dance for you.'

'Yes, you can. But right now, practise your song,' said Belle, trying to calm her down. 'It has to be perfect, otherwise you won't be able to go on stage.'

'But you promised, Mama! And Daddy's the boss and he said I can, can't I, Daddy?' Shelley patted the side of Artis's head to get his attention.

'Not if Mama tells me you've been misbehaving. Now do what Mama says before I change my mind,' said Artis.

Shelley sang her song with zest as they proceeded to the site, just a short walk from town and the railway station. When they had set up the marquee and tents, Artis checked Belle, the children and Olivia into the Royal Hotel to settle in, then headed out to check sales at the ticket office.

'Just when I thought I was done with this miserable hard slog, it starts all over again. If only you'd taken up Vinnie's offer,' said Olivia.

'You didn't have to come, Mother.'

'Well, it's not like you can afford to hire someone. It's just another step backwards every time Artis has to hire someone to replace me.'

'Mother, you know we appreciate everything you do on the tour, but please don't keep using the guilt trip on me. It causes so much tension between us.'

Olivia sniffed and kept herself busy unpacking and getting

organised for the tasks ahead.

***

The guttural sound of a motorcycle reverberated in the distance, but everybody was too preoccupied with their duties to pay any attention to it. Stan cut the engine and dismounted. He leant against a tree, far enough away so as not to be seen, and eyed the young girls unloading their costumes. He downed a few Benzedrine pills as he tried to figure out a way to carry out Rose's dirty deed without being caught. A rush of energy pumped through his body as he lit a cigarette and waited for the ticket stand to open so he could purchase a ticket.

'Do you reckon Tommy will notice my costume's two inches shorter?' said Gracie.

'You kidding? Any shorter and you'll have the coppers locking you up,' said Birdie.

'Behave yourself, Gracie,' warned Jean.

After some skilful bartering, Artis presented Olivia with a couple of shins of beef, a leg of lamb, some bacon, eggs, a couple of plucked chickens, and an assortment of vegetables. By the time she arrived at the campsite, the men had already unloaded the cooking facilities and set up camp. She set up the packed food supplies and got one of the young lads to fill the 20-pint aluminium soup kettle with water. She tossed the shins into the soup kettle with some pearl barley and left them to simmer for a couple of hours whilst they ran the matinee show.

Fredric was always perfecting his acts and adding something new for variety. Hours before a performance, he would meticulously check his props, apply his make-up, and get dressed. Influenced by his

European heritage, his appearance was always immaculate, both on and off the stage, even in the hottest weather. One act he would perform that night was extremely risky, as it required him to climb up a high ladder and jump headfirst into a portable pool. The trick was that just before he hit the water, an elasticised rope would keep him suspended in the air and he would wave his arms about as if he was swimming. It was a very effective trick, and the audience loved it. Fredric did a final check to ensure the elasticised rope was securely fastened before joining the others for a publicity walk around town before the show started. What he failed to notice was Stan in the shadows, watching with interest.

***

Containing Shelley's excitement as Belle fitted her into the pirate costume Betty had made for her was near impossible. Belle was thankful she'd set Shelley's curls hours before, when she was calmer. Considering Shelley was bursting to get on stage, he decided against putting her in the act as the chaser. Once the music started, Artis strode downstage centre with arms outstretched in a welcoming gesture.

'Welcome, ladies, gentlemen, and children. What a pleasure it is to visit your beautiful town once again. It looks as though nothing much has changed except these delightful children seem to have grown before my very eyes.' The children reacted with toothy smiles; their chests puffed out with pride as they sat up straight. 'Well, let me tell you, somebody else has been doing some growing. It's our very own baby, Shelley. We can't keep the little trooper still. At just three years old, she's been learning to tap, tumble, and sing, just for the chance to come on stage and entertain you. Now, as announced, we have a special treat for you today. This is Baby Shelley's debut performance. She'll be singing 'On the Good Ship 'Yacki Hicki Doo La'. I hope you'll make her feel very welcome.' As the audience applauded, Artis took a bow and exited the stage.

Artis could see Belle and Shelley waiting in the wings. Belle was holding onto Shelley to prevent her from running onto the stage before her cue. A second before his exit point, Artis winked at Belle as a cue to let her go. Shelley skipped to centre stage in her tiny pirate costume, an eye patch, and her golden curls tucked under a pirate hat. Her bright smile won her an applause that triggered the shaking of her tambourine, just as Belle had taught her. She showed no signs of shyness as she took her bow and sang with perfect pitch and timing. Once finished, she curtsied and was rewarded with rousing applause. As the applause died down, Belle motioned from the wings for Shelley to come off. Shelley shook her head.

'I wanna sing some more!' she said and began the song all over again. Olivia, at the piano, let out a hearty laugh and replayed the accompaniment. Artis joined Belle in the wings, waving for Shelley to come off. Other cast members joined in, trying to coax Shelley off the stage, but she would have none of it. In response to the growing applause, Shelley took another bow and started the song all over again. Olivia, helpless in the pit, had no option but to continue playing. There was no stopping Shelley, who had fallen under the spell of the limelight and the waves of applause and admiration. After beaming at the audience, she took another bow and restarted the song. The audience howled with laughter as Artis appeared onstage to carry her off. She continued to sing and wave her tambourine with vigour as she disappeared offstage. Clearly, a star had been born.

'I want to sing more,' she pleaded.

'You were wonderful, darling, but it's Mama's turn now,' laughed Belle.

The crew had to keep Shelley distracted so she wouldn't run back onstage. She watched the other acts and made a few escapes onto the stage, much to the delight of the audience, until she slipped and fell headfirst into the orchestra pit. Tommy scooped her up as she screamed blue murder from the pain. The audience was silent as Shelley's wails diminished as she was carried backstage. Despite the mishap, the matinee received a standing ovation, leaving the troupe in high spirits. Shelley had suffered a gash to her temple that required a doctor's visit for a few stitches. She was lulled with a lollipop, and lots of praise to help take her mind off her sore head.

'What did I teach you about backstage etiquette?' said Olivia. 'Let that be an important lesson never to run onto the stage again. Now sit here a minute while I fix you up.'

Shelley was reluctant but didn't dare defy her grandma. Olivia cracked a fresh egg and peeled off the membrane, which she masterfully placed over Shelley's wound to promote healing before covering it back up with the gauze dressing. Samson cheered Shelley up by getting Metza to perform tricks, and Tommy sat her on his shoulders and paraded her around the campsite. She was so hyped up she refused to take a nap before the evening show.

As the sun shifted in the sky, the sweet aroma of the cooked meat from the shin of beef soup that had been left simmering made the troupe salivate.

'Gracie and Coco, can you prepare the vegetables and Birdie, make the damper, please,' instructed Olivia as she separated the meat from the bone. She then added the shredded meat back to the cooking pot along with carrots, turnips and a couple of heads of celery to absorb the flavour of the simmering meat, plus a little allspice, cloves, savoury, thyme, parsley, salt and pepper. They boiled a mound of potatoes to be served with a smothering of butter and finely chopped parsley. The preparation of their meals was as well-rehearsed as their performances. By this time, the men had completed their errands for the evening show and had gathered around the campfire with a billy of tea on the brew and a space amongst the glowing coals reserved to cook the damper.

Samson, whose consumption of food was always double what the other men ate, tore up a loaf of Vienna bread and thickly sliced a baton-sided salami. Taking a chunk of cheese that had been wrapped in a linen tea towel, he trimmed the crust before slicing it up. He jammed the cheese and salami into the spongy white interior of the crusty bread before shovelling it into his mouth, chewing with gusto despite some missing teeth. With a brisk twist, he unscrewed the lid from a jar of green olives, popping three into his mouth to accompany the masticated paste of cheese, salami, and bread he was yet to swallow. Birdie wrinkled her nose at the sight of him licking his fingers, noting his middle one was amputated at the tip. The troupe, accustomed to

Samson's unfamiliar odoriferous food that reeked of garlic and spices, ignored his customary double meal. Whenever they returned to Melbourne, Samson would stock up on his Italian delicacies. He kept his goodies carefully wrapped in a hessian bag, which he would keep wet and hanging from the rear-view mirror of his car.

'Mangiare … eat,' said Samson, offering a slice of salami to members of the troupe. They recoiled, wrinkling their noses as if he had offered them a dead rat. 'You lose,' he said. This supplementary food gave him the extra nourishment he needed to perform his incredible feats. Once he had run out of his delicacies, he hunted for rabbits or ducks for extra food and bartered or sold the excess. Metza was well trained at fetching the doomed catch and enjoyed her just reward. Samson offered his hunting skills for hire to farmers who needed to reduce the abundance of kangaroos that were destroying their crops.

Stan was loitering around the marquee while the troupe was gathered around the campfire. Making sure he wasn't noticed, he entered the marquee and waited for Fredric to do his prop checks for his swimming skit. When Fredric left, he loosened the rope, taking care to make it look like it was untouched. The faint sound of voices approaching the marquee floated towards him, prompting him to take cover.

'You think anyone'll notice we're gone?' whispered Gracie.

'Nah. We just need to be real quiet. If anyone comes, we'll just tell them we're rehearsing,' said Tommy. Within minutes they were necking, the sound of their passion arousing Stan's curiosity.

Word had got out about the matinee's standing ovation, resulting in a queue of buzzing bodies lined up at the ticket stand. Much to Artis's delight, the evening show was packed to maximum capacity. Backstage, however, things began to go wrong. Some props were missing, and a few costumes were ripped. The frantic backstage buzz to get things in order was creating friction amongst the troupe. Artis noticed the audience getting restless, with a few letting out groans and boos. This raised the troupe's anxiety as they absorbed the negative energy.

Fredric stood in the wings, getting ready for his diving act. He attached his swimming costume to the elasticised rope and once he heard Bert announce him, he entered the stage. He began climbing the ladder for his plunge into the pool. With trembling legs, he climbed the ladder, his face showing utter terror. The audience laughed at his antics.

'Hurry up! Don't be a chicken!' yelled Bert.

Fredric was wobbling around on his shaky legs and pretended to fall off the ladder a few times as he edged his way higher and higher. The audience's increasing tension was relieved by outbursts of laughter at Fredric's exaggerated facial expressions. When he reached the top of the ladder, his head was wobbling around in circles, signifying he was suffering from vertigo. The audience howled at his comical crying. His antics resulted in his foot slipping between the ladder rungs, causing him to hang upside down, screaming for help.

'Enough of the antics. Jump already!' shouted Bert, his hands cupped around his mouth like a loudspeaker. Fredric's comical attempt to untangle his foot from the ladder rung had the audience in stitches, although on tenterhooks. Once Fredric had untangled himself and was perched at the top of the ladder, Bert looked inside the pool, gave an exaggerated leap in the air and screeched, 'Argh! Stop! There's no water in the pool!'

The audience gasped as Bert's screech startled Fredric, who fell from the ladder headfirst with a blood-curdling scream and arms and legs flailing in all directions. As soon as he jumped, Fredric felt the slackness of the rope, his heart sinking as he waited for the impact.

It was serendipity that backstage Samson happened to be walking past the rope. He snatched it within a fraction of a second as it unwound, pulling it tightly around his arm to support Fredric's weight. Fredric's head was inches from hitting the bottom of the pool when the elastic bounced him back up. He caught his breath and imitated swimming through the air as if nothing untoward had happened.

'Well, if it ain't the swim fairy!' called out Bert, confused by the discrepancy in the act. The audience laughed, unaware of the near fatality. Regardless of how shaken they were, Fredric and Bert masked their emotions and continued with the show, absorbing the audience's appreciation of their antics.

After the show, Artis gathered everyone to debrief and to work out what had gone wrong. Nobody could figure out how the elastic had come loose. Fredric was quite shaken by the incident, considering he had always been so meticulous at ensuring the safety of his stunts. He thanked Samson for saving his life. He was sweating profusely, causing the greasepaint on his face to dissolve into a mess of blended colours.

'You better fix your face. It's falling off.' Samson patted Fredric on the back.

'I'm gonna ask that from now on we take more care with keeping an eye on things and double-checking all equipment and props before performances. It's a team effort. We need to look after each other,' said Artis.

Whilst the troupe packed up the set and started loading up the trucks, ready to leave the next morning, Larry noticed that Tommy and Gracie were missing.

23

Financial Ruin

After the show, Tommy and Gracie had snuck out and headed to a bushland area behind the troupe's campsite. Their youthful passion had prevailed against their fear of being reprimanded and dropped from the troupe. What they didn't realise was the danger they were putting themselves in as Stan watched them leave the marquee. He pulled out a bottle of bootleg he had in his bag and followed them into the bushland, close enough that he could follow the light from their torch without having to use his own.

When they had found a spot far enough from the campsite, Tommy laid out the blanket he had brought with him and lay down with Gracie. They wasted no time necking and fumbling around, undressing with wild abandon. The light of the moon enabled them to switch off their torch and still see each other's supple bodies.

Stan stood behind a tree, taking pleasure in watching them. When they had finished, he stepped out and tried to hide his amusement when they jumped out of their skins in fright at the stranger standing over them. They scrambled to get their clothes back on, terrified of what was coming.

'Well, what have we here? It looks like someone's misbehaving.' Scared out of their wits, they backed away when Stan took his knife from its holster. 'Where do you think you're going? Settle down. I'm looking for some company to share my bootleg.' Stan held out a bottle.

'I'm sorry, sir. We need to get back,' said Tommy, visibly shaking, as was Gracie.

'Come on! Are you trying to make me mad?' he thrust the bottle into Tommy's hand. Out of fear, Tommy took a swig and handed it back, gagging and coughing as his throat caught fire. 'What's your name?'

'Tommy.'

'Tommy, has nobody taught you to drink like a man? Have another go at it,' insisted Stan. Tommy took another swig. 'Keep going, keep going,' said Stan, holding the bottle to Tommy's lips, making him swallow mouthfuls until tears slid from the corners of his eyes and he began to cough and splutter. He pushed the bottle away from his mouth. Stan laughed. 'Sit down and tell me all about yourself. It gets lonely drinking by myself.'

'This is Gracie. We're part of a troupe performing in town,' Tommy said, trying to compose himself. His throat burned as though he'd swallowed acid.

'Gracie. Such a sweet name. Here, try some.' He held out the bottle. Regardless of the tone in his voice, it came across as a demand. Paralysed with fear, she did as she was told. Stan pushed her to swallow mouthfuls until she, too, was spluttering and coughing, her eyes streaming tears. Stan laughed. 'Relax. Looks like you two know how to have some fun.' He pulled out a bag of peanuts from his pocket and offered it to them.

'We need to get back before our boss notices we're missing,' stammered Tommy.

'Sit down!'

They immediately sat. Gracie started crying.

'Here, have some peanuts and take another swig. I want to have some fun too.' Stan shoved the bottle into Tommy's hand.

***

Artis grew frantic as the hours passed and Tommy and Gracie were still missing. It wasn't easy keeping the younger members in line. Bert, Samson, and Larry helped him search around town until the early hours.

When they had not returned by morning, Artis headed to the police station.

'I want to report two missing youngsters,' said Artis.

'How long have they been missing?' asked the officer.

'Since after ten last night.' Artis gave the officer a rundown.

'Let's hope it's not related to the murder we're currently investigating.'

'Murder! Who's been murdered?'

'We have officers out at the scene. I won't know any details until they return. I'll have an officer come and see you when we have more information.'

Artis returned to their campsite, where everyone was busy packing and loading up the trucks.

'We need to stay put. Police are looking into it. I've called the booking agent in Cressy to transfer the matinee tickets to the evening show for now.'

Rather than alarm everyone, Artis withheld the information about the murder investigation. He and a few of the men continued to search for Tommy and Gracie.

It was lunchtime when they returned to the camp and found Tommy and Gracie looking the worse for wear as the women tended to them. Artis felt the stress in his body replace itself with anger. 'Damned youngsters,' he muttered under his breath as he approached them.

'You better have a damned good explanation! We thought you'd been murdered!'

'I'm sorry, sir. It's all my fault,' said Tommy.

'They both reek of alcohol!' said Bert.

'Where on God's earth did you get alcohol?' Nobody had seen Artis this rattled before. 'You better start explaining yourself, boy!'

'A man forced us to drink it.'

'Forced you?' Artis pinned Tommy down with squinted eyes. 'What man?'

'I dunno, but it made us sick, and we blacked out. We only just woke up and came straight back.'

'Where the hell were you?'

'Just over there in the bushes.'

'Right under our bloody noses! What the hell were the two of you doing in the bushes?' Tommy and Gracie's silence and shaking bodies confirmed what everyone suspected.

'Did either of you have anything to do with untying my elastic rope?' said Fredric.

'No, sir! We didn't touch nothing. I swear on my mother's grave,'

'You know the rule for fooling around is instant dismissal,' said Artis. Gracie burst into tears. 'I'm responsible for you and now you've broken my trust.'

'Sir, please give us another chance. We promise it won't happen again.'

'I've been watching the both of you, and I can see you're smitten with each other, so I don't think you can make a guarantee like that, as far as I'm concerned. I'll be asking Jonesy to make plans to replace you and get you back home.' Gracie began howling.

'Please, sir. I can't go back home. My father's a drunk and hurts me,' said Gracie. Tommy put a protective arm around her.

'Sir, we're old enough to get married. I already asked Gracie, and she said yes, so we were planning to get ourselves hitched.'

'You're just kids!' said Artis.

'Please, sir, give us another chance,' begged Tommy. 'We're gonna do the right thing and make it up to you.'

'Can you replace the loss of ticket sales your stupidity cost us?'

Tommy shook his head as he stared at his feet. Gracie looked a mess with her dishevelled hair and dirty clothes. Remnants of her make-up were streaked all over her face as her tears kept flowing.

'Artis, I think if we head off right now, we should be able to set up for the evening performance in Cressy,' said Bert.

'Let's do it. I'll stop into town and let the police know we've found them, and let the booking agent in Cressy know we're on track for the evening performance.'

It was no surprise that tempers flared after driving the thirty-eight miles to Cressy, then rushing to unpack the trucks and set up for the evening show. Tommy and Gracie walked on eggshells after being forbidden to be anywhere near each other. Tea that night was a simple meal of damper with Vegemite or jam.

They recouped some of the money from the cancelled matinee and the show went ahead without incident. The following day was Sunday, the only day of the week performances were forbidden. It was a day to attend church, for those inclined, or spend the day relaxing. Samson would attend the Catholic Mass and then go hunting, hoping to shoot a kangaroo or wild boar to feed the troupe or sell. The young lads admired him and asked to accompany him on his hunting missions.

Next, they packed up and continued another eleven miles to Beeac, where they were able to enjoy a refreshing swim in the lake before the show. They continued the week in better spirits.

'Jonesy's lined us up at Alvie, which is about eleven miles from here, and then we're booked at Colac, another nine miles away, followed by Deans Marsh, which is nineteen miles away,' said Artis, running his finger along the map. 'We need to stock up with enough petrol to get us through to Forrest. Taking that wrong turn just before we got to Beeac cost us about a quarter of a tank, so we're cutting things a little fine,' he said to Larry, Samson, and Bert, who were driving vehicles.

Finances were tight. They were managing to break even, with just enough people attending the shows to keep them out of trouble. After the incident in Meredith with Tommy and Gracie, Stan laid low, even though he doubted they would remember his face, considering it was dark, and the alcohol had hit them faster than he expected. Their drunken state made it easy to extract information about their touring schedule so he could plan how to execute his dirty deed on Artis and Belle.

Stan waited for them in Forrest. He had stopped for a feed at the bakery on the main street when some of the local lads stopped to admire the 247cc Waratah's twin nickel exhaust pipes and two-gallon petrol tank. The one thing Stan liked to talk about was his Waratah. He was so engrossed in conversation that by the time he noticed the troupe's entourage of trucks rattling through the main street, it was too late for him to get out of sight.

Bert noticed the Waratah and pointed it out to Tommy, Charley and Fredric, who were his passengers.

'What a beauty!' said Charley.

'Hey, that looks like the man from Meredith that gave Gracie and me the alcohol,' said Tommy, craning his neck to get a better look at his face.

'You sure?' said Bert.

'I'm pretty sure, but what's he doing here?' said Tommy as they drove on. 'Come to think of it, I think I've seen that motorbike before.'

The town of Forrest was a welcome sight, with its lush trees, their branches dancing with the wind's currents. The earthy smell of plant life was invigorating. Samson and Charley had the bright idea of camping by the water's edge at Lake Elizabeth. They found what they thought was the perfect spot to pitch their tents. Not everyone was as keen to camp so close to the water. The girls made a trade of mending costumes, socks and personal garments in exchange for having the men set up their temporary living quarters, albeit at a safe distance from the water. Afterwards, they enjoyed a refreshing swim before the matinee show.

Relaxing by the lake before the matinee, Belle and Jean watched some of the younger troupe members playing with Shelley and Joe. Belle's realisation that her dream was slipping away had settled into her subconscious. The constant disappointments and struggles of touring made her long for a stable life where she didn't have to pack and unpack every day.

'This isn't the life I'd envisioned for myself,' said Belle.

'Me neither. It kills me to think we could have been touring in London,' said Jean.

'And Jim Stapleton had talked about a possible role in a Hollywood film.'

'Really? You never mentioned that before.'

'What was the point? It never happened.'

'Thanks to Vinnie. He'll get his own back one of these days,' said

Jean. 'He and his wife have got all the fame and money they could possibly want and yet they're still miserable. You should have at least reported Rose's attack to the police. Things are getting out of hand.'

'She got what she wanted. I'm far away from her husband and she's reclaimed the spotlight as Melbourne's star performer.'

'You know it's only a matter of time before all hell breaks loose and everything's exposed.'

'I know. The thought scares the life out of me.'

'When are you going to tell Artis about Vinnie?'

'Every time I'm about to, something stops me. He's stressed enough as it is, trying to keep us afloat.'

'He's going to take it badly, but you know I'll support you, no matter what.'

'Thanks, I'm going to need it.'

***

When Stan paid a heckler to sabotage the matinee performance, he got his money's worth. The heckler rattled the younger girls in the troupe with disparaging remarks directed at their dancing, singing or body shape. The troupe had dealt with hecklers in the past, but this one was relentless and had the lads in the troupe vowing for his blood. True to their word, after the show, they followed the heckler out as he left the marquee and cornered him.

'What the hell do you think you were doing, disrupting our show?' said Tommy, grabbing the heckler by his shirt collar. When Samson's six-foot-two stature approached, the heckler's face turned ashen.

'Hey, I don't want any trouble. A guy bought me a ticket and paid me to heckle and not hold back.'

'What did this guy look like?' said Samson, grabbing a fistful of the heckler's shirt and lifting him off the ground, so that seams tore open and shirt buttons flew in all directions.

'Ah, ah, ah. It was a guy with a Waratah motorcycle. I never saw him before in my life, I swear!'

'Where-a does he live?' Samson positioned his fist in the air, ready to strike the ashen face.

'I swear I don't know. I don't think he lives here. I know pretty much everyone in town and I'd remember someone with a Waratah.'

'That's the Waratah we saw when we drove into town. So that man must definitely be the one who gave us the alcohol in Meredith,' said Tommy.

'If we have trouble tonight, I will find you and break your face. Capisce?' The heckler looked puzzled by the last word that came out of Samson's mouth, but nodded regardless.

The evening performance went without incident. After the show, they retired to the rhythmic sounds of the forest. Some of the lads started a small fire near Samson and Charley's tents and indulged in a late-night swim and liquid supper before being lulled to sleep by the sound of lapping water.

In the morning, Charley ran screaming from his tent. He was covered head to toe with fat, furry caterpillars. The creepy crawlies had made their way into Charley and Samson's tents to get shelter from the rising water during the night. In a panic, he ran around in circles, leaping into the air and shaking himself violently to get them out of his hair and undergarments. When he realised one had crawled up his nostril, he added snorting and yowling to his incredible dance performance.

'Jump in the water,' said Fredric, who was laughing hysterically, along with a few of the other early risers. Charley made a dive for the water, reacting with a loud squark to the icy liquid.

When Fredric checked in on Samson, the only sign confirming that he was still in the tent was his snoring. The whole interior of the tent was decorated with a blanket of thousands of caterpillars moving in unison. Not a speck of canvas could be seen. Samson's face and hair were also covered with caterpillars. Metza was nowhere in sight. Fredric called out to Samson, but after his liquid supper, it took some time to stir him from his deep slumber. When he finally stirred and his brain computed his surroundings, he put on such a song and dance that, in his state of horror, he practically demolished the tent. By the time he found the tent's exit flap, he'd left behind a slushy mess of caterpillars. The troupe was in hysterics as they watched Samson running towards the water in his birthday suit, with furry caterpillar carcasses smeared over his body. Samson dove into the water with a mighty leap, almost sinking a stupefied Charley in the process. Peals of laughter echoed through the forest. Metza eventually crawled out from her hiding spot under the truck to inspect the damage.

A barrage of curses coming from Artis's truck soon cut the laughter short.

'If it's not one bloody thing after another! Some thief's stolen my money tin!' yelled Artis. 'All the money from the ticket sales is gone!'

24

The Accident

Beech Forest, Timboon, Camperdown, Carmut, Illowa, Victoria, 17 December 1934

After losing all their takings, Artis had to arrange a bank transfer of funds to keep them going. The little savings he had left from the *Little Red Riding Hood* profits were almost gone. Any more setbacks and they would have to shut down the production and he would have to go back to running the family bakery. With Christmas only three weeks away, Artis had to make the most of the time before the troupe would take a month's break to spend with their families over the summer.

'I know we're doing it tough, but I'm doing my best to keep us going. We need to work harder than ever to keep this show going. Any more mishaps and it'll be the end of us. I'm proposing we run three shows a day to help us keep afloat till Christmas.' Most in the troupe complained about this proposal, as running two shows was gruelling enough. Artis stood his ground, even though the decision caused discord among them.

Entering Beech Forest only further darkened their mood as they drove into the heavily blanketed sky that soon turned into a darker shade of grey, with an ominous tinge of green. The battle between the trees and the wind had such intensity that it sent thousands of leaves swirling like confetti through the restless air. Metza panted anxiously. It was only a matter of time before torrential rain would assault them. Setting up the marquee would be a nightmare, creating a muddy mess and limiting the number of people willing to brave the weather and walk through the slush to watch the show.

Noticing there were no posters advertising the show anywhere in sight, Artis felt his anxiety levels rise. He located the commissioning agent to find there were only a handful of tickets sold.

'How are we supposed to put on a show with only a handful of tickets and no posters anywhere?' said Artis.

The agent shuffled around his desk before pulling out a telegram.

'This came for ya last Wednesdee,' said the agent, his bulbous belly oozing onto his lap as he leaned forward to hand Artis the telegram. Artis's heart sank as he read it.

Death in the family. Must return home. Jonesy.

'Did the posters and tickets arrive?'

'Buggered if I know,' said the agent, a wisp of his hair dancing atop his balding head as a gust of air blew through the window. 'Ya'll need to pay ya invoice today,' he said, waving a sheet of paper at Artis.

'What the hell? You've charged us a flat fee even though you've done nothin' about selling tickets?'

'Ya got yourself a few there. What ya grumbling about?'

'A few won't cover your invoice, mate!'

'Not my problem, mate,' he said, taking a puff of a sausage-sized cigar.

Artis knew better than to argue with the old codger. He was clearly one of those crafty, calculating town agents who preferred to charge a flat fee rather than a percentage of tickets sold, giving him little incentive to fill seats.

Some smaller towns wanted to keep money circulating within their town rather than see it go to touring companies who would pitch their tents, make money on ticket sales, and disappear the next day. Artis checked the newspaper and found their advertisement listed in the back of the classifieds. It seemed like the locals always got the first pick of the prime advertising spots in this town.

'Oh, and another thing. Storms gonna be a cracker. We're expecting flash flooding, so the grounds will be outta bounds.'

'You can't be serious! Where are we supposed to perform?'

'Not my problem, mate.' The agent aimed a puff of smoke towards Artis's face.

'Well, I'm gonna make it your problem! You want your lousy invoice paid, you better find me a venue, quick smart.'

'Righto, don't get ya knickers in a knot. I can't control the weather, mate. All ya gotta do is ask nicely. Ya city folks got no manners.'

'Fine, I'm gonna ask nicely. What are my options?'

'Well, there ain't any,' said the agent, biting down on his cigar.

Artis moved up close to his face and tried to keep his voice steady.

'Think harder, *please.*'

'Well, there's an old hall a couple of streets away. Not as big as ya marquee, though.'

'I'll take it.'

'I'll need an upfront payment of 3 pounds and ten shillings.'

'Are you outta your mind!'

'There's those bad manners again.'

Artis bit his tongue, wanting nothing more than to get out of there before he knocked the old codger's lights out. After paying the invoice and the hall fee, he was left with only a few shillings and a bad taste in his mouth. Their next town, Timboon, was over fifty miles away. They were going to need to purchase fuel and supplies before they left. He prayed for a miracle to get enough seats sold to get them through to the next town.

As soon as Artis left the agent's office, Stan stepped out from the other room holding the posters.

'Make sure you burn these,' he said, throwing the posters on the agent's desk and slipping him a pound note. He waited for Artis to be out of sight before leaving the office.

While the troupe was relieved at not having to set up and pack down the marquee in miserable weather, their gratitude was dampened as soon as they opened the door of the old, abandoned hall. The women let out shrill screams as hundreds of mice scrambled in every direction at the intrusion. The troupe eyed the hall in dismay, knowing they faced back-breaking work to turn a filthy hall into a place of wonder where people could leave behind their worries and indulge in a few hours of entertainment.

They promptly unpacked the trucks as the wind had picked up to such an extreme that the troupe thought the massive branches, arching with the force of the wind, would snap at any minute and be hurled in their direction. Someone had to be stationed at every door to keep them from slamming shut. The wind forced their eyes shut, and they had to bow their heads to protect themselves from their whipping hair and flying debris. Others had the job of sweeping out the mice, some of which were trampled underfoot as the men worked swiftly to unpack the vehicles. They finished unloading just as bolts of lightning zapped the sky, followed by claps of thunder that shook the air. By then leaves and debris had swept into their vehicles and the hall, leaving them the task of cleaning up and transforming the hall in a matter of hours.

Usually, when ticket sales were down, Artis would ask the performers to parade the streets in costume to entice the townsfolk to purchase tickets. However, due to the wild weather, this was not possible. Instead, Larry drove around town, manoeuvring around potholes, while Tommy and Gracie announced the arrival of the show on the loudspeaker. Meanwhile, the makeshift stage was transformed with colourful backdrops and props, creating the illusion of good things to come.

As the start time for the matinee grew near, Larry, Tommy and Gracie's promotional efforts had paid off. Townsfolk began to dribble in, but there were no more than forty people when the overture started. There were still mice scurrying across the room, causing women to squeal and lift their feet off the ground, though some were used to the critters and didn't bat an eyelid. It wasn't the first time they'd experienced a mouse plague.

Artis opened the show and signalled for Birdie to take her place, followed by Bert and Jean as the soubrette. Shelley, dressed in a matching soldier costume, ready for her performance with the dancers, tugged at Belle's dress.

'Why do I have to be last?' said Shelley.

'Because you're the littlest. The dancers enter the stage from the tallest to the smallest. I've told you that many times. Now pay attention or you'll miss your cue.'

A few seconds later, when Shelley skipped onto the stage, the audience applauded the tiny performer. Shelley took command of the stage as she sang 'There's Something About a Soldier'. The admiration on Belle's face was evident as she watched Shelley from the wings. At the end of the song, Shelley searched out her mother in the wings for further instructions. Belle demonstrated a curtsy for Shelley to mimic, then signalled for her to come off stage.

The evening show welcomed a motley crew. Audiences in these small towns were not ladies in gowns and gentlemen in cravats. They were sheep shearers, farmers, or loggers. The men were unshaven, wore bib overalls, and sometimes stank to high heaven. Many of them lived in remote barracks and hadn't seen a woman in weeks. They were usually the most appreciative audience, as they were starved for company and entertainment, especially if it comprised beautiful dancers displaying shapely legs. They would howl, laugh, applaud loudly, and overlook any mistakes a performer might make. Belle and Jean were masterful singers who knew how to connect with the audience by singing directly to them as if they were the only ones that mattered in the room. With each verse of the song, they would pick someone else to focus on. The men loved it.

The following morning, they set off for Timboon. Their supplies were getting low and with little income or barter exchange from the last two shows, things were tight. They were counting on near full houses to keep them going. Artis's heart ached as he saw the exhaustion on Belle's face as she unpacked costumes and props. Her dreams of fame and fortune were diminishing, yet she never once complained.

Just before the start of the late morning show, Belle advised Artis that Shelley was sick with a fever and still asleep from her nap. Shelley had become their star performer, and those who attended the late morning show would rave about her, which helped with ticket sales for the matinee and the evening performances.

'Better keep her warm in bed,' said Artis as he prepared to open the show.

'Welcome, ladies and gentlemen, boys and girls,' boomed Artis. 'Have we got a show for you! Birdie is going to tie herself up in knots, Fred will be clowning around and performing his amazing acrobatics. Samson will perform magnificent acts of strength that are sure to take your breath away. His little dog, Metza, will also delight you with a few tricks of her own. Sadly, Baby Shirley is sick in bed and won't be making an appearance.'

'Boo!'

'Now, folks, we have the beautiful Belle and Jean here tonight to sing and dance your troubles away. There'll be plenty of magic tricks and surprises to keep you entertained. And now, without further ado, please welcome the extraordinary Birdie!' Artis exited the stage as the overture began.

Shelley was floating in a zone of semiconsciousness, in a makeshift dressing room. Beads of perspiration dotted her forehead. Her mind was about to be swallowed by the darkness of deep sleep when the tune of 'When the Saints Come Marching In' threw her into full alert. It was her cue! She ran, in a state of delirium, towards the stage, pushing past bodies and ducking through legs and costumes before scrambling onto the stage to take her place. When the audience saw her wearing her nightgown, with strips of ribbons through her hair to set her curls, she received an exuberant response. Shelley performed like the professional she had become. As soon as the act was over, her fever got the better of her and one of the troupe managed to get her back to bed to sleep it off.

The pressure of three daily performances was taking its toll on the troupe. Frayed nerves were causing tempers to flare, and disputes broke out, bringing some to breaking point. With Jonesy gone, they had little time to rest as they marketed for extra ticket sales by parading around town in costume prior to the shows. Samson, in his leopard-print costume, attracted the admiration of many. It was a lure. He had spiced up his evening act by performing a muscle dance, wearing nothing more than an artificial fig leaf on his well-oiled body. He flexed his arms, back, pectorals and buttocks to music, whilst Metza danced on her hind legs in a pink tutu, with a big bow tied around her neck.

Before he disappeared, Jonesy had booked the Theatre Royal in Camperdown. It was an elegant theatre that held 800 people on the floor and another 250 upstairs in the dress circle and had the psychological effect of boosting morale after playing under a marquee or in decrepit halls. The Camperdown community appreciated the arts, making it easier to get full houses, or close to it, for the three daily performances. The troupe was given the royal treatment, with rooms at the Hampden Hotel, sponsored by the mayor. Artis returned the kindness with tickets to the best seats in the house. Playing at the Theatre Royal gave them the opportunity to make a lot more money and meant he could pay the troupe a few extra bob to show appreciation for their hard work and commitment.

Fredric performed his comedy routine in baggy pants, a brightly checked suit and a big red nose which he honked from time to time. The audience squealed with delight during his orange juggling act, when his hands got caught in his suspenders, causing his pants to fall down around his ankles. Still juggling, he began to pull his pants back up and kept adding oranges until he had seven circling in the air. He ended the act with all seven oranges disappearing into his baggy pants, then, looking embarrassed, motioned for the curtains to close.

Next, Jean entered the stage in a glittery gold gown that highlighted her shapely figure and draped itself across her slender legs. After she had performed her song, Belle, Bert and Gracie joined her, dressed in black tuxedos and white gloves. They performed a skilfully choreographed tap dance that started with small foot gestures, tiptoeing and shuffling, showing off their intense discipline. The rhythmic tapping of eight shoes that went from a gunfire rat-a-tat to slow syncopated taps lifted the mood of the audience. They ended the routine by leaping into the air and landing in the splits position at Jean's feet, with broad smiles that hid the wild pumping of their lungs. The performance won them a standing ovation.

The show climaxed when Artis strode onto the stage with a handful of scimitars and machetes. Artis held up a poster advertising their show, then rapidly slashed it with a machete to demonstrate the sharpness of the blade. Then he casually flipped three of his deadly weapons upward, one after another, deftly catching each as it descended, his hands skilfully clasping the handles, seemingly only narrowly missing the blades. The audience was aghast as he juggled faster and faster, making the loop smaller, a prodigy of deft manoeuvring. He slowed down only to add another scimitar and another machete until he had five deadly weapons flying through the air, a feat almost beyond imagining requiring the most delicate propulsion. When the tension had reached its peak, Artis collected the scimitars and machetes with ease and bowed to the audience. People studied his hands, looking for missing digits or scars, but none were visible across the footlights. Some of the audience had hoped to see a disaster, while others had feverishly prayed that they not be witness to bloodshed, readying themselves to cover their children's eyes should there be a sudden slip of the hand.

It had taken Artis years of practice to make this dangerous skill look easy. He had worked up a sheen and as he bowed, he showed his appreciation of the respectful applause he received and noted the relieved look on people's faces.

Fredric teamed up with Bert for the Drink Driving skit, with Bert playing a police officer, and Fredric a drunkard. Bert entered centre stage right, while Fredric staggered on from centre stage left. He was holding a bottle wrapped in a paper bag. They met centre stage.

Fredric: (slurring his words) G'day, officer!

Bert: You again! Shouldn't you be at home with your wife and kids?

Fredric: Well, I would be if I could find 'em. They seemed to have disappeared.

Bert: Disappeared! How long ago did they go missing?

Fredric: (swaying with his feet on one spot) Ah … let me see … It'd be about … (rubbing the stubble on his chin) at least … six or seven … um … (struggling to get the words out)

Bert: Hours?

Fredric: Ah … years … as a matter of fact.

Bert: Years! Well, for heaven's sake, shouldn't you stop drinking and get them back?

Fredric: Yes, sir. That's good advice. And you'll be pleased to know that last night I had a couple of drinks, and I took your advice.

Bert: What advice was that?

Fredric: To take the bus home.

Bert: You took the bus home? That's wonderful!

Fredric: Yeah, but you never told me how hard it is to drive those things when you're pissed!

Bert: That's the last straw. You're under arrest!

The audience roared with laughter as Bert chased Fredric around the stage. Samson entered and intercepted Fredric, scooping him up and holding him over his head. With a doomed look on his face, Fredric started swimming through the air, froggy style, while Samson paraded him around. Then Samson spun Fredric around above his head as Fredric begged for mercy. He threw him up high in the air, and Fredric's antics and screams as he was being thrown about were hilarious. When Samson placed him back down, Fredric was swooning. Bert handcuffed him and Samson carried a stiff Fredric offstage, under his armpit, as the audience clapped.

Things were looking up. They were making enough money to cover wages, the ticket agent's cut, the printers for the playbills and newspaper advertisements. They could replace broken props, or the props used to make cream pies that were splattered on faces. They could afford balloons, painting competition prizes, laundry costs, petrol, and their food and accommodation.

They continued to the town of Caramut and were back to setting up the marquee and tents. Since they had recouped enough money, Artis reduced their performances to two shows a day. After the evening show, as everyone was heading back to their sleeping quarters, they heard an anguished bellow cut through the thickness of night. Samson was standing beside his tent, torch in hand, bent over something lying on the ground. Everyone ran over to see Metza lying in a pool of blood beside her master's tent. Distraught, Samson tenderly picked up her lifeless body. A trickle of blood escaped her slashed throat. Witnessing the sobs coming from Samson was more than the troupe could bear. They joined the gentle giant in his grief, some weeping with him.

'What monster would do this?' said Fredric, his hands fisted.

'I bet it's that man with the Waratah. I seen him in the audience tonight. He must be following us. He's the man from Meredith, I'm sure of it now,' said Tommy.

'Are you sure, Tommy?' said Artis.

Tommy nodded. 'Vinnie's gotta be behind this. We need to find this guy.'

'This is a warning. Something worse is coming,' said Samson, stunning everyone. The blood drained from Artis's face. He felt a knot in the pit of his stomach. Samson disappeared into his tent with Metza in his arms.

At a loss for words, Artis waved the troupe away. They dispersed to their sleeping quarters in a state of shock and grief. He consoled Belle and the children until they had fallen asleep. So far, he had protected Belle from knowing the financial strain he was under, but this imminent threat had shaken them all. Restless, he returned to the campsite to speak with Samson in private. He approached Samson's tent and called out to him in a low voice. There was no response. The campfire begged to be revived, the glow of embers beckoning. Artis added a log and twigs and fanned the life back into it. Spotting a pack of cigarettes, he pulled one out of the pack, and using the flame on the end of a twig, lit the first cigarette he'd ever smoked. Coughing and spluttering, he wondered why anybody in their right mind would smoke as he tried to steady his spinning head. He tossed the cigarette into the fire and sat staring at the dancing flames.

Artis felt a hand on his shoulder and almost jumped out of his skin. Samson was standing over him with a bottle of bootleg in his hand. He handed the bottle to Artis, who took a swig of the foul-tasting liquid.

'Sam, I'm so sorry about Metza. But what makes you think there's worse to come?'

'Vinnie's wife comes from a bad famiglia.'

'What do you mean by bad?' Artis felt nauseous.

'Rose's stepfather, Carlo, killed my uncle.' He saw the horror in Artis's eyes.

'Why?'

'Carlo loaned my uncle money to start a ristorante. When Carlo demanded protection money on top of the loan repayments, my uncle could not pay so much money.'

'So they killed him?'

Samson nodded.

'Was Carlo arrested?'

'Carlo has police friends.'

'You're kidding me!' Artis stood up and paced. 'I don't understand.

Why would Carlo want to kill me?'

'Not Carlo. Maybe Vinnie arranged this with one of Carlo's men. The man with the motorcycle.'

Artis regurgitated his swig of bootleg.

'This is getting outta hand. I didn't think Vinnie would sink this low.' He took another swig of bootleg. 'What should I do? I have to protect my family.'

Samson was pensive, his eyes fixed on the lapping flames of the fire that were gnawing away at the charcoaled log.

'Take your family far away. They will not stop until you are destroyed,' he said as he took another swig.

'No, I'm putting an end to this.'

'I will get my revenge first.' Samson got up and disappeared into his tent.

Artis's head was throbbing. The bootleg had turned to cement inside him. He left to get some sleep, medicating himself with a cup of tea and a Bex.

***

When the first crack of light appeared over the horizon, Samson took a shovel and headed towards the bushland, holding the blanketed bundle containing Metza's body.

Out of respect for Samson, and because the sky was predicting rain, Artis decided to cancel the evening show so they could leave town earlier.

The matinee bombed. The tension amongst the troupe made it difficult for them to concentrate. Samson was particularly on edge after performing without his beloved Metza. They held it together as best as they could, but the audience could sense something was amiss. Artis closed the show after announcing the painting competition winners. They were all keen to head to Illowa for the final leg of their tour and skip the storm that was brewing. As they were packing, the weight in the sky emitted an aura that felt like a bad omen. Everyone just wanted to get moving before it hit.

***

When Stan woke up covered in blood, he was still in a drugged stupor. The pills Rose had given him to enable him to commit murder had sent him on a wild, psychedelic ride. He tried to recall what he'd done after washing a couple of the pills down with bootleg. Flashing visions came back to him. He had lured Metza with a piece of meat and when he had her in his arms, he felt a malevolent spirit enter him as he sliced Metza's throat. The visions intensified as he recalled her struggle to escape from his arms and her warm blood on his skin. The recollection made him nauseous, confirming he could not slice the throat of a human.

Time was running out. He had procrastinated long enough. The only other plan he felt he could pull off would risk more than just Artis and Belle's lives, but would cause him less trauma than what he'd experienced by killing Metza.

The cancelled show meant he had to carry out Rose's deed that day. As he dragged himself into action, he saw that the troupe had packed the trucks and were getting ready to leave. The rain had started and was running down his jacket into a muddy pool under his boots. Fairly certain the rain would increase; he purchased some heavy rope and looped it across his shoulder and waist. The rain would facilitate his plan, although it would cause more carnage than was needed. Wiping the rain from his face, he straddled his Waratah. He was in a foul mood. A rage was stirring inside him against the troupe, Vinnie, Rose, and the bastard Carlo for keeping his wife and daughter from him. His heart had grown cold when the malevolent spirit had entered him. The fear that had kept him procrastinating had escalated to the point where the pressure had to be released before he had a nervous breakdown. He focused all his energy on getting the deed done so he could regain his freedom and disappear with his family. He jerked his motorcycle to a start and sped off ahead of the troupe.

As Artis and his entourage left town, the rain came with force, slowing their travel. The clouds had darkened the daylight, making it appear that night had fallen. Belle sat in the front seat with Joe wrapped in a blanket asleep in his bassinet tucked between herself and Artis. Shelley and five of the troupe, including Olivia, had made themselves comfortable in the truck, cocooned in a mound of blankets and pillows.

Stan kept his eye out for fallen branches as the wind continued to whip the trees into a frenzy. Then he spotted it. A trunk lay hazardously close to the side of the road. Knowing he only had a short time to put his plan in place before Artis's truck caught up with him, he got off his motorcycle and tied the rope around the tree trunk. He tied the other end of the rope around his motorcycle and attempted to manoeuvre the trunk across the road. The wheels spun mud in every direction as the engine screamed and the motorcycle slid around in protest, but Stan managed to pull the trunk across the road. When he saw the headlights from Artis's truck approaching, he ran to untie the rope from the tree trunk. He opened a bottle of oil and spilled it across the road, then sped off, hiding his motorcycle behind bushes.

The rain at this stage was torrential. Artis felt the truck sliding across the road, the weight of it making it difficult to control. Straining against the grit in his eyes from lack of sleep, and the fogged-up windscreen, he began to unconsciously grind his teeth. Belle kept wiping the condensation from the windscreen with her handkerchief so that Artis could see where he was going. His nose was inches from the windscreen when in a split second, as the truck rounded a gentle bend, Artis saw the tree trunk in the middle of the road and swerved to miss it. This caused the truck to fishtail out of control before heading for an electric light pole and hitting it with full force. Chaos erupted as screams and the sound of brakes mingled and they heard the crushing sound of metal as the truck came to an abrupt stop.

The entourage of trucks following Artis skidded across the slippery road before coming to a stop. Samson, Bert, Jean, and Larry ran out of their vehicles demanding the others stay put, the horror of the scene etched on their faces. Bert noted the Waratah motorcycle he'd seen in Forrest drive out from the bushes and disappear into the grey mist.

The heavy impact of Artis's truck against the light pole had torn away the left front wheel and demolished the radiator, pushing it through the cabin and crushing Belle's legs against the twisted metal. Her head had slammed against the side of the door, knocking her unconscious.

The sight of Belle filled Artis with fear. He looked behind him to check on Shelley and the others sitting in the back, expecting to see carnage. Once panic had gripped them, they had begun to cry aloud, intensifying Artis's anxiety.

'My God, you've killed her!' screamed Olivia.

Seeing Belle's limp body pumped a shot of adrenalin through Artis, prompting him into action. He scrambled to reach her and gasped as he saw drops of blood dripping onto Belle's dress from a gash on her head. He choked back the sobs that were welling in his throat, but they exploded once he saw her cut and mangled legs and a pool of blood spreading on the floor.

'Belle!' Artis felt the paralysis of panic overwhelm him when he caught the distinctive smell of petrol.

'Everybody get out!'

As if in slow motion, Artis got everyone out of the truck to safety. Shelley was screaming for her mother while Birdie and Coco tried to calm her down and soothe Joe, who was also howling. Olivia pushed past him and was trying to pull the door open.

'You've killed her! You've killed her!' She bashed at the window. 'Get her out!'

In his panicked state, Artis tugged at the door handle with superhuman strength. He cursed when it broke off in his hand. The relentless rain was making his attempt at prying the door open more difficult as his shoes slid around in the mud. He ran his hand across the window to wipe away the rain that was obstructing his view of

Belle. She was still not moving.

'Belle!' both he and Olivia yelled as they banged on the window.

'I'll never forgive you. Because of you, she's lived a life of misery on the road when she could have been a star if she'd stayed with Vinnie!'

The shock of her words sliced through Artis. Larry, Bert and Samson rushed to help.

'Fredric has run to the house down the road to see about calling an ambulance,' said Larry. Samson found a large rock, smashed the glass, and reefed the door open before getting to work on dislodging Belle's legs from the twisted metal, cutting his hands in the process.

'Belle, wake up! Please wake up, love.'

'You've killed my daughter!' screamed Olivia, writhing in despair. Alarmed, Shelley started screaming for her mother.

Jean came to assist. She took Olivia and the children away from the scene, into the care of other members of the troupe, before returning to care for Belle with some improvised bandages.

'We need to wrap her head to stop the bleeding,' she said. She took one of the fabric strips and wrapped it tightly around Belle's head. 'Her foot's badly damaged. It's best if I leave her shoe on. I'll wrap around her feet and legs the best I can to stop the bleeding.'

'I've lost her!' cried Artis as he cradled Belle's head.

25

Tainted Love

The Newmans' accident made front-page news. A stunning photograph of a smiling Belle in costume accompanied the image of the crumpled touring truck. Rose poured herself a glass of brandy and sat on the armchair to read the details.

Heavily laden with the Company's properties, and carrying about seven members of the cast, a bus conveying the touring Newman Pantomime Company was involved in a serious crash near Illowa at about 7 o'clock last night. The bus, which was travelling from Koroit to Melbourne via Illowa, was approaching the turn about a third of a mile this side of Illowa, during the heavy storm which swept the district. As it rounded the turn, the bus swerved to avoid hitting a tree that had fallen across the road when the wheels got on the slippery side of the road, and assisted by the high camber, skidded, and crashed heavily into an electric light pole. So heavy was the impact that the pole tore away the left front wheel and smashed through the radiator section and crushed the cabin, jamming Mrs Belle Newman, aged 27 of St Kilda, who was seated in the left-hand seat of the cabin ...

When she had finished reading the rest, she picked up the phone.

'Stan Jenkins has a letter addressed to Frank Rogers and a stack of cash that belongs to me. You need to get it now and make Stan disappear. I'll meet you at the usual place in an hour.' Rose hung up the phone, then redialled for a cab. She threw the newspaper into the fireplace and lit a match. Once the newspaper had turned to ash, she climbed the stairs to change her clothes, fix her hair and make-up and instruct the maid to look after the children while she was out. She returned downstairs, put on her coat, hat, and gloves, and left the house.

***

Artis paced the hospital waiting room with Larry, Shelley and baby Joe. Some of the troupe had sustained cuts and bruises and were being treated by the nurses. After what seemed an eternity, a doctor approached them and reported that Belle was going to pull through.

'Thank God,' said Artis, the air leaving his lungs like a released pressure valve.

'Unfortunately, her foot was partially amputated, and her legs are badly injured.'

'But she's a dancer!'

'I'm sorry, Mr Newman. The damage was significant. Had she not been bandaged up, she would have bled to death.'

'But she's a dancer.'

'I understand this is a shock. But she's going to have difficulty walking again, let alone dancing.'

Artis was silent, zoning out from the hospital din and retreating into the turmoil of his thoughts. When he regained his composure, the doctor had gone. His heart was pounding as he stood outside the door of Belle's room, not wanting to open it for fear of what he might see. With trembling hands, he pushed open the door. Belle was sleeping, her bandaged foot hanging up in a stirrup. He diverted his eyes away from it and approached her. She opened her eyes and offered him a weak smile. Tears welled in his eyes, and he broke down and sobbed as he held her hand.

'I'm so sorry, Belle. I'm so sorry.' They both held onto each other and wept.

***

Vinnie was devastated when he heard about Belle's injuries. Rose watched him drink himself into a stupor. After days of watching him medicate his grief with the aid of a bottle, she snapped.

'This needs to stop. Do you want to ruin our lives as well?'

'What the hell's that supposed to mean?'

'You need to pay attention to me and the children. We're your family.'

'What do you want from me? You've got everything a person could want and you're still not happy.'

'I just want you to love *me*.' His silence rattled her. 'Do you still love her, even now?'

'Aye,' he whispered.

That one word was a dagger to her heart. It was the brokenness in his voice that cut her the deepest.

'You only love her because you can't have her.'

'Aye, maybe you're right. But what eats away at me the most is if *he* hadn't taken her from me, none of this would've happened.'

'I hate you!' she spat the venomous words from her mouth as an incredible surge of rage exploded from within her. 'I wish she'd died in that accident!'

A flash of anger sparked Vinnie's eyes, warning her she'd crossed the line. But she was past caring. She wanted to hurt him as much as he had hurt her.

'How can you still love a cripple?'

Vinnie slapped her across the face. Rose retaliated by swiping at his face with her nails. He grabbed her hands and dragged her across the room to the front door. Her sobs grew louder. Possessed by his fury, he opened the door and pushed Rose out. He picked up her handbag and coat from the coat stand and threw them out the door before slamming it shut and locking it. Shaking, he made a beeline for the liquor cabinet and drank greedily from the bottle, shocked and remorseful. It was his first act of violence towards a woman.

***

It was late evening when Artis returned from visiting Belle at the hospital. Olivia, who had been minding the children, went home soon after he got home. Just as Artis was about to heat the dinner plate Olivia had prepared for him, he was startled by a loud banging on the door. He glanced through the curtain and saw Rose leaning against the door.

'Open the door!' she screamed, prompting Artis to oblige before her screams attracted the neighbours' curiosity.

'What are you doing here?'

'I need to talk to you and wifey.' She reeked of alcohol, and before Artis could stop her, she barged through the door.

'Belle's still in hospital.' He ushered Rose into the lounge room, hoping the neighbours hadn't seen her.

'Well, that's too bad 'cause it's time to clear the air about your darling Belle and my husband!'

'What?' A lump tightened in the pit of Artis's stomach.

'Oh, come on! You don't know that Belle and my husband have been having an affair all these years?'

'What? You're drunk!'

'Truth hurts. I should know,' said Rose, her body swaying from side to side as she tried to keep her balance.

'You need to go home.'

'I hired someone to follow Vinnie when I suspected he was having an affair. Sure enough, he caught Vinnie at your house with Belle.'

'You're lying!' The colour drained from his face. Rose pulled some photos from her handbag and waved them under his nose.

'Photos don't lie.' She handed them to him.

'When was this?' he whispered.

'A couple of years ago, while you were off touring. Your hussy wife had Vinnie's son.' Artis sat on the couch in a state of shock. The memory of Belle's behaviour came flooding back. Rose revelled in the blow she had struck.

'No! You're lying!'

'Keep looking.'

Artis flicked through the rest of the photographs. He sucked in his breath when he saw the photos of Vinnie kissing Belle at the park, with Shelley looking up at them. He flung them back at her.

'Bloody hurts, doesn't it?' Rose moved closer towards him. 'We can play that game, too. What better way to get back at them than to give them a taste of their own medicine?' While making a move to kiss him, she swayed in her drunken stupor, catching him off guard. They sprawled on the couch. She kissed him while attempting to undo his belt. Shelley, who had awoken because of the commotion, came out of her room and saw Rose on top of Artis. She screamed and scurried back to her room. Artis reacted by pushing Rose off him and dragging her to the door, shocking himself at his rough handling of a woman.

'Get outta my house!'

He shuffled her outside and slammed the door, his heart pumping with fury. Leaning his back against the wall, he slid down it and sobbed. The shock made him nauseous. On hearing Shelley's faint cry, he did his best to compose himself before making his way to her room. He sat on her bed, smoothing her hair away from her face. Using the bedsheet, he dabbed at her tears, unsure what to say.

'Don't you and Mummy love each other anymore?'

'Of course we do,' he said, with a heavy heart.

'Then why are you and Mummy kissing other people?' Her words stabbed his chest.

'It was a mistake,' he said, stroking her cheek. 'It's best if you don't say anything to Mummy. She has enough things to worry about for now. You better get back to sleep.'

'Can you sing me a song?'

'I'm not up to singing tonight, love.' Artis kissed her on the forehead and looked over at Joe sleeping in the crib. With a shredded heart, he studied him. His love for him was intact. *It can't be true.* Visualising Vinnie being intimate with Belle made him regurgitate, leaving a vile taste of bitter acid in his mouth. He brushed his teeth with vigour until his gums bled.

Alone with his anguished thoughts, Artis wondered how he would handle the revelation of Belle's affair. He blamed himself for leaving her in Melbourne. He'd been so sure of her loyalty. Olivia had made her disappointment in Belle's choice to marry him clear. Over the years, she'd never missed an opportunity to point out Rose's rise to stardom under Vinnie's guidance. *It's Olivia's fault. She's been in Belle's ear the whole time about lost opportunities and grumbling that touring like rogues and vagabonds was no place for her and the children. She probably encouraged Belle to be with Vinnie,* thought Artis.

The following evening, Artis waited in the shadows outside Vinnie's home. When Vinnie arrived and got out of his car, Artis pounced on him, releasing his rage as he punched him full force in the jaw. The searing pain that shot through his knuckles to his forearm did not stop him from causing further damage to Vinnie.

'Stay away from my wife, you bastard!'

Vinnie hit back. They kept throwing punches, battling for dominance.

'I'd bloody kill you, but you're not worth the jail time.' Artis took a final slug before walking away.

'She loves me! You stole her from me, but she loves me. Look what you've done to her!' Vinnie's words resonated to the core of Artis's heart, slicing it to shreds as he disappeared into the night shadows.

***

For the next few days, Artis's tormented soul prevented him from visiting Belle. He gave Olivia the excuse that he had to make arrangements to start a new tour, as they had no more savings after the cost of repairing their truck and the medical bills. But both Olivia and Belle knew something was amiss due to the dramatic change in his demeanour.

'He's repulsed by me,' lamented Belle, trying to hold back tears that came regardless.

'That's nonsense.'

'I'm a twenty-six-year-old cripple who's no use to him now.'

'Don't say that word.'

'I'm a cripple, Mother. My performance days are over and so is your dream of having a famous daughter.'

'My dream?'

'Yes, your dream. You put pressure on me after Margie died to pick up where she left off. She was the favourite. The talented one that everyone loved.'

'But you said you wanted to be famous and make Margie proud.'

'I was a child, Mother. I idolised Margie. After she died, that's what I wanted, but not anymore.'

'But you love performing!'

'Of course I do. But after Vinnie ruined our chance to tour London with *Red Riding Hood*, I was done working hard and getting nowhere. My family means more to me than fame. Artis was trying so hard to make me happy and now he doesn't want me anymore.' Fresh tears surfaced.

***

Artis's eventual visit was as sterile as the hospital, elevating Belle's fears of abandonment.

'I've arranged for a new tour to start at the end of the month,' said Artis, avoiding eye contact as he fiddled with his fedora.

'You're leaving me here?' Belle's eyes instantly filled with tears.

'Your mother said she'd stay to look after you. I managed to find someone to replace you both.'

'You spoke to my mother? Why didn't you discuss this with me, like you always have?'

'You need time to recover, and I need to make money to pay for the medical bills and keep the troupe together.' Watching Belle cry was tearing him apart, but his hurt overrode his compassion. 'I'd like to take Shelley. She's a big part of the show.'

'You can't take her away from me!'

'I thought it would give you time to recover if you didn't have to worry about Shelley as well as Joe.'

'Well, you thought wrong,' she cried. 'Why are you being so cruel?'

'Fine, I'll leave Shelley with you.'

He turned and walked out the door, keeping his head down and his hat low on his forehead. Once he was in his car, he broke down.

I can't believe I've lost him. God help me! Belle sobbed. The sight of the bandages covering her mangled foot and scarred legs caused her to lash out and smash anything she could get her hands on. A nurse came running into the ward and settled her down with a sedative and pain medication, leaving her in a heavily doped state, oblivious to her brokenness. While sedated, she felt a presence in the room. She opened her eyes and was shocked to see Vinnie standing beside the bed.

***

Morale was low among the troupe as they started their tour without Belle, Olivia, Shelley and baby Joe. But it was Artis's demeanour that threw off the dynamics of the troupe. Sombre silence replaced his jovial spirit. Even his performances lacked energy, resulting in a few hecklers booing him. Those performing alongside him had to work twice as hard to prop up his weak performances. It got to the point where Bert took over the management of the tour as Artis sank deeper into depression, refusing to speak to anyone.

Bert had been rehearsing a Protean act based on a whodunit. He'd mastered playing both genders and five different roles, complete with make-up and costume changes. The act required the stage to be prepared before the show. Bert laid out several hats, a scarf, a shawl, a moustache, lipstick and a pistol in specific spots. Costumes were hung from hooks behind doors, chairs or desks so he could complete his costume changes in a split second by either turning his back to the audience, ducking down behind a piece of furniture, or on the run as he stepped out one door and ran back onstage from another entrance. The fast pace of Bert's movements was exhausting but very effective, and he received a standing ovation.

Fredric had mastered the art of pickpocketing and created a comedy act where he made his way to the stage while weaving through the audience. Unbeknownst to them, he was lifting their wallets, watches, bracelets, jewellery, and even their hair combs while shaking hands with as many people as he could. By the time he reached the stage, his pockets were bulging and his pants sagging from the weight. Gracie, who acted as his assistant, would then return the items to their bewildered owners.

'Ladies and gentlemen, please don't take offence. I was just checking no one was carrying any explosives or rotten eggs,' said Fredric. The audience responded with peals of laughter.

While Artis was driving to the next town in a trance-like state, his truck got bogged in a ditch on the side of the road, the front wheel entrenched in mud. Artis's attempts to reverse out resulted in packing the tyre in more firmly. Regardless of how many broken branches, rocks and leaves they tried to pack under the tyres for traction, the truck was not budging. The incident triggered memories of the accident and after wasting an hour trying to dig around the tyres to no avail, Artis spectacularly lost his temper.

'It's just one bloody thing after another!'

'We'll have to find a farmer with a tractor to pull us out,' said Bert. He'd never seen Artis so fired up.

'Someone'll have to drive ahead and cancel the bloody matinee,' he ranted. 'I tell you what, cancel the whole bloody tour. I'm done! I'm through with this bloody business!' He marched into the bushland in a rage, sending a few grazing kangaroos hopping in all directions.

26

Reap What You Sow

Melbourne, Victoria, 19 December 1934

As soon as Stan walked into his cramped lodgings, he knew he was a dead man. All his belongings had been turned upside down, seat cushions were ripped open and within seconds of opening his door, he was struck in the head with a blunt object, felling him. A shooting pain paralysed him momentarily, and he strained to focus on the man standing over him, ready to strike the next blow, which again caught him unawares. When Stan's blurred vision regained focus, he saw a gun pointed at his head.

'Where's the letter Rose De Luca gave you?'

'What letter?' The man booted Stan in the stomach. Stan's reflexes and adrenalin kicked in and when he saw the boot coming at him for a second kick, he caught the man's foot in mid-air and twisted it with a swift motion, sending him crashing to the floor. Stan manoeuvred himself into a stronger position, clasping the hand that was holding the gun. Both struggled for control, pointing the gun at each other before it fired, blasting a hole in the wall. They jumped to their feet. Stan lunged at the man and attempted to wrestle the gun from his hand, his muscles burning from the exertion. In a split second, the man lost his balance as another shot was fired. His head hit the corner of a chair, rendering him unconscious. A trickle of blood began spreading across the floor. Stan wrenched the gun from his hand and moved swiftly to retrieve the stash of cash Rose had paid him, and her letter. He was packing some of his belongings into a bag when he heard police sirens. Fuelled by adrenaline, he left his life behind, with hopes of a fresh start.

His frazzled nerves were made evident by the full-throttle screams of his Waratah as he sped towards his wife's ramshackle house. For the first time since his youth, Stan began to pray. He begged God for forgiveness and a second chance to start over with his family. As he pulled up outside the house he'd seen Lulu walk into, he prayed they were home as he raced towards the front door.

'Betsy, open the door!' he banged on the door like a madman, straining to hear any signs of movement before continuing until he heard footsteps.

'Who the hell is it?' shouted a woman.

'It's Stan, your husband. Open the door!' He heard the lock click and saw Betsy's gaunt face staring back at him in disbelief.

'Stan? My God! Where have you been all these years?'

'Something's happened. I need to get you and Lulu outta here, right now.' Betsy's face turned from a look of annoyance to fear as she processed Stan's anxiety.

'How did you find us? I thought you was dead.'

'I went back to your parent's house to get you and you were all gone.'

'We got evicted. Dad went on the wallaby and never came back. Mum died seven months back.' Stan responded with a sympathetic shake of his head.

'What about the man you're shacked up with? I'm still your husband.'

'What are ya talking about?'

'When I dropped off the flowers and dough and asked to see you, Lulu said she had to ask her Pa.'

Betsy snorted. 'Ya knucklehead. Pa's an old man. This is his house. Lulu and I board here, and he and his wife look after Lulu when I'm working. They'll be back a bit later and you can meet them.'

'You're working?'

'At the pub. What's happened that you got a bee in your bonnet?'

'I got myself in some trouble, and the people that told me where you live are gonna come after you to get to me. You either come with me now or you'll be reading about me in the obituary page in the papers. You're not safe either.'

'For the love of God, what have ya done?'

'The only job I could get was working for the mob and things have gone bad.'

'Why would ya do that?'

'I didn't know who they were at the time, and I was desperate to make money to get my family back. One of the mob just tried to kill me.'

'Bloody hell, Stan. How did they find me?' Her eyes were so wide he thought they'd pop out of her head.

'I dunno. These guys have got connections all over the place.' He pulled out wads of notes and Rose's letter from his jacket and handed them to her. 'At least now I can look after you. I'm gonna trade my Waratah for a car and come back to get you and Lulu. Things will be better now I've got money and my debts are cleared.'

'Holey moley, this is a lot of dough, Stan. Tell me ya didn't steal it!'

'I didn't steal it, but I can't explain now. You have to trust me. If anything happens to me, give that letter to the cops. Actually, have you got a pen, paper, and envelope?'

'Crikey, what's going on, Stan?'

'I need to right some wrongs.'

'With a pen and paper?'

'Please, Betsy, just do it quick smart. I'll explain everything later.'

Betsy went to find a pen and paper, returning minutes later.

'Thanks. Now go pack what you need. You ain't coming back here.'

'For the love of God. I can't just pack up and leave!'

'Betsy! You need to trust me. Do you really want to stay in this dump?'

She left to pack while he wrote his letter. When he finished, he gave it to Betsy.

'What's with the letters?'

'Some of that money I gave you was payment to keep the letter safe. I can't explain it now. Just think of it as an insurance policy. It'll keep you safe. Give my letter to the cops as well. It'll explain everything.'

'Where we gonna go?'

'As far as we can go. I'm thinking Queensland. I'll go call a cab to pick you up and take you to the train station. If I'm not there to pick you up by late arvo, get that letter to the cops quick smart and take the first train outta here that's heading for Queensland. Then go to the nearest church from the border and let them know where you're staying, so I know where to find you … if I get outta this alive.'

'You're scaring me, Stan. Can't I wait for you here and we go together?'

'I already told you, Betsy. I can't risk it. They're gonna come get you. Now, will you stop flapping your gums and just do exactly what I said? You got enough dough there to buy whatever you want. We'll be able to start fresh and buy a nice house in Queensland.'

Betsy looked down at the money in her hands and drew comfort from it.

'I've always wanted to go to Queensland. I heard it's nice and warm there.'

'We're going to have a nice life there, Betsy. Where's Lulu?'

'Lulu!' called Betsy.

Lulu had been peeking from behind the couch and ran to them, her pigtails bouncing to the rhythm of her steps.

Stan kneeled to greet her. Lulu stared at him before wrapping her arms around his neck and kissing him on the cheek. The sensation of her eyelashes brushing against his skin stirred his memory. He held her tight, feeling hot tears prickling behind his eyes.

'I'll not fail you this time,' he said.

'Lulu, go pack up all ya belongings, quick smart. We're going on a trip,' said Betsy.

'Goody!' said Lulu before running to pack.

'She's a beauty. Looks just like you.'

'She's got a dimple on her chin, like you.'

'I've missed you both so much.' Stan embraced Betsy, triggering an overwhelming moment of passion. They kissed, releasing a torrent of suppressed emotions that had them fumbling their way into the bedroom. Tears of mingled sadness and joy fell as they stripped themselves bare and united their bodies with intensity, revelling in the ecstasy of the physical bond that had once been so familiar.

'I'm sorry I've failed you, Betsy. I'm not proud of what's become of me, but I'm gonna make it up to you. I promise. I've asked God's forgiveness for everything I've done.'

'I've missed you too.' Betsy kissed his eyelids, knowing the softness of her lips always aroused him. As much as they wanted to indulge in further lovemaking, Stan's sense of urgency prevailed.

'We need to shake a leg, love.'

'I thought we just did,' smiled Betsy.

'You know what I mean.' Stan laughed and kissed her. 'We need to get outta here, quick smart.' Betsy made haste in packing a couple of ports and Stan helped Lulu.

'I'm gonna go find a phone booth and call a cab to come get you. Stay put and don't let anybody in the house. If anybody comes here, make a run for it, and use some of the money I gave you to get another cab. Don't tell anyone where you're going, you hear me?'

'I was gonna leave a note for me landlords.'

'You can't, Betsy. They'll find you. Not a word to anyone. Promise.'

'Yeah, righto. Let's hope to God they don't come home any minute. Ya really gonna sell the Waratah?'

'I have to. It's a dead giveaway.' He scooped Lulu up.

'You got a butterfly kiss for me?'

'Only if you promise to come back for good.'

'Yes, love. I've missed you, but we're back together now.'

Lulu handed him a piece of paper with a drawing of a man and girl holding hands in a garden filled with birds and butterflies. At the bottom of the drawing, she'd written 'My Dad' next to a love heart coloured pink, with 'Lulu' written beside it.

'It's for you,' whispered Lulu. 'Mama said you might come back.' Stan felt the years it had taken to harden his heart begin to unravel. He folded the drawing and put it in his top shirt pocket.

'You'll always be with me now, close to my heart like you've always been.' He smiled and kissed the top of her head. 'I'll see you soon.'

For the first time in years, he felt hope and happiness as he mounted his Waratah and sped off. He found a phone booth and called a cab for Betsy and Lulu. With a spring in his step, he remounted his Waratah. He hadn't gotten far when he noticed a car speeding up behind him and getting dangerously close. In an attempt to increase the distance between them, Stan accelerated. The car gave chase, confirming his worst fear. Panic made him accelerate. When he looked back and saw the car was gaining ground, he made an abrupt turn and sped down a road that would lead him away from the city. He pushed his Waratah to maximum speed and in a matter of seconds, he saw the car was losing ground. His tension eased until he noticed the road ahead change to a dirt track, causing him to lose traction. It forced him to slow down, which allowed the car to catch up to him. The chase became more perilous as the car sped up and came close to clipping his motorcycle. Stan gained some ground, then lost it again as they spun around a bend. He heard the rev of the car engine before it rammed him. As if in slow motion, his body was thrust from his motorcycle, arms and legs flailing, before he hit the ground and blacked out, the sound of the Waratah's screaming engine reverberating through the air.

The car pulled up beside him. A man got out, gun in hand, to examine the damage. Stan's lifeless body lay battered on the ground in a mangled mess. The man flinched at Stan's broken body. His eyes were wide open. Warily, the man aimed his gun at Stan's head and kicked his body. Once he was convinced he was dead, he searched through his pockets, pulling out the photograph of Betsy and Lulu, a few coins and notes, and Lulu's drawing. He put them in his pocket and returned to the car before speeding off back toward the city.

279

27

Bringing Down the Mob

The pounding on the front door aroused Vinnie and Rose from sleep. Vinnie got up and peered through the curtain from the second storey of their terrace home.

'Who is it?' asked Rose.

'Coppers.' Vinnie wrapped himself in his dressing gown, rammed his feet into his slippers, and made his way downstairs to silence the pounding. Rose strained to hear the muffled voices below. A few moments later, Vinnie returned, looking pale.

'You need to come downstairs.'

'Why?' The pitch of her voice betrayed her panic.

'Apparently Stan might have caused the accident with the Newman's truck,' he said, noticeably shaken by the news.

'What's that got to do with me?'

'They found out he works for us. His flat was ransacked, and he was found dead on the side of the road. They think I had something to do with it.'

'Did they say anything about Carlo?' Vinnie noted the pinched look on Rose's face.

'What are you talking about?'

'Things are going to get very bad for us if they're asking about Carlo. Why do they want to see me?'

'You need to come downstairs.'

They made their way down.

'Good morning, Mrs McIntyre. I'm guessing your husband has explained why we're here?'

Rose gave a curt nod.

'The first matter concerns your stepfather, Carlo De Luca.' Rose stiffened. 'He was assaulted a couple of nights ago. He's currently in hospital in a critical condition.' The colour drained from Rose's face.

'Who assaulted him?'

'We thought you might be able to answer that.'

'Why would I?'

'Your mother, Sofia De Luca, has disappeared. Do you have any idea where she is?'

'Why would I?'

'Mrs McIntyre, the police department received a very detailed letter signed by you with several photographs of the sort of activities your father was involved in—'

'Stop, please!' Rose was visibly shaking.

'What letter?' Vinnie looked at Rose. When she didn't respond, he looked at the police officer.

'A woman brought it into the police station. Said she was Stanley Jenkin's wife. We need you to come to the station for further questioning.'

'Questioning about what?' said Rose.

'Your letter, for starters, your father's assault, and your connection with Stanley Jenkins. We need a statement from you,' said the police officer.

'Our children are asleep. I'll come. Leave my wife out of it.'

'We need to question both of you. We can come back for your wife if that's the case.'

'Can I have a word with her first?'

'Do you have something to hide, Mr McIntyre?'

'No.'

'Then I suggest we get going.'

'At least let me get dressed.'

'This isn't a tea party invitation.' The police officers led Vinnie to the door. His mind was racing, fearful that the crime he had committed on the farm all those years ago would be uncovered.

***

Rose reached for a cigarette to calm her nerves. Pacing the floor, she inhaled the smoke deeply into her lungs so that only a sliver of smoke escaped her lips. She poured herself a brandy and downed it. The tip of her cigarette was fiery as she sucked the life out of it. Reaching for the brandy bottle, she lifted it to her lips and drank until she felt the burning sting of alcohol mingled with hot smoke in her throat. Ignoring the ache in her throat, she continued to suck on her cigarette until the ash dropped onto the floor. The shrill ring of the telephone startled her. She stared at it, hesitating, as if it was going to bite her if she reached out. Her hand shook as she pressed the receiver to her ear.

'Hello.'

'You and your family will die a slow death for what you've done.' The phone went dead. A chill ran through Rose. She ran up the stairs.

***

Vinnie sat in the interrogation room, trying to look calm. The senior officer seated himself in front of him, while another officer stood over Vinnie.

'Let's start with what you know about Stanley Jenkins,' said the senior officer, a cigar clenched between his teeth. His prominent belly showed years of inactivity as he leaned back in his chair.

'Nothin'.'

The officer beside him punched him in the temple, sending his head jerking sideways. Vinnie growled as he steadied himself.

'What was your reason for employing Stanley Jenkins?'

'I want to speak to my lawyer,' said Vinnie, his jaw set.

'It's been reported that several witnesses sighted Stanley Jenkins's Waratah motorcycle at the scene of the Newman truck accident. Police matched the tyre marks at the exact location of the accident to his motorcycle. It was also sighted at several towns visited by the Newman Players. A Waratah is a standout motorcycle. Not something you would easily miss.'

'What's that got to do with me?' said Vinnie.

'We found flyers promoting the Newman Entertainers in his apartment for starters.'

'He was obviously a big fan,' said Vinnie, prompting another blow to the head.

'We tracked the printers. They said you arranged, paid for and picked up the flyers. So how did they end up at Stanley Jenkins's apartment?'

'Dunno.'

'Jim Stapleton heard the news of the Newman's accident and came into the station to make a statement. He said you were hell-bent on bringing Artis Newman to ruin. Said he was roughed up by some salamis to make sure he didn't renew Artis's contract at the Playhouse. Sounds like you sent Carlo De Luca's mob to do your dirty work, if you ask me.'

Vinnie remained silent.

'He's willing to testify against you in exchange for police protection to make sure it doesn't happen again. You starting to connect the dots?'

Vinnie stared at a speck on the wall.

'Look, mate, we can do this the easy way or the hard way,' said the officer.

'Let's do it the easy way. Talk to my lawyer.'

Vinnie remained withdrawn, his brow creased under the weight of his thoughts. After what seemed an eternity of silence, the officer stood, prompting his comrade to pin Vinnie's arms behind him as he squashed his cigar onto Vinnie's neck, twisting the life out of its embers.

'Argh!' Vinnie struggled to free himself, resulting in a punch to the stomach.

'Maybe you'd rather talk about your illegal dealings with Carlo De Luca?'

'Illegal dealings? I was running shows for him!'

'You run a burlesque show that's a cover-up for a brothel. You've got a bank account that's running hot with transferred funds that would make Rockefeller's head spin. And now we're investigating a crashed touring van and a dead person that all link back to you!'

Vinnie's world came crashing down when he heard the accusations. He began to sweat profusely.

'I don't know nothin' about a brothel, or about Carlo De Luca's illegal businesses. My wife never told me about no letter.'

'Are you saying you weren't in business with Carlo De Luca?'

'I used his venues to run our shows, that's all.'

'You made a hell of a lot of money running shows. What did you charge for entry?'

'I dunno. Carlo's accountant handled all the finances. He told me to open a bank account for the business.'

'You expect me to believe you knew nothing about the money going in and out of your account?'

'Aye.'

'So you were just a pawn covering his illegal businesses?'

'Aye.'

'That's not going to hold up in court when the man in question is fighting for his life and you stand to gain financially. What do you know about Carlo De Luca's assault?'

'Nothin'. Talk to my lawyer.'

'You better have a bloody good one, mate,' said the officer, spittle and the odour of tobacco escaping his mouth. 'Stanley Jenkins's wife gave us a letter written by Stan that has details about an affair between you and Belle Newman. It also states that your wife hired him to report details of your affair, and you hired him to destroy Artis Newman's business. Then there's an old report we dug up from a farmer who said you tried to kill him after he caught you stealing his cash. Said you also stole and wrecked his truck and disappeared.'

'You got the wrong man on that one,' lied Vinnie, relieved he could clear his conscience—he had not killed his owner.

'Have it your way. I'm bringing you down one way or another.' The officer grabbed him by his collar and tossed him out of the room to where two officers waited outside the door. 'Take him home and bring his wife in.'

The two police officers escorted Vinnie into a police car. Once they were underway, the police officer sitting next to Vinnie cuffed him and pulled a hood over his head.

'What are you doing?'

'Shut your gob or I'll crack your skull.'

The cop driving turned up the radio and began taunting Vinnie to distract him from tracking their direction.

'What did you tell them?'

'Nothin',' said Vinnie.

'There's nothing worse than lying scum.'

'Won't take him long to talk after they finish with him,' said the other officer.

Vinnie's heart was galloping, but he remained silent and unemotional. The car came to a stop. Vinnie was pulled out, dragged into a building and tied to a chair. When the hood was ripped from his head, he found himself surrounded by Carlo's men and the two crooked cops. Without warning, he was slugged across the face, causing the chair to topple sideways. Vinnie's head hit the floor. He groaned as pain exploded inside his head. His arms, which were tied behind his back, felt like they were going to be ripped from their sockets.

'What did you tell the cops?'

'Nothin'.'

'We got cops everywhere asking questions, so don't tell me you told them nothin' or I'll kill you right now.'

One of the men walked over to a table laid out with pliers, a hammer and a scalpel. He picked up the pliers. Vinnie struggled against the ropes, recalling the times he was beaten with a chain at the farm.

'Who beat up Carlo?'

'I dunno! I woke up this morning with cops at my door.'

'Something's gone down, and we need to know now! Our bank accounts are frozen, and that makes me very angry!' said one of Carlo's men.

'Everything points back to you and your wife,' said one of the cops. 'Even I've been questioned at the station and mark my words, if I go down, you're a dead man. Now you better start talking, 'cause I'm in the mood to finish you off right now.'

'I don't know what you're talking about,' said Vinnie.

The man took the pliers and ripped out one of Vinnie's fingernails. His scream was silenced with a punch to his face. He hit the floor with force and was promptly pulled back upright.

'Anytime you want to talk, mate. I got all day.' He took hold of a scalpel, yanked Vinnie's shirt open and sliced his chest. Blood trickled down his abdomen. Vinnie muffled a growl, steeling his body against the pain.

'What did you tell the cops?'

'I told you, NOTHIN'! I said I wanted to see my lawyer and they let me go.'

The man slashed Vinnie's chest again with the scalpel. The sensation of warm blood trickling down his chest made his heart pump furiously.

'You and Rose double-crossed us. Someone's at your house right now, paying Rose a visit. You better tell me what the cops know or your wife and children will suffer a slow and painful death.'

Vinnie flew into a rage, struggling to break free with all the strength he could muster. It resulted in him toppling the chair, triggering the men to kick him in the head and give him a merciless beating until he blacked out.

As he came to consciousness, his memory flashed back to the

beatings he would get as a child enslaved on the isolated rural farm. He saw his mother's face, so similar to Belle's, calling out to him from across an ocean. The memory of her face brought him peace. 'I love ye, Vinnie,' whispered his mother through the image of Belle.

Before he could fully get his mental bearings, Vinnie felt himself being untied from the chair and dragged outside towards the open door of a car. Pandemonium broke out as police cars with sirens screaming cornered them. He heard a crack of gunshots and immediately fell to the ground.

***

Terror paralysed Rose when Carlo's men broke into her house shortly after she received the threatening phone call. She had raced to pack their ports when they ambushed the house and dragged her into the basement by her hair. As three men circled her, acid churned in her stomach. She resisted the urge to regurgitate.

'Who tried to kill Carlo?'

'I don't know.'

Immediately, she received a punch in the face that sent her to the floor. Shaken, she steadied herself on all fours. The pain made her eyes water and blood drip from her nose. One of the men grabbed hold of her hair and pulled her up to within an inch of his face. She dug deep for the steely determination she had used many times before to survive the pure evil she endured at the hands of these monsters.

'Cops raided the club and froze our bank accounts. Why?' he screamed.

'Where's Vinnie?'

'He's dead. Now start talking! What do the cops know?'

'I don't know,' she said, shaken by the news that Vinnie was dead. Her only hope was that the police would return soon to take her in for questioning.

'You know what's coming if you don't talk.'

She braced herself, keeping her face frozen, refusing to let them see the turmoil raging inside her.

'Take your clothes off.'

Rose didn't move.

'Either you talk, or we work you over.'

Paralysed with fear, she was too numb to think or respond.

'Do you and your kids want to stay alive or not?'

Rose clenched her jaw as she mechanically undressed, hoping her submission would save her children.

'Turn around and bend over.' Catching the lustful glare in his eyes as he unzipped his pants and approached her, she steeled herself, her mind screaming her hatred. Bracing herself to endure the humiliation, she mentally checked herself out as he groped her breasts and thrust himself inside her like a crazed animal. When he was spent, he motioned for the next man to take his turn while the others watched and waited for theirs. Once she was in a broken, exhausted state, they interrogated her again. Her tenaciousness infuriated them, and they worked her over again.

'Go find the kids so they can watch. That'll make her talk.'

***

When Vinnie entered his house, he heard whimpering sobs coming from the basement. He found Rose in a foetal position, her naked body battered, deep red marks all over her body and breasts. Her inner thighs were bloodied, and blood trickled from a gash on her head. Her nose was caked with congealed blood. Seeing her in this state filled Vinnie with rage.

'Bastards!'

'They said you were dead.'

'Not far from it.'

Relieved, Rose released the tension that had cramped her body and sobbed hysterically as she clung to him. 'Did they take Lola and Frank?'

Panic rose in Vinnie, desensitising his aching body as he ran towards the children's bedroom. The air left his lungs at the sight of the empty beds and the bedcovers in disarray.

'No!' he wailed, dropping to the floor and covering his face. Intense rage exploded within him as he thought to kill every one of Carlo's mob and finish Carlo off. His sobs brought the comfort of a tiny hand on his neck.

Startled, he turned to find a terrified Frank next to him, with Lola emerging from the open door of the cupboard where they had been hiding. Vinnie picked Lola up and engulfed them both in a protective embrace, kissing their heads.

'Are you hurt?' A wave of relief washed over him as they shook their heads. A sense of urgency had him scrambling for their ports.

'I need you both to pack your clothes and some of your favourite toys as quickly as you can. I'm going to help Mummy, then come back to help you.'

'They hurt Mummy. I heard her screaming.' Frank was crying, triggering tears from Lola as well.

'Yes, they did, Frank. They're very bad men. That's why we have to pack our ports and go away from here.'

'I'm scared,' said Frank.

'Me too,' said Lola, her eyelashes glistening. Vinnie hugged and kissed them again.

'I need you to be my brave soldiers now and pack your ports as quickly as you can.'

'I want Mummy,' said Frank.

'I want Mummy too,' said Lola.

'Stay in here and pack. I'll bring Mummy in soon.' Frank nodded and began to put his toy cars into the port.

'Don't forget to put some clothes in there as well,' said Vinnie before making his way back to Rose, who had managed to crawl out of the basement.

'Vinnie, they're going to kill us. We have to leave town now.' Rose's fear was contagious, her tears streaming.

'Aye. I need you to be strong, love, for the children's sake.'

Vinnie's compassion sparked Rose's hope that he could love her after all. She found comfort in the strength of his arms as he carried her upstairs.

'I need to wash. Can you finish packing the ports.'

Vinnie packed everything he could into their car. He emptied their safe and went back to help Rose, who hadn't stopped crying and was still shaking. He tended to her wounds and helped her get dressed.

'My God, what happened, Rose?' he said, trying to contain his rage.

'They broke through the door and came at me so fast,' she said. 'I wouldn't tell them anything, so they went looking for the children. That's when the police came, and all hell broke loose. The bastard watching me cracked his gun across my head before escaping.' She wiped away her tears with shaking hands.

'Tell them what? What's this letter the police are asking about?' said Vinnie, as he attempted to dress the gash on her head.

'It exposes Carlo's illegal activities.'

'So what the cops said was true? He's running a brothel?'

'That's only one of his businesses. I was forced to service Carlo and his men since I was a child. He'd drug me to stop me from screaming while they raped me. Once they broke me in after weeks of being raped and beaten, drugs were the only way I could cope with the humiliation of the things I was made to do.'

'My God, Rose! I want to kill that bastard. Where was your real father?'

'I was too young to remember him. Carlo had him killed after he met my mother and wanted her. Carlo made me believe I was a bastard child.'

'Why didn't your mother protect you?'

'She went through her own hell. Carlo's men tied her up and made her watch me being raped when I was six. We've all been broken and held together with alcohol, drugs and every luxury money could buy to shut us up.'

'Bloody hell, Rose! Why didn't you tell me Carlo was such a sick son of a bitch?' Vinnie had never imagined someone else's life could have been worse than his.

'You never cared about me, Vinnie. Your obsession with Belle and Carlo's money made you easy bait for him. Carlo's generosity comes at a high price.'

'I can't believe you never told me this until now.'

'That's the tip of the iceberg. Carlo's other income comes from drug dealing and black market weapons.'

'For the love of God, what kind of mess are we in?'

'A very bad one. I tried to warn you not to go into business with him.'

'But you didn't tell me the truth about it.'

'Would it have made a difference? You chose not to ask questions. Revenge was more important to you.'

'Yes, Rose. It would have made a difference. But you're right. I chose not to ask questions even though I sensed your desperation.'

'Hold me, Vinnie. I need you to hold me.' As they embraced, she noticed the cuts on his chest.

'Who hurt you?'

'I'll explain later. We need to go. I'm taking you to the hospital to have your head stitched, and I'll find us a safe place to stay until I work out how to get outta this mess.'

'Kiss me, Vinnie.' He lifted her chin, bringing her mouth to his, and kissed her. It was their first kiss that didn't stem from lust. It filled her with hope and gave her the strength to face whatever lay ahead.

They all piled into the car and Vinnie dropped Rose at the hospital.

'I need to arrange a few things. I'll be back in about an hour to pick you up from this exact spot.'

***

Before leaving the house, Rose had done her best to cleanse herself from the filth of her assault and covered up her battered body, concealing any visible bruises. Her head wound was still bleeding and with each throb of her violated body, her desire to avenge the humiliation she had suffered at the hands of Carlo's men grew. Familiar with hospital protocol, she dodged the nurse's questions, insisting that she had fallen down the basement stairs. The nurse gave her a look insinuating she didn't buy her story. As Rose was getting stitched up, she thought about Carlo, in the same hospital, fighting for his life. Fuelled by pain and rage, she devised a plan to find Carlo and ensure his fight for life ended.

Once the nurse had finished, Rose made her way along the familiar hallways in search of Carlo. The demons in her mind egged her on until she found him. Taking great care not to attract the attention of hospital staff, she approached the bed, checking the name on the bedhead matched the monstrosity lying there. Bandages formed a helmet over his head, revealing the black, blue, and red discolouration of his face. His eyes were swollen shut, his mouth gaping, exposing broken teeth and releasing the foul stench of his breath, which had always revolted Rose. Seeing him so vulnerable gave her a strange sense of satisfaction, yet the demons in her head demanded she slay him.

As she stood over him, waves of nausea and rage rushed through her. His lifestyle of indulgence had resulted in a grotesque body that had grown more repulsive with age. She thought of her mother, who would also be free from this monster. Under his control, Sofia became an unemotional, drug and alcohol-addicted *madam* who witnessed Rose's misery but was powerless to protect her.

The sound of his strained breathing made her nervous. She feared he would snap his eyes open and grab her by the throat. Doubt began to override whether she could commit the deed. Carlo was known to police as the most dangerous, villainous man in Melbourne, and now with her letter in their possession, they had all the evidence they needed to bring him down. She thought about the corrupt police and lawyers she'd mentioned in the letter who would defend Carlo to protect their own interest and who would now hunt her down to silence her. *What if they got him off all charges?* Her mind was racing, knowing that her death, and no doubt her children's, would be slow and torturous at the hands of Carlo and his mob. Yet as she reached her hands out to him, they were shaking so uncontrollably that she aborted the plan and left the room.

But the demons in her mind ran amok. *Kill him. Kill him. He has to die. Kill or be killed!* In a trance-like state, with her body pulsating from the pain of her brutal rape, she returned to the room and faced the monster who, for decades, had terrorised her and her mother. Without a second thought, she submitted to the demons of hate. This time, when she left the room, Carlo was no longer breathing.

28

Circus Life

Adelaide, South Australia, 1935

Rose looked pale as she left the hospital. Vinnie was parked on the street, waiting for her with the children. They drove away, fully aware that returning to their house or former way of life would put their lives at risk. In the safety of their car, Rose sat close to Vinnie, trying to find solace in the strength of his body. Pain was still pulsating through her body and any bump on the road made her wince. The only consolation was Vinnie's compassion. He was remorseful that he hadn't been there to protect her and the children, and apologised for his behaviour when he had kicked her out of the house only days before.

What she regretted, but couldn't bring herself to confess, was her retaliation. When she had told Artis about Vinnie and Belle's affair in her drunken stupor, it was the catalyst that toppled the house of cards.

'I found somewhere we can stay that's out of the city,' said Vinnie.

'No, they'll find us before nightfall. We need to get out of Melbourne today,' she said.

'Where do you suggest?'

'Carlo has connections everywhere. We need to leave the state.'

'Sydney?'

'He has connections there, too. Adelaide should be safer.'

It took them a couple of days to drive the 450 miles. The drive was excruciating as both were recovering from their injuries and the bumpy roads made it feel like they were being jabbed with knives. Frank and Lola sat in the back seat, nestled amongst their possessions, which filled every nook and cranny of the car. Their demeanour reflected the trauma they had experienced seeing their parents battered and bleeding.

Once they had found somewhere to stay, Vinnie got to work searching for opportunities to restart a production. They knew they would no longer be living the high life, as Rose especially was accustomed to. An unexpected opportunity arose when Vinnie caught sight of a newspaper headline that read 'Morris Bros. Circus Folds!'

'I'm buying a circus,' said Vinnie.

'Have you lost your mind? What do you know about running a circus?'

'You got any better options? It'll have to do. I made a deal with Max, the owner, to buy the circus and have him stay on to help run it with the option to buy it back in a year, once the dust settles back in Melbourne.'

'Why's he selling?'

'Said the railway transportation costs were killing him. He's paid over a million pounds to the railways, plus the double entertainment tax.'

'Why would you buy it then?'

'I won't be using the railways. Max reckons the marquee holds between two to three thousand people and the takings are around 500 pounds from a packed house, which isn't too shabby. We need to stay low, so we'll just tour regionally. He's got some solid Ford trucks to transport the animals …'

'Animals!'

'It's a circus, Rose. Of course there are animals. We got ourselves lions, equestrians and their horses, an ancient elephant, a midget couple with a miniature pony, bicycle acts, contortionists, trapeze artists, multi-talented clowns that swallow swords and fire, juggle, spin plates and perform highwire acts, and a bunch of circus hands.'

Rose's jaw dropped.

'Did you say lions?'

'Don't worry, they come with a lion tamer.'

'To think I sold my soul to be in a Hollywood film and now I'm expected to perform in a circus. Excuse me if I don't jump for joy.'

'What's the problem? You can keep doing what you're famous for—flaunting your body in a glitzy costume.'

'Maybe I should take my chances back in Melbourne. I'm hating this already.' She got up and left the room.

***

Vinnie met up with the Morris Bros. advance manager, Wal, the business face that gave the circus credibility. His keen determination, aptitude and negotiating skills won Vinnie over.

'Give me a rundown on your business tactics,' said Vinnie.

'For starters, I know how to negotiate the best price for venues and I've got a list of all the agricultural shows in the region, so I can line up your shows to coincide. I also have all the contacts of the regional newspaper reporters who can get the buzz happening in town before the show rolls in. And I have connections in the printing business who'll do a mighty fine job on your flyers and posters at a reasonable price.'

'I want to know what all the other circuses are doing,' said Vinnie. 'Where they're performing, what they're charging, what their acts are and how many tickets they're selling.'

'Of course. I can tell you straight up that Wirth's Circus print a souvenir program that has top brand ads all the way through it, so not only does it pay for the printing but they make dough on it.'

'Is that so? What kind of ads?'

'Anything from Barrett Bros. Cordials, Max Factor cosmetics, Peters Ice Cream to the State Savings Bank of Victoria.'

'Let's do the same. Line it up,' said Vinnie.

True to his word, Wal ensured Morris Bros. Circus got a good start with their first tour. They would hit the road at eight o'clock every morning. Their touring schedule consisted of one-night stands covering up to 94 miles a day. Country folks craving a bit of entertainment didn't want to miss out, so as gruelling as it was to unpack and pack up again each day, it was a profitable way to operate. The trucks were fitted with loudspeakers on their roofs to announce their arrival in the country towns.

Vinnie, keen to project the air of prestige and respectability that he had grown accustomed to, ensured he and his family stayed and ate in hotels. This deflected the gypsy image with which the circus profession was often identified. The circus families' homes were large tents on the circus lot and children were schooled by correspondence. Those who didn't have tents slept inside the Big Top. Vinnie demanded they cook their meals over a campfire positioned behind the Big Top so as not to be seen from the street and made it clear that he wouldn't tolerate any gambling, brawling, drunkenness or swearing, especially in front of customers.

The circus hands were a rough bunch of drifters. They did the routine manual work such as preparing the circus ring, and erecting and dismantling the Big Top, plus handling all the rigging and lighting, setting up the seats and tending to the animals. They had mastered the art of erecting a tent in windy conditions and setting up tiered seating on sloping ground.

Only a month into the tour, a downpour of rain beat down mercilessly on the troupe. Town after town and day after day it rained until everyone's tents were completely soggy and mould-ridden. The many feet required to set up the marquee and tents caused a slush pile of mud that spread into everything and made the perimeter of the circus grounds look like a war zone. The troupes' beds were soaking wet and trying to keep bodies and costumes clean was stressful, as was washing mud off edgy circus animals and keeping them calm. Nerves were frayed to breaking point. Curses were heavy in the air, mingled with threats to leave that left everyone walking on eggshells. Even Vinnie turned a deaf ear to the colourful language, as he succumbed to cursing, although never around customers.

The days of miserable rain turned into weeks. The lions in particular were pacing after having their accustomed daily exercise routine minimised to a quarter of the time. One truck got stuck in the mud and had to be unhooked from the caravan to get it out. The men dug around the wheels and put stones and logs underneath for traction. With the help of Zulo the elephant and a long rope, they managed to pull it out. This was when Vinnie realised elephants were an excellent investment. Not only did they live a long time, but they were also valuable for such tasks as loading and unloading circus equipment, raising and lowering the circus tents, and occasionally hoisting trucks out of the mud.

After a few more soaking weeks, the sun finally broke through the gunmetal grey clouds to reveal a welcome striking blue sky. That meant a town full of people would fill the marquee, ready for showtime. The hellish weeks of trying to keep dry and keep the mud and mildew at bay were forgotten as they erected seats in anticipation of a bumper house for the matinee show.

One performer had modified his truck so that the sides folded down to reveal a small stage with a honky-tonk piano and drum kit inside. Vinnie had the idea of using this as a pre-show warm-up where the band played inside the truck while it drove around town, enticing people to the show.

'Get Zulo and the circus animals positioned next to the ticket sales booth to draw in the townsfolk before the show opens,' said Vinnie.

Regardless of the challenging circumstances, Vinnie took pride in his work. The weeks of relentless rain had set them back financially, but Wal had been working hard to pre-sell tickets and get a buzz going about their new circus show. He promoted the matinees to the schools and had the midgets, Pixie and Rick, visit the school to give them a teaser with Pixie's special breed dwarf pony, Tiny Tilly, who was a favourite with the children. Pixie dressed Tiny Tilly up in an elaborate costume and paraded her, to the children's delight.

Pixie and Rick were very versatile performers, as they could pass as children and perform acts accordingly. The children in the audience loved Pixie and Rick's balloon act. They would laugh hysterically every time the balloon popped. As Rick and Pixie waited for Vinnie to announce them, Rick checked the pin was securely taped to Pixie's finger and gave her the thumbs up as he walked to the centre of the ring, holding three balloons.

Rick: Balloons! Balloons! Get your big shiny balloons here! Sixpence each. Lovely balloons! Balloons, sixpence each!

Pixie: (entering the circus ring). Hey, mister. What are you selling?

Rick: Balloons. Sixpence each.

Pixie: How much are they?

Rick: Sixpence.

Pixie: What? For one?

Rick: Yes, for one.

Pixie: I've got sixpence. I'll take the green one. (There is no green one, only a red, yellow and blue.)

Rick: (does a double take) There isn't a green one.

Pixie: Oh, alright then. I'll have that one. (She points to a balloon, which pops, then runs off when she sees Rick's reaction.)

Rick: Balloons, only sixpence each. Get them while they last. Lovely balloons. Sixpence each. Going fast.

Pixie: (re-enters the circus ring) Hey mister, what're you selling?

Rick: Balloons. Sixpence each.

Pixie: How much are they?

Rick: Sixpence.

Pixie: What? For one?

Rick: Yes, for one.

Pixie: I'll have the one in the middle. (There are two.)

Rick: (double take) There's no balloon in the middle!

Pixie: Then I'll take that one! (She points to a balloon, and it pops. She runs off when she sees Rick's reaction. With only one balloon left, he is sad and tearful.)

Rick: Balloon! Sixpence. One only! The last of its tribe. Lonely. Singular. All by itself. Solo. The one and only. A beautiful balloon. Only sixpence. The lucky last.

Pixie: (re-enters circus ring) Hey mister, what're you selling?

Rick: A balloon. Only sixpence.

Pixie: What? For one?

Rick: There is only one. It's sixpence.

Pixie: I'll have the one on the left.

Rick: (does a triple-take) There is no balloon on the left. There's only one left!

Pixie: Then I'll have … (Rick snatches the balloon away protectively, but Pixie manages to pop it. Rick is left looking forlornly at a handful of rubber. Pixie throws a full-blown tantrum with tears.)

Pixie: I want a balloon! I've got sixpence. It isn't fair! I want a balloon! Get me a balloon, mister!

Rick: Alright, don't cry! You can have a balloon. (He pulls a balloon out of his pocket.)

Pixie: (looks at it distastefully) Put some wind in it.

Rick: (Gives it a few puffs and hands it to her. She is not impressed.)

Pixie: More wind! (Rick keeps puffing.) More wind! More wind!

Rick kept blowing faster and faster until he was out of breath. Finally, the balloon exploded, and Rick was left looking pathetically at his exploded balloon. Pixie started howling. She exited the circus ring, making a racket and stomping her feet as Rick chased after her.

Each circus act brought laughter, wonder, amazement and exhilaration. The townsfolk were not disappointed, nor were they any the wiser to the absolute misery the troupe had suffered over the last five weeks. Physically and emotionally, it was a hard enough life already, setting up tents and seats and pulling them back down, let alone being subjected to the elements.

Rose hated circus life and struggled with the vagabond lifestyle. She missed the luxury she was accustomed to and resented the fact that she would remain a marked woman in Melbourne. She was homesick and concerned for her mother, who was left to deal with the repercussions of the content of her letter. Thankfully, she had read in the newspaper that Carlo had succumbed to his injuries and no suspicion of foul play had been raised. His men were being arrested as a result of the evidence she had provided in her letter. It would be a while before she could contemplate a secret visit, in disguise, to her grandparents' house. Under their protection, they would be able to arrange for her to see her mother.

On the other hand, Frank and Lola enjoyed circus life and were eager to learn circus skills. They had the company of other children and were fascinated by the animals and the amazing circus performers.

Circus training was tough, regardless of a performer's age. Heavy falls that could render a performer half-unconscious were ignored, and they were expected to keep going as if nothing had happened. To overcome their fear of mastering a difficult trick, performers were told to repeat it immediately after each attempt.

***

It was late morning when Vinnie and his entourage of trucks, following behind his sturdy Ford, were hit by a splattering of locusts across the windscreen. They kept falling like rain until they were engulfed by a cloud of them. By the time they had wound up all the windows, locusts were crawling all over them. As the trucks moved forward, disturbing those lying on the ground, they fluttered in all directions. Millions of them, as far as the eye could see, were pelting the trucks, creating an eerie noise and atmosphere. The children and Rose were screaming hysterically as they tried to pull the sticky locusts' legs away from their hair and clothes. Vinnie was trying to see through a layer of them that covered the windscreen. The sun was only just filtering through the clouds of locusts.

'I can't see a bloody thing!' said Vinnie, his nerves rattled by the blood-curdling screams. 'Will you shut the hell up!' he yelled as his eyes flitted from the windscreen to the rear-view mirror to check the entourage was still following. The crackling sound of wings beating ferociously heightened everyone's anxiety. Vinnie gripped the steering wheel, unconsciously grinding his teeth.

They continued at a slow pace until they reached the town. The place looked deserted as people had shut themselves indoors.

'Bloody hell! It doesn't look like there'll be a show tonight,' said Vinnie, his mood dire as his deep-seated resentment of having to tour regionally made itself felt. He hated running a circus after having worked his way up to performing at classy venues in Melbourne.

'I can't bloody take this anymore!' He thrust his foot against the accelerator and sped on down the road, hoping to high hell there was nobody in front of him to cop his fury as he strained to see through the locust-smeared windscreen. The entourage of trucks followed Vinnie and kept up as best they could. They drove aimlessly, under a darkened sky of locusts, looking for some relief. They found none. Exasperated and exhausted, Vinnie pulled over into an open field to rest. He estimated that he and the others had roughly a quarter tank of petrol left. The rest of the entourage pulled up alongside him. Nobody wanted to get out of their trucks, so they sat inside, trying to calm their nerves. They had no option but to spend a miserable night barricaded in their trucks, smashing locusts until the early hours.

The locust plague had cost the circus thousands of pounds in lost income from cancelled shows. Dreading the cold bite of winter, which was fast approaching, Vinnie decided to return to Adelaide and have the circus go into hibernation for a month. Running a circus had been a steep learning curve. He'd met with resistance from the performers and circus hands who were used to doing things a certain way. The most challenging adjustment was the responsibility of taking care of the animals. They were expensive to maintain. The cash he'd taken from his safe before leaving Melbourne had afforded him the purchase of the circus, leaving them with very little left over.

Vinnie felt the sting of remorse when he thought of how difficult life must have been for Belle and Artis, forced to tour because of his determination to destroy them. They had the added frustration of Stan's sabotage tactics to deal with. Vinnie's losses, because of the rain and locust plague, left him no option but to have money wired from his Melbourne bank account—a mistake that would cost him dearly.

A few days later, as he was contemplating how to get himself out of this mess of a life, a knock on his door changed the course of his life. Two police officers barged into his house.

'Vinnie McIntyre?'

'What's this about?'

'You are under arrest for running illegal businesses, money laundering, and suspected murder.'

'Are you outta your mind!' Within seconds, they had handcuffed him in front of Rose and the children. They watched him being hauled into the police car, leaving them alone to run a circus.

The day after Vinnie's arrest in Adelaide, the police had returned to the house to interrogate Rose about her letter and Vinnie's involvement in the family business. While she signed a statement that the content of her letter was true, she was adamant she would not return to Melbourne to testify in court, even under police protection. Rose had included an assortment of photographs with the letter, some of which included multiple corrupt police personnel performing lewd acts. She knew she was not safe until all of Carlo's mob and the corrupt police who took bribes from him in exchange for immunity were behind bars. The police officer allowed Rose to speak with Vinnie at the police station before he was to be transferred back to Melbourne.

'I can't go back there, Vinnie. You know they'll kill me, even with police protection.'

'But you need to testify that I've been set up. I've been made a scapegoat, Rose. You need to help me. You pulled me into all this.'

'I told you not to go into business with Carlo.'

'You never told me he was a criminal.'

'You chose not to ask questions, Vinnie. You reaped the financial benefits of the business to get back at Artis.'

'Your time's up,' said the police officer.

'Rose, you need to testify, or they'll send me to prison.'

'I'll see what I can do.' Rose got up to leave.

'I need to see my children, Rose!'

Vinnie didn't get to see Rose or Frank and Lola before he was transferred to Melbourne to stand trial and await his fate. Everyone had turned on him, and once again he found himself abandoned and in a place of darkness, but this time there was no lucky escape. Carlo's lawyer tried to get him a death sentence by pinning Carlo's attack and ultimate death on him after he had apparently succumbed to his injuries at the hospital. However, that backfired when the letter Stan had given Betsy to hand to the police along with Rose's letter included Stan's confession of bashing Carlo with the intent to murder him for all the misery he had caused him and his family. Once the trial was over, Vinnie wished he had received the death sentence than face the verdict handed to him.

29

Fall From Grace

Brisbane, Queensland, 1935

Rose had no choice but to continue running the circus in Vinnie's absence, as it was their only source of income. All their assets and bank accounts had been seized by the authorities after Vinnie's arrest. For their safety, Rose insisted on renaming themselves Circus Spectacular. Unable to trust the police for long-term protection, she moved to Brisbane, in Queensland, to get as far away from Carlo's men as possible. However, moving to a state so far away where she had no connections made the responsibilities of running a circus even more overwhelming for her. It was difficult to find supplies, especially to feed so many animals, performers and crew. To calm her nerves, Rose took comfort in the bottle a little more often than usual and doubled her cocaine dose.

Knowing no other way, she used her sexual prowess to lure Max, a willing target, to take Vinnie's place in her bed, but her lack of morals made him lose all respect for her, and her addictions made her an easy victim. It wasn't long before he was calling the shots and controlling the money. Any objections from Rose resulted in a busted lip or black eye.

Max took advantage of the situation by regaining full control of the circus without buying it back from Vinnie, as discussed during the sale—leaving Rose with all the liability should things go wrong. Although he resented the name change and the move to Brisbane, he preferred it to a visit from the mob. Trying to acclimatise to the humidity of Queensland summers was draining. The cyclone season, when strong winds could demolish the circus tents or prevent their erection, was particularly stressful. Rose wore the full brunt of Max's resentment.

The most stressful situation was when a lion escaped after his cage was overturned on rough roads. Max, with the help of others, spent hours attempting to lure the anxious lion with a chunk of meat attached to a rope. After much difficulty, they captured him.

***

The trauma of seeing his father taken away had a tremendous impact on Frank. He was given no explanation as to what had happened and why Max had now taken over his father's role. Not understanding how to process his feelings, he suppressed his fears by playing the role of a clown. He also became a masterful acrobat and was taught how to perform on stilts. His love for the circus animals brought him solace as he related to their entrapment in a life they didn't choose. His special bond with Zulo the elephant ensured she received extra snacks and attention. Her usual stubborn nature abated when he was present. She was always well-behaved around him.

It didn't take Lola long to master riding Tiny Tilly once she'd created a strong bond with the miniature pony. The next and most difficult step was learning how to perform on her back without the assistance of a lunge. Max saw her natural ability and took a particular interest in training her. He held the end of a long rope tied to a belt around her waist that was threaded through a ring inside the dome of the circus tent. The technique led to some humorous incidents, such as the time when Tiny Tilly moved too fast. Lola was left swimming in the air as Tiny Tilly disappeared from underneath her. It took countless hours to learn basic techniques and years to learn more spectacular manoeuvres.

While for Rose, circus life was hell, Frank and Lola found it an escape from the hell they'd experienced and wanted to forget. Their father was gone, and their mother was at the mercy of a man who abused her. They both feared Max and thought the only way to appease him was to impress him with their circus skills. They missed their great-grandparents, who spoilt them and had been their soft place to land when they were feeling out of sorts.

30

No Escape

Melbourne, 1935

Vinnie was sentenced to twenty years in prison. Bitterness seeped through him, creating a storm of rage that increased in intensity as he drowned in self-pity. These emotions were released through fist fights which soon landed him in solitary confinement for the third time since being imprisoned a few months prior. Revenge had cost him everything. Instead of winning Belle back, he had to endure the torment of knowing that, because of his conceit, he was responsible for her damaged body and subsequent ruined career at the peak of her youth. To twist the knife deeper, the image of Belle and Artis's hatred mingled with pity was imprinted in his mind. Deep down, he knew Artis was a decent man. Not only had his deluded obsession with revenge destroyed lives, but it had also clouded his better judgement about going into business with Carlo. Now, he was not only carrying the weight of his sins, but also the sins of others.

As the first year of his incarceration approached, he lay in his prison cell in the early hours of the morning, contemplating the years ahead. Nobody had come to see him. He missed Frank and Lola and wondered whether they missed him. The thought of the years ahead made him want to end his life. Like an overinflated balloon, he released everything he'd been holding back from the time of his childhood. His clenched abdomen spasmed as he spat out sobs.

Time became a blur of no hope. The prison chaplain's words of encouragement were met with rebuke, yet he would consistently visit Vinnie every day, greeting him as if he were a long-lost friend, regardless of how many insults Vinnie had hurled at him over the past year.

'Have you ever been to church, Vinnie?'

'You can shove your church where the sun don't shine! Be gone!'

And then he had the audacity to quote Vinnie a Bible verse that triggered a memory.

'For God so loved the world, that He gave His only begotten Son, that whosoever believeth in Him should not perish, but have everlasting life.'

'John 3:16,' said Vinnie.

'You know it!' said the chaplain.

'Aye, I know it. Now leave me alone.' He shooed the chaplain away, annoyed that he had let his guard down.

Vinnie reflected on the John 3:16 Bible verse his mother would recite to him and his sister often. She would say, '*We can bear the hardships of this world when we know that everlasting life awaits us in the next life. Where do you want to spend eternity, Vinnie? Your soul needs a resting place. Make sure it's with the Lord.*' Whenever she had a chance, she would take him and his sister to church to pray for better days, when his father would stop beating her in his drunken rages. Flashbacks of his mother having to clean up her blood after a merciless beating so as not to enrage his father further at the sight of it retriggered his trauma. He recalled the guilt he felt at not being able to protect her, despite his interventions, which resulted in his small body being hurled across the room, sometimes knocking him unconscious when he hit the wall. *Where was God then?* he thought.

Having now mellowed towards the chaplain, Vinnie's hostility ebbed. Even though he had rejected the prison chaplain's offer for prayer at every visit, the chaplain continued to offer it. Finally, Vinnie relented, when he couldn't overcome the torment of desperation and loneliness he was feeling, and the chaplain's offer of friendship gave him some source of hope. The chaplain's simple prayer surprised Vinnie. He addressed God as his Heavenly Father, and he asked Him to soften Vinnie's heart and protect him. The power of his words paralysed the anger, sadness and fear that had a stranglehold on Vinnie. Before he could stop himself, Vinnie began pouring out his heart to the chaplain.

'Were you born here, Vinnie? I've noticed you use Scottish words here and there.'

'My ma's English. She had the misfortune of marrying a Scottish drunkard who made our lives a living hell.'

'I'm sorry to hear it. So, you grew up in Scotland?'

'Till I was seven. Then we moved to London to get away from him. Lived with my grandma and her new husband.'

'Just you and your ma?'

'And my sister.'

'How did that work out for you?'

'Ma found a job. She was working long hours to get us our own place. Grandma's husband didn't like us being there. I got on his nerves. He wanted me gone and tried to talk Ma into sending me away to get disciplined. Reckoned I was uncontrollable.' Vinnie chuckled at the memory. 'I did have ants in my pants. "Quit your tomfoolery!" he kept yelling at me. My sister thought I was funny. So did Ma.' Vinnie became pensive. The chaplain sat calmly, respecting the moment. 'I loved me ma, more than anything,' said Vinnie, almost whispering. 'She always made me feel like I was the centre of her universe. She would have put up with anything for the sake of my sister and me, but when my pa started hurting me, that was the last straw. So it was 'cause of me we left him. That's how much she loved me.'

'That must have been tough,' said the chaplain.

'It was hard for a single woman with children. No one would rent her a place. Told her to go back to her husband. So she was caught between a rock and a hard place because of me. And my grandma's husband wanted us out quick smart.'

'It sounds like your mother was a very brave woman.'

'That she was. I promised to take care of her when I was old enough, so she'd never have to work again. I told her she could have anything she wanted, 'cause I'd buy it for her. *Anything* she wanted, I said.'

'Did your grandma look after you?'

'She tried to keep the peace, but her husband was hell-bent on getting us out of his house. Kept telling me Ma we'd overstayed our welcome.' Vinnie stood up to leave. 'I need a smoke.' With that, the conversation ended.

The following day, the chaplain returned.

'Thanks for sharing your story with me yesterday.'

'Why are you interested?'

'Your story has made you the person you are today. I don't say that disrespectfully. It's just that revisiting the past has a way of unravelling the knots we've tied ourselves in. If we don't look back, we can't move forward.'

'I got a twenty-year prison sentence and you're talking about moving forward?'

'Do you want to be a tormented prisoner filled with anger or find peace with what you can't control?'

'Let sleeping dogs lie. The past can't be changed.'

'No, but you can change your future.'

'What future?'

'You're still young, Vinnie. You'll manage the rest of your time much better if you change your thinking. The Bible says in Romans 12 verse 2 not to conform to the pattern of this world, but to be transformed by the renewing of your mind. I can help you with that if you want me to. If I can do it, you can.'

'Easy for you to talk.'

'Fifteen years ago, I was serving time in this very prison, and a chaplain was talking to me just like I'm doing with you, so believe me when I tell you that our past makes us the people we are today.'

'I never pegged you for a criminal.'

'We're all sinners, Vinnie.'

'I was set up with a bad business deal. I already told you.'

'Sounds like you chose to do business with the wrong people. What you didn't choose was your childhood. How did you end up in Australia?'

Vinnie snorted at the question.

'My grandma's miserable husband packed my port one day and told me he was taking me on an adventure. I could smell a rat when I saw my grandma's face was white as a sheet. My sister started crying. I told her to fetch Ma as I was shuffled out the door. Next thing I know, we're at the dock with hundreds of boys and girls getting shuffled on board a massive ship.' Vinnie lit a cigarette. 'They take us to a dining hall decked out with the finest spread of morning tea I'd ever seen in my life. I was so fixated on the food I didn't pay attention to the pompous speeches from some high and mighty toffs.' Vinnie drew deeply on his cigarette, trapping the smoke in his lungs. 'We finally got to scoff the morning tea. I stuffed as many cakes, biscuits and sandwiches as I could into my starved mouth. It was the best feed I ever had in my life. With the food to distract us, the next thing I know the ship's getting ready to sail and I'd been left there with the other bairns. I raced to the deck to get off, but it was too late. I could see the old miser on the dock and shouted out to him, but he kept walking. Then just as the ship pulls away, I see my ma running along the dock, and I scream out to her. She sees me and yells for them to stop the ship. She's hysterical, but nobody cares, so I climbed over the rails to jump off the ship when someone caught hold of me and held me back. I kicked and screamed so much I vomited up all the food.' Vinnie's eyes welled. 'I could hear Ma's screams as the ship got further away. I've never been so scared in my life. I can still hear her like it was yesterday. The anguish on her face is burned into my memory. Her screams faded away and then I couldn't see her anymore.' Vinnie wiped his tears on his sleeve.

'I'm sorry, mate.' The chaplain gave Vinnie a moment to compose himself. 'How old were the other children?'

'Five to eleven. They were orphans. Said a man came to their orphanage one day and asked if they wanted to go on a grand adventure where the sun always shines.' Vinnie snorted. 'It was no grand adventure. It was hell. We were scared and sick, and at night we were packed together like sardines in a tin, falling asleep to the sound of gut-retching sobs.'

'How old were you?'

'I got here just before my eighth birthday. Got loaded into the back of a jalopy and driven miles away to a farm in the middle of nowhere. Lived in a shed that was not fit for a dog and was put to work on the farm barefoot and wearing only a pair of shorts, summer and winter, so they wouldn't have to bother washing my filthy clothes. The shed leaked when it rained and was freezing in winter, so I'd spend the night in the stable, lying next to the horses to keep warm. The mongrel farmer told me he owned me and the only way I could ever return to England to see my ma was to work off the debt it had cost him to ship me to Australia. Then he'd come into my shed at night and tell me to take my pants off. He'd take his clothes off and try to make me do things to him.' Vinnie's voice wavered, and his fists clenched. 'When I refused, he'd beat me so bad I could barely walk for days. But I'd rather take the beatings than what he wanted me to do.'

Vinnie became agitated and paced the cell.

'Did anyone help you?'

'Nah.'

'How did you get out of there?'

'The other farmhand needed a hand to shoot the kangaroos, rabbits and wild boars that were destroying crops, so he taught me to drive. We'd haul the dead things into the jalopy, take them back to the shed, bleed them out, then skin and dry the kangaroo and rabbit hides ready to sell, as well as the meat.' Vinnie lit another cigarette. 'It was a miserable life. All I could think about was getting back to my ma. I tried to escape a few times, but got caught and beaten to within an inch of my life. I endured eight years of hell before I finally escaped. By then I was filled with hate.'

'It must have felt good to be free.'

'I was scared out of my wits. I had nowhere to go.'

'What happened then?'

'I jumped into the back of the Association for the Advancement of the Blind's touring truck and begged them for a job.'

'Divine intervention, you think?'

'A lucky break, I thought.'

'Did you try to get back home?'

'It took me a while, 'cause I had no identification. No birth certificate, nothin'. And I wanted to go back to England with money in my pockets so my ma could be proud of me. It took me years, but when I turned up at my grandma's house in London, my sister answered the door. She didn't recognise me at first. Nearly dropped dead from shock when I told her who I was. She was married with a bairn and looking after my sick, widowed grandma. Which was just as well, 'cause I was aiming to knock her husband's lights out.' Vinnie paused and used the tail end of his cigarette to light another one.

'And your mother?'

'She died two weeks before I got there from tuberculosis. How's that for a loving God? So don't be giving me no lectures about confessing my sins, repenting, and asking God for forgiveness.'

'I'm sorry to hear it, mate. It's clear you loved your mother very much.'

'I adored my ma. She was the only person I ever wanted to impress until I met Belle. I couldn't believe my eyes when I first saw her. It was like seeing my ma again. She looked exactly like her.' Vinnie flicked his cigarette ash onto the ground then tapped it with his shoe. 'I couldn't work out why she didn't love me.' Vinnie turned his back on the chaplain and sucked on his cigarette. The chaplain watched swirls of smoke dance around Vinnie's bowed head. He put a hand on

Vinnie's shoulder before excusing himself.

Over time, Vinnie confessed what he had done to destroy Artis's business and the mess he had got himself into with Carlo.

'Artis was a decent man, really. A hard worker—always had a smile on his face,' said Vinnie.

'Do you really believe Artis deliberately stole Belle from you?'

Vinnie lit a cigarette, calming his thoughts by sucking in smoke and holding it in his lungs. Deep in thought, he puckered his lips and expelled the last thread of smoke, ignoring the question.

'Maybe the anger you aimed at Artis was related to the trauma of what your grandfather did when he sent you away from your mother.'

'He wasn't my grandfather!' Vinnie's body stiffened. 'It's time for you to go.'

'Sure, mate. I'll call in tomorrow.'

'Just let me be,' said Vinnie, drawing on his cigarette before turning his back on him.

31

Australia's Shirley Temple

Melbourne, Victoria, 1935–1941

After months of rehabilitation, Belle managed to walk again with the assistance of a cane. She did her best to hide the excruciating pain she was suffering, but it was evident from her pinched face and pained movements.

A gust of wind disrupted the warmth of the house as Olivia walked through the door. She took off her hat and scarf and peeled off her gloves.

'Manton's Department Store is looking for child mannequins!'

Shelley ran to greet her grandmother, wrapping her arms around her hips.

'Did you bring me a lolly?' beamed Shelley. Joe was quick to join her at the mention of lollies. Olivia hugged them.

'I saw a sign on Manton's window. I thought Shelley might enjoy modelling, seeing as she's getting restless about not performing with the troupe,' said Olivia. Belle flipped through *The Australian Women's Weekly* magazine. 'Would you mind if I took her in tomorrow to see if they'll take her on?' Belle shrugged. Olivia took the children into the kitchen for their afternoon snack.

Within the week, Shelley had her first modelling assignment. Shelley admired Manton's collection of tweed coats, velvet hats, long socks, brogues and gloves. But when they made her model summer clothes outside in the freezing weather and asked her to stand still and smile, pretending she was thrilled, she protested. Although she had been taught to always be professional, it wasn't long before she point-blank refused to cooperate, whining that she wanted to go home. Opposite Manton's was the Tivoli Theatre, which captured Shelley's attention.

'That's where I belong,' she said, pointing at the Tivoli. Her modelling career was short-lived.

***

Olivia slapped the newspaper down in front of Belle, hoping this discovery would shake her out of her state of depression, considering Shelley's modelling for Manton's hadn't enthused her.

'Read it, Belle. Hoyts Theatres are holding a Shirley Temple talent competition. This is a wonderful opportunity for Shelley. I always said she had an uncanny resemblance to Shirley Temple. The best part is the prize money. It would solve your financial problems.'

When Belle showed no interest, Olivia picked up the newspaper and read it to her.

> STATE-WIDE interest has been aroused by Hoyts Theatre's quest to find a Victorian Shirley Temple. The competition is open to girls between the ages of three and seven. The prize will be awarded to the entrant who bears the closest resemblance in looks and personality to the famous child screen star. Prize consists of a cash payment of 100 pounds and a one-year touring contract as Hoyts Theatres Australia's Shirley Temple. The winner will be required to sing and dance renditions of Shirley Temple songs.

'What's the point, Mother? Haven't we had enough disappointments?'

'Nobody gets through life unscathed, Belle. Learning to navigate the storms and believing there are better times to come is what'll get you through the hard times. In the meantime, you have no right to rob your children of opportunities that could change the course of their lives.'

'Do whatever you like. You always do anyhow,' said Belle before leaving the room.

***

A few weeks later, Olivia received notice that Shelley had been chosen amongst the finalists. Hoyts management booked an audition that required Shelley to sing Shirley Temple's latest song, *On the*

Good Ship Lollipop. The night before the finals, Olivia curled Shelley's wet hair by rolling a section of hair around her finger and securing the curl with a bobby pin until they were all joined together like honeycomb, in three perfect rows. The excitement rubbed off on Belle and ignited a much-needed spark that brought some life back into her.

'Come on, then. Let's practise your steps.' Belle coached Shelley through the exact choreographed tap-dancing routine Shirley Temple performed in *The Littlest Rebel* with Bojangles, then worked on her vocals to get her audition song perfected.

Olivia looked after Joe whilst Belle and Shelley attended the audition. They sat in the lobby of the Hoyts Cinema with about twenty other hopefuls, all dressed and coiffed to look like Shirley Temple. One by one, the girls were called in to audition. When Shelley's turn came, she skipped inside, her bouncing curls reflecting her excitement. Belle followed, leaning heavily on her cane and trying to minimise her limp. Three judges sat at a table at the far side of the room and a lady sat at the piano.

'Shelley Newman?' called out one of the judges.

'That's me. Can I sing and dance now?' beamed Shelley.

Each judge asked Shelley a series of questions about herself. When they asked her to present her audition song, Shelley got into position, nodded at the pianist, and sang *On the Good Ship Lollipop,* then tap danced her choreographed routine. Once she'd finished, the judges applauded and thanked her. They advised Belle that the winner's name would be published in the newspaper in a week. After days and hours of painstaking preparation, the audition was over in five minutes.

'Thank you. I hope you pick me!' said Shelley, before skipping out of the room. Belle thanked the judges before following Shelley out.

A week later, Olivia rushed to buy the newspaper, accompanied by Belle, Shelley and Joe. As she flicked through the pages, Belle and Shelley watched as her eyes scanned the newspaper.

'Shelley, you won!'

Belle and Olivia burst into tears and hugged each other. Not only was Olivia happy for Shelley, she was relieved that the news was the breakthrough she'd been hoping for to get Belle out of her depressed state. 'Think of the possibilities this opportunity might bring, like a Hollywood contract to star in films, just like Shirley Temple,' said Olivia.

'Forever the optimist,' said Belle.

That afternoon they received a phone call from the public relations office at Hoyts congratulating Shelley and Belle and asking them to call in to the studio to sign a contract and have Shelley fitted for her costumes. As much as the Hoyts competition had lifted Belle's spirits, when she went to sleep at night, alone in her bed, her mood plunged back into darkness. She pined for Artis and continued to cry herself to sleep.

Seeing Shelley so happy was the balm Belle needed to push forward as she absorbed the massive change to their life. The following day, they made their way to the dressmaker's studio to have Shelley measured to make replicas of the costumes Shirley Temple had worn in her latest film. Next, she was sent to the dance studio to begin rehearsals. Thanks to Belle's training, Shelley was able to pick up the dances with ease. She was full of energy and continued to dance her way out of the studio.

The afternoons were reserved for the singing teacher, who taught Shelley the latest Shirley Temple songs. Shelley put her heart and soul into every song and dance. Olivia watched Shelley rehearse with renewed hope of living her dream through her granddaughter.

Once the costumes were ready, they began dress rehearsals so Shelley could get used to them. She was scheduled for a photo shoot at a studio set up with a replica setting of Shirley Temple's latest film. Shelley was shown photographs of Shirley Temple and asked to replicate her poses. Her natural ability to take direction impressed the photographer and the Hoyts manager. Shelley was booked to tour all the major Hoyts cinemas around Melbourne.

***

A few weeks before the tour was due to start, Artis returned. Although Belle was shocked to see him unshaven and dishevelled, she rushed to embrace him.

'Artis!' To her dismay, he pulled away from her. She detected alcohol on his breath.

'I'm done with this business.'

'What do you mean?'

'It was cursed from the start, thanks to your lover.' She recoiled at the remark, stunned to hear Artis speak in this manner. 'I'm going back to Yarra Glen to run the family business.'

'You can't be serious. You're leaving us?' Belle felt a tingle of electricity run through her body. She sat down to settle herself, tears springing from her eyes.

'You'll be free to be with him. Isn't that what you want? Or would you prefer to sneak around behind my back?'

'What are you talking about?'

'Rose showed me the photos of you and Vinnie, and Shelley told me, so don't bother denying it.'

Belle covered her face and sobbed. Her reaction confirmed Artis's worst fears.

'I'm so sorry, Art. I should have told you right from the beginning, but things were going so badly, the last thing I wanted to do was upset you even more by adding fuel to the fire. Believe me, those photos were a set-up to use against me. How could you possibly think that I was having an affair?'

'Maybe hearing my own daughter telling me she saw you kissing him was convincing enough. You didn't even have the decency to hide it from her.'

'I told you, he set me up and had someone there to take photos. You know him. He'll stop at nothing.'

'I'm not convinced. You were kissing him at our house, Belle. You had plans to marry him!'

Belle's renewed sobs heightened his anxiety.

'He came to our house before we left for our first tour and forced himself on me.'

'He forced himself on you! You kept this from me? Why, Belle? Why would you not tell me?'

'I don't know,' she cried. 'After what he did to you, I was scared to anger him any more in case he hurt you again. I was trying to appease him, but he became more persistent once he knew I was pregnant. He started stalking me in public, hoping someone would see us and expose us as lovers. He was hell-bent on ruining our marriage.'

'Bloody oath, I'll kill him!'

'That's why I didn't tell you. I knew you'd react this way and it would destroy everything, which is exactly what Vinnie wanted. He thought I'd go back to him if your business failed.'

With tears in his eyes and a mask of fury, Artis paced the room, muttering curses. 'I swear, I'll bloody kill him!'

'And go to prison for someone like him? Hasn't he already taken everything from us?'

'Why didn't you go to the police?'

'We're public figures, Artis. Reporters would have had a field day. I couldn't bear the humiliation. I was in shock. We were leaving that day. I didn't know what to do.'

'He forced himself on you, Belle! You kept this hidden all these years? I had a right to know!' He moved towards her and put his arms around her. The embrace had a calming effect on them, and they sat in silence as the affection rekindled between them. 'I'm so sorry, Belle. My job's to protect you. How could you not tell me?'

'I'm sorry. There were so many times I wanted to. I know what a struggle it's been for you to keep the troupe in business and how angry you were with him, and yet you kept your integrity. It's what made me love you even more. I remember your mother asked me years ago what would fame bring me that I don't already have, and after losing everything, including you, I realised that only the love of my family matters, not being famous. I was trying to live my sister's dream.'

'I'm gonna make him pay.'

'Artis, please don't confront him. He's not worth going to prison for.'

'Don't worry, I won't kill him. But I'm gonna ruin him and make him suffer.'

***

A stroke of serendipity presented itself to Artis when he saw Vinnie's face plastered on the front page of the newspaper. He had been arrested for illegal business activities, money laundering and suspected murder. The police issued a call for anyone with incriminating evidence to come forward. Artis made a beeline to the police station.

Although Belle and Artis worked at resolving their first major marital fallout, their relationship had been marred. The youthful naivety that had fuelled their passion became tainted with insecurity and a hint of mistrust. They handled it the only way they knew how— by burying it and never speaking of it again.

Their saving grace was the extraordinary opportunity Shelley's contract with Hoyts offered them. It sparked Artis to continue running his shows around Shelley's commitments. There were many benefits linked to the prestigious role of playing Australia's Shirley Temple. The publicity Shelley generated was beyond belief. Hoyts had the budgeting dollars to spend on media coverage and marketing.

Photographs of Shelley were featured regularly in newspapers, and posters of her were all over town. Hoyts movie tickets were regularly sold out. Artis capitalised on Shelley's success by featuring Shelley as Australia's Shirley Temple in his advertisements and publicity. The public loved her. The last time things were going so well for them was when they played *Little Red Riding Hood* at the Playhouse. Their financial struggles were over.

With Christmas approaching, Hoyts management arranged for Shelley to perform on a float at Luna Park in St Kilda. Her manager, Eddie, gave them the rundown. They were required to be at the park before it opened for a photo shoot at the front entrance with the giant moon face.

'After the initial shoot at the park entrance, we'd like to shoot some photos around the other park features, like the carousel, the Big Dipper rollercoaster and the Dodgem Pavilion,' said Eddie.

'Can I propose that my star performers be included? Imagine the publicity if you had some clown acrobats performing among the public,' said Artis.

'I think that would work out well,' said Eddie. They shook hands to seal the deal.

The crisp, salty air of St Kilda greeted Shirley and her entourage with a speckling of the sun's rays that brightened up the iconic Luna Park merry clown face that was about to swallow them as they passed through the gate to begin their day of publicity. Fredric, Birdie and Charley performed in clown costumes, and the troupe's musicians were also engaged in traipsing around the park, creating merriment.

Shelley showed no fear as she rode the roller coaster, giant slippery slides and Ferris wheel. She posed for photographs with great aplomb. Shortly after the park opened to the public, she performed for the eager crowd. An invitation was given to anyone who purchased Hoyt's memorabilia to have their photograph taken with Shelley on a swing seat made in the shape of Luna Park's smiling moon, with a starry background.

Just before Shelley's contract came to an end, Eddie called them to a meeting in his office. It had been an extraordinary year for Shelley, and her performance skills had been polished to a high level of professionalism. Not only had she made Hoyts buckets of money, but she had also won the hearts of the public, who claimed her as Australia's Shirley Temple.

'Shelley, you've been doing a wonderful job, not only promoting Shirley Temple films but the Hoyts brand.'

'Thank you,' said Shelley.

'Most importantly, the public adores you, and we don't think they're going to want to see you disappear anytime soon. Therefore, management has decided to extend your contract for another five years. Would you like that?'

'Oh, yes!' said Shelley, jumping for joy.

'Thank you very much. This is excellent news,' said Artis.

***

After many years of struggle and broken dreams, Artis and Belle were rewarded with success. Vinnie and Rose were out of their lives, enabling them to enjoy peace and prosperity. When it was getting close to Shelley's birthday, Eddie called them into his office. He greeted Shelley warmly and had soda, popcorn and candy served before he started their meeting.

'I believe you'll be turning ten in a month?'

'Yes, sir.'

'Well, we'd like to give you a great big party for your tenth birthday, since you've been working so hard.'

'Thank you!'

'We were planning on inviting your fans and making a giant birthday cake you can hide in. When the music starts, you'll surprise everyone by jumping out of the cake and singing and dancing for your fans. Would you like to do that?'

Shelley nodded enthusiastically.

'Can I eat the cake too?'

Eddie laughed.

'We're going to have lots of cake and food and photographers. Afterwards, we'll be running a double Shirley Temple feature at the cinema. Does that sound like an exciting party?'

Shelley nodded, hiding the exhaustion she was feeling.

32

Broken Legs

Melbourne, Victoria, January 1941

A week before her tenth birthday, Shelley woke up with a splitting headache and stiff neck. Her body was aching, she was having trouble breathing, and her arms and legs felt like lead. With great effort, she tried to lift herself out of bed and fell to the floor, betrayed by the weakness of her legs. The pain searing through her body made her cry out. Shocked by the loud thud and Shelley's cry, Belle raced into the bedroom.

'Shelley, what's wrong?'

'Mama, am I going to be paralysed?'

'Oh, darling, why would you say such a thing?'

'My legs are broken, and my head and neck hurt.' Belle saw she was struggling to breathe and looked deathly pale. 'Nanma was reading the newspaper, and I heard her say lots of children were getting sick and paralysed. I don't want my legs to be broken,' cried Shelley.

'Oh, darling, don't cry.'

'How will I dance at my special birthday party?' When vomit projected from her mouth, Belle panicked and called out to Artis.

'No, no, no! This can't be happening,' she cried, rejecting Artis's attempts to console her.

'Don't fret, love. She'll be alright.'

'No! This is exactly what happened to my sister. I'm going to lose her. We need to get her to the hospital.'

'Love, you need to keep it together, for Shelley's sake. Watch what you're saying.'

'Can I still have my birthday party?' sobbed Shelley, her eyes watery from the fever.

They made haste to get her to the hospital, as her condition deteriorated.

'Don't leave me, Mama!' cried Shelley, reaching for Belle, who was trying to conceal her fear as the medical staff took over.

After waiting in the hospital hallway for over an hour, Artis and Belle were called into the doctor's office. He confirmed their worst fears. Shelley had contracted infantile paralysis.

'We've put her into the quarantine ward,' said the doctor. 'She'll need to be in isolation for two weeks.'

'Will she be alright?' said Belle.

'Your daughter's condition is quite serious. Not only is she struggling to breathe, but she has developed a very high fever and will need to be closely monitored. If her breathing continues to deteriorate, we'll need to place her in an iron lung. This could also pose a problem, as the influx of polio patients requiring an iron lung means we don't have enough to service all patients.'

'We'll pay whatever we have to for her to have the best care,' said Artis.

'Mr. Newman, it's not a matter of paying your way out of this situation. She's very sick and at this stage, there's the possibility that she may not recover.'

'No bloody way!' boomed Artis. Belle broke down.

'I'm very sorry.'

'What are her chances?'

'I'm not sure. Some children develop flu symptoms and nothing more, but there's a small minority that suffers more severe symptoms. Once poliomyelitis hits the nervous system, it depends on the individual child as to the outcome.'

'I want the best doctors to see her,' said Artis.

'I've already conferred with my colleagues. We're doing the best we can. We'll need to keep her quarantined for at least two weeks, whilst she's at her most contagious.'

'She was worried she'd be paralysed,' said Belle, her face soaked in tears.

'The fact she can't move her legs at this point is not a good sign. If the poliovirus has destroyed her nerves, the paralysis will be permanent and there's no chance of your daughter walking again.'

'What do you mean, she'll never walk again? She's a performer,' said Artis. 'God Almighty, she's Australia's Shirley Temple!' said Artis.

'I'm sorry, Mr Newman.'

'No, I won't accept it. You better bloody do something. She can't die. I want the best doctors. And she has to walk again. That child comes to life on stage. It's what she lives for. You can't take that away from her!'

'Mr Newman, this is out of our control. Of course, we will do everything possible for her recovery, but her legs are paralysed. What I'm more concerned about at this point is not whether she'll walk again, but how well her body copes with the virus. She's very sick, Mr Newman. There's a very real possibility she may not pull through.'

Artis studied the doctor's face in disbelief. Belle squeezed his hand as she sobbed.

'No!' He pounded the doctor's desk with his fist, then pointed a finger at his face. 'You'd better find a bloody way to save her and make sure she can walk. That's your job! I don't care what it bloody costs.' He helped Belle up and led her out the door.

To add to their grief, they couldn't see Shelley while she was in quarantine, and with her health in a precarious state, the possibility of never seeing her alive again was very real.

Neither of them slept that night. Belle's heaving sobs echoed throughout the night. The next day, Artis phoned Eddie at Hoyts to tell him about Shelley's situation. It pained them to have to end her contract and cancel all her remaining bookings.

'This is devastating news, Artis. I'm very sorry. This is such a loss, not just to us but to all her fans. We'd like to support you in any way we can. I'll have my secretary post you a cheque to help with medical expenses.'

'Ta, mate,' said Artis, his emotions raw at the enormity of their situation. He could not bear the thought of losing Shelley. She was larger than life, on and off the stage. He hung up the phone and broke down crying. Belle heard him from her bedroom and a wave of despair washed over her. Belle checked on Joe countless times, fearing he might also have contracted the virus. She spent all day cleaning Shelley's bedding and all her clothes, then disinfected the entire house, pouring all her anxiety into the tasks.

Hoyts informed the media and word spread that Australia's Shirley Temple was fighting for her life. Larry and Bert took over the management of the troupe and did their best to keep the show running, despite their low morale.

***

The following days were torturous as they waited for news of Shelley's condition. It wasn't until the third day that Shelley awoke after having passed through the worst of the polio fever and symptoms. Her entire body was paralysed. Frightened by the strange sensation, she used her peripheral vision to see rows of boxes with children's heads poking out of them. Thinking they were coffins with dead children inside, she screamed for her mother and had to be consoled by one of the nurses.

Everyone was relieved to hear Shelley had come through the first hurdle. Trying to grasp the extent of the damage caused by the virus was just as frightening.

'Belle, take a look at this newspaper article,' said Betty. There's a nurse who's been doing amazing work in recuperating polio patients with a very high success rate of them becoming fully rehabilitated.'

Belle read the article about Sister Elizabeth Kenny, who used natural therapies involving heat and massage.

'I'll show Artis.'

'If you follow the doctor's orders, Shelley will never walk again. I've seen the results of doctors putting children into splints. They'll be crippled at best, or in a wheelchair for the rest of their lives. I'm begging you to give her a try,' said Betty.

Anxious to see Shelley, Artis and Belle were disappointed when all they could do was peer through a tiny window into the ward where she was being held. The sight of rows of children's heads poking out of iron lungs was alarming. They caught a glimpse of Shelley in the back corner, looking frail and helpless. Belle couldn't control her tears. When the doctor was ready to see them, they were nervous about hearing the prognosis.

'Can she move her legs?'

'Mr Newman, your daughter is very fortunate to have pulled through. It's unreasonable for you to expect there to be no repercussions from this illness.'

'She needs to walk. She's a performer. What needs to be done to get her walking again?'

'The next step is to have your daughter measured for a full bodysuit and have a Thomas splint put in place before her muscles become deformed. She'll also require braces on her legs.'

'We heard about an alternative treatment offered by Sister Elizabeth Kenny that's getting excellent results. She's had a very high success rate, with her patients walking again without assistance,' said Belle.

'Yes, I've heard of her. I'm sorry to advise you, Mrs Newman, but Sister Elizabeth Kenny is what we call in the medical profession, a quack. She has no qualifications. There's no way I can recommend her.'

'So your only other option is to strap our daughter up to a splint and braces?' said Artis.

'That's the standard procedure, yes,' confirmed the doctor.

'Well, you can shove your standard procedure where the sun doesn't shine! I expected more from you, doc. I told you she's a special girl who's entertained you all as Australia's Shirley Temple for years. She puts her heart and soul into every performance and deserves for you to at least make a better effort than your standard procedure!'

'Mr Newman, I assure you we're using new techniques and making excellent progress with patient recovery. We've just purchased Plywood lungs, a revolutionary device created by Edward Both of South Australia.'

'What are Plywood lungs?' asked Artis.

'They're a portable respirator made of plywood. It's quite ingenious and affordable. At the moment we have patients dying because we can't wait for them to be imported from America.'

'When we looked into the room, she wasn't in a respirator,' said

Artis.

'As I mentioned, we don't have enough respirators for every patient. We placed her in that ward because initially her respiratory muscles were paralysed and she couldn't breathe on her own, so she had to share a respirator. Fortunately, she made a marvellous recovery and appears to be breathing well enough on her own. She's a real little fighter, Mr Newman. If she keeps up that fighting spirit, there's a possibility she may walk again eventually, but with the severity of her paralysis, it could take years.'

'She needs to dance again,' pleaded Artis. 'We've been told Sister Elizabeth Kenny's treatment can have her walking again within the year,' said Artis.

'That's poppycock. I think you're making a huge mistake. I don't believe your daughter will have any chance of ever walking again if she chooses Sister Kenny's treatment. She's not a qualified doctor.'

'Maybe so, but strapping a child up with a full body splint and leg braces is barbaric, if you ask me.' Artis rose from his chair and helped Belle up. He placed his hat on his head and nodded his farewell. 'G'day, doc.'

Artis made arrangements for Shelley to be transported to Sister Kenny's small hospital quarters in Hampton. The Hampton Convalescent Home was attached to the Children's Hospital. The opposition Sister Kenny met with from the medical profession meant she was given minimal support. She had to make do with twelve beds on a verandah with only a canvas screen between the patients and the elements. This was not exactly ideal in a beachside suburb, especially during winter.

The poliovirus had done significant damage to Shelley's muscles. They wheeled her into her quarters and laid her on a makeshift hospital bed. Belle and Artis sat with Shelley and explained the arrangement to her.

'You'll be walking again in no time, darling.'

'Will I be able to sing as well? I still can't breathe properly.'

'Well then, do the breathing exercises Nanma Oli taught you and you'll be singing again in no time.'

'Gracie made this for you,' said Belle, opening a small box that held a bracelet made of tiny, colourful beads. Shelley smiled as Belle put the bracelet on her wrist. 'And this is from Fredric.' Belle put a milk chocolate Freddo Frog on Shelley's bed, followed by a Cherry Ripe chocolate bar. 'The Cherry Ripe is from Charley.' Belle continued to put gifts on Shelley's bed. All the attention lifted her spirits, but her mood darkened when it was time for Artis and Belle to leave.

'Don't leave me,' cried Shelley, her face crinkling as the tears came. Belle and Artis tensed up, their guilt cutting through them.

'Darling, it's only 'til you get better. You understand we have to keep the show going.' Shelley nodded, but it didn't stop the tears. 'I need you to be my little soldier and make me proud.'

'I want to go home,' she cried through heartbroken hiccups. As the tension mounted, a nurse intervened.

'Good morning, Shelley. My name is Sister Evangeline. I'm one of the nurses who'll be looking after you.' Her smile made her plain features beautiful. Shelley tried to focus her waterlogged eyes on her.

Sister Evangeline scanned the pile of sweets, books, a jigsaw puzzle and small toys on Shelley's bed. 'Look at all these gifts! You are a much-loved little girl.' Her smile and soothing voice put Shelley and her parents at ease. 'It's time for your treatment. Your parents need to be on their way now.' She smiled at Belle and Artis. They kissed and hugged Shelley, who was now putting on a brave face for Sister Evangeline.

'Sister Flanagan is waiting for you in her office to explain Sister Kenny's procedures,' said Sister Evangeline. She escorted Belle and Artis there, and Sister Flanagan immediately made them feel at ease.

'Sister Kenny's treatments involve using hot packs for up to twelve hours a day until the muscle spasms stop. Then the muscles are massaged gently at least twice a day to stretch them out, to prevent them from becoming deformed,' she said. 'I understand you're touring performers and will be leaving Shelley with us until she's rehabilitated?'

'Yes, we'll visit as often as possible, but it won't be for a few months,' said Artis.

'It'll take some time to get her walking again, but you needn't worry, she'll be well looked after.'

While reassured that Shelley was in good hands, Belle could not hold back her tears. She had never been separated from Shelley, let alone for an undetermined extended period.

***

Recuperation was slow and painful. Shelley eyed the aluminium cart that was plugged into the wall next to her bed. The nurse pulled out strips of wet wool that had been soaked in hot water and then put through a wringer to squeeze out the excess. Shelley's first treatment left her in a state of self-pity. As if the summer heat wasn't unbearable enough, the hot packs wrapped around her limbs burned her skin and were itchy, adding to the torture.

When the wool cooled down, Shelley was left shivering. It wasn't long before the nurse came back and reapplied more hot strips. Just when she thought the worst was over, the nurse began to massage her muscles and stretch them out. The pain was unbearable, and Shelley howled in protest.

'Be brave, darling. I need to loosen up your muscles, so they don't become deformed.'

As loving as the nurses were, the stretching and kneading of her muscles was pure torture. By the end of her treatment, the emotional and physical trauma left Shelley exhausted. She fell into a deep sleep and dreamt about performing. It lifted her spirits until she woke up, her muscles stiff and lifeless again.

The excruciating treatment strengthened her sheer determination to perform again and in just a few months began yielding positive results in her recuperation. The nurses thought that her training as a tumbler had given her a huge advantage, as Shelley knew how to stretch her muscles to maximum capacity. Once she was past the worst stage of the paralysis, heliotherapy became part of the daily treatment. The nurses lifted the awnings from the balcony, allowing the sunshine to spill over the beds. Shelley bonded with the other children who shared the balcony. The impact of their illness and separation from their family had left some of them traumatised and withdrawn.

Another downside was Shelley's delicate stomach when it came to food. She gagged whenever tripe or brains were served at mealtimes. The larrikin spirit came out in the children, regardless of their broken bodies. They found creative ways to dispose of the offensive food. Attempts at flinging the food across the balcony into the bushes resulted in pieces of brain or tripe dangling from the canopy or stuck on a balcony post.

'Can someone please explain why there's food dangling all over the place?' said nurse Clara when she came to collect their plates. When one child explained that they had lost control of their fork when their body spasmed, nurse Clara made a point of assisting them by feeding them their next meal of tripe, as it was one of the foods that regularly decorated the balcony.

There was a moment of terror when a gigantic huntsman spider fell on one girl's bed, causing utter panic and ear-piercing screams. Sister Evangeline came armed with a broom, swinging it with force, her face just as terror-stricken. The spider moved so quickly up the body of the horrified girl that her blood-curdling screams further panicked Sister Evangeline, and she smacked the broom straight across the girl's face, causing the spider to fall under her sheets.

'Kill it!' screamed the terrified girl. The commotion ranged from screams of terror to fits of laughter as the children watched Sister Evangeline continue to smash the broom about wildly, turning it into a weapon of mass destruction. Moments later, the girl had fallen out of bed, her body weighed down by her paralysed limbs.

Once the spider's carcass was found, everyone calmed down. It was a brutal death, with spider juice squashed between the sheets and amputated spindly legs scattered about the bed. Regardless of the sheets having been changed, the poor girl, who had a small egg-sized lump on her forehead to commemorate the battle, refused to get back into her bed.

The summer heat sometimes became intolerable when there wasn't a breath of wind and the air was heavy, causing their skin to prickle from the lack of moisture. The gardener took pity on the row of perspiration-soaked bodies lying trapped on their beds and would hose down the tin roof. It helped to cool the temperature for a short time. If the nurses were out of sight, he covered the hose with his thumb to create a fine spray and doused the children. There were squeals of delight at the welcome coolness of the water as it dripped from hair and bodies.

What they dreaded the most was when the sky turned a ghastly green, and gusts of wind agitated the canvas blinds until they came loose. Then the rain started to patter on the roof, gently at first, then coming down like artillery. The children screamed out for help. Several nurses rushed outside and tied down the canvas blinds. It helped, but it didn't stop the rain from spraying across the beds.

As the weather cooled down and autumn approached, trying to keep the children warm at night became a concern. Family members would bring additional blankets or newspapers that they could layer between the blankets. Some children had blankets piled up on top of them, and others shared a bed during the night when it was particularly cold. The evidence they were still breathing came from the wispy mist that rose like frozen feathers into the air. The children were rugged up in knitted bonnets, scarves and mittens or gloves, their noses red and usually runny. They all eventually caught a cold. The unfortunate ones came down with pneumonia. It was the most miserable time of the year.

Mrs Brown was a retired teacher who volunteered her services to teach the children for a few hours every morning. One child's parent brought in a radio. The children looked forward to listening to *Chatterbox Corner* every afternoon. It was a godsend that distracted the children from a pitiable existence for the short time it was on air. Nancy Lee, the Ukulele Lady, delighted the children with her pure, crystal voice, which held their attention and took their minds off the painful process of their treatment.

***

Months had passed without a word from her parents since their last visit. Shelley struggled with feelings of abandonment as she wondered whether they'd found someone to replace her and wouldn't be coming back to get her. The day Sister Evangeline announced that her parents were in the visitor's room, she was overjoyed. Tears came the instant she saw her beautiful mother dressed in an elegant sapphire blue dress, her hair cropped short, a cascade of waves to one side. Artis looked handsome in light grey pants, a vest, and a Walker hat with a crisp white shirt. They made an admirable couple.

Much to their delight, Shelley stretched out her arms for a hug as Sister Evangeline wheeled her in.

'Oh Shelley, you can lift your arms!' said Belle.

'I'm so proud of you,' said Artis, his smile warming her heart.

'Watch this!' she said as she mustered all her strength and stood up while she held the sides of the wheelchair. She could only hold herself up for a few seconds before she sat back down.

'That's my girl! I knew you could do it.'

When their emotions had settled, Belle took out gifts from several bags Artis was carrying.

'You can probably guess what Grandma Betty got you,' said Belle.

'Another jigsaw puzzle or a book,' said Shelley. 'I hope you brought something yummy to eat. There's nothing nice to eat here.'

'Will this cheer you up?' Belle pulled out four packets of Smiths potato crisps, an assortment of chocolates, four packets of Pufnel biscuits, and two bottles of Dr Williams' Pink Pills.

'Pufnels!' Shelley reached for her favourite biscuits.

'These will help bring your strength back. It's important you take them every day,' said Belle, as she placed the bottles of Dr Williams' Pink Pills on the bedside table. 'I've also brought some warm clothes, slippers, and a woollen blanket.'

Artis filled Shelley in with news from the troupe and stories of funny things that had happened on tour. Their moods were further lifted when they had a sing-along to Belle's favourite song, 'Give My Regards to Broadway', which they all sang with gusto.

In one of his bags, Artis had brought some props and he put on a show for Shelley, with Belle joining in with her beautiful singing voice.

When it was time for them to leave, Shelley clung to Belle as they both cried. It was difficult to pry Shelley's fingers away from the grasp she had on her mother. Promises to return as soon as they could did nothing to console Shelley.

Little did they know it would be longer than expected. Bert was waiting for them when they got home with another devastating blow to their circumstances.

'A fire broke out in the storage van. We've lost everything. Costumes, props—everything's gone.'

33

A Boy Called Chico

Melbourne, Victoria, 1942

It was late November, and the birds appeared to be in a particularly chirpy mood, perhaps in anticipation of warmer months ahead. Shelley was one of the few children still recuperating at the Hampton Convalescent Home. The other children were permitted to go home and be brought in for their daily treatments.

As she sat soaking in the sun on the balcony, reading a book, the sound of shuffling from behind a bush distracted her. She spotted a shock of wavy caramel hair, cut near to the scalp on the sides and back. Craning her neck, she saw a boy, around the same age as her, in navy overalls and a beige shirt kneeling in the dirt holding a jar. His right arm was wrapped in plaster.

'Hello! What are you doing?' called out Shelley. The boy looked up. His smile took Shelley's breath away.

'Catching bugs.'

'What happened to your arm?'

'I fell over when I was clowning around. Are you sick?'

'I got polio.'

'What's that?'

'It's a virus that makes your legs stop working.'

'What d'you mean? Are your legs broken?'

'No, they got paralysed, so I suppose the muscles are broken.'

'Can't you walk?'

'I can now, but not for long.'

'How long have you been here?'

'I've had two birthdays and one Christmas here. I'll be twelve soon.'

'Fair dinkum! That's a long time. I broke my arm a week ago and I'm bored stupid.'

'Are you staying at the hospital?'

'Nah, I'm staying with my nonni down the road till I get the plaster off.'

'Nonni?'

'My great-grandparents.'

'They must be really old.'

'Yeah. Do you wanna see what I caught?'

Shelley nodded. He lifted the lid on the jar, revealing a couple of cicadas. He had made a home for his trapped victims with grass and tiny flowers he picked from the garden. Shelley smiled as they let out their vibrating, tinny hum.

'What's your name?'

'Chico. What's yours?'

'Shelley. What do you do with them once you catch them?'

'I look at them for a while. Then I feed them to Nonno's chickens.'

'Oh! Poor things,' she said.

Chico shrugged.

'They're just bugs. Chickens love them.' Chico's new hobby helped ease his boredom and get him out of the house.

From that day on, Chico visited Shelley every day. Part of her therapy was to take short strolls to help strengthen her legs. Having Chico with her made her push herself harder so she could go on adventures looking for bugs around the garden. One afternoon, they found a crippled blue wren on the grass that was struggling to fly. It was so tiny and helpless. Chico found a shoebox at home and lined the bottom with one of his knitted woollen socks. They put the blue wren inside so they could look after it while it recovered.

'Let's call him Bluey,' suggested Chico. Shelley agreed.

'We better go find some worms to feed him. He doesn't look real good.'

They scrounged around in the dirt, their hands and faces smeared with earth. Grass and mud stains had ruined Shelley's dress. Chico's knees were caked with oval patches of dirt.

When they presented Bluey with a fresh worm, he showed no interest. His eyes kept closing as he let out pathetic little tweets.

'Oh, no! I think he's dying. He's tweeting for help,' said Shelley.

'Shelley! It's time for your treatment,' called out Sister Evangeline.

'I have to go. What are we going to do about Bluey?'

'Nonna has some medicine. I'll bring some back after lunch.'

'We better hide him in the bushes for now.' Shelley placed the shoebox under the shade of some bushes and made her way inside.

Chico waved to Shelley and ran down the path towards home. She watched his bobbing head growing smaller in the distance.

As soon as he entered the house, his Nonna announced she was taking Chico to his doctor's appointment after lunch. Ignoring her, he raced to the cabinet in search for the medicine he saw Nonna use. Once he found it he made a beeline for the door to get it back to Shelley before Bluey died, but Nonna stopped him in his tracks.

'Na, na, na! Vieni qui,' called out Nonna.

'I'll be back. I have to get this medicine to my friend so we can save a bird we found.'

'Bird? Na, you stay-a here. We go dottore.'

'But it's important. I'll only be five minutes.'

'Chico, no make-a me angry!' She knew Chico enough to know that his five minutes would turn into hours. She plucked the medicine bottle from his hand. 'Madonna! This is not for bird! Sciocco ragazzo!'

'Please, Nonna. Five minutes!'

Nonna positioned herself at the entrance to the door with her hands on her hips and a frown that could darken the brightest day. This was the first step of her warning. The next step was to wave a wooden spoon in the air. The final step would be to use the weapon. Chico thought it over and decided getting back to Shelley was more important than a beating. He made a dash for the back door, bumping slap bang into Nonno, who was coming in from tending the vegetable garden, laden with a large basket full of potatoes, tomatoes, spinach, parsley, basil, and strawberries. He knew he was in for it now.

'Chico! You disrespect Nonna?' boomed Nonno. In a flash, Nonna had hold of his ear, pulling him back inside and letting fly with the wooden spoon. Nonna's hefty arms were a power to be reckoned with. The beating took less than ten seconds, but the burning welts on his buttocks lasted hours and would be felt for days whenever he sat down. He took pride in not shedding a tear, the way his father had taught him.

'Go wash your hands, presto,' said Nonna, as if nothing had happened.

When Chico returned, he sat down under the watchful eye of Nonno, trying not to wince from the pain of his burning buttocks. Nonna served her lunch of beef ravioli with tomato sauce, basil and chopped olives. It made up for the spanking—only just. Nonno poured him a glass of water with a splash of red wine. As a special treat, Nonna gave Chico a big serving of her strawberry gelato and aniseed biscuits.

'Change your clothes. We go dottore,' said Nonna. Chico went to his room and saw his clothes already laid out on the bed. He changed into his tweed shorts, jacket, and matching cap. All he could think about was Shelley waiting for him, with Bluey on the verge of death.

As the hours passed and Chico had not returned, Shelley worried about what to do about Bluey. The air was getting chilly as the sun slipped over the horizon. Shelley's muscles had seized up and her skin was an eerie shade of speckled purple.

'Shelley!' This was the third time she heard Sister Evangeline calling her. 'Shelley Newman, I've been looking everywhere for you! Where have you been?'

'I'm sorry. I fell asleep in the garden,' lied Shelley.

'That was a silly thing to do. Look at you. Your legs are purple, and you can barely walk. We need to get you into a hot bath.' Shelley felt the prickle of hot tears behind her eyes. *Where are you, Chico?*

While the hot bath helped relieve her muscle spasms, the kneading required to release the tension in her muscles was painful. With her nerves already frazzled, Shelley had to restrain herself from screaming.

When Shelley awoke the next morning, her legs were still stiff, making it difficult to get out of bed. By the time she had completed her morning routine and was allowed to go outside, the air had warmed somewhat. She made her way to the shoebox only to find Bluey lifeless. Her heart was heavy. She longed to see Chico bounding around the corner with his cheeky smile and mischievous eyes that sought adventure. After what seemed an eternity, Chico sped around the corner at breakneck speed.

'Chico!' Shelley's heart lurched at the sight of him. He skidded on the gravel, scattering rocks everywhere. His cheeks were flushed, his hair tousled. Shelley noticed his arm.

'Your plaster's gone!'

'Yes, that's why I couldn't get here yesterday. Sorry.'

'Does that mean you're going back to your parents?'

'Yes, Nonno's taking me back in the morning.'

Her heart sank at the news, although she didn't understand why she was reacting so strongly. She hadn't realised the depth of her loneliness until Chico had filled it. Now she would have nothing to look forward to. He noted her sadness as she handed him the shoebox.

'He's dead,' she said.

Chico lifted the lid, acknowledging that the sadness he felt was not related to Bluey. It was his last day with Shelley. They were kindred spirits who'd felt lost until they found each other. Now, just like Bluey, their friendship was destined to die.

'We'll have to bury him before he starts to stink,' said Chico.

'And worms start crawling out of him. We should give him a decent burial.'

'We're going to need something to dig a hole, and a Bible.'

'A Bible?'

'Have you never been to a funeral? We have to read something out of it.'

Shelley shrugged.

'I can borrow Sister Evangeline's. I'll go and get it.' Shelley left and came back with a Bible and a metal spoon to dig a hole.

They found a burial spot among some flowers, and Chico started digging. Shelley busied herself making a cross out of two sticks. She tore out a clump of ornamental grass from the garden and used the long stems to tie the sticks together. When she had finished making the cross, Chico placed it at the head of Bluey's burial site. They checked Bluey one last time, just to make sure he hadn't miraculously come back to life. Shelley picked a bright pink flower from the garden and put it next to Bluey.

'Wait!' Chico placed the worm that had died in the shoebox next to Bluey's beak.

'Just in case he gets hungry in heaven.'

Shelley rolled her eyes.

'They have fresh worms in heaven, silly.'

Chico shrugged.

'What do we do now?' said Shelley.

Chico picked up the Bible and flicked through the pages, looking for something appropriate to read out. Perplexed, he gave up and closed the Bible. He held Shelley's hand. She felt a shiver run down her spine and wished he would never let her go.

'Bow your head and close your eyes,' he said to Shelley as he prepared to conduct the ceremony.

'Hello, God. We are standing here today to ask you to look after Bluey. Maybe you could take care of the worm as well, so it doesn't go to waste.' He paused, unsure of what to say next. Then he remembered.

'Amen.' He nudged Shelley, who looked at him, puzzled. Prompting her, he whispered the word 'Amen'.

'Amen,' said Shelley.

Chico used the spoon to shovel dirt on top of the shoebox until it was buried. He framed the burial site with some small rocks, and Shelley picked more flowers from the garden for decoration.

'Well, that's done, then. I better get home for lunch before my

Nonna flips her lid.'

'Will you come straight back?'

'Sure.'

'Don't let me down.'

'I won't. See ya!'

He burst into a sprint, his mop of hair tousling about wildly. Shelley felt her heart swell. She resented the fact that she was the only child left at the hospital. The others, once they were strong enough, were able to go back home to their families and come in for treatments. But since her family was touring, she had to stay. Now she was going to lose Chico, whose vibrant personality had brightened up her days and given her much to look forward to. It made her want to leave as soon as possible and get back to the life she missed, surrounded by people who loved her. She was not going to be left behind anymore.

After lunch, she sat down to make Chico a goodbye card. She laid out her coloured pencils and asked Sister Clara if she could have a little flour and water to make some glue. Her garden adventures with Chico had resulted in her starting a collection of leaves and flowers that she pressed between the pages of her books. These were now used to decorate the card, along with her coloured pencils. She pondered over what message to write, and when she was satisfied with its contents, she put the card in an envelope and went outside to wait for him.

The sun prickled Shelley's skin even in a shady spot. It wasn't long before Chico came running along the path, carrying something in a paper bag. She smiled as the joy of seeing him energised her body.

Chico returned her broad smile, his face flushed a rosy pink with the exertion of running.

'I brought some of Nonna's ciambelle!' Inside the bag was a white linen tea towel. Chico took it out and unwrapped it, revealing two giant doughnuts coated in sugar and cinnamon.

'Mmm, looks delicious!'

'Nonna's the best cook in the world. She made these especially for me because I'm leaving tomorrow, and she knows they're my favourite. I wanted you to taste it.'

'Thank you.'

'Let's go down to the beach and eat them.'

'I'm not allowed to leave the property.'

'No one will know. They've never come looking for us before. I think it'll be a special thing to do for our last day together.' It would be Shelley's first visit to the beach since arriving at the hospital. Every night, she was lulled to sleep by the sound of the ocean, which seemed louder at night. Many times she had wished she could go there. 'Come on.' Chico took her hand and assisted her down the pathway that led to the beach. The heaviness of walking through the sand made Shelley's legs ache, so they found a little nook on the beach, close to the path, and sat down.

'The best part of being at the beach is digging your toes in the sand. Try it.' They took their shoes and socks off.

'Won't those little crabs bite me?' she said, pointing to the ghost crabs scurrying around.

'Nuh, they're harmless.' He picked one up and showed her. He unwrapped the tea towel and offered Shelley a ciambelle. He bit into his with gusto, rolling his eyes with delight at its sweet taste. Shelley sank her front teeth into the soft, sugary dough.

'Mmm, it's delicious.' Apart from the occasional raspberry jam tart or fruit cake at Christmas time, she was not fond of sweets, preferring a SAO biscuit with butter and Vegemite. The ciambelle, however, was not overly sweet, and she relished its unique yeasty taste.

They spent the rest of the afternoon exploring rock pools, finding beautiful shells the ocean's battering waves hadn't marred and colourful rocks. The exertion of walking on sand was difficult for Shelley, so Chico piggy-backed her back to their nook near the pathway.

'I made something for you.' Shelley pulled the card out of her pocket. It was bent and damp from sharing space with the treasures she'd found. 'Read it later.'

'Thanks. I've got something for you, too.' Chico took out a small gemstone from his pocket and handed it to Shelley. She studied the vibrant colours.

'It's beautiful.'

'It's an opal. I found it when we went fossicking in Coober Pedy. People live underground there.'

'Under the ground? Why?'

'Because it's cooler in summer and warmer in winter,' he said, before blurting out, 'One day I'll marry you and I'll make you a ring from that opal.'

Shelley's heart leapt.

'You want to marry me?'

Chico mustered his courage and kissed her on the lips, stirring their senses. They sprang back and looked at each other wide-eyed.

'Come on, jump on my back. We better go,' said Chico, trying to cover up the awkwardness of his arousal. Shelley closed her fist around the opal, afraid of losing such a precious gift.

When they got back, Sister Clara was not pleased. She observed the sandy bare feet and Shelley's damp, soiled dress.

'You need to go home now,' she said to Chico.

'Bye, Shelley.'

'Bye, Chico.' Shelley watched him take off down the road, dragging her heart behind him.

'I'm very disappointed in you, Shelley.' Sister Clara took her by the hand and led her inside. Shelley hid the opal amongst her possessions while Sister Clara ran her a bath. As she undressed, a stream of sand fell out of her underpants onto the bathroom floor.

'Shelley, you are never to see that boy again. Is that clear?' Shelley nodded, her eyes downcast. 'Boys will get you into trouble, and then you'll never hear from them again. A boy like that corrupts good character. You've been such a good girl until now. From now on, you'll not be allowed to go outdoors without supervision. What would your parents say if they knew about your conduct today? You gave us quite a fright, leaving the premises without permission.'

After Sister Clara had finished her lecture, she remained silent, her lips pursed in disapproval. The thought that there would be nothing to look forward to when she awoke each morning weighed on Shelley's heart. Sister Clara's words rang in her ears: *Boys will get you into trouble, and then you'll never hear from them again.* Surely that wasn't true of Chico.

34

The End of an Era

When war was declared in Europe in September 1939, it made it increasingly difficult for Artis to keep the show going, as more and more men were forced to enlist or had gone to war of their own accord. After the fire that destroyed all their costumes and props, and with Shelley's medical bills continuing to drain their finances, Artis's only option, as much as it pained him, was to approach the bank for a loan. Dressed in his best suit, tie, hat, and polished shoes, he walked into the Commonwealth Bank building with his paperwork tucked under his arm. He did everything in his power to charm the bank manager into approving a small loan to help them get back on their feet. He presented him with records of their ticket sales, publicity clippings, a circuit booking schedule, pre-sales, a list of expenses, and reassurance that he had no other debts. Once his cards were on the table, he held his breath whilst the bank manager crunched the figures. After what seemed an eternity, the bank manager acknowledged Artis had done well to keep his troupe afloat during the worst of the Depression, attributing his current situation to a series of unfortunate events.

'Unfortunately, Mr Newman, when the glitter fades, it's hard to get the sparkle back. As much as I would like to help you, your figures are based on sales when your daughter was a prime attraction for your show. As she's now sick, with no prospects of ever returning to the stage, and her recovery being a long and costly one, we can't take the risk of loaning you money, especially considering we're still facing a challenging economic future as this war continues. I'm very sorry.' He brought down the stamp marked *REJECT* on the paperwork, jolting Artis into his new reality.

Of all the highs and lows Artis Newman's Pantomime Players had experienced over the years, having the business he worked so hard to build finally fold was devastating. Even with Vinnie in prison, it appeared the curse could not be lifted. The tragic events and losses both parties had experienced in order to inflict revenge had only succeeded in fuelling hatred between them.

After much pleading from his mother to return to Yarra Glen until they got back on their feet, Artis relented when Betty disclosed his father was suffering ill health. Larry, Bert, and Tommy announced they were enlisting in the military. The rest of the troupe dispersed to find work elsewhere. Olivia returned to her house and continued to take in boarders and teach piano as a source of income.

Returning to the family bakery reminded Artis of why he had left all those years ago. His heart wasn't in it, but it allowed Shelley to come back to live with them. To ease his displeasure at having to run a bakery, Artis worked hard and was frugal until he had saved enough money to open a roller skating rink he ran on the side. The skating rink offered the locals an inexpensive way to entertain themselves and was a popular after school activity. Artis hired out the roller skates or sold new skates to those who took the activity seriously enough to want to hone their skating skills. Roller skating appealed to all ages. Young couples who were dating or hoping to find a mate would attend on a Friday or Saturday night when Artis hired a live band who played the latest hit songs as skaters attempted to skate to the beat of the music with their sweethearts by their side. These nights usually attracted a small crowd. It was a far cry from running a show, but it gave him a sense of accomplishment to ease his feelings of failure.

For the first time in their lives, Shelley and Joe were enrolled at school. Shelley, a social butterfly, preferred it to learning by correspondence. If anyone felt the loss of no longer being an entertainer, it was Shelley. Although she had recovered well enough to walk again, her legs were too weak to dance at a professional level. The taste of fame she had experienced as Australia's Shirley Temple had left her hungry for more. She made a vow to somehow find a way back to the life she loved.

The war placed restrictions on everyone's lifestyles, leaving no chance for Shelley to escape country living. She settled down to school life, friends, and helping Artis run the roller skating business, and tried her best to look happy about it. On the upside, she found skating an excellent and enjoyable way to strengthen her leg muscles.

'Why don't you teach skate classes and choreograph a routine you can present at the end of the evening?' suggested Artis.

Shelley took him up on his offer. It gave her some extra income that she put away for a time when she could leave Yarra Glen and perform on an actual stage again.

Belle and Artis knew the light had gone out of their bright young star, so in the spring of 1949, they had some news for Shelley.

'I've received a letter from Jean. She's invited you to stay with her for a while in Sydney. Would you like that?' said Belle.

'Oh, yes! That would be wonderful. When can I go?'

'Once you graduate from school—with good grades, might I add— you'll be free to spread your wings and see what the world has to offer you,' said Artis.

'I'm so excited. Sydney!'

'Jean will appreciate your company. It's been hard on her losing poor Bert in the war.'

'Don't worry, I'll cheer her up!

Giving Shelley something to look forward to completely changed her disposition. It was perfect timing as it meant she put in a mighty effort to pass her final year exams at school and worked extra at the bakery and skating rink to save as much money as possible for her time in Sydney.

35

Refuelling the Fire

Sydney, New South Wales, 1949

'You look even more like your mother now!' Jean said as she hugged Shelley.

Shelley was thrilled to be in Sydney. Her curiosity about their touring days resulted in them spending hours reminiscing. As an adult, she relished hearing Jean telling her all the stories she couldn't remember as a child.

'Those were the happiest days of my life,' said Shelley.

'Your father kept his struggle to make ends meet and keep the show on the road throughout the Depression hidden. Putting on the best show, taking care of everyone, and making your mother a star were his top priorities.

'I miss those days.'

'Me too. You were our little shining star. I'm so glad to see you walking again. You truly are a miracle.'

'I have a limp.'

'I didn't notice.'

'I can't dance like I used to.'

'But you can still sing.'

'Not as good as you.'

'It's not about how well you sing, Shelley. It's about how well you capture your audience's heart. That's the secret.'

'I miss performing.'

'Then maybe it's time for a fresh start.'

'Do you really think so?' Shelley's spirit soared.

'You must! I still sing in nightclubs on the weekends and at special functions. It's good for the soul' Jean smiled. 'I needed to do something to lift me out of the doldrums and pay the bills after I lost Bert. I begged him not to enlist.'

'I remember how upset Ma and Pa were, especially Pa. I'd never seen him so sad. He was relieved when Uncle Larry came back.'

'Let's go for a walk and I'll show you around. You're going to love it here.'

Shelley spent the following weeks filled with thoughts of resurrecting her dream. Jean helped her rehearse a few numbers, and Shelley watched her perform at a nightclub. Jean had spoken with the nightclub manager about allowing Shelley to perform a duet with her. He agreed, and Shelley was thrilled to perform in public for the first time since contracting polio.

Things were looking promising for her until Circus Spectacular rolled into town on a summery morning. Shelley watched with excitement as the crew bustled around, erecting the Big Top. Memories came flooding back of her days touring regional Victoria. With her heart fluttering, she scanned the grounds, looking for the circus manager. She approached a robust lady with a moustache to make her enquiry.

'Hey, Chico!' the woman called. 'This sweet pea's looking for Max.' Shelley's heart leapt when she heard the name Chico. She scanned the faces of the svelte males unloading the trucks. A young man turned in response.

'Chico! Do you remember me? I'm Shelley from the hospital in Hampton all those years ago.' Chico, whose face was now chiselled and bore evidence of facial hair, squinted through the sun's rays until her familiar face registered with him.

'Shelley!' His surprise meant all eyes were now on Shelley. The men responded with wolf whistles that made Shelley blush. Chico rushed to her, lifting her in an awkward hug. 'It's really you!'

'I thought I'd never see you again.' Shelley's exuberance matched his.

'I've moved around a lot since I last saw you.'

'I can't believe you work in a circus!'

'That's how I broke my arm—clowning around, remember? I got sent to stay with my nonni till it healed.'

'You never mentioned the circus.'

'Yeah, I wasn't allowed to talk about it.'

'Why?'

'Long story. You gonna come see the show tonight?'

'I was actually hoping to get some work.'

'What kind of work?'

'Anything to start with.'

'So you're all fixed up now?'

'Pretty much. I've been keeping up my gymnastics, and I started roller skating. It helps keep my muscles strong. Remember Bluey?'

'How can I forget conducting my first funeral?' Chico laughed.

'Chico, get a move on!' yelled Max.

'I've gotta go, but come to the show tonight. I'll see what I can do about getting you some work.'

'Thank you. That's wonderful.'

'Wait for me at the ticket box after the show.'

Shelley's smile was infectious. Chico smiled, pushing his hair away from his eyes the way he had when he was a boy. Shelley's heart swelled as she waved him goodbye.

After years of living without purpose, Shelley felt revived. Her enthusiasm created a stir as she burst through the door, rattling Jean's peaceful state.

'I've got the most wonderful news!'

'Seems like it!' Jean put down her book.

'When I was in the hospital, a boy who'd broken his arm would come to visit me. Well, I can't believe it, but I just bumped into him! He works at the circus that's just come into town.'

'That's exciting!'

'Will you please come with me to see the show tonight?'

'How could I resist such an offer to reminisce about the good old times?'

'Thank you!' Shelley hugged Jean.

The hours and minutes seemed to drag for Shelley. Her mind was a whirl of romantic fantasy in which she created scenarios of a romance she had suppressed in the innocence of her childhood. Chico had lit up her world during a time of despair and loneliness. She thought that maybe Bluey's demise represented a love they had had to bury, only to have it resurrected all these years later.

***

The surprise of seeing Shelley, all grown and beautiful, had revived feelings of happiness and hope Chico had long ago buried. As the time approached for the show to start, he searched for her in the audience, scanning faces until he finally found her. She looked radiant, with her hair pulled away from her face, a touch of lipstick highlighting her lips, and a smile that stirred his heart. He waited impatiently for Max, who was acting as the ringmaster, to announce his act. Finally, his turn came. The spotlight followed Chico as he entered the arena and walked across the floor, eating a banana. Shelley leapt from her seat.

'That's him!' she said, elbowing Jean.

'Ooh, he's handsome.'

As Chico paraded around, the shape of his body began to change, causing the audience to do a double-take as he morphed into an ape. With a quick motion, unseen by the audience, he had attached an ape mask with enormous ears to his face and slipped on hairy gloves. Then he began dancing around in an ape-like manner. Pandemonium ensued as he moved through the audience. He made his way towards Shelley, her face illuminated by the soft rays of the spotlight, which was still focused on Chico. He took the last bite of his banana and made an exaggerated gesture of admiration at the sight of Shelley. Then he tossed the banana peel so that it landed on a man's head. This caused squeals of laughter from the audience.

Chico patted Shelley on the head before snatching her handbag and foraging around it. With a look of surprise, he pulled out a lipstick and looked at it inquisitively, then looked back at Shelley, motioning for her to kiss his cheek by tapping the side of his face. Laughing, she obliged him with a peck. In response, he jumped up and down, making ape-like gleeful squeals, much to the audience's delight. He ran back to the centre ring and sat on a stool, examining the lipstick. He sniffed it and licked it before attempting to smear it over his rubber lips and face as the audience howled. After parading around for the audience to get a good look at his handiwork, he morphed back into Chico, much to their amazement.

Once Chico had left the arena, Shelley settled back into her seat. It was obvious to Jean that she was smitten. They were enjoying the acts when Max introduced the lion-taming act.

'Please welcome my beautiful assistant, Rose!'

When Rose entered the arena, Jean stared in disbelief—could it be Rose McIntyre? She knew Vinnie was in prison, but none of them knew what had become of Rose and her family. They had simply disappeared all those years ago. The rest of the show was a blur for

Jean. Her thoughts were dominated by the strange coincidence that Shelley should come across a boy she had met years ago, who happened to work in a circus with Rose McIntyre.

'Chico asked me to meet him at the ticket box after the show.'

'Why?'

'He was going to ask about getting me some work here.'

'Shelley, why didn't you mention this to me?'

'You sound upset.' Shelley sensed the tension in Jean's voice.

'I thought you'd discuss something like this with me first. Are you planning to move on when the circus leaves?'

'I guess I hadn't really thought about it. I was just excited to see Chico and get an opportunity to perform again.'

'This is not the place for you, Shelley. Your parents wouldn't approve.'

Just as Shelley's mood took a dive, Chico came bounding around the corner like a lovesick puppy. His electric smile zapped her back to life.

'Chico, this is my godmother, Jean.'

'Pleased to meet you,' beamed Chico, lifting his cap in greeting. 'Did ya enjoy the show?'

'Yes, you performed very well. Chico, is it?'

'Yes, ma'am.'

'Is that your stage name?'

'I suppose. I've been called Chico since I can remember. My real name's Frank.'

'Frank!' Jean tried to steady herself. 'Is Rose McIntyre your mother, if you don't mind me asking?'

'Sure is. She owns the circus.' He looked at Shelley. 'Ma said she'd like to meet you tomorrow and she'll see what she can do about a job.'

'Oh, that's wonderful! Thank you so much.' Shelley avoided eye contact with Jean.

'It was nice to meet you, Chico. Shelley, we'd better go. It's getting late.' Jean hooked her arm around Shelley's and jostled her forward. Shelley turned her head back to mouth her goodbye to Chico.

Jean was quiet on the way home. It was clear to Shelley that something was brewing.

'Are you upset with me?' asked Shelley, hoping to break the tension as they entered the house.

'No, darling. It's just that I don't think your parents would be too pleased with you associating with Chico and his family.'

'Why? They don't even know them.'

'Actually, they do, and their acquaintance is not a good one.'

'What do you mean?'

Jean paused as past misdemeanours resurfaced in her memory.

'They caused your family a lot of pain, Shelley. You need to trust me and just let it go.'

The weight of Jean's words lay heavy in the air. Shelley didn't want to hear any more and excused herself. The knot in her stomach prevented her from falling asleep. She spent a restless night pondering her situation. By the time dawn broke, she concluded that there had to be a reason why, after so many years, she would be reunited with Chico and, most importantly, why she was so attracted to him.

Taking advantage of the stillness in the house, she quietly got dressed and slipped out of the front door. Her every step was filled with doubt and turmoil. The battle with her conscience made her change direction several times as she contemplated having to face Jean after disregarding her warning. No doubt Jean would write to her parents, informing them of the situation. By the time she reached the circus, she was still in a state of confusion and turmoil. She had decided to let Chico know she had changed her mind about wanting work, but changed it back again as soon as she spotted him, running to greet him with the enthusiasm of a child. His familiar exuberance wiped every negative thought from her mind.

'I'm so glad you came. I was hoping you weren't going to change your mind. Come and meet my mother.' Chico took Shelley's hand and led her in a half run towards a caravan. Rose was seated at the far end, covered in a thin, loose robe. Shelley couldn't help but notice her breasts were close to being exposed. Spider veins and bruises marred her crossed legs. What her body revealed, her face concealed under heavy greasepaint. Wisps of cigarette smoke escaped her painted lips. Her eyes pierced Shelley, causing her to feel intimidated. Noticing Shelley's hesitation, she broke into a slithering smile and motioned for Shelley to sit.

'Welcome, welcome. Do sit down. I've been very eager to meet you. Chico, go do your chores and let me have a moment with your friend.' Chico smiled at Shelley and left them alone.

'So, Shelley, tell me about yourself,' Rose said in a raspy voice, followed by a cough that rattled her chest and exposed a breast. Rose noted Shelley's embarrassment as she averted her eyes. She adjusted her robe but made no apology for not bothering to dress for their meeting.

'Well, I've been performing since I was a child, until I got polio.'

'You were Australia's Shirley Temple, were you not?'

'Yes.'

'Your parents are Artis and Belle?'

'Yes.'

'You have a brother called Joe?'

'Yes.'

'How is your dear brother?'

'He's well.'

'Looks just like your daddy, does he?'

Shelley was puzzled by the question. 'I suppose.'

'You look just like your mother. What are your parents doing these days?' Rose dragged deeply on her cigarette, then blew smoke in Shelley's direction. A wave of caution washed over Shelley. She began to fidget and wished Chico would come back. Jean's words were echoing in her mind, and she wished she'd asked more questions.

'They're running my grandfather's bakery and a roller skating rink.'

Rose's crisp laugh took Shelley by surprise. 'A bakery and a roller skating rink! How disappointing for them.'

Shelley's silence and obvious discomfort made Rose change tactics.

'Chico tells me you're looking for work here.'

Shelley nodded.

Rose became pensive, drawing on her cigarette as if her life depended on it, then coughing as her lungs protested. After a few moments, her demeanour transformed itself through a smile that broke the ice.

'You're no circus performer, but I'm sure you'll have no trouble selling popcorn and sweets, if that interests you.'

Shelley's joy at this chance to be with Chico overrode her disappointment at not being able to perform.

'Go find Chico. He'll show you the ropes.' Rose waved Shelley out with a flick of her wrist as she stubbed out her cigarette with forceful jabs.

Shelley felt strange, as if she had had a spell cast on her, but once she found Chico, any feelings of doubt dissolved. She watched his lithe body working rhythmically before he caught sight of her. Flicking his hair away from his eyes, he smiled at her, and in that moment she didn't care who tried to discourage her from spending time with him. This was the Chico from her childhood. He'd made her happy then, and she was sure he would do so again.

'How did it go?' he asked.

'She said I could sell popcorn and sweets.'

'So you're in! She probably thinks you won't stick around. Most people move on once the circus leaves town.'

'I'm very grateful. Not only do I have a job, but I get to see you every day. I better go tell Jean the news. She was asleep when I left.'

'Okey-doke. Come back around two so I can show you the ropes before the matinee,' he said, with a grin.

Shelley waved and left, her spirits high until she was nearing home and rehearsing the speech she was hoping would placate Jean.

'Good morning!'

'You've been to see him.'

'Yes, and I met his mother. She gave me a job.'

'Why would you do that after what I told you?'

'I don't mean to disrespect you, but I'm eighteen and I need to make my own decisions.'

'You're in love with him, aren't you?'

'Yes.'

'You need to tell your parents.'

'Yes, of course.'

'I think you should telephone them, rather than write to them.'

'It's so expensive to telephone them. I'll write a letter now.'

'No matter the expense. It's best if we telephone them.'

'Can you speak with them, please?'

***

Once Chico finished his chores, he sought his mother out.

'Thanks for giving Shelley a job.'

'You like this girl?'

'Yes.'

'Well then, have your fun with her. If she cares for you, she'll let you have your way with her.' Rose lit a cigarette, smiling at him as she left to find Max.

***

News of Shelley's association with the McIntyres did not go down well with Artis or Belle. They made plans to drive the 520 miles to Sydney once they had made arrangements to have someone cover their work commitments. In the meantime, Jean watched Shelley's youthful passion dissolve all logic. Before Artis and Belle had a chance to leave Yarra Glen, Jean had to make the dreaded telephone call to tell them to cancel their visit. Circus Spectacular had moved on and taken Shelley with them.

36

Deadly Revenge

Regional New South Wales, 1949

Rain escorted Circus Spectacular's departure from Sydney. It seemed an allegorical farewell that spurred Shelley's tears, knowing her impulsive actions would devastate her parents. As an added burden, she carried the guilt of leaving Jean nothing more than a note telling her she was leaving town with the circus. It was uncharacteristic of her to be so defiant and headstrong. Her infatuation with Chico overshadowed any logic. She was not thinking of the consequences of her actions, but was driven by her passion and determination not to be left behind this time.

'I'll look after you, Shelley. I promise,' said Chico, whose alluring eyes melted her anxiety. They embraced and stole kisses away from prying eyes, each time igniting a passion that grew in intensity. They were once again inseparable. Rose kept a watchful eye on them. Shelley overcompensated with acts of kindness towards Rose to not only show her appreciation for giving her a job, but to ensure she gained Rose's approval to be with Chico. Her efforts were not bearing fruit. Whenever Rose spoke to her, Shelley detected a bristling tone.

'All the girls are crazy about Chico. They throw themselves at him any chance they get,' Rose said, noting Shelley's discomfort. 'The way to keep a man is to give him what he wants. Show him you love him before someone else does.'

'I'm not sure what you mean.'

'Oh, you're a virgin? How quaint,' Rose said, laughing, in a manner that embarrassed Shelley. 'Well, dear, what can I say? If you want to keep your man, you might want to try taking your panties off and show him you're a woman, not a girl.'

Shelley blushed. 'But we're not married.'

Rose's laugh echoed. Confused and mortified, Shelley swiftly excused herself, vowing to stay out of Rose's way as much as possible from then on. The vision she had had of returning to the stage was far removed from her current reality. The familiarity of the troupe she loved, and who doted on her, was replaced with a clique of circus folks who were not particularly welcoming to an ornamental girlfriend hired to sell popcorn and sweets. Even Lola and the other girls, who she had to share sleeping quarters with, were polite around Chico but otherwise shunned her. Her growing insecurities made her gravitate towards Chico every chance she got.

Circus Spectacular had its share of hardships. The heavy rain that had begun the previous week had caused their travel between towns to become a boggy battlefield. A convoy of cars and caravans were banked up and stranded in the thick mud, requiring them to hire a tractor from a nearby farm to pull them out. The men helped guide the caravan whilst the tractor pulled it out of the ditch, churning up the road and covering the men in mud.

One evening, over two thousand people were seated in the Big Top when some of the tiered seats gave way, throwing about a hundred people to the ground. A general uproar ensued, with some women fainting and children screaming. The commotion caused other people to leave. Then another section of the seats gave way, throwing another hundred people to the ground. Those inconvenienced were given free tickets for the following night's performance.

'Your girlfriend's a bad omen,' said Max. Chico threw him a look of disdain.

The troupe felt the strain of working long hours and six-day weeks to compensate for their losses. They drew comfort from the serenity offered by country nights that soothed even the most shattered of nerves after a long, arduous day. Sunburnt skin was refreshed from the day's heat with a swim in a nearby river. Although Rose had agreed that Shelley could tour with them, she would not let her perform. Besides selling tickets and snacks, she was made to wash the performers' costumes and do Rose and Max's bidding. Chico would always help her whenever he finished his chores. Then they would find a quiet spot to fool around.

On a night when the full moon created a romantic aura, their passion intensified as they kissed. They hurried to find a secret place away from prying eyes, choosing a spot near the river. The rhythmic sound of hidden insects pulsated through the reeds that formed a curtain of privacy around them. The moon cast an angelic light on Shelley's face. Their eyes confirmed the depths of their passion. Melting into Chico's arms, she breathed in the scent of his skin as he stroked her hair and face before kissing her. The plumpness of her lips caressing his soon aroused him.

'You want to have a swim?'

'In our clothes?' She looked at him, wondering if he could sense the wild beating of her heart. When he began to lift her dress over her head, she thought her heart would explode, and yet she yielded to him. Rose's voice echoed in her head, fighting against her conscience, which was warning her to stop. As he peeled off her petticoat, her legs started to shake. He comforted her with a lingering kiss. An electrical current ran through her body. She felt on fire but was shivering. Chico unbuttoned his shirt and pants, and within seconds, they were standing in their undergarments, their arousal heightened. Their bodies shook with nervous anticipation. Chico slid off his undergarment and proceeded to remove Shelley's, with her help. Feeling vulnerable, she covered herself with her arms. Chico pulled them away to look at her beauty. The cool night breeze tickled their sunburnt skin. They embraced. Chico gently pulled her down onto a carpet of reeds.

Shelley trembled as Chico lay on her. She quietened the voices in her head by focusing on the warmth of his body, which was arousing new senses within her. The sight of her with her hair splayed across the ground, her eyes in a dreamlike state, lips parted in ecstasy, made him wild. The moon cast its spell, illuminating them as they explored their newfound love. Her inexperience made her unsure of her movements, yet she submitted herself to him as he parted her legs and entered her.

The moment she felt the pain of penetration, the spell was broken, and she cried from shame. Chico, still spellbound, was fixated on climaxing. Moments later, after groaning with satisfaction, he rolled on his side to catch his breath. He stroked Shelley's hair and tried to soothe her, but her tears kept coming. Feeling unclean, she stood up and walked into the calmness of the water, bathing herself as if this would cleanse her sinful act. An image of her parents came into her mind and made her sob. Chico followed her in and wrapped his arms around her. The trance had dissolved and left them in a state of awkwardness.

The days that followed were strained. Shelley rejected further private encounters.

'We can't do this anymore. It's wrong.'

'Are you saying you don't love me?'

'We're not married. It's not right unless we're married.'

'Do you love me or not, Shell?'

'You know I do. More than anything.'

'Then you need to trust me. I told you I'd look after you.' Chico wrapped his arms around Shelley and attempted to kiss her, but she resisted.

'No, Chico. You need to do right by me.'

'It's not like I can marry you right this minute. I've got to get you a ring, for starters.'

Shelley took him by the hand and led him to her port, at her bedside. She took out a small box, opened it, and handed him the opal he had given her when they were children.

'You kept it!'

'It's my most precious possession. I always have it with me. You promised me you'd marry me when you gave it to me, remember?'

'Well, now you've ruined it by forcing a proposal from me.'

'I'm sorry. Please don't be angry. My parents will be so upset with me.'

'Well, they're not here, are they? What they can't see won't hurt them. Besides, you're an adult now.' Nodding, she caved in and embraced him. It didn't take them long to get aroused. He led her to a quiet spot where she resigned herself to surrender rather than risk losing him.

The proposal never came, and a few months later Shelley wondered why she had not menstruated the previous month and was vomiting throughout the day. Rose pulled her aside.

'So you've been fooling around with my son?'

Shelley was mortified by her accusing tone, considering it had been her suggestion that yielding to Chico's wishes was the only way to keep him from other girls.

'You're obviously pregnant. I wonder what your parents will think of you.'

Shelley burst into tears and crumpled in a heap on the floor.

'Stop acting like a baby. If you're mature enough to spread your legs, you need to start behaving like an adult.'

Shelley's tears turned to sobs.

'Quieten down!' she hissed. Do you want the world to know about your predicament?'

Shelley calmed herself.

'What should I do?'

'Go home to your parents. Let them figure it out.'

'I can't do that!' cried Shelley.

'Well, you can't stay here. I can't have a pregnant woman working in the circus. I suggest you pack your bags. The sooner the better.' Rose left Shelley in a state of remorse and confusion. She summoned Chico, who was preparing for the matinee.

'Your lover is pregnant. You need to get rid of her.' Chico, in a state of shock, looked for Shelley, finding her sobbing in a foetal position in her bed.

'Your mother wants to get rid of me! You promised to look after me. You promised!'

He didn't know how to deal with her hysteria, let alone the situation.

***

When the days turned into weeks and Shelley had not left, Rose began to antagonise her.

'Why are you still here? I told you I can't have a pregnant woman working here, especially when you're vomiting in front of customers. And don't count on any pay this month. You're off the payroll.' Rose left to find Lola.

'Lola, Shelley's expressed an interest in performing. I want you to train her on the trapeze swing.'

'Now?'

'The sooner the better. If she asks, make it sound like it was your idea.'

Her mother's request puzzled her, but she knew from her mother's tone not to ask questions.

Lola's sudden friendly approach surprised Shelley.

'Hey, can you help me rig the trapeze swing? It'll give you a chance to try it out. You'll love it.' The suggestion made Shelley realise Lola didn't know about her pregnancy. Although relieved it was still a secret, the thought of climbing up high to rig the trapeze swing terrified her, let alone swing on it. Regardless, she obliged, thankful for Lola's change of heart towards her.

'I don't know if I'm cut out for this,' said Shelley.

'Once you get a taste for it, you'll be addicted to the adrenaline rush.'

'Did it take you long to learn?'

'Not as long as performing on horseback.'

Rose watched, out of sight, waiting for the girls to reach the swing.

'Bravo!' she bellowed. The girls got a shock and Shelley almost lost her balance. Lola caught hold of her arm to settle her.

'Ma, you know better than to scare us when we're up here. Are you trying to kill us?'

Rose flipped her wrist in dismissal.

'It's good to see you girls bonding. Teach her something simple so she can perform next week. Isn't that what you wanted, Shelley?'

Confused and in shock, Shelley said nothing.

'Next week!' said Lola.

'I'm sure you can make it happen. She has a performance background.'

Rose left them in a state of bewilderment.

'Does she hate me?'

'She's giving you a chance to perform, which surprised me. Aren't you pleased?'

Shelley nodded, wondering whether to confide in Lola about her condition, but held back.

'My mother's a complicated woman. Don't take things she says to heart.'

When Shelley discussed his mother's suggestion that she learn how to perform on the trapeze swing, Chico thought it was a breakthrough.

'Do you think it's safe? Your mother said she didn't want someone in my condition working in the circus. Why do you think she changed her mind?'

'I don't know, but at least it will buy us some time 'til I can work out a plan for us.'

'I'm not sure if I can cope with the height. I get dizzy and the urge to vomit hits me unexpectedly.'

'Then tell her you can't do it.'

Shelley sensed Chico's frustration.

'I'll do my best. Have you told Lola about the baby?'

'No. We need to keep it to ourselves 'til I can figure things out.'

Lola and Shelley kept working on a simple routine that Shelley could cope with. She gave her first performance at a matinee. Its simplicity met with lukewarm applause, but that didn't seem to bother Rose. The energy absorbed from a live performance thrilled Shelley, regardless of the level of feedback.

All went well for a few weeks until Rose tampered with the rigging of the net and rope securing the swing. Her mind ran amok as she watched the show unfold. Performers and crew were flitting about, and the audience's energy was at a peak when she began wrestling with her conscience. She wondered whether to put a stop to the performance. All she had to do was tell Max not to announce it. *This is going to be bad publicity for the circus. But she's going to ruin Chicos life. I don't want him anywhere near her family.* She kept hesitating, pushing the boundaries of her evil thoughts. Shelley, dressed in her costume, stood ready to perform. Her abdomen showed no evidence of her condition. Time was ticking. She looked at Chico. Her handsome son, whom she adored. The strain of his situation was evident only to her. Shelley had to go. She looked so much like Belle that it grated on Rose every time she looked at her. And Artis had helped put her husband in prison. She hated them. She hated her life, and she hated Shelley. It was the ultimate revenge.

Max walked to the centre of the arena to announce Shelley's act. Rose moved to the sidelines, waiting with heightened anticipation. Shelley went to take her position behind the scenes. Max began his introduction. Rose could feel her heart beating. Her mind was in turmoil, counting down the seconds before she could stop the madness dominating her mind.

'Ladies and gentlemen, please give a big round of applause to the amazing Shelley Newman!'

It was too late. The audience applauded as they waited for Shelley to appear. There was a pause that confused Rose. Then she appeared, climbing nimbly up the ladder with confidence. But it wasn't Shelley, it was Lola. Rose ran to the arena and saw Shelley crumpled on the floor in pain, holding her ankle. The applause and music drowned out Rose's protests.

'Lola, stop!'

When Lola reached the top, she stretched out one arm and gave the audience a winning smile before moving to sit on the swing. In that instant, the rope gave way. Screams of horror permeated the Big Top as the net gave way and Lola hit the ground. Rose heard the thud and cracking of bones as she ran screaming to Lola's side. Every fibre of her being was on fire. A knot of tension grasped her stomach, causing waves of nausea that made her head reel. She held Lola in her arms, cradling her lifeless, broken body, her loosened gold tresses cascading to the ground. Rose sobbed, demanding that Lola wake.

'No, please no,' wept Rose as she rocked Lola back and forth, squeezing her body as if that would bring her back to life. She did not hear the sobs of the troupe that had formed a protective circle around her, blocking the prying eyes of shocked members of the audience as they were ushered out of the Big Top.

It took the ambulance almost an hour to arrive. The officers pushed their way through the circle of people to where Rose and Lola lay. It was clear Lola's spirit had left her. Rose's despair was raw as she felt Lola's lithe body grow cold. The paramedics tried to coax Rose to release Lola to them.

'No, you're not taking her!' said Rose, tightening her grip. Distraught, she hissed at anybody who came close. Max and a few of the other men managed to pull her away from Lola, and the paramedics took her away. Rose caught sight of Shelley.

'You were meant to be performing!' She lunged at Shelley, who was being propped up by Chico. A few of the performers got hold of her, pulling her back as she continued to lunge at Shelley, possessed with supernatural strength.

Chico carried Shelley out to her quarters to protect her from Rose. He hastily wrapped her swollen ankle and helped her pack her belongings, then borrowed a car to drive into town. They spent the night in the car, both in an inconsolable state of shock. In the morning, Chico paid for a bus to take Shelley back to her parents.

37

Abandoned

Yarra Glen, Victoria, 1950

A broken-spirited Shelley returned home. Her parent's joy was soon replaced with deep concern when she refused to speak and spent her days in bed crying. She had no energy to move and no appetite.

'Shelley, darling, you're scaring me. Please tell me what's wrong,' said Belle. Shelley rolled over in her bed to hide the new flow of tears that dampened her pillow.

A breakthrough came almost two weeks later when her grandma, Betty, visited for the fourth time.

'Shelley, we can't help you if we don't know what's wrong. You're tormenting us as well as yourself,' said Betty. Shelley stared trance-like out of the window. 'We can only imagine the worst.' Shelley's eyes teared up.

'You're going to hate me.'

'I could never hate you.'

'Everyone hates me.'

'Who's everyone?'

'Rose McIntyre hates me. She blames me for her daughter's death, but it wasn't my fault.'

'What do you mean by her daughter's death?'

'Lola fell off the trapeze swing when it should have been me.'

'What do you mean it should have been you?'

'I was meant to be on the swing, but I twisted my ankle and Lola took my place.'

'That's a terrible thing to happen, Shelley, but it wasn't your fault. Why would I hate you for that?'

'I'm pregnant, Grandma.'

Betty sucked in her breath.

'Oh, Shelley.'

Shelley turned her head away and cried. Betty wrapped her arms around her and cradled her head, which prompted Shelley to sob.

'What am I going to do?'

'Who's the father?'

'Frank McIntyre. Vinnie and Rose's son. Mother and Father's enemies.'

'Do you love him?'

'Very much.' Tears splashed from Shelley's eyes.

'Why has he left you in this condition?'

'His sister was killed, and his mother was trying to hurt me. He thought it best I come back here.'

'What are his intentions?'

'He said he'll come back for me.'

'Does he plan to marry you?'

'He said he would.' A heaviness stifled the air. 'Are you ashamed of me, Grandma?'

'I'm disappointed in the situation, Shelley, but that doesn't change my love for you.'

'I'm going to hell, aren't I?'

'Have you repented and asked Jesus for forgiveness?'

'Many times.'

'Then all is well. What's done is done. We must move forward.' Betty cradled Shelley in her arms and soothed her, as she had done many times in her childhood. The relief Shelley felt after releasing her secret overwhelmed her with exhaustion, and she fell into slumber.

Belle and Artis were anxiously waiting for Betty. One look at her face as she was shutting the bedroom door behind her made their hearts sink.

'You might want to put the kettle on and make a brew.'

The news did not go down well with Belle and Artis. Shelley awoke to raised voices coming from the kitchen, then heard the front door slam, followed by the high revs of her father's car tearing down the street. The sound of her mother crying pained her, and she stayed in her bed until the sun set and her room was cast in shadows. It was then that she heard a knock at her door, so faint she thought she'd imagined it until she heard it again.

'Come in.' The sight of her mother's troubled face made her cry. 'I'm sorry, Mother.' Belle's eyes welled, and they both cried as they held each other until the room darkened to black.

Artis did not return until the early hours. Belle was waiting up for him. She made him a cup of tea and they talked under the calmness of morning twilight.

'I'm gonna find him and kill him.'

'You'll do nothing of the sort.'

'How can you be so calm about this?'

'She loves him, Artis.'

'How can she love a rapist that leaves her in this state?'

'He didn't rape her, Artis. She said they love each other, and he promised to come back and marry her.'

'How can you not hate him after his father raped you? Joe is his half-brother, for God's sake!'

Belle froze. She stood up and paced the room.

'No, Artis, no! How could you think that? All these years you thought Joe was Vinnie's son?'

The blood drained from Artis's face.

'You said he forced himself on you at our house.'

'He forced his affections on me. He didn't rape me! He had completely lost his senses and kissed me. He tried to take it further, but I stopped him.'

'You mean Joe belongs to me?'

'Yes!'

Artis hid his face in his hands and cried.

'All these years, Belle! I had so much hatred for the man that I made sure he went to prison.'

Artis took a moment to process the information.

'He still had the intent to have his way with you.'

'Yes.' Belle paused to collect her thoughts. 'He came to see me at the hospital after my accident. He was inconsolable and begged my forgiveness for all the pain he'd caused us.'

'Belle, why didn't you tell me all this?' There was a hint of anger in his voice.

'I meant to, but the last thing we needed was more drama. I was angry at him for making things so difficult for us. From the time he first hired me, there was always such a sense of desperation and intensity in him that made me pity him. But it also frightened me. When I left him for you, I tried to appease him so he wouldn't harm you.'

'So you encouraged him?'

'I was trying to keep things under control, Artis. He was a loose cannon.'

'And letting him kiss you and put his hands on you in front of Shelley was the solution?'

'I told you he set me up for that so he could use the photographs to blackmail me to come back to him.'

'For the love of God, Belle! What did you expect when you were leading him on.'

'Did you think it was easy for me? What would you have done?'

'I would have knocked his lights out!'

'Exactly! As if we didn't have enough troubles that we needed to add scandalous publicity that would have ruined both our reputations and the business. Did you think I didn't know the strain you were under keeping the business going and paying the troupe?'

'Why did you stay with me when he could have made you famous and given you everything you dreamed?'

'Because when I fell in love with you, fame wasn't important anymore, especially after Shelley was born.'

Artis held her, and after a few moments of silence, they both felt years of tension begin to dissipate.

'Thank you for choosing me, Belle. I'm sorry I didn't make your dreams come true.'

'Oh, but you did. Not everyone dreams of becoming famous, but most dream of finding the love of their life to grow old with and being blessed with children.'

'I love you more than you'll ever know, Belle.'

'I do know, and I love you just as much.'

***

As the months passed, Shelley's apprehension grew at Chico's absence. There was no way to communicate with him, and she was beginning to wonder whether he would keep his word and return to her. She had written to Jean, apologising profusely for her actions, and asking for her forgiveness. She explained her situation and asked if she could check the newspapers for any advertisements Circus Spectacular may have published indicating their touring dates. Jean's reply included a newspaper clipping announcing Lola's death and that the circus was on hiatus. It was dated not long after Shelley had left.

Sister Clara's words came back to haunt her. *Boys will get you into trouble, and then you'll never hear from them again. A boy like that corrupts good character.* Shelley sought comfort from her grandmother, Betty, whose strong faith taught her that all would work out for good. Every day she would recite the Bible verse in Psalm 55:22: '*Cast your cares on the Lord and He will sustain you.*'

***

The knock at the door came after dinner, when they were sitting in the lounge room listening to the wireless. Artis went to the door. Shelley strained to hear the muffled voices. When Artis returned, he had Chico with him. Her swollen belly slowed her excited attempt to stand. Chico hastened to her aid. They embraced. Artis switched off the wireless and motioned for everybody to leave the room to allow them some privacy.

'I thought you'd abandoned me!'

'I'm sorry it took me so long to come, but I'm here to marry you, Shell.' He took a small box out of his pocket and got down on one knee. When he opened the box, Shelley gasped at the opal ring. 'Will you marry me?'

'Yes, yes, yes!' She hugged him. 'You had it mounted,' she said, admiring the ring as he slid it onto her finger.

'Do you like it?'

'It's beautiful.' They kissed. 'I honestly thought you'd left me.'

'I'm sorry, Shell. All hell broke loose after you left. We had to shut the circus down. My mother had a nervous breakdown at the funeral.

When Lola's coffin was lowered into the ground, she threw herself on top of it and refused to let go. It was the worst day of my life, seeing her so broken,' he said, his voice wavering.

'Oh, Chico. I'm so sorry.'

'It took about five men to get her out of there. They drove her to the hospital, and she's been locked up in a mental institution ever since.'

'Chico, that's awful.'

'Then Max disappeared and took all the money we had. I found out they were up to their eyeballs in debt. I had to sell everything.' Shelley stroked his arm. 'I should have told you before I proposed that I don't have much to offer you.'

'I'm so happy you're here now. We can work the rest out.'

Shelley placed Chico's hand on her belly. His wonderment at the baby's movement pleased her. All the tension of the past few months melted away as she held her man, snuggling into the strength of his arms and nestling her head on his shoulder.

Artis and Belle returned to the lounge room with refreshments of tea and fruitcake. Shelley showed them the engagement ring.

'As I told you at the door, sir, I'd like to marry your daughter as soon as possible, and I also need a job. I'll do anything.'

'I'd like to speak with you in private,' said Artis.

Chico followed Artis into the kitchen.

'I'm guessing you're aware of the rivalry between our families?'

'My mother told me.'

'What'd she tell you?'

'About the affair. That Joe's my half-brother and you testified against my father in court.'

Artis winced.

'While it's true that your father was in love with Shelley's mother, there was no affair and Joe isn't your half-brother.'

'Why would my mother say that?'

'She was misinformed.'

'Did you send my father to prison?'

'I gave evidence in court. I can't say I was fully responsible. He had multiple convictions.'

'Growing up without a father makes you crave to know everything about him. From what I remember, he was good to us, so I couldn't think of him as a bad person, even though he was in prison. I don't know why my mother wouldn't let me visit him when we were children, but when I got older, I needed to see him. So, a few years back, I started visiting him in prison. He was sorry for what he did to you, but he said he was framed for money laundering and running illegal businesses. My father's not a criminal.'

'I never said he was. Revenge is a spirit of destruction that makes people do unreasonable things.'

'He said something happened to him in prison that changed him. He said he woke up in the middle of the night to find a man standing in his cell. It scared the living daylights out of him when the man said He was Jesus and told him things about his childhood that nobody could have known. Then He repeated the very thoughts my father had been thinking only minutes before. My father said what really broke him was when this man told him that his mother had never stopped praying to see him again, after he was taken from her. It was the first time I'd ever seen my father cry. He said he got to his knees and begged for forgiveness and has been reading a Bible the chaplain gave him ever since. He said now he knows he's going to see his mother again, as a richer man than when he first tried to find her.'

Artis was quiet as he collected his thoughts.

'Well, he's a better man than me. I was raised a Christian, and I can't say I've been living life the way I should have been. I put all my effort into chasing money and fame, and for what?'

'When I met Shelley at the hospital, we found a little bird with a broken wing. We tried to keep it alive, but it died. Even though we didn't know what we were doing, we gave it a funeral, and a few days later, I left and didn't think I'd ever see Shelley again. When we met again, we talked about how that bird represented a relationship that was destined to die, but later be resurrected. When I told my father that story, he said God had it all planned out and that Shelley and I were meant to be together. He couldn't believe I was going to have a child with your daughter. He told me we'd gone about it the wrong way by not getting married first, but I told him I was going to make things right.'

'I'm glad to hear that. We can't mess with love. It wins out every time,' said Artis, misty-eyed. 'But while you're in my house, you'll sleep on the couch 'til you're married. Is that clear?'

'Yes, sir.'

'Good. I'll see you in the morning.'

38

Meeting Evie

Yarra Glen, Victoria, 1955

The news of Lola's death hit Vinnie hard. He fell into a dark depression. The chaplain's visits helped him through his grief and kept him focused on the Bible's promises and the one thing that gave him hope—he had his son back in his life. Chico visited when he could and wrote to Vinnie often. Lola had been feisty and strong-willed, but Chico's character was softer, like Vinnie's mother. Rose's involvement with Max did not surprise him. He acknowledged he had not been a good husband and barely knew his wife on a deep, personal level. Their relationship had been based on sex and convenience, and while he believed she deserved better than him, Chico told him she had been worse off with Max.

When Vinnie was finally released from prison, the freedom he had craved brought him more anxiety than joy. He had no money, nowhere to live, and, with a criminal record, limited work prospects. As much as it pained him, he had no option but to swallow his pride and seek the help of his son. Chico and Shelley were still living in Yarra Glen with their five-year-old daughter and two-year-old son. They told him he could stay with them as long as he needed.

Chico arranged to pick Vinnie up from the bus station. Shelley thought it best to wait at home, to give them time together before meeting the family. As the passengers descended from the bus, Chico paced as he searched for his father. Once people parted ways, he spotted him, looking respectable, in his once fashionable suit and shiny black shoes. His roughly shaved hair was the only giveaway of his release from prison. The regrowth had a tinge of ginger and was flecked with grey, as was his beard, making him look older than his years. When their eyes met, Chico noted a flicker of joy.

After being deprived of physical contact for twenty years, Vinnie's intention to hold his son was clear. He approached Chico with open arms, and Chico fell into them. Their embrace exploded into a barrage of emotions as the realisation of Vinnie's freedom hit home.

'I'm glad you're home, Pa.'

'I'm sorry, son. I'll make it up to you.'

'I love you, Pa.'

'I love you, too, Frank. I'm so proud of the man you've become.'

They heard the bus rumble off.

'That's a mighty fine-looking machine. Real comfortable too. I couldn't believe how smooth the ride was,' said Vinnie thumbing at the bus. 'I feel like an alien. Everything's changed. There are buildings and cars everywhere.'

Chico led Vinnie to his car.

'Now, *that* I recognise,' he said, pointing to Chico's car. 'It's as old as me! Is this thing going to make it home?' He laughed.

'You're a praying man now. You tell me.'

They both laughed.

'I can't wait for you to meet my family,' Chico said, once they were on the road.

'Aye, looks like you live out in the sticks.'

'Yeah. I have to make sure you don't escape.'

'Cheeky bugger!' said Vinnie, giving him a playful punch in the arm that caused the car to veer to one side of the road.

'Whoa, steady on! This thing's got dodgy brakes. You're gonna run us into a ditch.'

'I doubt it. You're driving like a grandma. Put your foot down!'

Chico sped up, only to have the car start shaking uncontrollably. They laughed at their jiggling cheeks.

'Alright, slow the bone-rattler down before my teeth fall out.'

Chico slowed down in time to miss hitting a kangaroo that had jumped out of the bush.

'Bloody roos!' said Chico. 'It's only a matter of time before I hit one and that'll be the end of my car, or me. It's been barely a year since my friend died after hitting one and rolling his car.'

Vinnie was quiet for a while as he watched the sheep grazing in the paddocks.

'Where'd you bury Lola?'

'We brought her back to Victoria and buried her next to Nonna. I'll take you there whenever you want.'

'Aye.' He wound down the window and leant his head out. 'Is your mother still locked up?'

'Yeah, I went to visit her a few times, but she refused to see me. She never approved of my relationship with Shelley.'

'I'll go see her and look after her. She's been through enough hell in her life.'

They arrived at the house and were immediately greeted by a boisterous four-year-old with pigtails bouncing in all directions. She wrapped herself around Chico's leg.

'Say hello to your grandpa.'

'Hello,' she beamed.

Vinnie got a jolt when he saw her face. Those golden eyes with flecks of chocolate, shadowed by an umbrella of lashes.

'You look just like your grandma Belle.'

Shelley joined them. She was holding Roy on her hip.

'Hello. I'm Shelley. Pleased to meet you. I see you've met Evie, and this is Roy.'

'You named her Evie?' A wave of emotion swept over Vinnie and tears sprang to his eyes. Chico and Shelley looked at each other, perplexed by his reaction. Vinnie got down on his knees and held his arms out to Evie, who, without hesitation, ran into them.

'My mother's name was Evie. You look just like her too,' he said, stroking her cheek.

'Are you alright, Pa?'

'Aye. I can't believe she's my granddaughter.' He took out a handkerchief and wiped his eyes before blowing his nose.

'Don't be sad, Poppy. Come see my swing under the apple tree,' said Evie, pulling him by the hand to the backyard, where they proceeded to immerse themselves in play like kindred spirits.

***

After twenty years of incarceration, sudden freedom in a world no longer familiar to Vinnie was overwhelming. There was no more daily regimen to abide by. He was free to do whatever he wanted and yet he felt paralysed. The changes in society were confounding. While he felt lost, any feelings of loneliness evaporated at the sight of Evie. Vinnie thanked God every day for her and the unconditional love she showed her new grandpapa that eased the trauma of this mammoth transition into his new life. Then Chico dropped a bombshell.

'Pa, we've invited Shelley's parents over for dinner on Saturday night. We're hoping you might be able to put the past behind you, seeing as we're all family now.'

'Oh, goodie! You can be best friends!' said Evie, who was sitting on Vinnie's lap explaining how he should read her favourite book to her and Roy by using a different voice for each character.

'Used to be once.'

'Evie, take Roy to Mama to have his nappy changed,' said Chico.

'Do I have to?'

'Yes, quick smart. Mama's waiting.'

'Don't move, Poppy. I'll be back.'

Vinnie chuckled as he watched Evie guide an obedient Roy, in awe of his big sister, out of the room.

'Is it too soon, Pa?'

'Do they hate me?'

'No, I told them about your conversion. Funnily enough, you inspired Artis. He and Belle have been going to church.'

'How about you and Shelley?'

'Shelley's embraced it. She takes the kids to Sunday school.'

'And you?'

'I dunno. Truth is, I barely know you. But to be honest, I was scared as hell of you as a kid even though you were good to us. And there are things I'm still really angry about, things I don't understand, and I just can't see God as the fix-it-man.'

'He fixed me.'

Chico was pensive for a moment.

'Yeah, I suppose. But He hasn't fixed me.'

'You just have to ask Him to, Chico. Get down on your knees and pour your heart out to Him about everything you're angry about, and He'll answer you.'

'I've tried. It's just not working out for me.'

'We got a lot to talk about, that's for sure. I said I'd make things up to you, and I will.'

Evie skipped back into the room and sat on Vinnie's lap.

'Can you read this book, Poppy?'

'What's this? Snugglepot and Cuddlepie. Those are funny names,' said Vinnie.

'They're gumnut babies. They're supposed to have funny names,' said Evie.

Chico shook his head. He had never thought he'd ever see his father become putty in a child's hands.

'Can I borrow your car to go see your mother this week?' said Vinnie.

'Of course, Pa.'

39

A Broken Spirit

Since his release from prison, Vinnie's sense of freedom was never more pronounced than when he drove Chico's car out of the driveway, on his own, just as the sun was rising. A map was spread out on the seat to guide him to Hillside Mental Asylum. The thought of Rose imprisoned in an asylum weighed heavily on him. During their marriage, they had never spoken about the personal demons they battled. The counselling he received from the chaplain in prison helped Vinnie piece together not only the madness of his actions but Rose's as well. He could only imagine that the abuse Rose had suffered at the hand of Carlo would have been extreme. *If only I had listened to her when she tried to warn me, things would have turned out differently. I knew he was trouble the minute I laid eyes on the bastard. He knew I'd take the bait. Who doesn't want money and fame? 'No man can serve two masters: for either he will hate the one, and love the other; or else he will hold to the one, and despise the other. Ye cannot serve God and mammon.'* If only I'd known that then, I wouldn't have let money and fame become my masters.

There was nothing to do but think during the drive. His thoughts became dark as he recollected Carlo's bribes, presented as very expensive gifts followed by 'instructions' on how to run his business to Carlo's liking. *How did I not see what was going on under my very nose? I was so obsessed with revenge that I didn't see the soulless eyes of those young burlesque dancers, nor my own wife's suffering. How did I not see that the signals given by men in the audience were not to order drinks, but to order a girl.* The memories of his past continued to torment him, even though he had asked for forgiveness.

The chaplain had taught him to catch and cast away negative thoughts before they had a chance to poison his mind. He had advised him to pray. *Talk to God like He's your best friend who knows everything about you.* It was a valuable piece of advice that worked every time. With a newfound understanding of Rose's delicate state of mind, he contemplated what to say to her. Being committed to a mental asylum was as cruel as being incarcerated for someone else's crimes. As if losing her daughter wasn't traumatic enough, she had also lost her freedom.

It was lunchtime when he drove into the driveway and parked the car in front of what could have been mistaken for a mansion had the building not had a painted sign on the gate with a name that cast a cloud of doom over it—*Hillside Mental Asylum.* An oppressive force was heavy in the air, sending a shiver down Vinnie's back as he climbed the stairs to the entrance.

The receptionist was as inhospitable as her environment. Leaving the room, she returned with a nurse who guided him through a bleach-scented corridor. His hair stood on end as he heard the faint moans leaching through the walls. The nurse led him to a courtyard at the back of the building.

'She's been medicated to calm her down,' said the nurse, pointing to a grey-haired skeleton sitting in a chair, her legs curled up under her.

Vinnie sucked in his breath as he approached the woman, trying to recollect the image of Rose from twenty years ago.

'Rose?'

She looked at him with vacant eyes, her stare piercing through him.

'Rose, it's Vinnie, your husband.'

Vinnie was taken aback when she began to cackle hysterically. He put his hand on her shoulder and knelt beside her with his eyes closed as he prayed until he felt her calm down.

'Vinnie's dead,' she said.

'No, Rose, I'm here.'

'Lola's dead.'

'Aye, love.'

'Lola's dead!' she screamed and tried to get out of her chair. Vinnie noted the straps that held her down. Enraged, he untied them.

'Don't fret, love.'

'Lola's dead!'

Vinnie knelt beside her and held her hands to calm her. He prayed quietly, then sang one of Rose's favourite songs, one she used to perform. Her heavy lids lifted as she looked at him in amazement.

'Vinnie?'

'Aye, love.'

Tears rolled down her cheeks.

'I'm gonna get you outta here, Rose. I need to get on my feet first, then I'll come get you.'

She stared, trance-like, straight through him, then started singing. Vinnie dropped his head into his hands.

'Rose, did you hear what I said?'

Rose concentrated until the words came to her and then continued to sing. The lyrics overpowered the effects of the sedative, and her spirit began to lift. Vinnie sang with her, watching her transformation as she came back to life. When they finished the song, Vinnie held her hands.

'Do you know who I am, Rose?'

'Vinnie?'

'Aye, love,' he smiled.

'You look old.'

He laughed. 'Time's got away on us, love.'

'Do I look old?'

'You look beautiful.'

'You've never said that to me before.'

'Haven't I?'

Rose shook her head, tears welling in her eyes.

'I've not been a good husband, but I'll make it up to you, Rose.'

'You want me? After everything I've done?'

'We've all done things we've regretted, love.'

'I killed Lola!'

She began to fidget when she saw the shock on Vinnie's face.

'No, Rose. Frank told me it was an accident.'

'I was so angry when I found out Chico was in love with that girl. Belle's daughter.' Rose spat the words. 'The person I hated most, who had stolen you and had your child, only to have her daughter pregnant with Chico. I wanted Chico to leave her, but he wouldn't. So I had to get rid of her.'

'Rose, I never had a child with Belle. But what do you mean you had to get rid of her?' Vinnie said. Rose rocked in the chair as tears rolled down her cheeks. 'I don't understand, Rose. What did you do?'

'I told Lola to train Shelley on the trapeze swing and then I rigged the ropes so she'd fall. Except that night she twisted her ankle and Lola took her place before I could stop her.'

'My God, Rose!'

Rose became hysterical as he pulled away from her. Two nurses came towards them.

'It might be best you go now,' said one of the nurses as they took Rose inside, screaming and struggling to get out of their grasp.

Vinnie sat in the chair Rose had vacated, his head cradled in his hands. He wrestled with his thoughts as time stood still. Drops of icy rain began to fall, slicing through his skin. He made his way back to the car, his mind a tempest the whole drive home.

40

Redemption

The prison chaplain who had helped Vinnie renew the way he thought through the teachings of Jesus had given Vinnie his phone number, inviting him to contact him any time after his release if he was ever in need. The turmoil Rose had caused with her confession had left Vinnie reeling and angry. He could not unburden himself to Frank, who would never forgive his mother, so he called the prison chaplain.

'You know, Vinnie, not only are we all sinners, but we're all capable of crossing the boundaries and doing something really evil, and even justifying our actions, especially when we feel threatened. When we allow ourselves to be tormented by our thoughts, we'll find ourselves reasoning why our actions are justified. We don't consider the catastrophic and long-lasting consequences. The truth is, it's impossible to be perfect. Only Jesus was the perfect human because

He was God in the flesh. We're all sinners and will continue to be until the next life when we go to be with Jesus for eternity. The good news is that He paid the price for everyone's sins by allowing himself to be crucified. It was the cruellest death penalty, reserved for criminals, yet He was the innocent sacrificial lamb required to reconcile us back to God.'

'So if we're all sinners and incapable of living perfect lives, should people not be held accountable for what they've done?' said Vinnie.

'Yes, we must hold each other accountable for our actions, but we must also forgive one another, and either keep our distance from the person, if they're incapable of changing their ways, or move forward making our boundaries clear of what we will not tolerate in future.'

Vinnie thought for a moment before he said, 'What should I do?'

'Forgive her and be the husband she needs you to be.'

'But she killed our daughter,'

'Not intentionally. Even though her intent to kill Shelley was very wrong, hasn't she been punished enough by everyone in her life, including herself?'

'Aye, that she has,' said Vinnie.

'Show her how to lay her burdens at the spiritual cross of Jesus, just as you did. Meditate on Romans 7:14–25 and find yourself a church, even if it's a small group of people who meet at home, so you're not walking this spiritual journey alone.'

***

The next hurdle Vinnie had to face was meeting Artis and Belle. He'd rehearsed what to say many times. As the time approached, he positioned himself in a lounge chair beside the window and pretended to be reading the newspaper. The chug of an engine made him look up to see an emerald green Terraplane pull into the driveway. He parted the curtain discreetly and watched as Artis got out of the car. His step was buoyant as he walked over to the passenger door to help Belle out. He looked in fine form. The only evidence of time was the dusting of grey through his receding hair.

The sight of Belle caused a stabbing pain in his heart as she emerged from the car. Her beauty was still evident, yet she looked frail as she leant her weight on a cane and did her best to camouflage her limp. Sadness washed over Vinnie at the realisation that the years of senseless revenge had brought nothing but misery to what could have been a formidable union of talent. For all its vibrant energy and promise, the hubris of youth also had the potential to wreak irreversible havoc. He was in deep thought when Chico poked his head into the room.

'Pa, Artis and Belle are here.'

The room filled with tension as they entered. In their proximity, Vinnie noted the silver threads through Belle's neatly styled hair. There was an uncomfortable silence between them and the absence of a handshake. They avoided eye contact as if that would ignite a nuclear bomb of emotions.

'Grandma!' Evie scampered into Belle's arms, almost knocking her over. Laughing, she stooped to embrace Evie. Vinnie was moved by the familiar sound of her laugh. He noted the crumpling of fine lines around her eyes. She was still as beautiful as when he first saw her all those years ago. Evie moved over to Artis for his embrace, and then Vinnie.

'This is my new grandpa. He's going to be your friend, aren't you, Grandpa?'

Vinnie smiled at Evie. 'He's a bit shy,' she said to Belle and Artis while she held his hand.

Artis raised an eyebrow but kept himself in check, thankful that only Belle had noticed. Vinnie was fixated on his shoes. Chico and Shelley, who had been lingering near the doorway, greeted Belle and Artis. Roy, who was propped on Shelley's hip, reached out for Belle. She put her cane down and held him, making him giggle when she covered his face with kisses.

Shelley motioned for them to sit at the dining table. It was laid out with an embroidered linen tablecloth, her best dinnerware, and freshly picked yellow roses from her garden as the centrepiece.

'Here's your mother's potato bake and date pudding.' Artis handed Shelley a basket.

'Thank you.'

'I'll come and help you,' said Belle, as she handed Roy to Artis.

'Come on, Evie. You can help too,' said Shelley.

The men sat at the table. Vinnie drummed the table with his fingers. Chico poured out drinks.

'Tell me how you met, Pa,' said Chico, trying to break the ice. Vinnie snorted.

'This laddie comes to my show at the Association for the Advancement of the Blind concert, then bombards me with compliments before asking for a job. Said he sold bread and reckoned there was no dough in it, so he'd rather sell tickets to my show.' Artis and Vinnie chuckled.

'You remembered my joke.'

'It's what got you hired. Tenacious thing you were. Didn't expect you to steal my sweetheart as well, though.'

'I'll swear on the Bible I had no idea you were sweet on her at the time.'

'I suppose I didn't give her a choice. I lost my head when I hired her. Felt like I'd known her my whole life. She reminded me so much of my mother.'

'I know what you mean about losing your head. When you told me to hire dancers, I saw her perform at the Glassy in a peacock costume and I was a goner.'

'Argh! I still feel like punching you in the nose. I have to say, when I found out Frank had hooked up with your girl, I knew it was divine intervention. Then I see my granddaughter looking just like Belle and named after my mother.' He shook his head as if to shake away the emotion that sprang back up.

'My parents said the same thing when Shelley told them the story about how she met Chico at the hospital, then years later in Sydney. It had to be divine intervention,' said Artis.

'It's time to bury the hatchet. We want our children to have good memories of their grandparents,' said Chico.

'Too bloody right,' said Artis. 'Look where all this feuding got us. I'm living back in the very place I was busting to get away from. Back selling bread with a sidekick roller skating business.'

'And I'm a convicted criminal,' said Vinnie, 'framed for illegitimate business practices I knew nothin' about and without a penny to my name.'

'I should've never testified against you. When Rose told me you'd fathered Joe, I lost my mind.'

'She told you what?' Vinnie abruptly stood up from the table and paced the room in disbelief.

'Showed me photos of the two of you in a park.'

'I was trying to win her back, and I crossed the line, but not to that extent.'

'I know. Belle set the record straight four years ago when Shelley came home pregnant.'

'All these years you thought your son was mine?' He sat back down and downed his drink. 'What a right bloody mess.'

'It needs to end now,' said Chico. 'Both of you need to wipe the slate clean for the sake of your grandchildren.'

Evie came into the room carrying a basket of bread. Chico was refilling the glasses when Shelley and Belle returned, carrying the roast and potato bake. The aroma of delicious food soon quelled the men. After Artis recited grace, they all enjoyed the meal in silence, pondering their conversation.

'Belle, I'd like to apologise again for my poor conduct over the years. You're the last person I wanted to hurt. I don't know what came over me.'

'Thank you. I never meant to hurt you, either.'

'Why did you hurt each other?' asked Evie.

'We both fell in love with Grandma and wanted to marry her,' said Artis.

'Is that why you stopped being friends?'

'Yes.'

'Are you going to be best friends now?' said Evie.

'As my mother would say, forgiveness has more power than revenge,' said Artis.

'Aye, no truer words,' said Vinnie.

Chico then guided the conversation to reminiscences of their show business days. As the hours passed, the children were put to bed, and they discussed how show business had changed.

'Vaudeville's dead. Since the war, everyone's been watching the talkies and listening to the wireless,' said Artis.

'Is that right?' said Vinnie.

'Television's the way of the future,' said Chico. 'There'll be plenty of new opportunities once the Menzies government launch ABC Television in Sydney. They're planning to televise the Melbourne Olympic Games. Now's a good time to get a foot in the door,' he said, with a twinkle in his eye.

'I'll eat my hat if you ain't been cooking something up, bringing us here together,' said Vinnie.

'Tomorrow will always bring new opportunities,' said Chico, smiling.

'Aye, laddie. That it will.'

'Bloody oath!' said Artis.

Acknowledgements

I'm very grateful to the people who shared this writing journey with me. Many thanks to the late Shirley Barnett, whose life story inspired me to preserve Australian entertainment history. She was very generous with her time and permitted me to use her collections of photographs. May the memory of her extraordinary life live on through this fictional story, based on some of her life events.

Hugh Stuckey was gracious enough to allow me to interview him during one of my trips to Melbourne. Hugh has been credited with being the first writer for Australian television. He worked with Shirley in the early years, writing comedy for *In Melbourne Tonight* and many other shows. He went on to gain great success in the United Kingdom and in the United States. He was writing his autobiography when I interviewed him. We kept in touch and in early 2018, he called me to ask if I would assist in publishing his autobiography. He said he would be turning 90 soon, and since he was suffering ill health, didn't think he had much time left on this earth. He told me he would email me the manuscript, but I never received it. He passed away on 21 June 2018— 10 days before his 90th birthday. I certainly hope his autobiography gets published one of these days. It would be such a colossal contribution in the preservation of Australian entertainment history.

Thanks to Robert Coenraads, my writing and travel buddy. A true gentleman whose generous support and encouragement I appreciate very much. Karen Le Rossignol, my lecturer from Deakin University, who supervised my writing project, then called *Broadway Star*. Gillian Arrighi, Honorary Associate Professor in Theatre and Performance at the University of New South Wales, Sydney, Australia. I'm very grateful for Gillian's exceptional feedback and guidance in ensuring the information relating to performances, circus, child actors, and much more was described accurately. Kylie Best, the librarian from the State Library of Victoria, who went above and beyond in helping me search for historical information, newspaper reports and everything in between.

I'm grateful to my children, Christian, Dillon, and Natalia, who kept encouraging me in my fourteen-year writing journey to complete my debut novel. Considering how long it's taken me; I now have grandchildren! Jett, Vaydah and Evie Lee, I adore you! You fill my heart with love. I feel like the most blessed Mimi in the world. Remember that Jesus loves you, and no matter how long something takes, how many setbacks you face, how hard it turns out to be, don't give up! Rely on the gifts God specifically gave you and persevere until the dream He's inspired you with comes to fruition.

Most importantly, I attribute any writing ability I might have to God. May any glory be His, because I find good writing a difficult craft to master. I'm not sure if having three languages bouncing around in my head has anything to do with my struggles. Stories float around beautifully in my head until, in my enthusiasm to write them down, I purge words out on the screen that end up looking like a literary mess. Sometimes words flow gracefully as I type and other times it feels like they're stuck in gluggy mud and it takes quite a bit of hashing and rehashing to create a coherent sentence, let alone a paragraph. Yet the strong desire to write never leaves me no matter how much torment I suffer in my attempts to beautify the prose. Why do I put myself through this? Because writing is a gift to the reader and a gift will only be cherished and appreciated if it is the very best gift you can give.

I humbly thank you for taking the time to read *When the Glitter Fades*. I hope it has touched you in some way and brought awareness that the sexual exploitation and abuse of children and women has been around since the beginning of time. It needs to stop! Please consider what part you can play in calling it out and helping the victims. You may be surprised how many people have been or are abused and are too afraid or embarrassed to speak up. It could be closer to home than you realise.

'As each one has received a special *gift, employ it in serving one another as good stewards of the multifaceted grace of God.'* 1 Peter 4:10 NASB20

References

Chapter 2 – Escaping the Family Business

Concert By The Blind poster wording was guided by the *West Gippsland Gazette* advertisement on Tuesday 11 November 1924 with character names replacing original names published.

Chapter 12 – Avoiding Poverty Point

The Boy Stood on the Burning Deck is a poem written in 1826 by the English poet Felicia Dorothea Hemans. It was originally titled *Casabianca* because it was about a boy named Casabianca, the son of the Admiral of the French *L'Orient*, who remained at his post, in obedience to his father, even after the ship caught fire and he lost his life.

Shirley Barnett told me the variation of the poem but could not recall the source.

Chapter 16 – Sinister Intentions

The House That Jack Built review was combined from the reviews given in the *Camperdown Chronicle,* on Tuesday 19 May 1931, and the *Portland Guardian*, on Thursday 21 May 1931.

Chapter 19 – House of Cards

The *Susso* was a playground rhyme that referred to people on government welfare payments introduced during the Great Depression.

Chapter 20 – Little Red Riding Hood

Costume descriptions taken from The Sun News-Pictorial Monday 28 December 1931

Circus: The Australian Story by Mark St. Leon

Glossary

Scottish words

Aye: Yes.

Bairn: Child.

Laddie: Boy.

Wee: Small.

Australian words and phrases

Ant's pants: Something extremely impressive; the best of its kind.

Anzac biscuit: A sweet biscuit containing rolled oats and golden syrup.

Arvo: Afternoon, as in 'See you Saturday arvo'.

Bex: A pain relief powder containing aspirin, phenacetin and caffeine.

Billy: A cylindrical container for boiling water or making tea over an open fire, usually made of tin, enamelware or aluminium, and fitted with a lid with a wire handle.

Billycart: A child's four-wheeled go-cart.

Bloody oath: A phrase that signifies you're in agreement.

Bonza: Excellent, terrific.

Cuppa: Cup of tea.

Damper: A simple unleavened bread baked in the ashes of an outdoor fire.

Dead soldier: An empty container of alcohol.

Face stretcher: An older lady trying to look young.

Fair dinkum: Used to emphasise the truth of a statement.

G'day: Good day.

Okey-doke: Okay.

On the wallaby: Roaming about looking for work (during the Depression).

Principal Boy: the young male protagonist in a play traditionally played by a young actress in boys' clothes.

Port: A suitcase.

Sambo: A sandwich.

Shake a leg: Hurry up.

Strewth: An exclamation of surprise or disgust.

Shut ya gob: Shut your mouth (shut up).

Susso: someone on a government welfare payment.

Ta: Thanks.

Tea: The evening meal (dinner).

Toff: An upper class person.

True blue: Loyal, faithful, genuine, dependable.

Italian words and phrases

Capisce: Understand?

Sciocco ragazzo: Silly boy.

Madonna: Good God!

Nonna: Grandma.

Nonno: Grandpa.

Nonni: Grandparents.

Australian author Jacqx Melilli's French and Spanish heritage blessed her with multiple language skills. It wasn't until she migrated to Australia and mastered the English language that her passion for writing stories was ignited.

Jacqx also pursued her love of acting. She joined a talent agency in Sydney and performed in theatre, minor roles in film, television series, commercials, and corporate films. She taught drama and wrote the one-act plays *Foreigners in Oztralia, Can Anybody Hear Me? Little Red Meets the Dingo, Goldisocks and the Three Koalas and Lost Child,* which were later published.

She was then commissioned to write the *Lights, Camera, Action* series of educational books on filmmaking and theatre production before the unexpected happened—she completed a Master of Arts degree in Writing and Literature as a mature-aged student in her forties.

While teaching drama, she met Shirley Barnett, who was the inspiration behind *When the Glitter Fades.* Jacqx passion for true stories resulted in her becoming an editor and writing mentor, to help others write their memoirs and autobiographies.

Jacqx has three children, three grandchildren, and a neurotic dog called Pablo, who's scared of his own shadow but acts tough around other dogs. She loves spending time on the beach, gardening, taking photographs of nature, spoiling her grandchildren, and has a mild addiction to Lindt chocolate and French pastries.